What Would This Golden Woman Be Like in His Fiery Embrace?

Black Cloud gazed from his forest hiding place at this woman, Caroline Fane. Fascinated, he stared at her full white breasts tumbling from her low-cut bodice. She was excitingly different.

Black Cloud imagined her lying naked on the soft skins of his bedding, this maiden with a mouth that was like ripe red fruit. Naked, he would stand over her, letting her admire his manhood. She would lift her arms, her fingers reaching out hungrily. He would feel her legs, like velvet snakes, inching up to clasp his waist, and then, not quite satisfied, going higher until they at last circled his neck. He thought of her as a wild mare bucking beneath him, and he the triumphant stallion.

Then Black Cloud moved forward, out of hiding, to seize Caroline Fane and turn his dream of lust into a savage reality. . . .

SS

Big Bestsellers from SIGNET

Rogue's Mistress

Rogue's
Mistress

by
Constance Gluyas

A SIGNET BOOK
NEW AMERICAN LIBRARY
TIMES MIRROR

SIGNET TRADEMARK REG. U.S. PAT. OFF. AND FOREIGN COUNTRIES
REGISTERED TRADEMARK—MARCA REGISTRADA
HECHO EN CHICAGO, U.S.A.

SIGNET, SIGNET CLASSICS, MENTOR, PLUME AND MERIDIAN BOOKS
are published by The New American Library, Inc.,
1301 Avenue of the Americas, New York, New York 10019

First Signet Printing, July, 1977

1 2 3 4 5 6 7 8 9

PRINTED IN THE UNITED STATES OF AMERICA

For my husband, Don,
with love.
And for my favorite star, C.M.,
the real Buck Carey.

Chapter 1

His hands loose on the reins, his long dark eyes narrowed against the brilliance that bathed his copper-skinned body in a fiery orange glow, the young Indian brave rode slowly through the lingering glory of the dawn. The girl perched behind him, her slim legs dangling, tightened her arms about his lean waist as he urged his mount up a rocky incline. Small stones disturbed by the animal's hooves rattled downward, the sharp sound of their progress loud in the monumental silence. Reaching the top of the incline, the brave checked the animal and allowed it to crop at the sparse greenery that sprouted from between crevices in the rocks.

The brave tensed, his eyes hostile as he stared at the raw new settlement far below him. The settlement was sprawled between the shadow of the brooding mountain on the right and the tall, irregular range of hills on the left that his people had named Giant Teeth. Beyond the makeshift shacks, hurriedly erected by the white settlers to preserve them from the elements, he could see the small lake. The lake, sparked to life by the glowing fingers of the dawn, looked, from the distance, like a shimmer of silver.

The girl behind him stirred. "I am cold, White Bird," she said in a petulant voice.

"Be silent, Lianne," White Bird said in sharp rebuke. He turned his head and regarded her briefly. She was a bold maiden, and she did not hesitate to speak, even when she knew that her man wished her to remain silent. Sometimes the deep feeling he had for her disturbed him, for she was like no other maiden he had known, unless it be Caroline Fane, the white woman with the hair like sunlight, whom he had known for a short, sweet time. Lianne's arrogance, so unseemly in a woman, troubled him, as did her willfulness, her disobedience to his will, and the white blood that ran so

1

strongly in her veins. So strongly, indeed, that it seemed to make nothing of the blood of Little Beaver, her Indian mother. Even worse, she appeared to be ashamed of the half of her that was Indian. This shame was shown in many ways, but mostly in her insistence upon using the name Lianne, given to her by her English father, rather than her Indian name, Sparkling Lake. Why, then, did he care for such a one, who might well bring shame to his lodge? Was it because both of them, for different reasons, were looked upon and sometimes even treated as outcasts in their own village? She because of her too proud flaunting of her white blood, and he because of the unfortunate delicacy of his constitution and the limp that made him a failure as a warrior and a hunter.

Frowning, White Bird dismissed Lianne from his thoughts and returned his attention to the settlement. In the past, he had often ridden this way. And not so long ago, before Caroline Fane and her white lover, Justin Lawrence, had entered his life, there had been, in this place that he favored, only the good fertile earth to greet his eyes, and above it, the vivid blue band of the sky that seemed to be attempting to draw mountain and hills together. Now the earth was pocked by the ugly wooden shacks that housed the white intruders. Soon, if he stayed long enough, he would see the men issue forth, sleepy-eyed, grumbling, but nonetheless eager to begin their task of taming the earth. The women, as women did everywhere, would see their men on their way. Then, the night's sleep washed from their faces, neatly clad in long strange dresses, sleeves rolled up and their hair hidden beneath something he had heard them call a sunbonnet, they would begin to move briskly about their own tasks of cleaning, cooking, washing, gathering wood for the fires, and their harassed, half-hysterical care of the numerous children who ran in and out of the shacks or played lightheartedly by the lake. Later, when the sun had climbed higher in the sky, the women would go to kneel beside their men, their perpetually busy hands now used to aid in the preparation of the earth to receive the seed.

From his hiding place, White Bird would be uncomfortably conscious of the hungry rumbling of his belly as the savory smells from the iron cooking pots hung over the fires began to drift toward him. But he was not deceived by the quiet domestic scene; he knew fear when he saw it, and it was ever present in the faces of the women. The men, though attempting to mask their own fear, could not altogether hide it. It was obvious that they doubted their ability to preserve their lives and to hang on to the sun-drenched stretch of land to which they had staked a claim.

There was good reason for their fear. The land belonged to those Indians whose village was on the high ground just beyond the hills. The last pale-skinned people who had attempted to settle near Beaver Lake had been brutally massacred when the Indians had swept down from the hills to remove the white intruders. The white men had fought well, but in the end they had been defeated, and they had died hard. The women, before dying, had been raped. Some of the children had been spared and taken back to the village, but others had been spitted on the feathered war spears of the warriors.

It was because of his wish to study these people who took such foolish risks with their lives and the lives of their children that White Bird had crept ever nearer, until, finally, he was hidden only by a screen of tall bushes a scant few yards from the settlement. He had seen the way the eyes of the women turned constantly to the hills, and he had felt their dread deep within himself. Fear! It was there in the shrill, rising note in their voices as they called to their children. In a man's nervous fingering of his musket, in a too-hearty laugh, in the grim lines graven about set lips. It was even reflected in the soberness of Justin Lawrence's dark eyes, and in Caroline Fane's quick, nervous movements.

Caroline! The thought of her made White Bird's hands tighten on the reins. On his secret visits, he had seen her slim young body change and ripen, grow heavy with the child she was to bear Justin Lawrence. She too looked always to the hills. He had seen how fixed her gaze became when she saw smoke wisping up into the still air. He knew exactly what she was thinking. That smoke reminded her that the Indians were there. Perhaps quite near. Watching, waiting their chance to steal upon the settlement and massacre the inhabitants. That stark look on her face would pain him in a way that he did not understand.

White Bird's frown deepened. His hide saddle creaked as he moved uneasily. It was he who, having heard that the white people had again made a settlement at Beaver Lake, had led Justin Lawrence and Caroline Fane to this place. He had had many misgivings, and because he looked upon Lawrence as a friend, he had spoken gravely of the dangers. Lawrence had listened attentively, but he had made light of the warning. His only comment had been, "You must not fear for us, White Bird. I believe that Carrie and I will be happy here. Besides, I doubt if Tobias Markham will send his search parties this far south."

White Bird knew the story of their slavery to Tobias Markham of Montrose Plantation. Looking at the tall, commanding Lawrence, and the blond, brown-eyed Caroline, White Bird had felt the usual touch of wonder that these two had known slavery under one of their own kind. The ways of the white man were indeed strange.

White Bird felt the warmth of Lianne's arms about his waist, but he could not divorce the past from the present, could not forget Caroline. It had been a full year and a half ago since he had led Lawrence and Caroline to this settlement that was called Pilgrim's Rest and since that time, not once had he spoken to these two who so occupied his mind. When he had left them among their own kind, he had vowed never to return. And yet, he had come secretly. Never showing himself, silently watching. Why? He had asked himself that question many times. Was it because he was drawn to the strength of Lawrence, the remembered sincerity in his eyes when he had clasped his hand in friendship? Or was it because he could not quite sever all connection with Caroline, who had once so bewitched him? He sighed. A year and a half ago, and in that time the hill Indians had held their peace and had made no move to drive the intruders away. But trouble would come. He knew it. These people knew it. Fugitives from Montrose Plantation Lawrence and Caroline might be, but that was a small enough trouble when one thought of what they might be facing. Perhaps Tobias Markham would never find them. But the hill Indians would.

White Bird became conscious of the little fidgeting movements Lianne was making. He heard her fretful sigh, but he did not turn his head. He felt his usual touch of regret for the loss of Caroline Fane, but for all that, he knew that Lianne was the woman for him. She had all of his devotion and time. It pleased him now to remain silent, and Lianne must endure it until such time as he saw fit to break that silence. He felt her fingers on his waist, almost pinching. With a sense of his own power over her, he deliberately shut her out of his mind and turned his thoughts back to Caroline Fane.

Caroline of the sunshine hair. The first white woman he had ever seen. He had found her deep in the forest. She had been dying from the flogging she had received at the Montrose Plantation, and from the venom of the snakebite that coursed through her body. He had saved her life. Even though, in her delirium, the name of Justin was constantly on her lips, he had vowed that the white woman should be his.

White Bird sighed. He would have kept that vow, had not Justin Lawrence come into his life. Lawrence had saved him from the savage mauling of a bobcat. Since Lawrence had saved him, he knew that he owed him a debt. When he found that the white man searched for Caroline Fane, he could not in honor withhold the woman from him.

Jealousy had raged in him when he witnessed their passionate reunion. But even so, he had stamped on his feelings, and he had led them out of the forest. After leaving them at the edge of the Pilgrim's Rest settlement, he had returned to his village, and to Lianne, who had always desired him. But he was restless, and it was not very long after that that he began making his secret visits to the settlement. There were many times, when Lawrence or Caroline passed near his place of concealment, that he was tempted to step out and face them. But he had never done so. There was always that battle within that stayed him. He had been taught that the white man was the enemy of his people. A ruthless and greedy enemy who sought to squeeze them out and take over the lands of their ancestors. More and more of the pale-skins were coming. Soon there would be no place for the Indian. No place in his own land! However much he desired to do so, it would be folly to meet with Lawrence and the woman. He could well imagine the cold, condemning faces of the elders in his village, were they to have knowledge of his secret desire to be with these two white people who were his friends. He could imagine, too, the judgment they would pronounce upon the traitor in their midst.

Lianne felt the shudder that went through White Bird's tautly held body, and the coldness of terror that had gathered inside her increased. What was he thinking about? Did he know what she had done? It would be like him to say nothing, and then to visit punishment upon her when she least expected it. He had done so before, and he could be harsh.

She lifted her hand and wiped her damp forehead. Wanting to speak, but unable to bring out the words that would arouse his anger, she stared at the back of his head, the left half of which had been newly shaved. On the right side, where hair was allowed to grow, his long braid had been freshly oiled. The braid was coiled neatly above his right ear and stuck through with three scarlet feathers. Yesterday, looking on at his painstaking preparations, she had wondered if this special grooming meant that he had something to celebrate.

At this last thought, tears filled Lianne's eyes, and she clung to him tightly. It was not for this lame youth to whom she had secretly given her body that she feared, but for herself. But for all that, she must speak out and warn him of the danger in which they both stood. Oh, why, after keeping the secret for so long, had she babbled so foolishly of the help White Bird had given to the two pale-skins? And why had she said that she too had helped? Even when she had seen the stony looks upon the faces of her audience, she had not been able to desist. Wishing to embroider the story and to impress upon them her own white blood, she had gone on to make more of it than there really was. She had said that she and White Bird often met with these people. That they were the greatest of friends. The fear in the eyes of Little Beaver, her mother, had not stopped her. Her wagging tongue had gone on and on. Why had she not thought of the talk that would result? The elders of the village would be told of her words. She would be punished!

"White Bird!" she cried out his name in a wailing voice. "There is something that I have done. But I did not mean to do it!"

Arrested by her tone, White Bird turned his head and looked at her. Then, without comment, he slid down from the horse. The copper chains about his neck glinted as he reached up. Gripping her by the waist, he swung her down beside him. "Now, then," he said, his grave eyes studying her, "tell me of this thing that you have done."

Lianne's soft mouth quivered. She lowered her eyes, afraid to look at him. "You will not beat me?" she bargained in a trembling voice. Her hand crept inside his buckskin shirt and softly caressed his chest. She felt his tensing, and despite her fear, she could not refrain from smiling. She knew well how her touch affected him. She twined her fingers in the copper chains. "You must promise me that you will not beat me."

White Bird controlled the slight trembling her touch had aroused. He looked at her consideringly, his eyes wary. "It may be that I will beat you," he said at last. "Do not ask me for a promise that I may not be able to keep."

"I meant no harm." Her dark-blue eyes rose, and she looked at him pleadingly. "You must believe me."

"Tell me."

Stumblingly, she began her story. White Bird listened, his face growing grim. When her voice faltered into silence, she waited for him to speak. When he did not, she flung her arms about him. Holding him tightly, she pressed her cheek against his chest.

White Bird stood very still. He felt her tears cold against his skin, the quivering of her slender body. She had done this thing! She had betrayed him!

"White Bird," Lianne cried. "I am afraid! I know that I will be punished. I cannot go back!"

I, White Bird thought wearily. It was always I with Lianne. She was so beautiful, but her nature did not match. She was selfish and cruel, and she loved and served only herself. "We will go back," he answered her in a toneless voice. "By now, the story will have reached the ears of the elders. If we do not return, we will be pursued. Rather than be brought before them in humiliation, I would prefer to await their judgment."

"No!" Lianne's voice rose to a scream. "It is you who have done this thing, not I. You who have befriended the paleskins. Why should I suffer because of what you have done?" She glared at him defiantly. "I will not let them hurt me. I will not go back!"

White Bird felt his agitation rising. Trying to master the heated words of censure on his tongue, he lifted his shoulders and shrugged indifferently. "Then you should not have twisted your tongue to lies. It is because of this that you must return."

She stared into his stony face. Then, like a small, furious cat, she dug her sharp nails into his shoulders. "I have done nothing!" she screamed. "Why should I be punished?"

Wincing, but still unwilling to lay violent hands upon her,

he drew back from the stinging pain. "You should not have lied."

"Lame one!" she hissed. Her hand lifted, and her nails tore a furrow in his cheek. "Weakling! Coward!"

White Bird made a guttural sound, and the welling fury inside him erupted. His eyes blazing, he caught at her hair and dragged her down to the ground.

Lianne screamed and writhed madly as his hard, punishing hands beat at her body. She tried to speak, but he had pushed her face against the ground, and she could not bring out the words. She heard the half-sobbing sounds he made as he continued to beat her. Even through her pain, she could not help wondering at this curious phenomenon. The other braves beat their women, and seemed to enjoy the pain they inflicted. But when White Bird was forced to beat her, it was almost as if he suffered with her. She despised him for those sobbing sounds, and she thought him less than a man. She did not understand the gentleness in him, and she called it weakness. Sometimes she had the feeling that, if he could have avoided it, he would not have beat her at all. But weak though he was, he knew that a woman, if she was to behave, must be frequently beaten. Had he given in to his weakness and stayed his hand, she would have been shamed before the other women. A beating was not only a punishment, it was a sign of strong feeling, of love. And above all else, she yearned to show those jeering, taunting women that she was greatly loved.

White Bird flung her from him. Rising to his feet, he looked down upon her, and he felt the pain move inside him. She was so lovely. She was like a small golden bird. The pain twisted deeper. He had hurt her!

Lianne rolled over on her back, and she caught the expression on his unguarded face. Soft! she thought. Soft and stupid! She hated him, she wanted a real man! The other braves laughed at him. Called him poet, dreamer, woman! She stared up at him with her tear-swollen eyes. Perhaps she could play on that weakness. She would make one last appeal. She inched herself forward and wrapped her arms about his buckskin-clad legs. "White Bird, I know why you so often go off on your own. I know why you came here today. It is because the pale-skins are living in the settlement. You like to watch them, these two people who have named themselves your friends. It is true, is it not?"

"It is true."

"Come," she coaxed. "Forgive me for my wickedness. Sit here beside me."

White Bird did not move for a moment. He stood there rigidly, trying to harden himself against her. Then, as her arms released his legs, he surrendered. With a little sigh, he sank down beside her and drew her into his arms.

Lianne snuggled against him. "You have never told me the names of these people. Tell me now."

Impossible to resist her, he thought. He shivered as she pressed her lips to his in the strange caress he had taught her. Heat flushed his body as he remembered the pressure of Caroline Fane's fevered lips against his own. She had kissed him, believing him to be the man for whom she called in her delirium. White woman! Strange white caress! And he had taught it to Lianne.

"Lianne!" His arms went around her. "Lianne!"

She turned her head away, avoiding his kiss. "Tell me their names," she said again.

She listened to his difficult pronouncement of the names, and she repeated them after him. "Justin Lawrence. Caroline Fane." She hesitated, not wishing to arouse his anger; then she said, almost timidly, "Tell me, is this Lawrence handsome?"

Repelled by the eager look in her eyes, he answered her in an indifferent voice. "He would no doubt be pleasing to the eyes of a woman. He is a man of a great height, and strong. He has hair as dark as mine, but it is not straight. It curls over his head."

"And his eyes?"

"As dark as his hair. He has somewhat the look of our people."

"Oh! But he is white?"

"He is. The woman is different. She has hair like the sun."

Lianne frowned. She was not interested in the woman. "White Bird"—she kissed him again, and touched his face gently—"let us not go back to our village. Let us stay here with your white friends."

"Stay here?" He looked at her curiously. "You would not be afraid to dwell among them?"

"Afraid?" Lianne tossed her head and gave him an angry glance. "No. Why should I be? Do you forget that I am half-white?"

White Bird shook his head. "How can I forget, when you remind me so constantly? It would not be wise. I do not think we would be welcome."

"But they are your friends."

"The two of whom I have spoken, yes. But what of the others?"

"Your friends would protect us," Lianne continued to coax.

A shadow touched White Bird's face. Drawing away from her, he stood up. "I need no man to protect me," he said in a cold, proud voice. He held out his hand to her. "Come."

Taking his hand, Lianne rose painfully to her feet. "Please." She peered at him hopefully. "Let us go to the white settlement."

"We go where we belong." White Bird lifted her into the saddle, and then mounted himself. "If punishment awaits us, we must endure."

White Bird felt the heaving of her body against his as she broke into loud, angry sobbing, but he made no move to comfort her. With that same fascination he had always accorded it, his eyes returned to the scene below. The settlement had come alive. Figures ran, walked, moved from place to place. They looked, from this distance, White Bird thought, like so many scurrying ants. A tongue of red licked upward, then another, as the cooking fires were lit.

White Bird averted his eyes. Abruptly he wheeled the horse about. He would look no more. Nor would he return to this place again. His knowledge of Justin Lawrence and Caroline Fane had been brief, and yet he could not help but feel that they had, in some subtle way, changed him. He could not define to himself in what way they had done this, or what the form of the change was; he only knew it was there. But the time had come to close his mind against them. They were white, he was Indian. This was his land. He would abide by the customs of his people. He would think no more of the strangers and the country from which they came.

He straightened in the saddle. "No," he said softly. "I will not return."

Lianne stirred behind him. "What did you say?" she asked in a tear-choked voice.

"It was nothing of importance."

Lianne slumped again. White Bird tightened his hands on the reins and dug his heels into the animal's sides. Beneath him he felt the bunching of responsive muscles. Wind rushed at his face and fluttered the feathers in his hair. Above the pounding of hooves, White Bird's laughter drifted high. It was a sound to banish sadness, and yet his heart was still heavy. No matter. Whatever awaited him, a man must be where he belonged.

Chapter 2

Dusk had fallen over the settlement, masking the ugliness of the raw wooden shacks and the much-trampled hard-packed earth. In the distance, the looming mountains and the neighboring hills, the last to surrender to the encroaching night, were wreathed in a purple mist that was faintly brightened by the last weak traces of daylight. In the dark velvet bowl of the sky, few stars were to be seen, but a half-moon, shedding a pale radiance whenever it appeared, sailed in and out of the veiling clouds.

The settlers, as was their uneasy habit of the past few nights, were gathered about a bright fire in the center of the clearing. They were exhausted, but it was as though they sought to put off indefinitely the heavy sleep that would surely claim them should they allow themselves a moment of relaxation. Sleep, they knew, would render them too vulnerable to the enemy who lived beyond the hills. Few of them spoke of their fear, but its shadow was there in their strained expressions and their haunted eyes. The day had passed—this was the thought in most minds—and they were still alive. But would they live to see another sunrise?

Firelight flickered over the dark, handsome face of Justin Lawrence. He listened to the halfhearted conversation of the men, the yawns, and the dragging weariness of the answering voices of the women, but he made no attempt to join in. He was thinking of the things big Jock McPherson had said. "The Indians will not attack at night," Jock had been at great pains to assure them. "Will ye not listen to me? How many times must I tell ye that 'tis the daylight ye must be fearing?"

The settlers did not believe him. They thought he spoke only to soothe their fear of the long nights. But the keenly perceptive Justin, studying him, knew that he spoke the simple truth. Jock, a big, gentle man, could be relied upon if

12

it came to a fight for their lives. He had, furthermore, lived in this country for a long time. He had lost his wife and two children in an Indian attack. And, as the long scar running down his right cheek and another at the base of his skull testified, he had done his share of Indian fighting. It was obvious to him, Justin thought, if not to the others, that Jock McPherson knew what he was talking about.

The mingled voices, as if too weary to carry on any longer with aimless conversation, faded into silence. Eyes, lackluster and heavy, stared broodingly at nothing. In the silence that had fallen, the chirping of the cicadas was a shrill, monotonous chorus. Straightening up on the wooden bench, Justin placed his arm about Caroline's thin, bowed shoulders. Hesitating for a moment, he placed his other hand on the mound of her stomach. He smiled as he felt movement beneath his fingers. Was it a son who kicked so vigorously, or a daughter? It mattered little to him what the sex of the child might be, for he would welcome either. The only thing that did matter was that Carrie should be safely delivered.

Justin looked quickly at Caroline as she made a small restless movement. Her eyes were closed, and in the bright firelight, the shadows beneath them looked like bruises. She was not sleeping; he could tell that by the flickering of her long dark lashes. He smiled again. Those lashes of hers which were so dark in comparison with her bright blond hair, had always surprised him. He tightened his arm about her as tremors began to shake her body. Poor Carrie, she had so many fears weighing her down. The Indians, the safety of the child she carried, and, an ever-present looming shadow over their lives, the thought that Tobias Markham might track them down and take them back to Montrose Plantation and bondage. At this time, the high courage with which she had met every situation in their stormy life together was momentarily quenched. Now, with the news of the Indian attacks of last month, a new burden on her strength had been added. The sickness that had attacked her at the beginning of her pregnancy had returned. Every morning now he would awaken to find her drained and trembling, her limbs icy cold against his. In his fear for her, he would sometimes speak to her roughly, but almost immediately he would regret it. The urge would come to him to take her in his arms and kiss the resentment and the anger from her mouth. He wanted to tease her, to laugh with her as they had once done.

Justin frowned as he thought of his recurring fantasy, which both plagued and shamed him. Lying there beside her, reluctant to get up and start the day, he would feel the spreading warmth in his loins, the sudden urgent thrusting of his manhood. He would think then of how it would be, once she was delivered. A slim and ardent Carrie, her limbs twining with his, her body jerking and shuddering beneath him. In this pleasant daydream, which, he was forced to admit, did little to quieten his turbulence, he would imagine her smiling at him as her robe slithered down her body and fell into a pool about her feet.

"Carrie!" All his yearning hunger was in his voice.

"Justin, it has been so long." Naked, she would stand there looking at him. Then, her arms held out, her breasts quivering, she would come slowly toward him.

"My love!" Naked himself, he would crush her against him, the warmth of her, the throbbing urgency of her that echoed his own. Lifting her up in his arms, he would carry her over to the bed. He would look at her slim, firm body for a moment, the long blond hair that spread itself about her; then he would lower himself until his body was covering hers. But he would not enter her at once. He would kiss her breasts, the thrusting nipples, then slowly, lingeringly, every part of her burning flesh. "Justin . . ." His name on her lips would turn into a moan of entreaty. "Now, my darling, now!"

Their joining would be a fierce, hot, frenzied explosion of delight. When he finally withdrew, they would both be only momentarily sated. Soon eyes would meet eyes, his asking a question, hers answering. His hands would touch her body, lingering there, subtly caressing, and then her returning hunger would leap out to match and mingle with his. So it had always been between Carrie and himself, and as soon as the child was born, would be again.

It was her movements, the small gasping sounds of strain she would make that would shatter his daydream. Looking at her, he would then be flooded with shame that he had allowed his thoughts such a sensuous turn. He could not kiss her in atonement for his previous rough words; the sullen expression on her face caused the impulse to die. Carrie, these days, seemed to retreat to a place where he could not follow her. He would have the dismayed feeling that a breach had opened between them and was slowly widening.

His frown deepened as he thought of the scene this morning. He had known for some time that there was something on her mind, just as he had known that it had no connection with the ever-present danger. He had questioned her, coaxed her, in his efforts to get her to reveal the thing that troubled her, but always before, she had changed the subject. Gradually her voice would begin to rise in shrill denunciation of something he had done, or had left undone. But he knew now what had changed his Caroline to the shrill-voiced woman who was so far removed from the girl he had once known. When words came bursting forth from her, he had listened to her in amazement that quickly turned to outrage. Trying to hang on to his self-control, he had thought with rising fury: Damn the shrew to hell! If she believed that of him, then she must go on believing it! Because he was afraid that his anger would make him forget her condition, he had walked out and left her standing there, her face still twisted with her emotion. The sound of her sobbing had followed him.

Justin's mind went back to the first time he had seen this woman who was to become so much a part of his life. It had been in a courtroom, and Caroline Fane had been on trial for her life. The second time he had seen her had been in that small squalid room in London. He had awakened from a long delirium to find her bending over him. Weak though he was, he had recognized her at once. The woman smoothing his damp, tangled hair away from his hot face was Caroline Fane, accused murderess and adulteress. Woman? Nay, she was a girl. He did not ask himself what she was doing there. He had not particularly cared; he was much too weak and tired to search for answers to the questions that sprang to his mind. Later, he had told himself, later.

Justin looked down into Caroline's tired face, and his simmering anger was swallowed up in a surge of tenderness. For all the infamous labels put upon her, she had seemed to him to be nothing more or less than a frightened child. And then, much later, lying in his arms in complete surrender, the child had disappeared and she had become a warmly passionate woman. There were so many sides to her, and until this time of false accusations and uncertainty, he had thought he knew them all. Carrie, the convict, fleeing from the law, her back raw and bleeding from the flogging that had all but crippled her. Carrie, his partner in crime, face flushed, laughing, enjoying the danger. Then there was the thin and overburdened girl who had nursed the plague victims on the convict ship. Carrie, loving him. Fighting for him. Going without food herself so that he might eat. And now, finally, this Carrie. Alien to him with her thin, pinched face and her perpetually scolding voice.

Again he thought of the scene between them this morning. The morning had begun when Tom Dayton had ridden into the settlement on his lathered mare. He had brought them the news of the Indian attack on the settlement that lay to the north. It had been razed to the ground, and the settlers massacred, every man, woman, and child. Dayton, who had been hunting, had returned just in time to see the war party riding off. One brave, he reported, had taken a grisly trophy. Spiked on his war lance was the severed head of a woman. As he described the atrocities that had taken place, a look of profound horror had spread over his face. His voice had faltered and broken, and the further words he struggled to utter had turned into wild sobbing.

Surrounded by a milling group of shouting, excited men and women, Justin had not at first noticed that Caroline had departed. When he became aware of it, he had broken free and made his way back to the shack. It took little, he knew, to bring on her sickness, and he feared the effect of Dayton's story on her already weakened constitution.

Entering the shack, he had found her leaning against the wall. Her face was colorless, her breathing rapid, and her unwieldy body was shaken by a violent trembling.

"Carrie!" In two strides he was beside her, gathering her into his arms. He felt the nervous jumping of her body increase, and hearing the soft moaning sounds she made, he had feared the child was coming.

"Those people!" She clutched at his shoulders. "Dead! All dead!"

"Don't think of it now, Carrie, love. Try, if you can, to put it from your mind."

"All dead!" She retched, and then put a hand to her mouth. Above her hand, he saw her wide, terrified eyes. Swallowing against the sickness, she began to moan again.

"Carrie . . ." He shook her gently. "Try to pull yourself together."

"We will all die! You know it, Justin, you know it!"

"I know nothing of the sort. The men are prepared in case of attack. We have a lookout. We will not be taken by surprise, Carrie. Trust me."

Her knees buckled, and he put his hands beneath her armpits to hold her upright. "But we are so few, and the Indians so many. You heard what Dayton said. The . . . the Indians took that baby and s-smashed her head against the wall. And that woman. They chopped off her head. The others, with their clothes torn from them, raped, broken! Oh, God in heaven, Justin, what are we doing here in this savage place!"

He tried to rally her, stroking her heaving back, pushing back the bright hair from her horror-stricken face. "Our savage Eden," he said gently. "We called it that, didn't we, Carrie? And we swore to conquer it together."

She began to turn her head from side to side, and there was a look on her face that reminded him of a trapped animal. The cords in her throat strained in a soundless scream. "It will conquer us," she gasped out at last. "I feel as though I can't go on. Don't want to go on."

"Where has my fierce, fighting Carrie gone?" He took her head between his hands and kissed her face. "It is the effort of carrying the baby that has changed you, I know." He kissed her trembling mouth, and then gently touched her full, thrusting breasts. "The old Carrie will come back, you will see."

"It is not the baby who has changed me." Her brown eyes were suddenly hard and bitter. "No, Justin, not the baby."

"Then what?"

She could not answer him; she was overtaken by nausea. Supporting her, he hurried her across the room to the white china basin that was set on a rough wooden stand. He looked on miserably while she vomited. Then, appalled by the violence of her retching, and afraid she would fall, he held on to her racked body.

When the attack was over, he pushed back her lank hair and wiped her damp face gently. Holding her close against him, he felt the baby kick. Fresh tremors began to shake her body, and panic overtook him. "The baby," he said hoarsely. "It's coming, isn't it?"

"Your baby." Laughing wildly, she pushed herself harder against him.

"Yes, mine. I will be glad when he is born."

"He? Perhaps it will be a she."

His brows drew together as he regarded her. He could not understand the wild look on her face. He stepped back a pace, his arms dropping away.

"Come, we made this child together. I, and my faithful lover." She grasped his hand and guided it to her belly. "Feel your child, Rogue Lawrence. Feel it!"

She screamed the last words at him, and he felt his patience snap. "Stop it, Carrie. Damn you, stop this nonsense." He drew his hand away. "You must lie down now."

She resisted his efforts to lead her over to the corn-shuck pallet. "There is no need," she said sullenly. "I feel better now, and I have no pain."

"Are you sure? Let me fetch Betty Forbes."

"No!" She looked at him with something that was close to hatred. "You will fetch no one."

Despite all his good resolutions, his anger had welled up. "What the devil is the matter with you now?" he snapped. "Whether or not the baby is coming, you will be the better for company. Betty is your friend. If I know her, she will be glad to stay with you."

"But you don't know her." She backed away from him. "You don't know any of them. I have no friends here." Her voice rose to a scream. "If you had been using your eyes, you would have noticed that the women shun me."

"For God's sake stop it! You can't know what you are saying."

"I know!" she spat the words at him, her eyes blazing in her pale face. "All these goodwives here were nice enough to me when they believed me to be your wife." Her mouth twisted in bitter mockery. "But now that they have found out that I am only Rogue Lawrence's mistress, a woman of little account, they behave as though I do not exist."

He felt a wave of relief. This, then, was the explanation for her withdrawal and her increasingly strange moods. His Carrie, as did most women at some time or another, hankered for respectability. He laughed, his dark eyes teasing. "And that has bothered you, Carrie, love? But I could not very well have married you without the services of a preacher, could I?"

She did not answer at once, and he said quickly, "We will be married, love, never fear. The next time the traveling preacher comes around, I will make an honest woman of you. I promise."

She took a hasty step toward him, her hand raised as though to strike him. Then, her hand dropping heavily to her side, she said in a strangled voice, "Before you put your child into me, you should have waited for the preacher to come. You . . . you should not have brought me so low."

His sympathy vanishing, he answered her coldly. "I see. But you know, Carrie, I have always understood that it takes two to make a child. Forgive me the impertinence, but you seemed willing enough."

"I will not forgive you!" Her eyes flashed with the old remembered fire. "How dare you talk to me like that!"

"In the name of Christ, don't be so bloody ridiculous!" Trying to conquer his angry impatience, he held out his hand to her. "Come, love, let's put an end to this nonsense."

"No!" She put her hands behind her back and glared at him defiantly. "Coaxing. Sweet talk. That has always been your way, Rogue Lawrence. But this time it will not serve. Do you think I don't know about you and Belle?"

Belle? The young black girl who had come to the settlement with the Fordyces. Confused, he snapped at her, "What the devil do you mean by that?"

"Surely it is plain enough. You were not content with one mistress, were you? You had to take Belle too. How many more will you gather on your way?"

"Carrie, don't be a fool! Belle! There is no truth in it."

"Liar!" Her voice trembled and cracked into hoarseness. "I saw you holding her in your arms. I followed you down to the lake. You kissed her!"

His confusion vanished, and he knew what she must have seen. The black girl, Belle, working with her usual energy, had stumbled and cut her foot. Happening along at that moment, he had picked her up and carried her down to the lake. He had bathed the ugly gash on her instep, and then, tearing a strip from his already ragged shirt, he had bound her foot securely. "There, Belle, that should hold you for a while. But have Nellie Fordyce look at it."

Belle had smiled at him gratefully. "Sure will." She touched his face with her small work-roughened hand, her fingers smoothing back the damp black curls from his heated forehead. "You a right handsome buck, and you kind, too."

He grinned. "Who says?" he answered her lightly.

"Me, Belle. I says." She moistened her full mouth with the tip of her tongue. "I like you," she said huskily. "I surely do." Her eyes turned slumberous and inviting. "I watch you whenever you near, and the more I watch, the more I like. You move so smooth and sure, like you owned the world. Like you . . . you a king."

"Not a king, Belle," he teased, faintly disturbed by the unmistakable look in her eyes. "And as for owning the world, I shall be content if I may own only a small part of this magnificence."

Belle moved closer to him, and he could smell the hot, almost spicy odor of her body. "You come to Belle whenever you feeling a need. I be waiting for you, and you be right welcome."

He smiled at her. She was little more than a child. Fourteen, he guessed. Yet already her breasts were prominent and inviting, and she had the wiles of a full-grown woman. "Don't be too generous with your favors, Belle," he said gently. "Save them for the right man. He'll be along someday."

Her mouth turned mutinous. "But Belle like you. You a big handsome buck, like I tell you. You fill me up and satisfy me." She looked furtively around. "Ain't no one near. Maybe you like to fill me up now?"

"Not right now." Unwilling to hurt her, he had tried to pass it off lightly. "We have work to do, you and I."

"It always work," Belle said sulkily. " 'Pears to me that there ain't never time for play." With a sudden movement, her arms lifted and circled his neck. He could feel the urgent thrust of her breasts against him. "And Belle, she like fine to play with you." She pressed her lips hard to his. "It be whenever you say," she said against his mouth. "I be waiting for you to come."

Pulling her arms down, he had risen to his feet, drawing her up with him. "Be off with you." He swatted her lightly on the buttocks. "Get, you disgraceful child!"

Giggling, Belle had fled. Before she disappeared, she had

turned a laughing face to him. "I ain't no child," she called. "I show you that when you come to me. Don't you forgit, big man. I be waiting for you."

Remembering the incident, conscious of Caroline's accusing eyes upon him, Justin had felt himself flushing. Because he felt guilty, when instead he was guiltless, he had felt himself hardening into stubbornness. Instead of giving her the explanation she so obviously waited for, he had said in an icily formal voice, "You should have used your ears as well as your eyes." Without another word, he had turned from her and walked out.

Tonight, when the others had gathered about the fire, he had expected that she would remain in the shack to nurse her grievances, real and imagined. Instead, she had surprised him. She had entered the circle of firelight and taken her accustomed seat beside him. Had it not been for her continuing silence and the sullen droop of her mouth, he might have thought that all was well between them, especially when she made no attempt to draw away when he put his arm about her.

Coming out of his thoughts, Justin looked up and met the smiling amber-brown eyes of Buck Carey. Returning the smile, Justin reflected on the firm friendship that had grown up between himself and Buck Carey. Buck was a man of medium height, stocky of build. A thick mop of graying black curls crowned a ruggedly handsome face, in which the high cheekbones and very slightly slanting eyes hinted at a faint strain of Indian blood in his makeup. He moved with deceptive slowness, as slow as his soft drawl, which had become overlaid with the slurred accent of the black. But Justin had found that there was nothing slow about him when it came to a fight, those fights that so often erupted between men of different races and opinions. Like Jock McPherson, Buck, now in his early fifties, had lived in this country for a great many years, and he was knowledgeable. Justin had often thought that Buck would be a good man to have beside one in a time of real trouble. Nodding to Buck, he thought gloomily that the time of trouble was not far off.

Buck looked at Caroline, the sun lines beside his eyes crinkling as he smiled. "Your li'l lady looking pure tuckered, Justin. Ain't it 'bout time she be going to her bed?"

Justin, who sometimes suspected that Buck had a tenderness for Caroline, grinned at him good-naturedly. "Mind your own damn business. Put your own lady to bed."

Buck guffawed. "You saying that 'cause you know I ain't got one. Can't get one."

Millicent Andrews, the spinster sister of Harry Andrews, leaned forward and laid a timid hand on Buck's black-clad knee. "What a terrible thing to say, Mr. Carey. You can get any girl you please."

Ignoring Harry Andrews' frown, Buck threw his arm about Millicent's shoulders and drew her close against him. "That including you, Millie gal? 'Cause iffen it ain't, I don't want you getting up my hopes."

Millicent blushed a fiery red, but she made no attempt to remove her head, which had somehow found its way to Buck's broad shoulder. Rather, she snuggled there, like a kitten who had found a home. Her precise little voice was somewhat smothered when she replied, "Yes, Mr. Carey, that includes me."

Buck's eyes widened slightly, and he looked faintly startled. Putting up his hand, he rumpled her light-brown hair. "That's right good o' you, ma'am," he said gently. "But can't rightly say that I'm deservin' it."

"You, Buck," Harry Andrews, coming to life, growled, "stop pawing my sister. Take your goddamned hands off her!"

"Well, now," Buck drawled, "me and li'l Millie here, we friends. Ain't nothing wrong 'bout it." Putting Millicent from him, he rose to his feet. "That being so, I reckon you done insulted me and this gal. Yep. Sure do reckon that."

Andrews rose too, his fists already clenched. "Depends how you look at it. If you want to make something of it, Buck, I'm ready."

"I reckon I does, Andrews." A light of pure joy flickered in Buck's eyes. "Ain't nothing like a fight to take the dust out of a man."

Caroline's eyes opened, and she got to her feet abruptly. "I'm sick of watching you fighting," she said in a rising voice. "Animals, all of you! Haven't we got troubles enough? Can't we somehow learn to get along?" She put her hand to her trembling mouth. "Oh, God, I'm so sick of this eternal brawling!"

Buck turned an abashed face to her. "You right, Miss Caroline, ma'am," he said in a contrite voice. "Men purely take too much joy in fighting. Ain't decent in front o' ladies, I knows that. It's my fault, and I'm right sorry." Turning to Andrews, he held out his hand, a grin lighting his face. "Same goes for you. I bin a mite hasty, I guess."

Andrews' wrathful expression softened into an answering grin. "Damn your hide, Buck, I've got nothing against you, except that you're a fighting fool. Never did know a man so ready with his fists. Not even Lawrence, and he's hotheaded enough. Still, I know you didn't mean wrong. Just don't hurt Millie, that's all."

"I ain't got no intention of hurting her." Buck clasped Andrews' hand warmly. Ignoring Millicent's look of disappointment, he added in a laughing voice, "You ain't got no need to worry. I'm just a mite too old for that pretty little filly." He looked at Millicent, inviting her to laugh with him. "Ain't that right, Millie gal?"

Millicent did not laugh. "No," she said, thrusting out her lower lip. "I don't agree with you, Mr. Carey. You're just the right age for me."

Buck rumpled his hair with an agitated hand. "Don't say that, gal. Of course I'm too old." Turning to Justin, he looked at him with imploring eyes. "You tell Miss Millie here that what I say is true."

His arm about Caroline, Justin began to laugh. "You did the sweet-talking, Buck, so you tell her. Personally, though, I think you're just right." Meeting the flame in Buck's eyes, he looked away, his mouth twitching.

"Now, you all look here, Justin," Buck began, "I don't—"

"Nobody has to tell me anything," Millicent interrupted in a passionate voice. "I can make up my own mind. I know what I want and what I mean to have."

"What's that?" Buck backed away from her, an alarmed expression on his face. "Now, you lookee here, Millie gal, I ain't the marrying kind." A flush overspread his face at the laughter that arose. "We friends, Millie. Friends, that's all."

Looking at him with glowing eyes, Millicent moved nearer to him. "You're right, Buck. At this moment we're just friends. But I don't intend things to remain that way. You might as well know that I mean to marry you."

"Don't say that, Millie gal." Buck's voice was anguished.

"But I do say it, Buck Carey. And I mean what I say."

Buck stared at her as though she had suddenly grown two heads. "Well," he declared in an outraged voice, "I'm right shocked at you, Miss Millie, ma'am. I never did hear a female speak so bold afore. You should purely think shame o' yourself. Sweet young ladies don't talk like that."

"But I am not a sweet young lady," Millicent said firmly. "I'm in love with you, Buck, and I mean to have you."

Even Caroline, her troubles for the moment forgotten, was smiling at Buck's dilemma. Silence fell, and the amused spectators settled back to enjoy the look of panic on Buck's face, and the determined look of the formidable little female who had publicly claimed him as her own.

They all heard the pounding of feet along the narrow, dusty trail that led into the settlement. Smiling faces tightened to startled apprehension, and hands curled about muskets and gripped them tensely.

Everyone was on his feet as a tall, emaciated man came out of the darkness and reeled into the glow cast by the fire. A woman screamed out as she saw the blood on his face, "Oh, dear Christ! Look at his head!"

A flap of skin flopped loosely at the front of the man's head, and it was from this the blood was pouring. Swaying on his feet, the man looked at them dazedly. "Indians!" His voice was high-pitched, fading even as he struggled to bring out words. "Tried to . . . to scalp me. I killed the brave . . . got away. They k-killed my wife. . . ." His eyes rolled up in his head. He would have fallen had not Justin leaped forward and caught him in his arms. Lowering him gently to the ground, Justin looked up at Buck. "What do you make of it?"

Shrugging, Buck got down on his knees beside the man and examined his head. "It's like he says," he said after a moment. "Injun tried to scalp him."

Justin looked up into the circle of faces. "One of you get some water. If we can bring him round, he might be able to tell us more."

Buck shook his head. "He cain't tell you no more, Justin. He's dead."

Buck got to his feet. "You men get the women into the shacks. Come daylight, I 'spect we got a fight on our hands. Injuns like to attack at first light. I aim to be ready for 'em."

Chapter 3

It was Justin who first saw the war party etched against the skyline. Unmoving, the Indians sat astride their horses. A brisk wind blew the vivid feathers in their hair, and the sun, coming from behind a rack of clouds, gilded their bodies and gave them the appearance of copper statues.

Justin swallowed, uncomfortably aware of the curiously hollow feeling inside him and the hard beating of his heart. He hesitated. It was not for him to assume command, but the lookout appeared to be dozing at his post, and there was, for the moment, no one else in sight. Making up his mind, he cupped his hands about his mouth and shouted, "Indians! Get to your positions!"

The lookout started violently. He cast a guilty look behind him, and then scrambled down from his platform to join the other men, who were already bursting from the shacks. The men were heavy-eyed, but their muskets were ready in their hands. Those men, who, ignoring the necessity of sleep, had gone to the fields at first light, were alerted by their own lookouts to the warning shout. They came on at a run, crouched almost double as they tried to gain the living area before the attack could begin.

Justin heard a gasp behind him. Caroline was staring at the Indians, her brown eyes wide with horror in her pale face. "Justin!" She made her awkward way to his side and gripped his arm with her trembling hands. "What can we do? What is going to happen now?"

"I imagine they will attack," he answered in a voice that he hoped was calm and reassuring. "But don't worry too much. We have some good men here, and all of them shoot straight." He pulled his arm free. Then, remembering her rooted fear of Indians, he said in a softer tone, "I won't let anything happen to you, Carrie. I promise. Get back into the shack! Go on!"

"Don't make me promises you have no way of keeping." A change came over her face. He saw the flash in her eyes, and it was as though her fear had vanished, swallowed up in a surge of indignation. " 'Get back into the shack!' " she said in an outraged voice. "What the devil do you think I am? Do you think I would ever leave you?"

"Carrie, listen to me. I—"

"No, damn you, Rogue Lawrence, I won't listen. I've fought by your side before, and I can do it again. I can shoot, you know that. I demand that you give me a musket."

He was touched by her determination to aid him, but at the same time he was impatient for her to be gone. "I know you can shoot, but I'm not risking your life. If you won't consider yourself, at least think of the child."

"I stay. I won't leave you to face those savages alone."

"Don't try me too far, Carrie, or you'll be sorry. You talk as though I will be standing off the Indians on my own. That's nonsense, and I've no time to argue with you." He gave her a slight push. When she did not move, his voice rose in harsh command. "By Christ, Carrie, will you do as I tell you! Another thing. If things go badly for us, you are to get out of here at once. Do you hear me?" He frowned. "In fact, it would be better if you did not delay." He cast a quick look at the Indians, and saw that they had made no move. "Round up the other women and make your way into the forest. You must hide there until you feel it safe to come out. If you take the narrow path behind the shacks, you won't be seen."

"And if you . . . if all the men are killed?"

"Go south. There is a settlement there. They will take you in."

Caroline's mouth quivered. "No, Justin! Let the other women do as they please, but I'm staying with you. Darling, don't you see, I love you, I want to be with you. If you die, then at least I will die by your side."

"There are worse things than dying. You know that."

She looked into his grim face. "I don't care. Let me stay. I love you!"

"Do you, Carrie? Lately I have not thought so."

She saw something in his dark eyes. Pain. And she had put

it there. "Forgive me!" she cried. "I lost sight of my love for a time. But I never will again, darling!"

"Carrie!" He wiped his sweating forehead on his sleeve, and then took her into his arms. "What a strange time you choose to declare your love. But the feeling is mutual. And we will have no more of this talk of dying." He released her. "If you would please me, love, then do as I tell you."

She shook her head. "No, Justin," she said firmly.

"Don't be a fool!"

"I've always been a fool, and I'm staying."

"You'll be no help." Justin's voice had an edge of desperation. "You'll just be in the way. For Christ's sake, Carrie, will you use your brains!"

"I haven't any. You've often told me that." Her mouth folded into the straight, stubborn line he knew so well. Short of violence, she was not to be moved. Goaded, he snapped. "Where is the necessity for both of us to die?"

"Ain't nobody going to die," Buck Carey's drawling voice said from behind them. "Leastwise, not today."

"What do you mean?" Justin swung around to face him. "That's a war party up there."

Buck shook his head. "No, it ain't. Ain't painted up for war, see?" He grinned. "Jock and me, we wasn't for trusting that lookout. He's a good fellow, but I reckon he ain't none too sharp. So we went out and did a bit of scouting on our own. We seen 'em coming a mile back. Ain't painted."

"Painted or not, Buck, they're there. What does it mean?"

"Come for a palaver, that's what it means." Buck pushed his wide-brimmed hat to the back of his head. Taking a crumpled handkerchief from his pocket, he wiped the sweat and the dust from his face. "This goddamned dust," he mumbled. "I reckon I must have ate me a peck or two of it." Meeting Justin's smoldering, impatient eyes, he thrust the handkerchief back into his pocket. "It's a warning," he elaborated. "Injuns want us to get off their land."

"That much I gathered for myself," Justin said, his shoulders straightening. "But we're not leaving."

Buck shrugged. "Know you ain't. That's what this is all about. That's why the other settlers got themselves killed. Me and Jock, we're going out there to meet up with them. Hear what they got to say, and maybe cool 'em off a mite till we're better prepared for an attack."

"Go out there?" Justin stared at him as if he had taken leave of his senses. "What's the matter with you, Buck? You want to get yourself killed?"

"Cain't say I'm hankering for it. I got me a lot of living to do yet. Still, cain't do no other but meet with 'em. That's what they're waiting for."

"But it's madness! Anyway, why you?"

"Ain't mad, if that's what you're thinking," Buck answered, his grin returning. "And it's got to be me and Jock, 'cause we know the Injuns. You're new to this country, Justin, and you ain't knowing how to go on as yet. And what's more, you ain't knowing their ways."

"That may be, but—"

"Ain't no but. We know what we're doing. We're going out under a flag of truce. That's Chief Running Fox up there on them hills. We're old enemies. I had me many a set-to with him and his braves. Last time, it was bad—I almost didn't get away."

"All the more reason to stay where you are," Justin said sharply.

Buck shook his head. "Running Fox won't break the truce."

Caroline looked wildly about her. This couldn't be happening! The red men poised like statues on the brow of the hill. The white, frightened faces of the women and children. The grim determination of the men to hang on to the land at whatever cost. Clad in their dusty buckskins, they crouched behind the barrier, ready to fire at the first sign of trouble, but what were their thoughts? Were they thinking of home and civilization, of quiet streets or country lanes? How did they feel, knowing that if they lost the battle they would be put to death in the cruelest way? That their women would be raped or killed, perhaps made squaws to some of the braves? And that their children, if they did not fall to the tomahawks of the Indians, would be taken as slaves and brought up as savages?

Caroline could find no answer to these questions. Perhaps men, caught in this situation, thought only of the moment at hand. Buck was still talking earnestly to Justin, but there was a faint smile on his lips. Buck was, she knew, a wanderer, never settling long in one place. Just lately she had heard a new term applied to these men who roamed the country and

were as much at home on the great plains as she would be in
an English country lane. The term was "saddle tramp," and it
was appropriate to him. He must have faced many dangers
and undergone many skirmishes with the Indians, but at this
tense moment she could not bring herself to believe in his
smiling self-confidence. Two men, without protection, so vulnerable to the enemy! She shuddered. "Buck," she said in a
trembling voice, "don't go out there. Stay here, please. You
can't seriously be thinking of trusting those savages?"

Justin noticed the warmth in Buck's eyes as he looked at
Caroline, and he wondered if he realized how that look be-
trayed the deep and growing feeling he had for her. Where
Justin had only suspected before, he was now convinced that
Buck was more than a little in love with her.

"Sure you can trust Injuns, ma'am." Buck's answering voice
was calm and reassuring, showing no trace of emotion. "They
got their honor, maybe more so than us, and they got respect
for a flag of truce. Still and all, I take it right kindly that
you're worrying 'bout me, even though there ain't no need."
His eyes fell on the white fichu about her shoulders. "If
you're wanting to do something for me, Miss Caroline,
ma'am, you can lend me that thing you're wearing 'bout your
shoulders. It'll make a right nice flag."

Meeting his smiling amber-brown eyes, she knew that no
words of hers would move him from his purpose. Nodding,
she unpinned the fichu with cold, fumbling fingers and
handed it to him.

As he took the fichu from her, Buck's fingers touched Caroline's in a brief contact. Color flooded his face, and he
seemed momentarily at a loss for words. Impulsively, Caroline kissed his cheek. "Be careful."

"I'm going with you, Buck," Justin said in a firm voice.

Caroline's heart plunged. "No, Justin, you can't!" She saw
the stubborn look on his face, and she knew that he had
made up his mind. "Please, Justin," she said in a breaking
voice. "Oh, please don't leave me, love!"

"It will be all right, Carrie." Smiling at her, Justin stooped
to kiss her trembling mouth. "I believe in Buck. He knows
the Indians."

"You did not believe in him a few moments ago," she
flashed. "Why now?"

"Because I've changed my mind. Any man who is fool

enough to go out there and face them head-on must know what he is doing."

"Justin, please!"

"Ain't no need for you to come, Justin," Buck put in quietly. "You'd do better to stay here with your lady."

Justin's eyes looked alive, Caroline noticed, as they had not done in some time. Almost, she felt, he was hoping for some trouble. It was the old Rogue Lawrence, hankering for excitement, who looked at Buck. Even his voice seemed to have changed. There was the old lazy, almost mocking note in it as he said, "Save your breath, Buck. I want to go with you." He laughed. "If I'm to live in this country, I must learn many things, and among them, how to handle Indians."

Buck looked compassionately into Caroline's white, strained face. "Now, you see here, Justin," he said uneasily, "maybe it ain't so easy as I make it sound. Could be a hot-blooded brave'll let fly with an arrow. It happens sometimes. It's risky, boy."

"It doesn't matter. I'll go with you."

"Maybe it matters to your lady. You're a stubborn mule!"

Justin opened his mouth to speak, but at that moment a man shouted, "The Indians are coming! See there! They're coming slow."

"Inside, lassies," Jock McPherson's voice bellowed. "Hurry the wee ones along. You, laddies, don't you be squeezing a trigger until ye're told. Anyone does, I'll bust his head!"

Some of the children, frightened by the tense atmosphere and the grim expression of the adults, began to cry as the frantic women herded them inside the shacks. One small boy, breaking free, ran to retrieve a fallen toy. He wailed loudly as his harassed mother caught up with him and dealt him a smart slap. The men stiffened, waiting. Some of them had been in the new country a scant few months, others only a little longer, and none of them could conceive of a peaceful palaver between Indian and white man. The stories they had heard of the savage atrocities practiced by the Indians sprang to their minds. Fingers hovered over triggers as they watched the slow advance of the Indians, and despite the comparative coolness of the early morning, a thick sweat broke out on their foreheads and trickled down their faces. Inside the shacks, the children still wailed, and the desperate, scolding voices of the women could be heard.

Caroline had not moved from her position. A door opened, and a sharp voice called her name. She was vaguely aware of the voice, but she did not turn her head. She watched with bleak eyes as the white fichu was fastened to a long stick. Hopelessness flooded her. She was sure that Justin was going out to meet his death. Had they survived Newgate Prison, the plague, the convict ship, slavery, only to meet death here in this wild country, at the hands of the savage red men? Her hands clenched tightly together. If Justin died, it would mean her death, too. She thought of all the foolish differences she had allowed to come between them, and she was bitterly ashamed. She had wanted to be respectable, a wife, and she had let these things prey on her mind, blinding her to the true values, the fact that they were together, that they were in love.

Caroline put a hand to her shaking mouth. She had been such a fool! Nothing was any good without Justin. He was her life, her sole reason for being. What had she been about in her mind? The answer came to her. Without knowing she was doing so, she had tried to make the eagle into a tame sparrow. But Justin would not be tamed, and she knew now that she wanted him exactly as he was. She had fallen in love with the eagle, and then she had tried to clip his wings. A wanton destruction of all she loved and cherished. But never again! Her lips moved. "God, keep him safe. Give us both another chance, please!"

Caroline looked at the makeshift flag fluttering in the wind. It was such a fragile protection against savagery. Let Buck be right. Let the Indians honor a flag of truce!

She started as the stockade gate was pulled open. The high, protesting squeal it made was like an explosion in her ears. With eyes that burned with the tears she would not allow to fall, she watched the three men walk through the gate. In an effort to master her terror, she became conscious of little things. Martha Briarley's frightened face peering through a crack in the door of the shack opposite her. Tom Lane's bright-red shirt, which he wore in preference to buckskin. The ceaseless and monotonous chirping of the cicadas, the fluting notes of a bird, the sunlight glinting on Justin's unruly black hair, on Buck's thick graying curls, and on McPherson's shock of sandy hair. She watched as a small bird with red breast feathers and gray wings came into sight.

Emboldened by the silence and the lack of movement, the bird skimmed low. Coming to rest on the ground, it commenced digging its thin, sharp beak into the hard-packed earth. Caroline moved slightly, and the sudden rustle of her gown startled the bird. It started up from the ground and flew rapidly away.

Justin's mouth felt dry, and his thoughts were chaotic, and yet he was conscious of an intense excitement. With the exception of the brief encounter with White Bird, he knew nothing about Indians, and now he was about to come face-to-face with a whole party of them. The feeling he had now was akin to feelings he had had in the past, a quickening, an almost pleasurable excitement that came to him whenever he was certain that he was about to walk into danger.

A grunt from Buck brought Justin's head around. At the same time, he heard the mutter of drums from beyond the hills, the sound carried to them on the wind. Buck's face, he saw, had taken on an intent, listening expression. What message, he wondered, did the drums carry? The sound thrilled through him, and his steps, even his heartbeat, seemed to keep time with the steady beating.

"You read them drums same as I do, Jock?" Buck asked.

"Aye, they're telling of another massacre." Jock's low voice sharpened. "Keep walking, Justin, lad. Whatever ye be feeling, don't be showing it in yere expression."

Justin's face flushed as he realized he had slowed. "You just worry about yourself, Jock," he answered stiffly.

McPherson chuckled. "Well, now, I wasn't meaning to be stinging yere pride, and ye're the last one I'd be worrying about, so don't be giving me that thundercloud look."

The Indians had reined in their horses. Faces impassive, their hands still on the reins, they watched the three men come nearer. An Indian astride a white horse sent the animal forward two paces. As they stopped before him, he lifted his hand in salute.

Buck and McPherson returned the salute, and Justin, watching closely, copied them. The white horse snorted and pawed the ground. "Greetings, Chief Running Fox," Buck said in a steady voice.

Running Fox inclined his head. "So it is you, Buck Carey. I had a feeling that we would meet again."

Buck grinned. "We're fated to meet, Chief. I've crossed your path more'n once, ain't I?"

"You have. But the next time you trap our game, you will not find it so easy to elude my braves. I will make sure of that."

"I believe you." Buck cleared his throat. "But I'm right surprised to see you so far from your village, Chief."

Running Fox stiffened as a murmur came from the braves behind him. His black eyes flashed imperiously, and the muscles beside his thin, straight mouth tightened. "This is strange talk from you." The yellow and green plumes decorating his thick braid of coarse black hair swayed slightly as he bent forward in the saddle. Wind whipped at the bright blanket about his broad shoulders and fluttered his necklet of scarlet feathers. "We roam where we will on our own land," he continued in a harsh voice. "Remember that."

At the pronounced hostility of his tone, Buck exchanged a disturbed look with McPherson. In an obvious effort to conciliate, when he next spoke he abandoned English and lapsed into the Indians' own tongue.

Listening to the odd clicking speech that was made up as much of gestures as words, Justin wondered what Buck could be saying. He noticed that McPherson, although not taking part in the conversation, was nodding his head at intervals, and occasionally smiling.

The chief appeared to be listening intently, and now and again he contributed a word of his own, but he did not look at the two men; his eyes were fastened on Justin. Abruptly he raised his hand, cutting off Buck in mid-speech. Nodding toward Justin, he said something in his own tongue.

"Him?" Buck turned surprised eyes on Justin. "Justin Lawrence," he answered the chief.

"Justin Lawrence," Running Fox repeated. Again the lean brown hand lifted, this time in a beckoning gesture.

Justin did not move. "Get closer to him," Buck prompted. "I don't know why, but he seems interested in you."

Meeting the piercing regard of the black eyes, Justin moved forward reluctantly and looked up into the fierce, hawklike face. "What is it you want of me?" he asked.

Running Fox did not answer. For a long moment he continued to regard him. The nostrils of his aquiline nose flared, and again his thin mouth tightened, but this time as if with some deep and painful emotion.

At a loss, Justin stood there stiffly, uncomfortably aware of the steady stare of the braves. His discomfort deepened as Running Fox reached out a hand and touched his hair. The thin hand hesitated there for a moment, then traveled lower to touch his features. He was about to speak again, when Running Fox took his hand away and straightened in the saddle. Turning his head, he said something to the braves.

"What is it?" Justin whispered to Buck. "What's going on?"

"He says you're like his son," Buck translated. "His son was killed by the firestick of the white man." He listened again, an incredulous, almost stunned look on his rugged face. "He says the gods have sent his son back to him and that he ain't liking to see his son returned in white form, but he must be grateful to the gods." Justin opened his mouth to speak, and Buck, forestalling him, hurried on quickly. "I know what you're going to say, but it's true, ain't it, McPherson? And he's telling them braves that . . ."

He broke off as the chief turned to face them. "While Lawrence remains with you, you may stay on our land." Running Fox spoke in English, obviously for the benefit of Justin. "We will not trouble you. But if Lawrence should leave, we will take back our land." He looked closely at Justin, and the fierce eyes seemed to soften. "It shall be my gift to you, Lawrence. Use it well."

"Thank you, Chief Running Fox." Prompted by some instinct, Justin laid his hand over the chief's. "I promise to use it well."

Running Fox allowed his hand to remain beneath Justin's for a moment; then he withdrew it. "Farewell, Lawrence," he said in his deep voice. His eyes turned to Buck. "Remember my warning, Buck Carey. The next time, you will not escape."

Unsmiling, he wheeled his horse about. As suddenly as they had come, the Indians were gone. Buck stared, his mouth slightly open. "Well, I'll be!" he exclaimed at last. Turning to Justin, he shouted, "You're our good-luck piece, boy, that's for sure." He began to laugh. "Jock, ain't this boy our good-luck piece? Ain't going to have no trouble from the Injuns, not while Big Chief Lawrence with us. Maybe I'll make up my mind to settle in one place now."

"You, Buck?" McPherson scoffed. "It's not in ye to stay long in one place. Ye say we'll have no more trouble from the Indians, but I'm none so sure. Did ye not see the look on Little Wolf's face? He was not for giving us the land. He'll go against the chief if he can, and I doubt not that the young one will work us a mischief in his own time."

"You're too cautious, Jock. Little Wolf ain't nothing. He's only the chief's third son." Overcome with exuberance, Buck snatched off his hat and flung it into the air. Catching it, he jammed it on his head and began to walk toward the settlement. "Come on, let's go tell the boys they can put away them muskets for good. Cain't hardly wait to see Miss Caroline's face when we tell her 'bout our chief here."

Following, Justin glanced at McPherson's sober face. He could not help thinking that McPherson was right. It was too easy. Something was bound to go wrong.

Chapter 4

Lianne lay full-length on the flat sun-warmed rock. She was aware of the eyes of the two braves upon her, and she knew that soon they would be taking her to face the elders. The elders would pass judgment upon her for having aided the white people. But that was only a story she had made up. She had done it to emphasize her own white blood and to make herself seem more important in their eyes. It had not worked out the way she had thought, and now, because of White Bird, she faced serious trouble. But not for long. She was certain that she could convince them that she had lied. White Bird must take all the blame. He had promised her that he would. And after all, it was all the fault of that lame one. She had never even seen Justin Lawrence and Caroline Fane. White Bird would tell the elders so. Nothing would happen to her. How could it? She was innocent.

Convincing herself, Lianne moved her fingertips caressingly over the purple and pink heads of the flowers that sprouted from the sides of the rock. It was one of nature's little miracles that these flowers could flourish in the crannies, seemingly without the benefit of the earth to nourish and sustain them. Just as she too was a miracle. Her mother, Little Beaver, who loved her and was proud of her, was always telling her so.

At this last thought, Lianne smiled complacently. She knew well that she was not popular with the other maidens of the tribe, but this did not worry her unduly. They thought her vain, and they ridiculed her white blood, the very thing of which she was so proud. They called her "half-breed," and they derided her at every opportunity. Let them, if it pleased them. She was superior to them, and they knew it, even if they could not be brought to admit it. They were dull too, having no time for enjoyment and the gay, bright things of life. The minds of the braves and the maidens too were wholly concentrated on war with the white men. They thought of little else. War! They were always planning it.

Frowning, Lianne moved impatiently. The example of the great chief who had led his braves against the white people in the famous uprising of 1622 had fired them all to a new fervor. That particular massacre had happened many years ago, but it made no difference to them. They continued to bow down in worship of his memory. A council of war was always being summoned, and the important men of the tribe and the war leaders would faithfully attend. The young braves, even though they knew well that it was as yet only talk and a continual rehearsal for the great wars that would surely come, would be carried away by enthusiasm. They would paint their bodies black and yellow, and their faces half-black, half-red, with white circles about their eyes. Afterward, as a finishing touch, the braves would throw handfuls of bright feathers against each other's paint-wet bodies. When the council was over, they came out of the wigwam to swagger before the adoring maidens, flourishing their tomahawks and boasting of the great deeds they would do.

Lianne pushed thoughts of war from her. It pleased her better to recall her mother's lavish praises on the glories and beauty of herself, Lianne, the perfect maiden. It was true. Was she not the glorious result of the union between her mother and a white man? Her father's name had been Jack Langley. It was true that he had forsaken her mother, leaving her lonely and desolate. But how could he, a white man, be expected to stay with a stupid and ignorant squaw? So he had returned to his wife and children in far-off England. Whenever her mother spoke of Jack Langley, she always cried bitterly, for she had truly loved him. Even though many years had passed, she lived on hope that Langley would one day return from that misty gray land that was girdled about by the sea.

Lianne's fingertips stroked the flower heads again. Before her father had taken his last farewell of her mother, he had named his child. He had given her his own mother's name, Lianne, and that was how she insisted on calling herself. Often she would stubbornly refuse to answer to her Indian name. She had been born beside a deep blue lake, and at the time of her birth the water had been radiant with sunlight. So her mother, in addition to her English name, had called her Sparkling Water. Sometimes, when the maidens wished her to do them a favor, they would address her kindly by her Indian name, but never could they be prevailed upon to call her Lianne. Mostly, though, they called her "half-breed." She did not care; they were only stupid Indian squaws. Their taunts were as ripples upon the waters, soon gone.

Shooting a look at the two braves, Lianne considered speaking to them. She hesitated, and then dismissed the notion. She went back to her favorite topic. Herself. She was, with her mingling of white blood, the most beautiful of the maidens. Her hair was thick and black and glossy, and when the sun touched her hair, it showed bright bronze lights. Unlike the other maidens, she was constantly washing it in the stream, and she disdained the use of bear's grease for grooming. Reluctantly, for even she was forced to bow to some things, she wore it according to the custom for unmarried maidens. It was cut into a straight fringe in the front, and the sides were short and came to just below the ears. The long hair at the back was braided, and she always twined the braid with little painted seashells. She liked the pleasant little tinkling sounds the shells made when she tossed her head. Her eyes were her father's, dark blue and slightly tilted at the outer corners. They were fringed with thick black lashes, of which she was extremely proud. She had likewise inherited her father's finely cut features and his winged black brows. Her mouth was full and soft and moistly red. She never had to use the juice of crushed berries on her lips to color them, as the other maidens did. She was always very careful of her skin, which was the color of pale honey, for she did not want the sun to darken it.

Lianne touched a finger to her lips. Leaping Stag, who admired her beauty and wished to make her his woman, had said that her lips were the color of the scarlet flowers that covered the slopes in the summertime. The compliment had pleased her, but she could wish that it had come from someone else. She did not like Leaping Stag, even though he was rich, and to prove it, wore his mantle of beaver in the summertime as well as the wintertime. He was thought by most of the maidens to be handsome and desirable.

A frown marred Lianne's smooth brow. She did not want

Leaping Stag, and she was tired of the lame one, White Bird. Her dream was to belong to a man of her father's race. One day, she was quite sure, the gods would bring this white man to her. From the first moment he saw her, he would look upon her with desire. His eyes would smolder and then kindle to flame, as Leaping Stag's did whenever he looked at her. The white man would take her for his woman, and she would be faithful to him. It had happened for her mother, and it would happen for her. But she did not want just any white man. He must be as strong and as handsome as Jack Langley, her father, had been. When he came to her, she would not be timid like her mother. She would be strong and aggressive in her love, and she would never let him go away and leave her. She would kiss him with her lips, in the strange way the white people seemed to find so pleasant. Her mother had told her of this custom. And later, when White Bird had learned of it through the woman Caroline Fane, she had experienced it.

Lianne fell to pondering on the custom of kissing the lips. At first she was frightened of the thought of having lips touch in such a close and intimate caress, but then she had found that the joy and the light-headed feeling to be obtained from this action far outweighed her fears.

Lianne laughed softly, so lost in her thoughts that she was now quite unaware of the eyes of the braves upon her. Two years ago, when she had risen to her fourteenth year, and the blood upon her thighs had told her she had become a woman, she had stalked a white man through the forest. Dark hair, the man had had, and strange light eyes in a brown face. Eyes that, when she encountered them, had made her shiver, for they were like ice overlaying blue water. While stalking him, she had tried in the way of the Indian to be very quiet. But she was too excited by the adventure, and she had stumbled over a stone and twisted her ankle. The pain had been so sharp that she had forgotten caution and cried out. Suddenly the white man was standing over her. His eyes, so pale in his brown face, had frightened her, but when he stooped to examine her ankle, she had been terrified.

When the man finally spoke, it was in a deep voice that she had found most attractive and pleasing to her ears. "Who are you?" he said. "To what tribe do you belong?"

Terror had been swallowed up by anger that he could so

easily class her as Indian. It had always seemed to her that she resembled more a woman of his own race. Sulkily she had answered him in her father's tongue, purposely leaving out the naming of her tribe. "I am Lianne."

"Lianne?" The man's light eyes had warmed with a twinkle. "That is a most unusual name for an Indian girl."

If she had dared, she would have spit in his face and clawed at his smooth skin; instead, she nursed her resentment and anger. Her head lifted proudly. "My father is a great Englishman," she said coldly. "He named me after his gracious mother. I am like her, I know, for she was very beautiful."

The man seemed to know that he had offended her, for he smiled and said softly, "I doubt that the lady could have been as beautiful as you."

She had liked that, and she found herself warming to him. While he busied himself binding her ankle with a spotted handkerchief that he had first dipped into a nearby stream, she had felt a great temptation to reach out her hand and touch his hair. It was thick hair, but it did not look coarse like that of the braves. She thought, if she could feel it with her fingers, it would be similar to the texture of her own hair. But then, when he looked up, the impulse to touch him had died. She was suddenly afraid that the icy eyes would bewitch her and perhaps bring down ill fortune on her head. It was a great pity that he was so old and had such chilling eyes. Had it not been for that, she might have taken him for her man, for she admired his looks.

He had asked her, after a little while spent in pleasant conversation, if she could get back to her village without assistance. She had told him that she did not require assistance, for she had feared that if the braves saw her in his company, it would lead to serious trouble for herself.

Before the man left her, he had told her that his name was Tobias Markham. He lived, he said, in a place that was called the Montrose Plantation. From his remarks, he seemed to wish for the friendship of the Indians, or so it had seemed to her. He had not hesitated to tell her in which direction the plantation lay. She had smiled at him shyly, and then she had cast down her eyes so that he might note and admire her long lashes. Perhaps, she thought, he wished to make her his woman.

He had returned her smile, and again commented on her

beauty, which she had found very pleasant, but only her due. When he had gone on to describe the wigwam in which he lived, she had marveled that it should have windows covered with glass, which was a thing that she found very strange indeed. At the thought of being enclosed within walls, and all the entries where air should penetrate blocked with this glass of which he spoke, she had felt stifled. But she did not tell him so, for she feared that he would think her to be only a stupid squaw. Even if she never saw him again, she wanted him to respect and admire her and to understand that she had great intelligence. So she had shrugged as though with indifference at this wonder, and she had told her lie in a lofty voice. "You must not think that this glass is new to me. The lodge of my mother is furnished in this way."

"I see." He had said it very kindly, but the smile was in his eyes again, and she had had the disagreeable suspicion that he was laughing at her.

She had tossed her head, making the little shells twined in her braid tinkle. "I have told you, Markham, that my father is a white man, a great chief in his own country. Do you think that such a great man would have neglected to furnish the lodge of my mother with this glass?"

"No, no, of course not." He had smiled at her, and then he had taken his leave.

"Farewell, Markham," she had called after him, and his answering voice had drifted back to her.

Since that time, whenever she could slip away, she had taken the long trek to the boundaries of the plantation. She had seen with her own eyes the wigwam that Markham called "house." It was a grand and beautiful building, so beautiful that at first she had found herself quite overwhelmed with its magnificence. But all the same, she shuddered at the thought of living in it. It seemed to her that she would die from lack of air.

She went to the Montrose Plantation many times, and although she had seen him pass by quite near to where she had hidden herself, she had never attempted to speak to Tobias Markham again. Through listening and observing, she had found out that the white woman with the strange reeling walk was Markham's squaw, but she looked much older than her man. There were many men who worked for Markham. Some had white skins and some had black, but there were no

Indians. This did not surprise her. The Indian was very proud, and she knew well that he would rather die before he would work for one of the pale-skins who had stolen his land.

Lianne thought of the killing fury in the heart of all the Indian braves. They worshiped the land of their ancestors, and piece by piece the pale-skins were taking it away from them. More and more of the pale-skins would come in the huge canoes with the great flapping white wings, and they too would take land. She had heard that the war chiefs, in their councils of war, spoke out against it. It must not be, they said. They could not allow the theft of their land to go on. If something was not done to stem the tide, then very soon there would be only a little space left to their own people. Chief Black Eagle, who was bitterly against the invading pale-skins, was often heard to remark that perhaps the plan of the invaders was to drive the Indian into the sea, while they took all the land for themselves. Lianne's thoughts drifted to the man who was called Justin Lawrence. It was true that she had never seen him, but White Bird had described him. With his great height, his dark hair and eyes, it seemed to her that he must be very like Jack Langley, whom her mother had so often described. Could Lawrence be the white man who was fated by the gods to become her own? It was a pleasant daydream, and she drifted with it willingly. She was half-asleep when the braves came to tell her that it was time for her to appear before the elders for judgment of her case.

Lianne arose slowly, and suddenly, looking into the grim faces of the men, her confidence that she would be found innocent fled. Terrified, she walked between them, and her terror almost overpowered her when each man took hold of one of her arms, as though they feared she would run away.

"Don't touch me!" She tried to drag her arm away, but Pale Sky, who walked on her left, instantly tightened his grip. Falling Arrow, on her right, looked at her with a certain sympathy, and she appealed to him. "Must you drag me along? I am not a prisoner yet. I am innocent. Have I not said so over and over again? Please do not march me along like a maiden of little account."

Falling Arrow felt Pale Sky's eyes upon him. He knew that Pale Sky was wondering if he, weakened by his desire for this half-breed maiden, would give in to her appeal. The hot blood flushed his face. Pale Sky should see that he was not too weak to do his duty. He dug his strong fingers into Lianne's arm, causing her to cry out in pain. "Be silent, woman," he said coldly.

Pale Sky gave a grunt that he thought might indicate approval, but Falling Arrow did not look at him to see if this was so. With his hand gripping Lianne's arm, he stared straight ahead, his mind filled with the picture she made. Today she was dressed in her finest garments, and the reason for the care she had taken in her dress was, he guessed, to gain the approval and sympathy of the elders. The sleeveless leather jacket she wore was fringed at the hem, and beaded in various designs. The jacket was not fastened at the front, and Falling Arrow had a clear view of her golden-skinned rounded breasts and rosy thrusting nipples. Her leather apron was slit on either side. It hung from her waist to just above her knees, and it too was fringed and embroidered in the same designs. Beneath the apron she was naked, and he thought of what it covered.

Pale Sky cleared his throat. Falling Arrow was a fool, he thought scornfully. If he were not careful, his desire for this foolish maiden would lead him into trouble. His lip curled as his thoughts gave way to his own lust for Lianne. Falling Arrow had a woman of his own, but he was sick with hunger for this maiden with the weak white blood. The one thought that gnawed at him night and day, the thought that he had put into words for his brothers to hear, was to drag her into his lodge, and tearing the garments from her body, throw her down on his bedding of skins and thrust himself inside her.

Again Pale Sky cleared his throat and thought what an animal Falling Arrow was. Even the old women trembled before his lecherous eyes. There was not a woman in the village that he had not desired, but never as strongly as he now desired this half-breed. He loved, too, to inflict cruelty on the object of his desire. Falling Arrow's own woman, Scarlet Blossom, cried out in agony when his huge penis was thrust inside her, for he took her like a dog takes a bitch. He had no shame or delicacy of feeling. Sometimes he would take Scarlet Blossom in the normal way that a man takes a woman, and on those occasions he would invite those brothers who, like himself, had no shame. He would bite at her breasts until her nipples bled, and then, when he had her screaming for mercy, he would mount her and ride her like a man crazed. It was fortunate for him that no one had as yet given him away. Should Chief Black Eagle come to learn of his conduct, he would be turned away from the village. Looked down upon by his brothers, he would become an outcast.

Lianne's fear mounted as they neared the village. Abruptly she stopped walking, and not even when the two men dragged on her arms would she move. "I am afraid!" she cried.

Pale Sky frowned at her. "Do not lose your dignity," he bade her.

Lianne turned a desperate face to Falling Arrow. If he had heard her outcry, he gave no sign. His tall, thin body shook with his rapid breathing, his mouth was half-open, and his mesmerized eyes were fastened greedily on her breasts.

Lianne looked at Pale Sky with her tear-wet eyes. "I am innocent, Pale Sky, but I fear they will not believe me. I boasted a knowledge of these white people, I said that they were my friends. But I lied. I have never seen them."

"That will show you the folly of lying," Pale Sky said sternly.

"Did White Bird tell the elders of my innocence?"

"I believe that he tried to do so. But the elders were angry. They would not listen."

Lianne's tears overflowed and ran down her cheeks. "Then what has happened to White Bird?"

"He has been found guilty. Did you not see the messenger who came to bring us the news?"

Lianne shook her head. She had been so deep in her thoughts that she would not have noticed the messenger. "No, no . . ." She faltered. "I did not see him. It may be that I was half-asleep. What will they do to him?"

"It has been done," Pale Sky said. "White Bird has already undergone torture. Tonight, when darkness falls, he will be banished from the village."

"Torture!" Lianne's voice rose in a hysteria of fear. "They will not do the same to me? Tell me they will not!"

"If you are indeed innocent, you need not fear," Pale Sky said in a grave, considering voice. "But if you are found guilty, it may well be that the same will be done to you." He took her arm. "Come."

Lianne's body stiffened, and a wailing came from her

throat. For a moment Pale Sky thought that a demon had entered into her, so rigid was she and so wild her appearance. The two men tried to move her, without success. Pale Sky became angry, and he decided that it was not a demon that had entered into her, but simply that, in her frenzy, she had taken on the strength of a man. "If she will not walk," he said curtly, "we must drag her along."

Falling Arrow looked at him, and his eyes were almost as wild as Lianne's. Pale Sky made his voice harsh, to bring him out of the heat of desire that was consuming him. "Take her arm. Do as I tell you!"

Falling Arrow's mouth tightened with resentment and anger, but he said nothing. Together they concentrated on pulling the stiff body along. Lianne hung between them, a deadweight. The thin soles of her moccasins scraped over the rough ground. Her mouth was wide open, the cords of her throat straining with her piercing, desperate screams.

Both men were sweating profusely when they came to the edge of the village. Relieved to be done with the prisoner for the moment, Pale Sky bade Falling Arrow to guard her. "I will go into the village and inquire if the elders are ready to receive her," he concluded.

A light came into Falling Arrow's eyes. He let his lids droop, afraid that Pale Sky's gaze would pierce through his eyes and see the thoughts in his head. "I will guard her well," he said in a thick voice. "You need not worry."

Pale Sky hesitated. "Do not touch her. You must promise me that you will not."

"I will not touch her," Falling Arrow mumbled.

Pale Sky nodded and turned away. He walked steadily, and he did not turn his head to look. Falling Arrow had said that he would not touch the maiden. To look back would be to degrade his word.

Lianne's screams had died to whimpers. Without looking at Falling Arrow, she sagged to the ground. Useless to run, she thought; he would catch her easily. An insect crawled over her leg, and she stared at it with hopeless, tear-swollen eyes. They would find her guilty—she knew it. If they tortured her, she would go mad!

Lianne looked up sharply as Falling Arrow grunted low in his throat. To impress her, he gathered air into his lungs and puffed out his chest. Then, expelling the air, he squatted down beside her. She saw the look in his eyes, and she knew what he would do to her. She spat at him. "I will tell!" she shouted.

Falling Arrow wiped the spittle from his chest with the palm of his hand. "Who will believe a maiden of such little account?" he said in a soft, mocking voice. "The women gather in the lodges and whisper of your lewd conduct with White Bird. The men laugh, and they spit at the mention of your name. They will remember the ease with which you opened your legs to White Bird. So who will blame me if I take what is so freely offered?"

"I do not offer it to you, you carrion!" She screamed as his heavy weight fell across her and pinned her body to the ground.

"Quiet!" Slapping her, he covered her mouth with his hand. Holding it there firmly, he lowered his head and began to bite her breasts. When he looked up again, he saw the agony in her face, and the sight of her pain fired him to madness. When her eyes rolled upward in her head and she lay there like one dead, he was not dismayed. Now she could not fight him. Now he could do anything he desired. Little bubbles of saliva formed at the corners of his mouth as he freed himself from his breechclout. Slowly, moving her about as though she were a doll, he took off her clothes. The madness flickered in his eyes again as he looked at her golden-skinned body. He had watched her for so long, his hot eyes noting her beauty, her slow maturing, the way her small breasts quivered beneath her jacket, the almost insolent swing of her slim, graceful hips as she walked about the village with that proud head of hers held high, and the longing for her had grown until it had mounted to an obsession. Lying in his lodge at nights, his woman tossing and turning beside him in her uneasy sleep, he would think of Lianne. That frightening throbbing in his temples would begin again as he imagined himself thrusting inside her. What he would not do to her! He would pound and pound, until, at last, his release came and his seed, hot and healing, would jet from him.

Falling Arrow made a low moaning sound as he crouched over Lianne. He could smell the perfume that always seemed to emanate from her skin. It was like crushed wildflowers, he thought. That wildflower perfume, mingled with her sweat, was a heady odor, the spur that drove all reason from him.

Panting with the forces that shook him, he bit at her, leaving behind abrasions in her flesh circled by beads of blood. His tongue licked at her greedily, going lower, until it entered the intimate place of her womanhood. He felt her convulsive leap as his tongue probed deeper, and his moaning grew in volume. She was conscious again. She would try to fight him off. She must not, not now! He would not let her.

Her body reared. "Don't!" Her voice, weak and unsteady, came to him faintly.

His head lifted. There were actual tears in his black eyes as he stared at her. Tears for himself, for the grinding pain inside him that only she could assuage. He crouched lower still, his nostrils flaring as he drew in her female odor. Then, with a hoarse, inarticulate cry, he was upon her.

Her brain blank with horror, Lianne went limp beneath him as he drove into her like a madman. Pain shuddered through her, and she felt as though her insides were splitting asunder, but still she continued to lie there like one dead. Only once did she move. Her arm lifted, with her fingers crooked like claws, her nails tearing a long furrow down his humping back.

Shuddering, sobbing, his dark face contorted, Falling Arrow did not even notice the pain she had inflicted upon him. When his release came, he fell heavily against her. Rubbing his sweat-slippery body against hers in the lingering remnants of his passion, he was already planning to possess her again. He did not ask himself what would happen if she spoke out against him. She was a witch woman, a madness in his brain!

Walking slowly into the village, Pale Sky listened with his usual pleasure to the frothy splash of the waterfall that spilled its bright, tumbling stream on the other side of the river. Halting, he averted his eyes from the crumpled, bloody figure of White Bird, who was tied to a post in the center of a cleared space. His hands on his hips, he stood there wondering if he should approach Chief Black Eagle at once, or wait for a few moments. Deciding to wait, he looked about him with proud eyes. He knew well that their village was finer than that of the brothers who lived beyond the waterfall.

There was reason for his pride. The village lay in a flat space between two slopes. It was so situated that it afforded a clear view of the broad river. There were few trees, for the ground had been ruthlessly cleared to make way for the dwellings and the crops, but here and there a mulberry tree had been allowed to remain. The spreading branches of the trees made a welcome shade for heated bodies when the sun was at its zenith. The wigwams were well-spaced. They were constructed of slender saplings that had first been driven deeply into the earth and then bent forward so that they formed a central point. Except for small spaces that had been left to allow the smoke from the fires to emerge, the points had been firmly tied together with flexible roots. The wigwams of the more prosperous Indians were covered with a natural bark. Those of the poorer members were protected from the changing seasons by woven mats.

Pale Sky looked at the largest of the dwellings. Seated cross-legged before it on a cushion of plaited reeds was Chief Black Eagle. Pale Sky studied Chief Black Eagle with the same pride that he had studied the well-laid-out village. Black Eagle was a majestic-looking man who had just entered his middle years. He wore a tunic and breeches, both fringed and lavishly embroidered with multicolored beads. About his broad shoulders he wore a cape that was composed entirely of vividly dyed feathers. His large head had been completely shaved on the right side. The length of hair on the left side had been pulled severely back from his face, and it was coiled into a large knot. His skin was a slightly deeper hue than the copper ornaments he wore. His black eyes were narrow, his mouth full and well-shaped. A great beak of a nose dominated the grim, craggy face. A black eagle with outspread wings had been painted on each cheek.

Pale Sky's eyes turned to the women. They were dressed in a similar style to the half-breed who insisted upon calling herself Lianne. His blood stirred as he thought of her, and he was ashamed. He placed his lips tightly together and continued to study the women. Some wore their leather aprons long, hiding their legs, for most of them were respectable women, and they did not care to flaunt their limbs as Lianne did, but, like hers, their breasts were unbound and visible between the loose folds of the short fringed jacket. Many wore their hair in the same way as Lianne. These were the unmarried maidens. Those who were mated wore their hair in two long braids that dangled to well below their waists. Some had bound their braids with strings of beads, others with strips of colored leather. Nearly all of them had painted upon their arms, their breasts, their shoulders, and their foreheads designs of various natures. Some depicted snakes, birds in flight, antelopes, and crouching beasts.

All of the men, except for the tall brave Leaping Stag, were wearing tunics and breeches that were similar in design to Black Eagle's, but they were not as heavily embroidered. Their heads, too, had been shaved, and the hair on the left coiled in a like manner. The hair knots were decorated with a variety of objects. One had the horns of a stag.

Perhaps, Pale Sky thought, frowning, Leaping Stag outdid him. It did not please him, but he had to admit it was true. His plain leather clothing and rich mantle of beaverskin made him stand out from the rest. He was never seen without this mantle, for he liked to flaunt the fact that he was above the other Indians in wealth. Pale Sky smiled inwardly. He had never liked Leaping Stag, and at this moment he was looking very grim. He had long desired the half-breed, and although he knew that White Bird had stolen her virginity, he pretended not to know, for he wished to make her his woman. No doubt he was thinking of the fate that would shortly befall her.

Pale Sky cleared his throat, waiting to be noticed and beckoned forward.

Chief Black Eagle was aware of Pale Sky's presence, but he was content for the moment to ignore him. Soon the half-breed maiden would be led forward to tell her story. He would listen, but he greatly feared that she was as guilty as White Bird. Black Eagle sighed. Three times had Little Beaver, the maiden's mother, come to him. She had crawled into his lodge on her knees, and she had laid her forehead against his feet while she pleaded for her daughter's life. He was not an unjust man, and he would not take the maiden's life from her, but he had not told Little Beaver this, for he was offended that she had thrust herself so boldly upon his attention.

Black Eagle looked across at White Bird, who was still bound to the stake. His head had fallen forward, and his knot of hair had come loose. It touched the ground, and the ends were wet from the thick spotting of blood about the stake. As he watched, White Bird raised his head slightly, and Black Eagle saw the dribble of blood coming from the corner of his mouth. His legs and his feet were scarred with burns. His buckskin shirt had been torn from his shoulders, and there were deep lacerations on his chest and his back that had been made by knives. Not once had he cried out under the torture. Even when the braves had demanded that a fire be kindled at his feet, he had folded his lips tightly together and shown no fear. It was because of this courage, which he could not help but admire, that he had forbidden the braves to kindle the fire. Like the maiden's, White Bird's Life would be returned to him. But because of his friendship with the pale-skins, he had lost both standing and honor. One does not aid the enemy or make a friend of them. So he would become an outcast from his tribe, and he would be an object of scorn to all his brothers.

From the corners of his eye, Pale Sky saw Black Eagle's hand lift. He turned quickly to face him. Black Eagle did not call him forward to have words with him, as he had hoped he might do; he merely pointed. The gesture meant that Pale Sky was to fetch the maiden before him. It was an honor to be seen in conversation with Black Eagle, and since this was denied him, his vanity was stung. His face flushing with humiliation, he hurried away.

White Bird felt his bonds loosen and drop away. With dazed eyes he looked up into the face of Gray Lake. Gray Lake placed one hand over his mouth, which meant that he was forbidden to speak to the traitor. With the other hand he pointed toward Black Eagle.

White Bird knew from this that he was to go before Black Eagle, who would formally pronounce his fate. Turning his head, he spat the blood from his mouth. Black Eagle was only a few yards away, but to White Bird it seemed like many miles. His vision was blurred, and he wondered if the heated sticks with which the women had poked him had blurred his eyes. The ground wavered beneath him, and he put out his burned hands to aid himself. Gritting his teeth against agony, he tried to square his shoulders and lift his head high. A man must walk like a man, not like a wounded animal. It was not until he had fallen to his knees before Black Eagle that he saw Lianne. She was lying on her back, her eyes wide open staring upward. Her stomach and breasts had been burned.

White Bird almost sobbed aloud when he saw her. As her eyes turned toward him, he bit down hard on his lip. Her eyes! Bright and blank, and yet with terror in their depths. He had seen such eyes on a wounded doe.

Lianne saw the blood on White Bird's face, the scars beside his eyes and his mouth, the deep gouge in his forehead where a rawhide thong had been twisted cruelly tight. There was a great gash on his cheek. It started from the cheekbone and swept down to his mouth, and there were burns covering his body.

Lianne felt no pity for him. Had she the strength, she would have spit at him. Or perhaps she would have taken her small knife and opened a gash in his other cheek. Her lips skinned back, showing her even white teeth, and her eyes glittered with hatred. It was he, the cursed lame one, who had brought her to this suffering and terror. Had it not been for him, she would not have known of the existence of Justin Lawrence and Caroline Fane, and therefore she would not have lied. She wanted to cry out, "Kill him!" But she did not dare, for perhaps they would kill her too.

Her agony seemed greater now than it had moments before. Tears streamed from her eyes and ran down into her hair. But far greater than the pain in her body was the injury to her vanity. They had burned her beautiful breasts! What if she were scarred? If ever she should see revulsion in a man's eyes, she would kill herself! She would take her knife and open the veins in her wrists and let her lifeblood flow away. She thought of Falling Arrow with a hatred that was greater than that she felt for White Bird. It was he who had held her while the flaming brand scorched her breasts and her stomach. It was also Flaming Arrow who had spoken out against her. He had told Black Eagle that she had taunted him into raping her; that she had taken off her clothes and undulated her body before him, until he, being only a man, had felt the blood racing through his thighs. He had tried to resist her, but she would not let him. And so he, for the sake of his sanity, had been forced to take her. Lies! He had said these things because he had feared that she would speak out and condemn him. Moaning, she began to turn her head from side to side. The moans built in her throat and turned into screams, and she did not try to stop them. She was not brave and had never been able to endure pain like the other maidens. They were not human!

Black Eagle turned his head and looked at Lianne's ravaged face and heard her scream. He felt shame for her, for he knew that an Indian maiden of pure blood would have suffered her pain in silence. He had seen other maidens, being punished for crimes, have too much pride to cry aloud as this half-breed was doing. He avoided looking at Little Beaver, knowing that her humiliation on behalf of her daughter was great, and a trial to endure. Instead, he tightened his upper lip to show his contempt and displeasure. "Silence her!" he said sharply. "I wish you all to hear my words."

A hard, calloused hand was laid across Lianne's mouth, the fingers pressing painfully into her cheeks. Suddenly, like a small wary animal, she scented danger. She ceased to struggle against the restraint, and she grew very still. Black Eagle, she knew, could be merciless, and there was a great fear inside her that he would order that she be burned again.

Black Eagle looked at her once more. It seemed to him that her eyes had a hunted look. He began to speak in a sonorous voice. "White Bird, Sparkling Water, I cast you from this village that you have dishonored." Again his eyes rested briefly on Lianne. She knew that he had deliberately emphasized her Indian name. As Black Eagle continued, Lianne shuddered when she heard they were to be stoned.

Lianne's heart began to beat furiously. The hand left her mouth, and she turned her head to her mother, seeking comfort and understanding. Little Beaver was staring straight ahead. Her face was like a carving in stone. Whatever her thoughts were, she would not reveal them. Her eyes were bleak, but there was no moisture in them. Lianne wanted to shout at her, to break through that terrible calm. Stupid Indian squaw! Was there nothing left in that dried-up breast of hers to give to the daughter she had borne?

Little Beaver clasped her hands together to still their trembling. Her daughter, her beautiful Sparkling Water, would be lost to her. They would drive her away with stones, and she would never see her again! She thought of Jack Langley, who had taught her strange joys. He had taken her love, and then thrown it to one side. But he had left her one perfect thing as a token of that love, her daughter. Something opened up inside her, and she thought of it as a cavern in her stomach where all of her many tears were stored. "Darling," Jack Langley had called her. "Sweetheart." Remembering with pain those endearments, she turned her eyes to her daughter and willed them to speak for her. "Darling!" their expression said. "My sweetheart, my little daughter!"

Lianne saw only the dry bleakness of her mother's eyes. She glared at Little Beaver. Curse the Indian hag! She had rejected her.

Black Eagle began to speak again. "Before I retire to my lodge, there is a thing that I must say." His piercing black eyes turned to Falling Arrow. Lifting his hand, he pointed a lean finger at him. "It is not a man who stands there, it is a slinking jackal! Lies flow from his tongue as easily as the streams flow down to the great river. These many months he has thought to deceive me, but my eyes and ears are everywhere. I know a lie when it is uttered, and shameless and disloyal though the maiden Sparkling Water has proved herself to be, yet even so, I know that she would not degrade her body by giving it willingly to Falling Arrow." Avoiding Lianne's eyes, Black Eagle drew in a deep breath. He was an old man, yet he could not deny that the sight of Lianne, bruised as she was, made the blood run more strongly in his veins and created a tingling warmth in his loins. Because of this weakness in himself, he spoke harshly to cover it. "Take him!" he ordered. "His tongue is to be cut out, and that part of him that has defiled the maiden also."

Falling Arrow began to struggle madly as his arms were seized and pinioned behind him. "I have spoken the truth, great Chief!" he shouted. "The maiden is unclean in mind, and lewd is her body. She did this thing to me of which I have spoken!" He broke off, his eyes widening slightly as Leaping Stag pushed his way through the crowd and came close to him. Seeing the hate-twisted face of the man who had loved Lianne and had hungered to possess her, he knew that there would be no mercy for him there. There would be no mercy anywhere. He was to become a mute. His manhood was to be cut away. He would be a thing, not a man. He would be lower than the yellow dogs who roamed the village. With a gasping sigh he let his body go limp between his captors.

Chief Black Eagle rose to his feet. "The jackal is unpleasant to my eyes. Do not let me see him again until his punishment has been completed." His back held stiffly, he turned about and entered his wigwam.

White Bird's pain was such that he felt as if a thousand fires had been kindled beneath his skin. His head pounded so violently that he had a great fear that it would burst. He winced as hands seized him and hauled him roughly to his feet, but he allowed no further sign of his agony to show. He was aware that he was staggering, but great though his pride was, he found himself unable to help it. He went forward again, but was halted once more by a hand that plucked at his bare arm. He turned his head as the fingers dug painfully into his burned flesh, and found himself looking into Lianne's distraught face. There were tears on her cheeks, and her eyes were feverish with the terror consuming her. "Help me!" she screamed. His heart moved in alarm as he stared at her. There was a look about her as though her reason had fled, and yet he knew instinctively that the brain beneath the madness of her terror still moved shrewdly. A rising sound came from behind White Bird. He saw Lianne's eyes stretch wide with horror and the color ebb from her face. Before he could turn and confront their persecutors, the first stone struck the back of his head. Another came, opening a cut beneath Lianne's eye. Then a shower, striking them in every part of the body. Oddly, the new pain, added to the rest, seemed to revive him and clear his head. With an inarticulate sound he grabbed Lianne's arm and forced her along at a stumbling run. He heard her babbling voice. "Great Spirit, protect me!"

Light flashed in his head as another stone struck, but still he forced himself on. He would not crawl before them like the dog they had named him. They would both live!

A wail came from Lianne as she was felled by a stone. He stooped and gathered her in his arms, his lips skinning back from his teeth with the agony it cost him. He could feel a warmth on his arm, and he knew that it came from the blood matting her hair. His breath labored in his lungs as he ran on, and he had the feeling that at any moment his legs would collapse beneath him. He must not collapse. He must reach the boundary of the village, for there lay safety. Once he had reached that, the pursuit would stop.

The last stone struck him as he reached the incline that led out of the village. Losing his footing, he fell down the steep side, with Lianne still crushed in his arms. His last thought, before unconsciousness claimed him, was that they were safe. The village had been left behind. The stoning was over.

Chapter 5

Seated astride his big chestnut horse, Justin Lawrence sent the animal galloping over the rough terrain at a reckless pace. He laughed aloud, exulting in the strength of the sun on his skin and the rush of wind that blew his long black hair away from his face. It was wonderful to be alive, he thought. The air was like strong wine. There was limitless space to roam, and he was here in a country that stretched a man's soul to its fullest capacity. It was a country that made you dream big dreams. It stirred ambitions that had never been there before.

A shout from behind him brought Justin's head around. He lifted his hand and beckoned Buck Carey and the rest of the party on. It had been Buck's idea to go hunting, but his own to take this wild gallop.

Justin smiled to himself as he recalled Jock McPherson's gloomy face. Jock had refrained from making one of the party. "Somebody has to think for the rest of you," he had grumbled. "Ye're crazy fools to go hunting in Running Fox's grounds. Nay good will come of it."

"Have you forgotten Big Chief Lawrence here?" Buck had said, grinning at him. "Running Fox favors him."

"I havna forgotten. Running Fox will keep his word, ye may expect nay trouble from him. But I am not for trusting Little Wolf. If he catches ye, 'twill be mayhem, and don't ye be forgetting it."

"I'll keep an eye on things, Jock. Don't you fret none."

"Will ye so, Buck," Jock had answered sarcastically. "And what of yeself? Ye've nay forgotten Running Fox's warning?"

"Ain't forgot, ain't mad enough for that. Justin and Harry Andrews will do the hunting, seeing as how I'm banned. I'm for taking a rest in the sun while they do the hard work. You satisfied, man?"

Jock was not to be appeased. "I am not. I dinna trust ye.

56

For the matter of that, why can ye not hunt nearer to home?"

"Better game farther in," had been Buck's laconic reply.

Jock had glared impatiently. "All right, all right! But why add to yere madness by lumbering yerself wi' a lass?"

Buck had grinned from Jock's indignant face to Millicent Andrews' flushed and determined one. "Cain't help it, Jock. Millie here won't take no for an answer. Ain't encouraging her, but cain't stop her if she's for trailing us."

"I'd stop her! The lassie's in need of a good thrashing, so she is."

Justin frowned. Jock was right—it was folly to bring a woman on a hunting expedition. But still, to do Buck justice, it was none of his doing. The fault lay with Harry. Millicent was strong-willed, and her determined pursuit of Buck had not abated. But if Harry had been doing his duty as her brother and protector, he should have knocked some sense into her with the flat of his hand. Justin dismissed the Andrewses from his mind and went back to his dreaming. Apart from the little irritations that could not very well be avoided in a colony of people, things were going very well. The crops were growing. Carrie was as she had always been, high-spirited, courageous, laughing at little disasters, encouraging him. The child had not yet arrived, but the complaining, bitter woman Carrie had fast become had disappeared as though she had never been. He remembered, after that confrontation with Running Fox, the softness in her eyes when he had returned to the settlement. "I needed these moments of danger to show me what a fool I have been," she had said, her hands caressing him as they were used to. "I love you, Justin."

"And I love you, Carrie. But you know, I really can't let you take all the blame. I have been short-tempered. Irritable. Understanding has never been one of my strong points."

"No," she agreed immediately, "it hasn't. But all the same, it was I who brought us to this pass. Forgive me, love."

"If you will forgive me about Belle," he said teasingly.

"Belle?" Outraged color had rushed into her face, and her eyes flashed with fire. "Do you mean to tell me, Rogue Lawrence, that it was true about Belle? Why, I'll—"

"No, it wasn't, and you know it. You made that little affair up in your own head."

"Are you sure? It would be like you to . . ."

"Like me to what?" He had grabbed her and kissed her hard. "Like me to what? Tell me!"

"You and your blasted women!"

"Carrie," he drawled, "if you will blame where no blame is, then you must expect me to prick you a little." Laughing, he had held her away from him. "And what if it had been true about Belle and me? What would you have done?"

"I would have killed you!" she had answered promptly. "Her, too."

"That would have been a shame. Think of all you would be missing. You know, Carrie, I love you in all your guises, but I must confess that I did not take kindly to your last guise. Now, attend me closely, woman. There was nothing between that child Belle and myself. Nor will there ever be. Do you believe me?"

Her eyes had slanted sideways at him as if she were assessing and weighing her answer. He knew that, where his relations with the various women who crossed his path were concerned, there would always be that slight distrust in her. It was inevitable, he supposed, since she knew so much of his past prowess with her sex. Her hesitation in answering irritated him slightly. "Well," she said at last. "Yes, I suppose I believe you. But when I think of all the women in your life, Rogue Lawrence, I am not disposed to—"

He had recovered his good humor, and his laughter interrupted her. "You will be suspecting me when I am a doddering old man."

"Yes, I will." There had been no hesitation in her answer then. "Can you blame me?"

"I can. I do. You are a narrow-minded, suspicious woman."

Her eyes had crinkled with laughter. "Suspicious, yes. Narrow-minded, never."

"Never mind all that twaddle. You must believe me wholly or not at all."

"Oh, all right, you damned blackguard. Yes, I believe you."

"And so you should. You see before you a reformed blackguard."

"Reformed, bah!"

He had lifted a threatening hand, setting her to laughing

outright. "Don't say any more," he warned, "or you will regret it."

"Would you beat a pregnant woman?" She caught his hand and held it to her breast. After a moment, she held his hand away from her and examined the fingers. "Ah! Do I see before my innocent eyes the hand of a thief?" She winked at him. "A gentleman thief, of course."

"No, you do not." He swatted her lightly. "You see the hand of a hard-working farmer."

She had opened her eyes wide. "You were never a thief, sir?"

"Yes, love, I was. But then, so were you."

She held his hand to her breast again. "Ungallant of you to remind me, but I forgive you." Her eyes had been full of a soft light when she looked at him. "I long for our child to be born, darling," she said in a voice that held a slight tremble. "I want so much to have you make love to me again."

"Even though we are not wed?" His eyes taunted her.

"Even so. And do not mock me."

"I will make love to you over and over again. You may count on that. I will even make love to you now, if you desire it."

"Desire it I most certainly do, and you know it. But I would not have you waste your energy, sweetheart, by climbing this shaky mountain." She had taken his hand again and guided it to her belly. "Feel how the child rages in his prison. He cannot wait to be born."

Feeling that leaping, quivering life beneath his hand, he had felt for her an overwhelming tenderness. "He is as impatient as his mother, I fear."

"As his father, you mean. I would have you know that I have within this belly of mine another Justin. When he is grown, may God save the ladies. For there is not a one who will be safe from him."

"So long as their jewels do not end up in his pocket, it will not matter."

"As they ended up in yours, eh? Let me tell you something, Rogue Lawrence. I am determined that my son will not end up with a rope about his neck, as you did."

He had seen the shadows of those old fears in her eyes. Wanting to dismiss them quickly, he had boasted lightly, "But

I did not end, for am I not here? Come, love, what rope could hold Rogue Lawrence?"

"Do not jest about that time," she had answered him sharply. "If Paul had not come along just at the right time, you would have strangled to death."

He felt her shuddering, and he had tightened his arm about her. "But Paul did come, and he saved me from hanging. That being so, why must you distress yourself needlessly? Besides, have you forgotten that you did not know me at that time?"

"No, but I nursed you through the aftermath. I listened to your delirious ramblings, and I saw your struggle to breathe. Added to that, I have a very good imagination."

He did not like to think of his young brother, Paul, whose life had so tragically ended beneath a hail of bullets.

Justin felt his mouth shaking, and he tightened it at once. It did no good to think of Paul, or of those who had murdered him. He was far away from England and the vengeance he had promised himself. Hastily he turned his thoughts to Chief Running Fox. Many weeks had passed since his dramatic encounter with him, but Running Fox had kept his word. Buck had told him that the drums continued to speak of massacres, but they had remained unmolested by the Indians.

His ears were caught by a steady throbbing, and he realized that his subconscious mind had been registering the sound of the drums for some time. Checking the animal's headlong pace with some difficulty, he reined in sharply. Narrowing his eyes against the glare of the sun, he looked toward the hills. He could see smoke wisping upward into the lazy air. It hung there like a gray veil against the harsh blue of the sky before drifting slowly away. He inclined his head forward and listened intently. He could not read whatever news was being relayed, but it seemed to him that the drums were giving out with a more mournful note than usual.

Buck and the Andrewses rode up and reined in. Justin turned his head and looked at Buck closely. At the sight of his unusually grim face, he felt his heartbeat quicken. "Well, Buck," he said in a quiet voice, "what are the drums saying?"

"They're saying that Running Fox and his second son, Flying Pony, were killed in the massacre at Ram's Head Pass." The grim line about his mouth deepened, and his nostrils had a pinched look. "Little Wolf is chief now. Reckon we're in trouble, Justin."

Millicent's frightened eyes looked huge in her pale face. "What will it mean to us?" She put a trembling hand on Buck's arm. "What kind of trouble are we in?"

"If Little Wolf don't mean to honor his daddy's word, it could mean a massacre, 'lessen we can fight 'em off." Buck thrust his hat to the back of his head and ran distracted fingers through his hair. "That Little Wolf is meaner than a snake."

"You think he won't honor Running Fox's word?" Justin put in.

"Cain't tell. Might, if it suits him. You all better get on back to the settlement. I'll catch up with you later."

"No!" Millicent gave a protesting cry. "Not without you, Buck. You must come with us!"

Buck's usual smile was absent. "Cain't," he answered her curtly. "I got me some scouting to do. I want to see how things go. Now, git along with you. Ride!"

"You go on with Millicent, Harry," Justin said. "I'm staying." As Buck opened his mouth to say something, he said quickly, "You might as well save your breath, Buck. I mean what I say."

Buck's set mouth relaxed into a grin. "You been a danged fool ever since I met you. Talking to you is just like talking to a mule."

"Then we understand each other. Millicent, you'll look in on Carrie, won't you?"

Millicent nodded. The tears standing bright in her eyes, she looked at Buck. "Be careful, please."

"I will, Millie. Don't you fret none 'bout that."

"All right, then." Millicent wheeled her horse about. "You coming, Harry?"

Harry hesitated, his fair face flushing. "I'd stay if it wasn't for Millicent. I hope you know that."

Buck laughed. "Sure we know it, Harry boy. But Millie, she needs you." He patted Harry's knee. "Get along with you."

Millicent was almost out of sight, with Harry riding hard to catch up with her, when they heard a sudden wild scream. They saw Harry's horse rear, paw the air, then topple over on its side. Harry was thrown clear, but even from that distance they could see the arrow buried in his back.

"Ain't taken them Injuns long to start up," Buck said shortly. "I reckon they been watching us for some time."

"Where are they? I can't see them."

"And you won't, Justin, not 'lessen they want you to see 'em." Buck dug his heels into his animal's sides and sent it streaking forward. "Come on," he shouted. "Ride low, Justin, that way you ain't so big a target."

Buck's musket was already in his hand when he reined in and slid down from his horse. "There's some shelter behind them bushes, Justin," he shouted. Bent double, he began to run, with Justin following. He had almost reached the tall bushes when the arrow came singing through the air.

Justin saw him stumble and fall. "Buck!" In three strides he was beside him. He fell to his knees, his hands reaching for the arrow in Buck's shoulder.

"Leave it be!" Buck gasped. "Cain't do nothing 'bout it now. 'Sides, it'll likely break off. Get on behind them bushes. Ain't no telling where them Injuns be."

Justin ignored him. Rising, he bent down and grasped him beneath both arms and began to drag him toward shelter.

"Don't be a fool, Justin," Buck protested. "I ain't wanting you to bother with me. Ain't no sense in us both dying. You get yourself hid, and you maybe got a chance."

Justin stopped his dragging. "Will you shut your mouth! You're not dying, and I'm not leaving you, is that clear?"

Buck smiled as Justin snatched a handkerchief from his pocket and wiped the perspiration from his forehead. "You nursemaiding me now?" He saw the expression in Justin's eyes, and he went on hastily, "Yeah, boy, it's clear to me. But them Injuns—"

"Curse the Indians!" Justin thrust the handkerchief back in his pocket. "You ready to go on?"

"I'm ready." Buck's eyes went beyond Justin, widening in apprehension. "It's too late, boy. I told you to leave me."

Justin tensed as the shadow fell across them. He turned his head and looked up at Little Wolf and the warriors grouped behind him. They had come up so silently that he had heard nothing until they were upon him.

"You smell 'em before you see 'em," Buck said in a labored voice. "It's that bear grease they use."

Little Wolf's fury flamed up. He had come across this Buck Carey many times, and each time the smiling Virginian had managed to defeat him with his skill and cunning, but he should not defeat him with his glib tongue. "Be silent!" he rapped out, prodding him with his moccasined foot.

Justin looked at the spreading stain on Buck's shoulder. If he did not soon have aid, he would die from loss of blood. His mouth tight, he faced Little Wolf.

A shudder shook Buck. He felt a creeping coldness, and it was hard to bring out words. "I cain't be silent, Little Wolf," he managed. "I got to remind you 'bout Running Fox's word. He give it in front of you, so you know 'bout it. You going to break that word?"

Little Wolf drew himself up. His eyes glittering, he said coldly, "Running Fox is dead."

"I know he's dead. Flying Pony too. You're the chief now. A chief's got to have honor."

Again Little Wolf felt that burst of killing fury. Honor! All his life he had heard that word. His father had been an honorable man. He would have died before he would break his given word. But that admirable trait in Running Fox had not stopped the pale-skins from stealing the land of his ancestors. Where was their honor?

Buck sensed what he was feeling. Seeing his advantage, he repeated softly, "No matter what, a chief's got to have honor."

The braves had heard the words of Buck Carey. Little Wolf did not turn; he knew their eyes were upon him. They waited to see if he would honor his father's word to these pale-skins. The certainty came to him that if he did not, he would lose standing with them. His fingers clenched about the knife in his belt. For a moment he played with the idea of snatching it out and plunging it into Carey's throat. He thought of the two who had died already. First the woman, and then the man who had followed after her. There was some satisfaction in that. Carey was watching him. He was waiting to see him lose standing before his braves. But that he should not see! An idea came to him, and he smiled inwardly. Forcing himself to pace his words so that his anger might not overwhelm him and rob him of calm, he said slowly, "My father gave his word to one whom he believed to be a man, and because he reminded him of his dead son."

His taunting eyes turned to Justin. "But your manhood has yet to be proved to me. Are you a man, Lawrence?"

Justin's hands clenched, and he did not try to hide his anger. "Why don't you find out, Little Wolf? Try me."

"I will. You will fight Red Morning, and that, you may believe me, Lawrence, will take courage. If you win, I will honor the word of Running Fox."

Buck's fingers plucked at Justin's ankle. "A word with you, lad."

Ignoring Little Wolf, Justin squatted down beside him. "How do you feel, Buck?"

"Never mind 'bout that. You listen to me. Little Wolf, he done this on purpose. He knows Red Morning cain't hardly be beat. I seen him fight, though the Injuns never knowed I was looking on. I'm telling, you, Justin, he's right good with a knife. You ain't got a prayer."

"But in any case, Buck, I don't have a choice. I've got to fight him." Justin laid his hand over Buck's cold fingers and smiled into his worried face. "Hang on, friend," he said in a carefully lowered voice. "If it will make you feel any better, I'm damned good with a knife myself. When you roam the London slums, as I did, you have to know how to defend yourself."

"I hope you're right 'bout your skill, boy," Buck said gloomily. " 'Cause if you ain't, you can say good-bye to tomorrow. It's you I'm worried about, 'cause even if you win, I'm done for."

Justin looked at him sharply. "What do you mean by that?"

"Little Wolf's been waiting a long time to trap me. Him and his daddy both. Now that he's got me, he ain't going to let me live."

Justin said nothing. Rising to his feet again, he studied Little Wolf. The Indian's face was impassive, and he bore the scrutiny calmly. But for all that, Justin could detect in him an eagerness to see him dead. That fierce glitter in his eyes gave him away. Like Buck, he believed that he hadn't a chance against Red Morning. "I will fight Red Morning," he said in an even voice. "But if I win, my friend and I go free."

"You are in no position to make demands, Lawrence."

"True. Are you afraid I will win, Little Wolf?"

"I fear nothing, Lawrence." Little Wolf looked at him imperiously. "You will not win."

"In that case, what harm is there in agreeing to my request?"

Almost, Little Wolf smiled. What harm indeed? The pale-skin was as good as dead. He pretended to ponder. It would not do for Lawrence to discover the secret mirth in his eyes. "Very well," he said at last, with the imperious air of one who confers a great favor. "If you win, you and Buck Carey will go free."

"I have your word?"

"I have said it. It shall be so."

Justin heard Buck's gasp, but he did not look at him. "In that case, Little Wolf, I am ready."

Little Wolf felt a great self-satisfaction. It was true that he could have slaughtered the pale-skins, but had he done so, there would always be a question in the minds of his warriors. But a fair fight was a fair fight, and they would be satisfied that he had meant to keep the word of Running Fox. If Red Morning's blade took Lawrence's life, they would not blame him or feel that he was without honor. He was about to raise his arm in the signal for the fight to commence when Buck Carey's weakening voice came to him again. "I know Harry Andrews is dead, Little Wolf, but what happened to the lady?"

"She is dead." Little Wolf spoke triumphantly. Hoping to further wound this man whom he hated, he added, "The woman took an arrow in the throat."

Buck had a flashing picture of Millie on that night when she had declared before them all that she would have him for her man. She had sounded hard and determined, and there had been no love in her voice. But in the days that followed, he had been given many glimpses of the core of love and tenderness that lay beneath the hard veneer. He was a saddle tramp. He was rough and ready in his approach to women, taking their bodies and then forgetting them when he rode on. And yet Millie had seen something in him to love, and he could not imagine why. When he had said this to her, she had looked at him in amazement. "You can't imagine why, Buck Carey? Why do you sell yourself so short?"

"I don't," he had answered her.

"But you do. You're handsome and attractive, and you are the only man I have ever wanted."

"I'm a saddle tramp and don't settle nowhere for too long." He had backed away from her, almost frightened by her intensity and the look in her eyes.

"Buck!" Millie would not let him escape her. She came close to him and put her hands on his shoulders. "I love you so very much!"

And so he had taken her in his arms and kissed her. But even as he did so, he knew that he did not love her, and never would.

Buck turned his head away to hide the tears in his eyes. No, he had not loved her, but he had liked her very much. He had found, to his cost, that he had no love to give to anyone. His capacity to love had died many years ago. He had a certain fondness for Carrie Fane, but he did not delude himself into thinking of it as anything stronger. Buck blinked. It would not do to think of Millie or Carrie now. He took a quick look at Little Wolf. He was smiling. No doubt in anticipation of Buck's reaction. "Maybe poor little Millie is better off dead," he said in a controlled voice. "It's likely a kinder fate than what you had in store for her."

Little Wolf's eyes narrowed to glittering slits. He had hoped to detect a weakness in Carey, but it seemed there was none. Always before, this man with his drawling, lazy voice had managed to confound him with words. He had done so again. With an effort, Little Wolf suppressed his flaring anger. There would be time enough later to deal with Carey. And he would deal with him in such a way that the man would beg him to kill him and put him out of his agony. He played with this pleasant picture, then put it firmly from his mind. Now was not the time. Turning, he raised his arm. "Let the fight begin," he said in a loud, clear voice.

Red Morning stepped forward at once, his knife already in his hand. He was a thin man of medium height, but his thinness was deceiving. Muscles rippled beneath his oiled skin, and he exuded strength and confidence. Between the black braids of coarse hair, his face had the sharp look of a fox.

Justin pulled his knife from his belt. The keenly honed blade glittered in the sunlight as he advanced upon Red

Morning. The Indian was not yet ready to make his thrust. He stepped back, his fierce eyes studying his adversary.

It was Justin who sprang first. Like the bullyboys whom he so often had fought in the back streets of London, he believed in boldness, not in a study of his enemy's weaker points. The knife took Red Morning in the side. It was not a deep wound—there was not enough power behind it—but it tore a long gash.

Red Morning put a hand to the wound. This man was bold, he thought, and he showed no fear. He liked there to be fear, and hitherto he had always seen it looking from the eyes of his opponents. Fear was a weakness that gave one the greater advantage. Gritting his teeth together and keeping his wary eyes on Justin, he stooped to wipe his blood-smeared hand on a tuft of grass.

Although Justin had drawn first blood, he did not make the mistake of underestimating the Indian. Which was as well.

Red Morning rose slowly to his feet. He filled his lungs with air, then, with a tigerlike spring that took him clear across the space between them, he cannoned into Justin and bore him to the ground.

For a moment Justin was dazed with the force of the fall; then he became conscious of the Indian's face close to his, but it took the prick of the knife in his arm to bring him back to a full sense of his danger. With the rank smell of the grease with which the Indian had smeared his body in his nostrils, he heaved up and pressed his thumb into Red Morning's eye.

Half-blinded, grunting with pain and rage, Red Morning threw himself backward. The pain in his watering eye had made him less than careful, and he fell awkwardly. As he made to rise, his ankle twisted beneath him. Panting, he fell back again, his lips twisting in a grimace as the burning pain shot through his ankle. His second attempt to rise was foiled by the heavy weight of Justin's body descending upon him.

Red Morning gasped as the knife stabbed first into his arm and then into his shoulder. The wounds were not deep, such as he would have inflicted upon the white man; they were designed to further incapacitate him, and he had a growing sense of defeat such as he had never experienced before. Snarling with frustration, he reached up and clasped his fingers crushingly about Justin's wrist in an attempt to force him to drop the knife. Fighting for supremacy, the two men rolled over and over on the dusty ground. It took all of Justin's strength before he managed to tear his wrist free, and then he saw that the Indian had lost his own knife. The sweat pouring down his face, his breath coming raggedly, he again managed to pinion Red Morning beneath him. He looked into the man's narrow black eyes for a moment; then, smiling, he raised his arm.

The Indian made a sound between his teeth, but there was no sign of fear in his eyes as the knife stabbed downward. The expected thrust did not come. The knife was poised within an inch of his stomach. "Do not insult me, pale-skin," Red Morning growled. "Yours is the victory. Finish it. Why do you hesitate?"

Justin shook his head. It was a lucky chance that had given him the advantage, no more. With an exclamation of disgust, he flung the knife from him. Getting painfully to his feet, he stooped over and dragged Red Morning up. The Indian gave an involuntary wince as his full weight went onto his injured ankle; then he closed his lips tightly against any further sign of pain.

Justin stared at the swaying man. No, he could not kill him. His inclination was to walk away and leave him standing there, but the conviction came to him that if he showed consideration for his enemy it would be construed by the other Indians as a sign of the weakness in the white man. Making up his mind suddenly, he doubled up his right fist and sent it crashing to the point of the man's jaw.

The blow felled Red Morning, but it did not render him unconscious. Knowing that he acted a part, the only one that his savage audience would recognize and understand, Justin walked over to the fallen man and placed his foot upon his stomach in the sign of victory. Wiping the sweat from his eyes with the back of his arm, he looked over at Little Wolf.

Little Wolf stared back at the white man. He felt the bursting, quivering rage gather into a tight knot inside him and then explode, but he allowed nothing of this inner turmoil to show in his outward appearance. The pale-skin had won. He had defeated Red Morning! But Little Wolf would meet up with Justin Lawrence and Buck Carey again; he was determined upon that. It was not the end.

His eyes were drawn to Buck, and the corners of his

mouth twitched. There were great drops of perspiration on the white man's forehead, and a white line of pain about his mouth. He was suffering. Perhaps he would die.

The thought consoled Little Wolf for what he now had to do. He turned his eyes away and ran his tongue over his dry lips. He was aware that the braves were looking at him and waiting for his words. Upon what he said now would depend his future authority over them. Narrowing his eyes to mask the too revealing hatred, he said in a loud, cold voice, "You have won, Lawrence. You may go in peace."

"And what of Buck Carey?" Justin said quickly.

"He too may go in peace."

"Little Wolf is a man of his word and a great warrior." Buck's voice was only a faint thread of sound now, but Little Wolf heard his words.

Again he looked at Buck, and this time he allowed his hatred to show. "Thank you," he said stiffly. "I shall value your words." He raised his arm. "Until we meet again." Turning, he made his way to his peacefully grazing horse. Signaling to the others to pick up the fallen Red Morning and follow after him, he vaulted onto the animal's back. Turning its head sharply about, he rode off without a backward glance.

Little Wolf's parting words still echoed in Justin's ears. "Until we meet again." He wondered if he had imagined the underlying threat.

Buck's eyes were closed. He opened them slowly when Justin knelt down beside him. "You did fine, Justin," he gasped. "I'm right proud of you."

"Thanks. How are you feeling, Buck?"

"Dandy. Ready to dance a jig."

Justin grinned at this. "You talk too much."

"I got to tell you what to do." Buck drew in a quivering breath. "Then I'll shut my mouth."

"You'd better." Justin made to touch the arrow in Buck's shoulder. He drew his hand back as he saw Buck's frown. "You don't trust me to pull it free, eh?"

"It ain't that I don't trust you. But there's a knack in it. Get me back to the settlement. McPherson will tend my shoulder."

Justin looked at Buck's drawn face with worried eyes. Seeing his teeth digging hard into his lower lip to hold back a cry of pain, he said quickly, "That's easier said than done. You're in no condition to ride."

"Settlement ain't far. I can do it."

"And if you should pass out?"

"Cain't fall forward if you rope me proper in the saddle. Get the horses. I'll show you how to do it."

"All right." Justin rose to his feet.

When he returned with the horses, he found Buck unconscious. More time was wasted while he revived him with water from the canteen. Looking at his colorless face, he had a feeling that he would die before they could reach the settlement.

With that uncanny ability that Justin had noted and marveled at before, Buck read his thoughts. "No, boy," he said in a hoarse, weary voice, "I ain't going to die. I'm too ornery."

They were almost in sight of the stockade gate when it opened and a rider came through. The animal's hooves raised a fine cloud of dust as the rider spurred toward them. "What happened, lad?" McPherson panted, pulling up sharply. "Andrews' horse came back a while ago, fair lathered was the creature. I was just readying a party to come out in search of ye." His eyes fell on Buck, and he sucked in a sharp breath. "It looks like that laddie is sore wounded."

Justin nodded. "Indians," he said briefly. "Harry and Millie are dead."

"I know 'twas an Indian attack. Ye have no need to be telling me. So the Andrewses are dead, eh?" Shaking his head mournfully, he cast his eyes over Justin's ripped and bloodstained jerkin. " 'Tis a fine sight ye are yerself."

Justin shrugged. "I'll tell you about it later. Let's get Buck attended to first."

"Aye," McPherson said, his eyes on Buck's unconscious face. "We'd best stop blathering like old women, for I am not wanting this laddie to die."

Justin caught a glimpse of McPherson's face as they rode on. It was devoid of expression. Had it not been for the tight set of his lips, he would have thought him unmoved. Buck was McPherson's longtime friend. Both of them had originally been wanderers in search of adventure. McPherson had married, but the friendship had not ceased. Then, when his wife and children had been massacred in an Indian raid, McPherson had once more joined Buck in his wanderings.

The man would take it very hard if Buck died. Justin put out a hand to steady Buck's swaying form. And so will I, he thought with a sudden rush of emotion. It occurred to him then that Buck, with his bursts of somewhat surprising shyness, his innate reserve, which was belied by his smiling good nature, had become for him an older edition of his brother, Paul. That was why, when he spoke to Buck, despite the pronounced southern drawl, he often had a haunting sense of familiarity.

His thoughts were scattered as they approached the stockade gate. It swung open to receive them, and they were met by a crowd of agitated men and women.

"Indians!" a woman screamed, her eyes taking in the arrow in Buck's shoulder and Justin's bloodstained appearance. As Justin dismounted, she came closer to him. "How far behind you are they?"

Justin pushed her aside, his eyes searching for Caroline. "You need not fear an attack just yet."

"I don't believe you!" the woman shrieked. She pointed a quivering finger at Buck. "Look at him! Look at yourself! And you tell me we need not fear."

"Willy Thompson," McPherson said sternly, "will ye clap yere hand over that woman's mouth? I'll not be having her creating such a hullabaloo."

The woman shrank back as Willy Thompson approached her. "I'll not be silenced. We all want to know what to expect." A murmur of agreement greeted this. Emboldened, the woman shouted, "I knew what we were in for when Harry Andrews' horse came back."

Parrying the questions from all sides, Justin helped McPherson cut Buck free. A silence fell as, carrying Buck between them, they made their way to McPherson's shack.

"I'll be taking this arrow from his shoulder now, lad," McPherson said, looking at Justin. "And ye could do with a bit of cleaning up yerself. I'll look to yere wound a bit later. Will ye bid one of the women to bring me some hot water and some clean rags?"

Justin had been aware of a feeling of weakness for some time. Ignoring it, he turned to the door. His fingers clung tightly to the handle as he nodded to McPherson. "Do you think Buck will be all right, Jock?"

"I dinna know," McPherson answered him gloomily. "I

can only tell ye that he's a strong laddie. Many an arrow he's had in him, and recovered fully from the wound."

Justin closed his eyes for a moment. McPherson's voice seemed to him to be far away. Frowning, he pulled himself together. "But this time, Jock, he has lost a lot of blood."

"Aye, I know." Now McPherson's voice, suddenly sharp and irritable, came clearly to Justin's ears. "I'll do my best for him. More than that, I canna say, not being God. And speaking of blood, ye have lost quite a bit yere own self. Off with ye. Find yere woman, for I can tell ye that she didna take it too well when she saw that riderless horse."

There was a lightness, a reeling in Justin's head as he made his way to his shack. His arm felt stiff and sore, and he could still feel the warm trickle of his blood. He felt very strange. He looked down at the spreading stain on his jerkin, and it occurred to him to wonder if there had been poison on the blade of Red Morning's knife.

Dismissing this notion as foolishness, he opened the door of the shack and reeled inside.

"Justin!" Caroline started toward him. "Justin, what—?" She broke off, her eyes widening as she took in his appearance.

He opened his mouth to reassure her, but the words would not come. He moved his lips again. "Carrie!" The single word he forced out was as loud as an explosion in his ears. He put out his hands in a helpless gesture as the room darkened and swung about him, and then he was falling.

Chapter 6

Lianne was afraid. She felt that the gods had turned their faces from her. Even though the sun was warm on her head and shoulders, it seemed to her that she walked in a world of darkness.

Sighing heavily, she blinked the tears from her eyes and asked herself how she could possibly feel otherwise. She had been publicly shamed. She had been cast from her village and left with only White Bird as a companion. Even worse, now that she had been forced to leave behind those people whom she had so despised, she could find no joy or consolation in the thought. She had a longing to mingle with them again and to be as she had once been. She put a hand to the healing scars on her breasts, and now she allowed her tears to flow freely.

Striding by Lianne's side, White Bird stumbled. He quickly recovered himself, but Lianne cast him a look of hatred and contempt. His eyes had been affected by the torture, and his limp was more pronounced. She could not find it in her heart to feel pity for him. He had brought his punishment upon himself, and she, the innocent, must share in that punishment. She glanced at him again. She was ashamed of him, this half-blind brave who walked so unevenly by her side. How could she have ever thought she loved him? She was meant for better things. One day, when the gods forgave her the sin of lying, as they surely would, she would fulfill her destiny. She would become the beloved and cherished woman of a white man, as her mother had been. A picture of her mother rose upon her mental vision. She had been the beloved of Jack Langley, but he had left her. But then, of course, her mother was only a stupid and ignorant squaw. It would not be for Lianne as it had been for Little Beaver.

White Bird stumbled again, interrupting her thoughts. Lianne made a hissing sound between her teeth to show her displeasure and drew farther away from him. She did not feel guilty about her withdrawal. Yesterday, when they had set out on this journey, she had somewhat shrinkingly, considering how distasteful he now was to her, offered him her arm to support him along the dusty trail. For this kindness on her part, she had been icily rebuked. She could understand a warrior's fierce pride, but White Bird, maimed as he was, could scarcely call himself a warrior.

Dismissing him from her thoughts, Lianne began to dwell on the nightmare days and nights she had spent in the cave, whose entrance was overhung with vines. The same cave that had once sheltered Caroline Fane. Lianne shivered. She did not like the gloomy cave, for it had seemed to her to be haunted by the white woman's lingering presence. At nights, lying huddled on the cold stone floor, her body writhing in agony from the painful burns inflicted upon her by the torture, she would think about Caroline Fane, and gradually there had grown up inside her a desire for vengeance. Had it not been for this woman whom she had never seen, she would not be here now, a despised outcast. Caroline Fane was the cause of all the misfortunes that now beset her.

Lianne drew in a deep, shaken breath. It was because of her that she, despite the pain in her own body, had been forced to care for White Bird. After the torture they had both endured, after running before the shower of bruising stones hurled at them by the people of the village, White Bird, who had been from his birth a cripple and a weakling, had fallen into a serious illness.

Lianne frowned. During that illness his feverishly babbling lips had called many times upon the name of Caroline Fane, the witch woman. And she, listening to him, had longed to use her knife on him and still his labored breathing forever. She would have done so, for the strength and power of her hatred would have guided her knife to a vital spot, but greater than her hatred was fear of being left all alone to fend for herself. Even the despised company of the lame one was preferable to that.

White Bird, walking stiffly erect and trying to avoid the occasional stumble, did not tell Lianne that his vision was slowly but surely beginning to clear. He felt shriveled by the contempt that she did not trouble to hide, and it was pride that sealed his lips. She would not have dared to act so before another brave, for fear that she would be punished. He would have beaten her for her insolent attitude; indeed, White Bird was greatly tempted to do so, but as yet the weakness in his body forbade such an action.

White Bird's lip curled in bitter self-contempt. He should be used to humiliation by now. From the day of his unfortunate birth, had he ever known anything else? His father, long since dead, had turned his face from his lamed and delicate son, and rarely, if he could avoid it, did he speak to him. Even his mother, who had quickly followed his father into death, had been unable to hide her shame in her son. But he had not thought to receive contempt from Lianne, who had so willingly opened her body to him. Lianne, as cruel as she was beautiful, who had caressed him and spoken words of love!

White Bird swallowed hard. He was ashamed of his bitter hurt. It was not manly to feel so deeply for a maiden. But, just as he had once done with Caroline Fane, he was allowing emotion to govern him. Why must he love her so much? If only he could cut all thoughts of her from his heart and mind. White Bird stared straight ahead of him, and he prayed that nothing of his feelings showed in his expression. Dust blew up from the trail, forcing a cough from him, making him feel the dreaded but familiar tightening in his chest. He did not look at Lianne, but he felt her quick, scornful glance burning through him. His hands clenched as he became aware of the other troubles afflicting his hated, delicate body. They had been walking for hours, and his legs, weakened by his illness, were beginning to tremble beneath him. To make matters worse, his head was pounding and his senses beginning to haze. He was suddenly shaken by rebellion and anger. Gods of health and charity, why did you endow me with the weak body of a lame man?

Lianne looked at White Bird, and her eyes narrowed to slits. What ailed the fool now? Why, if she had to be cast adrift, had it not been in the company of a real man?

White Bird heard the hissing sound of contempt Lianne made, and his back stiffened. Were these the only emotions he roused in her now? He experienced a longing to sit down beside the trail and rest, if only for a few moments, but he could not face the scorn in her eyes, were he to do so. The cough caught him again, and he sucked in his breath sharply in an effort to control the coming spasm. He had had these coughing spells from childhood, and he feared and dreaded them. Helpless before the cough, he would feel his eyes water with the strain, and as he fought to draw his breath, harsh rattling sounds would come from his laboring chest. His mother, hearing these sounds, had once said to him, "There are devils fighting inside you."

He had been a child, and when she said this to him, he had been very frightened. There was hurt there, too, for after one of these spells his mother would withdraw herself yet further, and her shame in him would be plainly seen. So, at a very early age, thinking this would please her and make her proud, he had learned not to cry. Tears, after all, were useless, bringing no rewards. His stoicism made no difference; he was too puny, too weak to please her. Dry-eyed, suffering, he had nonetheless believed that his mother's attitude, under the circumstances, was natural. He could not blame her, he reasoned, since his birth had brought shame upon their lodge. But for all his reasoning, he could not deny the longing in himself to have her touch him with love, or perhaps now and again to comfort him. Sometimes he would stare at her for a long time, hoping to see her expression soften. It never did. Not once had he seen her grim face relax into a smile.

White Bird drew in a gasping breath. He was a fool. It did not do to dwell on such things. The cough was striving to escape and he tightened his lips against it. Do not let it come! he prayed. Not now, when I am already brought so low. There were only a few more hours of walking to be accomplished, and they would be in sight of the Pilgrim's Rest settlement. Lawrence had no knowledge of their coming, but remembering their last meeting, that smile in his dark eyes and the friendly clasp of his hand, White Bird was in hopes that they would be welcome. He would not lie to Lawrence. He would tell him that they had been cast out by their own people, but the reason for it he would keep to himself. He did not wish to place a burden of guilt upon the other man.

White Bird's thoughts broke off abruptly. Not all his will and concentration could control the cough. A burning sensation filled his throat. It traveled lower, clamping his chest and bringing with it a hard stabbing pain. The cough came, bursting out with such violence that the strength left his legs and he collapsed to the ground.

Lianne started back. Her dark-blue eyes wide and full of fear, she stood there rigidly, staring at his hunched figure. His hands were clawing desperately at his throat and his chest, as though he would tear apart his very flesh to let in the life-saving air. Her heart beating so fast that it sickened her, she listened to the harsh, ugly sounds of his struggle to breathe. She hesitated; then she got down on her knees. Pulling back his head, she looked into his face. His features were contorted with agony and thickly glazed with sweat. His lips had a blue tinge, such as she had once seen about the lips of a dying warrior. Quite suddenly her fear turned into fury. Had she nursed him through his illness only to come to this? He was choking to death! He was going to leave her all alone. "Lame one!" She snarled the words at him. Allowing his head to drop, she pushed roughly at his heaving shoulders. "Weakling! You are not a man, you are a maiden!"

He could not breathe! This time he was surely dying. Through the thundering in his ears, White Bird heard Lianne's berating voice. With a tremendous effort he raised his head and looked into her face. He saw the hatred reflected in her eyes. He had always known that there was no compassion in her. There was only a greed to grasp at the good things of life and a self-love that went beyond all bounds. And yet, even though he knew this, to see her hatred now, at this desperate moment, was a shock so profound that it was like having freezing water thrown into his face. But, strangely, it had the effect of calming his agony. The tight stranglehold on his chest relaxed its grip, and the precious air rushed into his lungs. Now his breathing began to ease rapidly. Closing his eyes, he pillowed his head on his arm and waited for his strength to return. He would not think of Lianne, not yet.

Lianne squatted back on her heels, watching him with glittering eyes. It would seem that, not content to frighten her, he must now ignore her. He should not sleep in her presence—she would not allow it! The pleasing thought came to her that she need not fear this one, who was more maiden than man. She could say what she pleased to him. Flushed with a sense of her own power, she dug her nails into his arm. "Open your eyes!" she shouted. "What, then, you weakling, you lame one, am I to be forced to carry you along on my back?"

White Bird heard her words, and he stiffened in outrage.

His hands twitched as the rage filled him. The half-breed bitch! How dared she speak to him so!

Lianne screamed as his eyes opened and his hand came out to grasp her wrist. His eyes looked clear now, as though his full vision had returned, but they were blazing with an emotion that set her heart leaping with fear. Trying to make amends, she faltered, "I . . . I did not mean it."

White Bird saw her easy tears filling her eyes. She had always been able to cry at will. But her tears, which he had always found touching, made no impression upon him now. Ignoring her growing terror, he dragged her down until her face was on a level with his. "Hear me well, Lianne," he said in a harsh voice. "For the insults you have offered me, you will be punished. I will beat you until your skin breaks." His hand tightened crushingly on her wrist. "Do you hear me, half-breed woman?"

Half-breed woman! She had never thought to hear those words from White Bird's lips. Cruelty looked from his eyes, and there was no mercy in him. She began to scream, loud, piercing screams, interspersing them with babbling words.

The force of his anger sent strength coursing through White Bird's body. The woman must be punished, and it must be now. He got to his feet, dragging her up with him. She was still screaming wildly when he pulled her off the trail and into the forest that bordered it.

Lianne's screams turned into sobs. White Bird meant what he said. She was to be punished, and no appeal would move him. Shivering, she sagged before him. Even when he released his hold on her wrist, she did not move. If she ran, he would only pursue her, and then her punishment would be worse. He had beaten her before when she had tried him too far, but it had always been lightly, regretfully, as though he hated doing it. There had, of course, been times when he had hurt her, but they had been rare, and, she felt, accidental. But this time, with that blaze looking from his eyes, she knew that it would be different.

White Bird walked over to a tree, examining it. Lianne watched with dilated eyes as, making up his mind, he withdrew his knife and cut a slender branch. Watching him carefully trimming the branch, she made one last appeal. "Do not beat me, White Bird," she begged him in a quivering voice. "I will ask your pardon on my knees, if it pleases you."

"It does please me." White Bird restored the knife to his belt. His face set and cold, he came toward her. "You will go on your knees, half-breed, make no mistake about that. Before I have finished with you, you will grovel before me." He grasped her hair, twisting it so that she was forced downward. He laughed as tears of pain spurted from the corners of her eyes. "For every insult you have uttered, for every slur you have put upon my manhood, you will pay."

Lianne heard the far-off scream of a wildcat as he stooped over her and tore the jacket from her shoulders, baring her back for the punishment to come. She shivered, for it seemed to her that the spirit, the cunning, and the cruelty of the wildcat had lodged within White Bird's body. He seemed to be in no hurry to start the punishment, and waiting for the first blow to descend, she whimpered, hoping still for his pity. The sight of his smile froze the words on her lips. It was a cold, deadly smile, and in that moment he looked hard and much older than his years. The delicate boy seemed to have vanished. It was a warrior who stood there, and she was about to feel the full force of his anger. She cringed before him, her head drooping and her hair trailing on the forest floor.

"Ask my pardon, woman." White Bird's voice grated in her ears. She opened her lips to speak, but he did not wait for her words. "Ask it, ask my pardon!" The slashing branch punctuated his words.

Lianne began to scream in earnest as she felt the trickle of her blood. Her skin had broken beneath the deluge of blows, and her back was on fire. "I . . . I do ask it, O White B-Bird." She managed to bring out the gasping words.

As if she had not spoken, White Bird ripped the rest of her clothes off, and the blows went on and on. There seemed to be no end to his avenging fury, and there was a great fear inside her that he would kill her.

Lianne's brain worked sluggishly, but she sensed what was needed to assuage his anger. As she had seen the women of her village do, she dropped flat on her stomach. Crawling painfully toward him, she laid her cheek against his moccasined feet.

White Bird looked down at her. He hesitated, and then allowed his raised arm to drop. This half-breed who cringed now before him had thought to rule him. She had scourged him with her tongue, and with each word she had uttered, she had stripped a little more of his manhood away. But no more. He had broken her domination over his heart and mind and spirit. That domination should never be allowed to return. He would beat her regularly, as his brothers did with their women.

The wildcat screamed again, and White Bird turned his head to listen. The sound sent a responsive tingle through his blood. He was man, the master. She was woman, his inferior. He would never forget it again. And even though he could not stop loving her, for that love was graven deeply on his heart, he would not allow her to forget it, either. A smile touched his lips as he drew one of his feet away and poked her in her side, and it seemed fitting that it should be the lame foot. "Get up, half-breed," he commanded. The words were sweet on his lips, for he knew that they put the final seal on her humiliation. "Follow after me. The hour grows late, and we have yet to complete our journey."

Lianne's drooping head rose. Even now, with the pain he had put upon her searing her body, she could not believe he had escaped his servitude to her. He must be feeling sorry now and looking for a way to make amends for his cruelty. Laboriously she got to her feet and stood there swaying slightly. Looking at him with her tear-swollen eyes, she said with unconscious haughtiness, "We will rest for a while, White Bird. For you must know that I am in great pain."

He stared at her in astonishment. These words from her now, and delivered in such a tone! The fury took him again in its grip. Lifting his hand, he lashed her hard across the face, sending her staggering back.

A cry escaped Lianne as her sore back collided with the trunk of a tree. There was no sorrow in him. He was enjoying her pain! She was suddenly afraid that he would see the hatred in her eyes and punish her again. Her lids drooped, and she said in a subdued voice, "I am ready. I will follow wherever you command, O White Bird."

Wherever he commanded. White Bird's head lifted. Why had he not beaten the defiance out of her long ago? It was a good feeling to see her thus. It was more than good, it was exhilarating. He said curtly, "Then follow, woman. I will hear no more words from you this day. Do you understand me?"

Lianne nodded. Confused thoughts seethed in her brain.

Then one thought, emerging clearly, told her that whereas she had once hated him for his delicacy and had felt a secret contempt for his weakness where she was concerned, now she hated him for his strength and the humiliation she was suffering. Half-breed woman, he had called her. For that alone, when she got the chance, she would sink her knife deep into his stomach, and she would laugh at his agony.

Breathing deeply and trembling with the force of her pain and her hatred, she followed him through the close-growing trees. Soon, now, they would be at the settlement. She would meet with Justin Lawrence, the white man upon whom she had placed her secret dreams. He would be to her as Jack Langley had been to her mother. She thought of White Bird's description of Justin Lawrence, and her tautly held lips relaxed into a faint smile. It would seem to her, judging from White Bird's words, that Lawrence's looks were a fitting match for her own feminine beauty. Soon, in an hour, or perhaps a little more, she would be able to see for herself. As clearly as though it was happening now before her eyes, she knew how that fateful meeting would be. Lawrence would take one look at her, and he would recognize her as the one whom the gods had sent to bless and enrich his life. He would put aside Caroline Fane. He would turn her from his lodge, and instead he would install her, Lianne, as his woman. In time, enslaved by her beauty and her devotion to him, he would take her for his wife in that strange ceremony they practiced. She would make her vows in the little house that they called a church, and he would put on her finger a band of gold, such as she had seen on the finger of the staggering squaw who was the woman of Tobias Markham. She thought of the great God of the white people, who lived in that church, and a shiver went through her. She would respect the great God, because Lawrence would expect it of her, but she did not really believe in his power. She believed only in her own gods, who had always guided her, but she need not tell Lawrence that.

Lianne put a hand to the scars on her breasts, and for the first time she wondered if she would find favor in Lawrence's eyes. She bit her lip, wishing she had one of those gowns that the white women wore, for it would hide the scars from Lawrence. Her dream broke off abruptly, and color scorched her cheeks as she saw that White Bird was looking back at

her. Once more, with his eyes upon her, she became fully
conscious of her pain. He must not suspect that her mind
dwelled upon Lawrence. For the moment, she must let him
believe that she was his true woman, or else he might abandon her. Trying to make her mind a blank, she dropped her
head and concentrated a hard bright gaze on the trail. To
further mollify him, she folded her hands before her and
crept along behind him, her attitude one of meek submission.

White Bird was not deceived. For the moment, she appeared subdued, but there was no meekness in her. She
boasted of the white blood that she claimed had civilized her
and made her superior, yes she was savage in all her emotions
and as untamed as a wild mare. He could feel the fury and
the hatred that emanated from her now. It would work inside
her, until, one day, it would blaze out at him again. The
thought that he would once more be forced to subdue her
gave him a strange pleasure such as he had never felt before.

White Bird glanced back at her again. He could not help
the ugly thought that had crept into his mind. Just now, when
he had seen her touching her breasts, he had known as
clearly as if he had been inside her head that she was thinking of Lawrence. His lips tightened as he thought of the
many times she had mentioned Lawrence's name. He could
tell that there was a great wish inside her to offer herself to
this man, as yet unknown to her, simply because he was
white, and because White Bird's description of him had so excited her that she had almost come to believe that he was another Jack Langley. It made no sense. But then, sense was
something that had always been lacking in Lianne. She was
composed of driving emotions, of greed and selfishness. She
was callous, and he knew that he would never touch her
heart. But for all that, half-breed though she was, she was
his woman, his property. No white man should have her, not
even Lawrence, whom he called friend. Rather than have that
happen, he would kill her. He moistened his dry lips. Perhaps
he would kill the man, too.

White Bird shook the disturbing thoughts from him as he
came to the first bend in the hitherto straight trail. Pausing,
he shaded his eyes with his hand and looked about him. Over
to his left, he could see the range of hills known as Giant's
Teeth. They looked very near, yet it would require another
hour of walking before they reached the settlement over

which those hills brooded. Clouds scudded across the deep-blue sky. Away in the west, the blue was tinged with purple, which meant, he knew, that the god of lightning would shortly stride across the sky. Following would come the god of thunder. And these two great gods would split the heavens apart and grant the gift of rain. The grass that covered the slopes would bend flat before the onslaught. The thirsty earth would drink deeply, and the god of the wind would sing his shrill song through the agitated branches of the trees and the rain-spangled leaves.

White Bird's eyes dreamed, and momentarily he forgot Lianne. When the deluge ceased, there would be the mingled perfumes of the grateful earth to delight the senses. Everywhere there would be the coming of new life. It was always so when the gods strode the sky.

A new life for him, too. White Bird felt a familiar pain as he thought of all that he had left behind. He had not been happy; from the day of his birth he had never been that, but it was the known, the familiar. Now he and Lianne were adrift, and the drums would whisper to other tribes of their shame. Outcasts, both, and about to enter an unfamiliar world. The white man's world.

White Bird shivered, his flesh crawling as he thought of mingling with the pale-skins. They were so alien to him. Even their smell was different. There were, of course, those two whom he called friends, but many months had washed over their last meeting. It might well be that they had forgotten him. White Bird frowned thoughtfully as he thought of the bitter anger and hostility existing between the two peoples. It had not touched him so much, for he, because of the infirmity of his body, had not been allowed to take part in the raids upon the pale-skins. Seated unnoticed on the outer edge of the fire, he had listened as the warriors told of great battles. The warriors never spoke of defeat, and so it had seemed to him that his people were well on the way to driving the white invaders from their land. He found that it was not so. The pale-skins still claimed and worked the land of their ancestors. Their number grew daily. Now, thinking of this hostility, for the first time he doubted if he and Lianne would be welcome at the settlement. But they would not go among them as enemies, he argued silently. It would be seen that they were horseless, weaponless. That they came, if not as friends, then at least with a willingness to be absorbed into the life there. Perhaps their presence would be considered as the first break in the hostility, and a cause for jubilation.

White Bird's frown deepened as doubt continued to prod at his mind. Had it not been for Lianne and her needs, her much-repeated statement that her blood gave her a claim on these people, he would as soon leap off a cliff and dash out his brains on the rocks below, for he did not want to enter into a white world.

Lianne stared at White Bird's back with brooding eyes and moved closer to him. When she leaned forward to look in the same direction, her breasts brushed his arm. With the contact, a shock thrilled along her nerves. She might hate him, but she could not deny that at this moment she wanted him.

Lianne stepped back, unable to believe this thing she was feeling. How could she even think in this way, knowing the pain would be unbearable? She moved in close, and again allowed her breasts to brush his arm. Her breath caught in her throat, and heat flushed her body. And then she knew. It was the excitement of the pain that made her ache for him. She wanted him to throw her to the ground and take her. Swallowing, she said his name.

White Bird turned slowly. His eyes widened as he saw her violent trembling. His eyes dropped lower, taking in her breasts with their pink, thrusting nipples. Despite the scars upon them, her breasts were still beautiful to him. Hardly daring to believe the demand he saw in her eyes, he said huskily, "What is it you want of me?"

She did not answer him. Impatience welled up in her. "White Bird!" She closed the slight gap between them. Fire coursed along his veins as her breasts were crushed close to his body, and he trembled with the force of his responsive desire. "Lianne," he said in a thick, difficult voice, "I have put pain upon your body. Would you have me behave as an unthinking animal?"

Again she crushed down impatience. Laughing, she said, "Yes, yes, have I not made it clear? Let us be as two animals, there among the dust and rocks." She stepped away from him, her fingers fumbling with the short leather apron that was all that covered her nakedness. Unfastening it, she threw it to the ground, and then removed her jacket.

White Bird stared at her, a blaze in his eyes. Her hair blew in the straightening wind, her body was golden and perfect in the strong light, and they were alone, with only the sighing trees, the sky above them, and the hills and the great mountain in the distance to see them. Now he forgot the wounds he had inflicted upon her and pulled her to the ground.

Lianne had not forgotten the pain. She kept it in the forefront of her mind, cherishing it. As the pain seared her body, her frenzy mounted. White Bird kissed her breasts gently, till her strained voice told him what she wanted, and he abandoned his gentleness. His lovemaking became punishment. He had caught some of her fever, and he wanted to hurt her even as she wanted to be hurt. His fingers gripped the soft flesh of her thighs, forcing her legs apart. His breathing harsh, his sweat dripping on her body, he entered her and took her with an almost mindless violence.

Lianne screamed aloud with delight as sensation shot through her body. Her legs came up to clamp tight about his waist. "More, Lawrence," she shouted. "More! Don't stop now!"

Through the pounding in his ears, White Bird heard her call upon the name of Lawrence. Hating her, he gave a last violent thrust and spilled his seed into her writhing body. He collapsed across her, and then, deliberately, savagely, he bit her breasts. "Do you like pain, then, half-breed? I will give you all the pain you desire!"

He had left her body before her desire was quenched. Her eyes blazed into his, and her fingernails tore a long furrow down his back. "Lame One!" she screamed at him. "Maiden!" Pursing her lips, she spat in his face.

He grabbed her. Seizing her hair, he banged her head against the ground. Her nails tore at him again. Her legs and arms locked tightly about him. Like the animals that passion and frenzy had made of them, they rolled over and over in the dust.

Lightning flashed across the sky, the thunder rumbling close on its heels. Lianne gave a loud, wailing scream of pure terror. She went limp beneath him, lying so still that it was almost as if the life had left her body.

The first light drops of rain began to fall as White Bird got slowly to his feet. His hands on his hips, he stood there looking down at her. Her eyes were tightly closed, and still she did not move. Before her fear of the storm, her frenzy had vanished as though it had never been. Dust coated her body, and beneath the dust was the darker stain of blood. The rain washed her face clean, and he saw the bruise upon her jaw.

Shrugging, White Bird turned away and picked up his scattered garments. Putting them on, he walked away from her without a backward glance.

He had walked for some time, and the rain had increased in violence. It was pounding heavily on the trail before he heard Lianne's stumbling footsteps behind him.

Chapter 7

Justin felt the heaviness of defeat as he waded through the sea of mud produced by the rainfall. He paused at the edge of the burned and blackened fields, sodden now with rain, and running with mud, and the heaviness inside him was shot through with a bitter anger. His hands clenched into fists as he thought of the vicious way that Little Wolf had honored the word of the chief, his father. Little Wolf had been present at that meeting between himself, Buck, Jock McPherson, and Running Fox. He had listened, as had they all, to the words of the chief. In his somewhat harsh voice, Running Fox had said, "While Lawrence remains upon the land, we will not trouble you."

Justin's dark brows drew together in a frown. The death of Running Fox and his older son had served Little Wolf's purpose well, for by their deaths, he had become the chief. He had chosen to interpret the word of Running Fox to mean that there should be no massacre of the people of the Pilgrim's Rest settlement. Instead, it should be the harassment of the hated pale-skins, and that harassment to be carried on at his will. In one way or another, he intended to drive them from the land.

Turning up the collar of his jacket against the bitter wind that had turned the mild, sunny weather into a semblance of winter, Justin stared long and hard at the ruined crops. Yesterday, when Little Wolf and his warriors had swept down in a surprise raid on the settlement and applied torches to the growing crops, there had been no defense against them. He, together with Jock McPherson and Buck, who was still weak from loss of blood, had attempted to rally the men. But, save for their own efforts, not one shot had been fired in defense of the fields. Unnerved by the howling Indians and the screams of their own womenfolk, the other men had broken and fled for the nearest cover. The Indians seemed oblivious of the three who stood their ground and of the occasional shots they fired. It was almost as if they were contemptuous of them and their haphazard shooting. They did what they had come to do. They fired the fields, but they did not let one arrow fly in retaliation. It was then that Justin had understood how Little Wolf meant to keep his father's word. It was to be a policy of bloodless harassment.

It seemed that Buck had understood this too. He continued to shoot, but he had fired low, and his shots had been more in the nature of a warning. "Can always grow crops, Justin," he had said in the carefully expressionless voice that hid his anger. "But kill one of them bucks, and you'll have a massacre on your hands. We ain't ready for that, as yet. But next time they come, we'll be good and ready for 'em."

Jack McPherson had nodded in agreement. "Buck's right. We'll just have to swallow this, I'm thinking. But if they come again, we'll be giving them a reception that they'll not be forgetting in a hurry."

The Indians had ridden away yelling their triumph. Justin's mouth tightened to a straight, grim line at the galling memory.

"It looks to me like you got blood in your eyes, boy," a drawling voice said from behind him. "You still brooding on them Injuns?"

Justin swung around to face Buck Carey. "Yes," he said through gritted teeth. "I'm still brooding on them, curse their mangy red hides! I've done little else since it happened."

"You ain't the only one."

"Maybe." Justin gestured toward the fields. "All our labor has gone for nothing. And what did we do? We just stood by and let them carry on!"

Buck nodded. "It does seem like that, I know. But wasn't much else we could do. We was three men against that crowd of savages. If we'd killed one of them bucks, it would have given Little Wolf the excuse he needed to do away entirely with his daddy's word. We did our best to warn 'em off. Reckon we can only hope that Little Wolf'll take the warning to heart."

"He won't. You know it."

Buck hesitated. He was not quite sure of the reaction of this city man, as he called Justin in his mind. Then, remem-

bering how well Justin had stood up to the fight with Red
Morning, he was ashamed of his doubts. Justin Lawrence was
a man who would always give a good accounting of himself,
no matter in what environment he might find himself. He was
a born leader. "Cain't deny that you're right," he said
frankly. "I was just trying to calm you a mite, that all. Can
see now that you ain't needing calming. Them Injuns will
come again, all right. Ain't likely they'll give up. I know their
way of thinking. But it's like I told you before, next time it'll
be different, 'cause we'll be ready for 'em."

"The three of us again, I suppose?" Justin said bitterly.

"Nope. Don't look like," Buck answered him slowly. "I
been talking to the men. They ain't none too proud of the
way they ran off. You might say that most of 'em is right
'shamed." Buck grinned. "I reckon their womenfolk been giving 'em hell. Ain't nothing like a woman for rubbing a man's
nose in it, seems like. Them men are willing to shape up now.
Don't you worry none 'bout that. Time Little Wolf comes
again, he'll be getting a right hot reception."

"I hope you're right about the men. They seem like a cowardly lot to me."

"Ain't you a mite hard on 'em, Justin?" Buck said mildly.
"This's a whole new experience to 'em. Don't reckon they
thought they'd have to stand up to painted savages."

"Nonsense!" Justin said curtly. "It's a new experience to
me, too, have you forgotten that?"

"Ain't forgot nothing. But you're a different stripe to them.
Ain't nothing going to make you cut and run. Leastways,
that's the way I see it."

"Thanks for the compliment," Justin said dryly. "But
you're wrong, you know. It's not so very long ago that I ran
from something."

Buck shrugged. "Don't know what it could be, and ain't
going to ask. But don't reckon it was a question of facing up
to a fight."

"No. I wouldn't run from a fight."

"Didn't think so." Buck's incurious eyes went beyond him
to the sodden fields.

Justin studied Buck closely. In many ways, he thought, he
could be called a mystery. He had never been known to
speak of his past life. And although he was open, honest, and
unfailingly friendly in his approach to people, Justin could

not help thinking that it was only a facade that covered the real man. He felt a sudden burning curiosity to know more about him. What was Buck Carey really like? Where did he come from, and how had he lived before he had decided to settle here? Justin was not the only one who was curious about Buck. On the surface, Buck was uncomplicated, but Carrie, who looked deeper than most, referred to him as "the mystery man." She had many times expressed a wish to know more about him.

With an unusual wish to have his curiosity satisfied, Justin moved neared to Buck and said impulsively, "You're an odd one. Do you always take things so lightly? Does nothing trouble you?"

Buck did not answer immediately. When he did, it was in a tight voice that was quite unlike his usual tone. "One time I didn't take nothing lightly. I've had my share of troubles, and they pretty near broke me. It wasn't till I told myself that it ain't no use to let life get you down that I began to grow up."

"Where do you come from, Buck?" Justin spoke half-hesitantly. "Where is your home?"

"You're all-fired curious, all of a sudden, ain't you?" Buck said, giving him a penetrating look. "What's behind it?"

Justin laughed, refusing to let the curt tone prick him. "Sorry. Just curious, I suppose. After all, we are friends."

"We're that, all right. But that don't mean I got to tell you everything, does it?"

"I've said I'm sorry. Forget I asked."

Buck did not seem disposed to forget. The hot blood of anger flushed his face, and his eyes glittered. "You hear something 'bout me? Is that why you're asking?"

Taken aback, Justin stared at him. "What the devil's got into you?" he snapped. "What could I hear?"

Buck's flush deepened. "Well, if you ain't heard nothing, how come you're askin'? I know you told me all about yourself afore you came to this country, but I don't have to do the same, do I?"

"No, you don't." Justin turned away.

Buck seemed unable to let go of his anger. He caught at Justin's arm, forcing him to face him, and then, almost as if driven, he burst out, "You want to know 'bout me, and I'll tell you!" Without their smile, Buck's eyes were hard. "Afterward, maybe you'll be wanting me to ride on out. Don't matter a blue hell to me if you do."

The last words, delivered so defiantly, had the effect of cooling Justin's rising anger. Buck was afraid of something. "I doubt I'll be wanting any such thing," he said impatiently. "Look, Buck, keep your mystery. You have no need to tell me anything."

"Know I ain't got no need. And it ain't no mystery. It's just something that I've always kept hid."

"Whatever you say, friend." To take the awkwardness out of the moment, Justin forced a smile and said lightly, "How about letting go of my arm? Damned if you haven't got a grip on you like a cursed bear!"

Buck looked down at his fingers clamped about Justin's arm. He looked faintly startled, as if he had forgotten they were there. As suddenly as it had come, his anger faded. "I reckon friends got a right, at that," he said in a voice of dragging weariness. "Not as you'll want to go on being my friend when I've told you."

"Nothing can alter our friendship, Buck. And I repeat, you don't have to tell me anything."

"I don't mind talking 'bout it to you. There's been something eating at me this long time. Maybe it's better I told someone." He swayed, some of the color draining from his face. Seeing Justin's quick step toward him, he said hastily, "I'm all right, Justin. It's just this goddamned shoulder acting up. You mind if we set ourselves down?"

Justin followed him to a roughly made bench.

Buck sat down beside him, and pushed his legs out before him. Thrusting his hands in his pockets and fastening his gaze on the tips of his boots, he said with a startling abruptness, "I was born in this country. Out west, a few miles from here. My ma came from across the continent when she was a bit of a girl. Hadn't been here long when her parents was killed in an Injun raid. They didn't see my ma, else they would likely have killed her too." Buck paused, then went on quickly, "Woman come across her. Took her in and cared for her. Later, when she growed, she met up with this breed." Again Buck paused, his eyes turning challengingly to Justin.

Justin ignored the look. "He was half-Indian, you mean?"

"That's right. Didn't look like no Injun, though, so I heard tell. Seems like he was mostly white. By the time Ma found out 'bout him, it was too late. She was in love with him. Weren't long after they was married up that I was born."

Justin nodded. "Then I was right. I thought there was some Indian in you."

Taken aback, Buck said belligerently, "My great-grand-pappy was a full-blood. You understand what I'm telling you?"

"Yes. Go on."

"Don't nothing rattle you, Justin?"

Justin smiled. "I asked you that. Remember?"

"Injuns ain't looked on kindly. After what happened here, I don't reckon you got any love for 'em."

"It depends upon the Indian, wouldn't you say?" Justin's brows rose in faint amusement. "What else, Buck? Is there more to your story?"

Buck took his hands from his pockets. Folding his arms across his chest, he nodded. "There's more," he said, without looking at Justin. "My parents died when I was three. Fever took 'em off. A woman took me in, same as my ma. Was fine and dandy at first. I was nine when this woman found out that I had Injun blood. She turned me out. Told me to go find my own people. And that's what I did. Wasn't hard. I knew my great-grandpappy's name. Swift River, it was. I had it in my mind that he was dead. It turned out that he was still alive. He was real old, but tough, and good, or so I thought then. Didn't have no love for the white folk, but he didn't make nothing of my white blood. I was the child of his grandson, and that's all he cared about."

"It must have been hard for you, since you had been brought up in an entirely different way," Justin remarked sympathetically.

"I soon got used to it. They were as kind to me as they knew how to be. Injuns ain't ones for showing too much feeling, and that was something else I had to get used to." Buck laughed, and to Justin's ears his laughter held a hint of bitterness. "Not as I could boast of much love in my life," he resumed. He looked at Justin with that faint challenge in his eyes. "You wanting me to go on with this?"

Justin nodded. "Please."

"When I was sixteen, I took me a wife. Small Flower, her name was. Loveliest little maid I ever did see." Buck's voice faltered. "Loved her, and ain't never loved anyone that much since."

Justin hesitated, wondering if he should ask the question. He decided that Buck would not have gone this far if questions were to be forbidden. "What happened to Small Flower?" he said gently.

Buck stared straight ahead of him, and Justin saw the muscles of his jaw tighten. "She's dead," he said at last.

"I'm sorry."

"My great-grandpappy had her killed."

Justin started. "He what! What do you mean?"

"It happened when I was out hunting. Swift River said that she'd been carrying on with another brave. Never believed him, though. I knew that Small Flower was true to me."

Justin saw the tears in Buck's eyes. Nothing would ever release him from the still-raw and bitter memory of the murder of Small Flower, but perhaps Justin could make it easier for him. "Look, Buck," he said awkwardly, "I had no right to question you. Your past life is none of my damned business. You don't have to go on with this."

"I want to." Buck's unemotional voice gave no clue to the agony inside him. "At the time she was killed, Small Flower was carrying my baby. After she was dead, they cut the baby from her stomach. It was a boy, and it was still alive. They smothered it and buried it with my wife."

Chilled, Justin turned stunned eyes to Buck. "What did you do about it?" he said in a strangled voice.

"I killed Swift River," Buck said simply.

Justin put out a hand and gripped Buck's rigid shoulder tightly. "I would have done the same." He groped for other words. Finding none, he sat there staring at the ground. A stifled sound came from Buck. He glanced at him quickly. He felt a cowardly relief when he found that his face was expressionless. "Never sorry I killed him," Buck went on. "Didn't feel nothing but hate when I did it. Still feel it whenever I think on it. I had to get away quick after that. Picked the swiftest horse I could find. Swift River's been dead a lot of years now, but I hear that the story of Buck Carey, man who murdered his own great-grandpappy, is still told when the braves gather 'bout the fire. The hate for me is still strong, 'cause it ain't never been allowed to die. It's been handed down from father to son, and the hunt for me still goes on. I'm only a name to them young bucks, but don't make no difference. It's almost a game with them to hunt me down. Someday they'll catch up with me. When they do, they won't be giving me no pretty death."

Justin thought of the hate he had seen in the eyes of Little Wolf. "Would Little Wolf have heard your story?" he said thoughtfully.

Buck nodded. "Could be. That tale spread out pretty far. But he ain't likely to do anything 'bout it. He wants revenge on me, all right, but he's not about to hand me over to another tribe." He smiled mirthlessly. "Little Wolf likes to do his own punishing."

"But these young braves who have grown up since that time have never seen you. How would they know you?"

"They know me," Buck said with quiet conviction. "They got their own special ways. Besides, along 'bout that time, I didn't care if I lived or died. Never did try to cover my tracks, and never did change my name."

"Why not?"

"Just told you. Wasn't thinking, didn't much care. Still don't. Them bucks ever track me this far, they'll likely get me. Been near to capture afore this, but always outrun 'em. But now I'm tired of running." Buck rose to his feet. "Well that's my story. You want me to ride out, I will."

Justin stood up. "You stay right here."

"You're a funny cuss, Justin. If you had to make yourself a friend, why'd you pick on a worthless saddle tramp?"

"I have a rooted objection to losing a friend. If troubles comes, Buck, we'll face it together."

"I ain't dragging you into it. Them bucks get down this far, they'll likely have themselves a taste for other blood 'sides mine."

"I'm already in. You stay."

"You ain't thinking 'bout Miss Caroline or any of them others."

"Carrie would say the same. You know that. If your Indian friends come for you, we'll take off for the hills. Let them give chase. That way, we won't be bringing trouble on the settlement."

"Could maybe work, but I doubt it."

"We'll see. By the way, does Jock know about this?"

Buck nodded. "He knows. He's been my pal a long time.

Lost him for a bit when he married up. I could have stayed with him and his missus, but in them times I had a bad case of the wanderlust. Couldn't settle too long in one place. Anyway, when the Injuns killed his wife and kids, we took up together again." Buck looked at him quickly. "You sure you're wanting me to stay on?" he said hesitantly.

"You make it sound as if the decision is entirely mine. It's not, and you know it. But since nobody else is going to know about it, it doesn't matter. For my part, I meant what I said. I want you to stay on."

His words seemed finally to convince Buck. His shoulders straightened, and the shadows left his eyes. "Reckon I'm tired of traveling on, like that," he confessed. He hesitated, and then went on quickly, "Ain't one for spouting off 'bout my affairs, but you can tell Miss Caroline, if you're wanting to."

Buck's mouth stayed open, as though he had more to say, but the only word that emerged was a muttered "Thanks." Without giving Justin a chance to reply, he turned abruptly and strode away.

Justin followed slowly after him. The heavy mood engendered by Buck's tragic story began to lift as he found himself recalling something he had said when speaking of Small Flower. "Loved her, and ain't never loved anyone that much since."

Chapter 8

With her hands clasped tightly over her head to protect it
from the expected blow, Lianne crouched before the assembled people and tried to make herself as small as possible.
Her mind whirled chaotically, giving back to her a variety of
sights and sounds and smells: the silvery hair on one man;
the heavy, sullen features of another; the rank smell of a
sweating body; the anger that glared from the face of a
small, thin woman; the babble of rising voices that were filled
with hatred; the blue sky, decorated by the gods with many-
shaped fleecy clouds; the half-tart, half-sweet smell of the
grass; the muddy, much-trampled ground; and the eyes that
stared at her. Those eyes seemed to her to be of many different hues, and they glittered with an anger so terrifying that
she feared at any moment she might vomit before them.

Lianne squeezed her eyes tightly shut. Then, as the alarm-
ing thought came to her that she had, in shuttering her soul
behind her lids, rendered it momentarily blind and unable to
give warning of her bodily danger, she opened her eyes again.
Why were these people so angry with her? What had she
done, and why must she cringe before them like a whipped
dog? She knew well that there was war between the Indians
and the pale-skins, perhaps there always would be, but she
was not responsible for the spilled blood of hatred and resentment that soaked the fertile lands. If these pale-skins would
only allow her to speak, she thought desperately, she would
tell them that she was one of their people and that her loyalty
lay with them. Lianne raised her head very slightly and allowed her eyes to flick in a quick, nervous searching. Which
one of these men was Lawrence? Not, she prayed fervently,
he of the dark hair and the brutal, sneering face. His eyes
were fastened greedily on her breasts, and there was some-

thing in his intent gaze that made her feel as if worms were crawling over her skin.

Shuddering, she looked quickly away, her heartbeat quickening with renewed panic. Her mind stirring, she began to think of White Bird's description of Lawrence. "Lawrence has the tall, proud look of a warrior, for there is that about him that reminds me of our own people," White Bird had said. "He has the handsome looks of a god, and in his hair there are slight touches of winter. I think perhaps that these touches were put there by suffering, for he is a young man."

Recalling this, Lianne drew in a deep breath of relief, and her heart resumed a steadier beat. As far as she could see, there was not one man present who could fit that description. No, Lawrence could not be among this hostile crowd, and so she had only White Bird on whom to rely. Lianne turned her head stiffly and cast a sidelong look at him. He was lying on the ground, and it seemed to her that the strength had gone from him. There were bruises on his face, the flesh about his eyes was swollen, and blood dribbled from his torn lip.

Lianne frowned heavily, her lower lip protruding sullenly. He had fought those men, but eventually he had allowed them to prevail and batter him to the ground. Therefore, he had failed her. When the women had touched her with their rough, hard hands, when they had pushed at her and spat vile names in her face, White Bird should not have lain there in that half-conscious condition. He should have jumped to his feet and aided her. For her, whom he had sworn to love forever, he should have been filled with the strength of the Great Spirit. Lianne's lip curled in contempt. It was said that men were more than mortal when they loved. More than mortal? Not White Bird. He was a lame weakling! He was nothing!

Lianne crouched lower, swept by a vast pity for herself. When first they had arrived, White Bird had stood proudly enough before these people. He had not seemed afraid, for his voice had been deep and steady as he said, "Stand aside, please. We come to see Lawrence." His words had been innocent and truthful enough, but they had seemed to fill the men with fury, for it was then that they had called him names and had used their fists upon him.

Lianne glanced at White Bird. She saw that he was trying to rise, but she gained no comfort from this, for almost im-

mediately a rough foot pushed him down again. Even were
he to regain his strength, what could he do for her? Could he
take the pain from her body? Tears started to her eyes. She
had been stoned and tortured by her own people, she had
been so ill-used that it was a wonder to her that the gods had
not touched her eyes and closed them in that last sleep. White
Bird had beaten her, and now these people had placed yet
more suffering upon her flesh. The women had pinched and
pushed at her, they had scratched her with their nails and
called her "Dirty Indian savage! Squaw! Red-skinned devil!"
But she was one of these people. Why could they not see
that? Her mouth quivered as she touched her hands to her
once beautiful breasts.

"Look at the squaw touching her titties!" The shrill voice
caused Lianne to start violently. Terror-stricken, she shrank
away from the tall woman with the light eyes and the untidy
gray hair. "Don't touch me," she whispered as the woman
loomed over her.

"Speak English, do you?" The woman bent over and
yanked at her hair, twisting it so savagely that fresh tears
started to Lianne's eyes. "I'll touch you, all right, you filthy
squaw! Who sent you here, eh? Did them dirty heathens who
burned our crops sent you here to scout for 'em? Tell me, or
I'll pull every hair out of your lousy head!"

"No one sent me!" Lianne screamed. The woman twisted
her hair again, breaking the small strings of shells that decorated it. "Lawrence," Lianne blurted out desperately, staring
at her scattered ornaments. "White Bird has told you that we
come to see Lawrence."

"Liar! You heard his name somewhere."

"No, no! Lawrence is the friend of White Bird."

The woman laughed harshly. "Justin Lawrence a friend of
a dirty, murdering heathen? You'll have to think up a better
tale than that."

"I'll get the truth out of her, Millie." The dark-haired man
moved in close. "Let go of her hair. I'll show you how it's
done."

Grunting, the woman obeyed. "Don't think you can make
her talk, Tom, but no harm in you trying."

"Just watch me." The dark-haired man got down on his
knees. "This way."

Lianne screamed as his fingers pinched and twisted at her

nipples. She flailed at him with her hands and tried to scratch at his face. "Let me go!"

"Look at her," a voice cried. "Ain't she a wildcat!"

Almost fainting with the agony inflicted upon her, Lianne thought of the knife in her belt. Swiftly her hand found the weapon and pulled it out, and almost in the same movement she plunged it into the man's upper arm.

"Why, you Indian bitch!" Blood spattered from the man's gashed arm as he lifted it and began smacking her face from side to side. "I'll teach you to pull a knife on me, you poxy squaw!"

"That's enough, Tom," a man's voice cried. "Keep that up, and you'll break her jaw. Why don't you try the brave? You'll get more from him."

Red-eyed with rage, the man turned a glowering face to the speaker. "Don't you tell me to leave her alone, Jack Barker!" The man's furious, bellowing voice hurt Lianne's ears. "You saw what this squaw did to me. What would you do?"

"Wouldn't treat her like that in the first place," Jack Barker replied. "Indian or not, she's a woman."

"Can't call her a woman," another voice cried. "Indians are all animals."

"Coming here with her titties hanging out of that thing she's wearing!" A woman's furious voice. "Almost naked, she is!"

"Says they've come to see Justin Lawrence. Did you ever hear the like of that!"

"All them Indians are liars!"

"Why ain't Justin here? We'd soon have the right of it."

"Gone hunting with Buck," a man called. "Be back shortly, I shouldn't wonder."

Somebody else made a scathing comment on Indians, and the comment was answered by an unexcited voice. "You can't keep saying them things. Nobody here knows the first thing about Indians. We ain't never met one face-to-face. Far's I'm concerned, don't want to."

"We know enough. Burned our crops, didn't they?"

"Did that, all right. But ain't nobody here knows them 'cept Buck and Jock."

"Where is Jock? Why ain't he here?"

"He's somewheres off on his own."

White Bird saw the three men he had fought standing nearby. It pleased him to note that his fists had made quite an impression on them. They were looking as battered as he felt. Lianne! His swollen eyes found her, and he felt a killing rage at the sight of her maltreated face. The cursed pale-skins had done this thing to her! Some of the men were grinning. Others wore expressions of disapproval, as though they did not like the treatment accorded to them. But not one of them had stepped forward to aid Lianne. Was Lawrence here? Was he too enjoying the spectacle?

The man kneeling in front of Lianne raised his hand again. The sharp sound of the blow sent a surge of strength through White Bird. On hands and knees he began to crawl toward her. "Do not put your hands on her again," he cried, "or I will kill you!"

The dark-haired man rose. Grinning, he waited until White Bird had reached Lianne's side; then he lifted his foot and kicked at him savagely. Lianne gave a wailing scream as White Bird's body fell heavily across her.

"I said enough!" It was Jack Barker, the man who had protested before. "Ease up, Tom."

In spite of the wound in his arm, the dark-haired man appeared to be in high spirits. He let out a bellow of raucous laughter. "Maybe the brave's a woman too, eh, Jack?" he spluttered.

"What is happening here?" A clear, slightly imperious voice cut across the growing tension.

"Why, if it ain't Mistress Fane," a woman's sneering voice said. "And there's Becky Forbes with her. You go running off to tell your dear friend all about it, did you, Becky?"

"Yes I did." The short, dark-haired woman standing beside Caroline spoke up defiantly. "I heard the Indian ask for Justin. I thought Caroline should know."

"You just wasted your time, Becky," the sneering voice answered. "We know well and good that Mistress Fane is living in sin with Justin Lawrence, but I shouldn't think she'd want to know anything about dirty, thieving, murdering Indians. She's not that low. Ain't that right, Mistress Fane?"

Caroline did not reply. She was staring with wide, horrified eyes at the two figures on the ground. "White Bird!" His name burst from her lips. She moved forward and stood there staring at him for a moment; then, with some difficulty, she got to her knees beside him. "Oh, White Bird, what have they done to you!"

"Done to him!" a woman cried in a shrill voice. "My man was all for shooting him on sight. Changed his mind when he saw the squaw with him. Tenderhearted is my man. Wish now that he'd shot them both."

Caroline did not even hear the voice. As White Bird struggled up to a sitting position, she put her arm about him. Her face soft with pity, she said gently, "You want to see Justin, is that it?"

"We have traveled far to see Lawrence," White Bird said stiffly. "But we did not know how it would be." He shrugged his shoulders, seemingly resentful of her touch. "I have no need of a woman's supporting arm, Caroline."

Aware that she had stung his fierce pride, Caroline hastily withdrew her arm. "I'm sorry, White Bird," she said in a suitably meek voice. "Please forgive me."

White Bird inclined his head. "A brave does not need a woman to supply him with strength."

"Hark at him!" the shrill-voiced woman gave tongue again. "To listen to him, you'd think he was a king instead of a stinking Indian."

"Never mind that," another woman cried out in a voice of outrage. "That Indian called her Caroline! Didn't you hear him?"

"Of course I did. Ain't deaf, am I? First names of white women for a bloody Indian! Well, it don't surprise me none. Likely she's lived in sin with him as well. I wouldn't put nothing past her."

White Bird saw Caroline's mouth tighten, and he guessed at the hot rage inside her. "Caroline," he said, touching her arm. "Their remarks are as the wind. Soon blown away."

Caroline managed a smile. "I know, White Bird."

"What is to happen to us, Caroline? Will they hang us, as, in the past, the pale-skins have hanged many of my brothers?" When she did not reply, he went on quickly, "You must understand that for myself I have no fear, but for Lianne I have much fear. You will help her, please?"

"Somehow I will find a way to help you both. She is your woman, White Bird?"

"She is my woman," White Bird answered her in his grave voice.

Caroline looked with pity at the crouching girl. "Don't be afraid, Lianne," she said softly. "I won't allow anyone to hurt you."

Lianne did not answer. She knew that these people did not like it because White Bird had called the woman by her given name. Now their faces were more menacing than before, and she could hear renewed threats of violence. She fingered the knife in her belt, and she was glad that she had stained it with the dark-haired man's blood. It was strange, she thought, but she seemed to have lost much of her fear. This pale-skin with the hair of sunshine who knelt now beside them was the woman of Lawrence, and she sensed that the position carried with it a certain authority. The people called the woman names, they insulted her, but they would not dare to harm her. It might even be that Lawrence was a great chief.

Lianne glanced at White Bird. She was convinced in her mind that Lawrence was indeed a chief. But why had not White Bird told her of his full glory? Struck by something, Lianne studied White Bird closely. There was a difference about him, a strangeness. It was true that he spoke to the woman coldly, as befitted the dignity of a brave, and his face held no expression, but his eyes were different. There was a tenderness in them, as though he looked on the woman and found her ripe and pleasing.

Lianne's fingers tightened about the knife as anger swept her. How dare he look at the pale-skin so! Her dark-blue eyes went disparagingly over Caroline. So the woman carried Lawrence's child. Just for a moment Lianne was dismayed; then she took heart again as she reflected upon her own charms. Almost, she laughed aloud. White Bird had told her that the woman of Lawrence had a rare and delicate beauty. She did not think so. She was ugly! Compared to herself, she was as nothing. What had possessed great Lawrence to take such a one to share his lodge? Despite the pain it cost her, Lianne's bruised lips smiled. Once Lawrence looked upon her, he would forget this ugly squaw.

Caroline looked up at the people who were standing over her. "You need not fear these Indians," she said, the imperious note back in her voice. "They are friendly." She indicated White Bird. "His name is White Bird. Once, when I desperately needed help, he gave it to me."

An angry muttering came from the crowd. Ignoring it,

Caroline pointed to the girl. "This is Lianne, the woman of White Bird. I would like to repay my debt to White Bird, and I can do that by caring for them both. Would you help me to get them to my shack, please?"

The silence of astonishment greeted her words. It was broken by a woman's angry voice. "Don't any of you men move!" she shouted. "Help her indeed! We're not having them Indians here."

"Are you, then, such cowards?" Caroline's voice was cool and scornful. "Even if they wished to do so, they are scarcely in a position to harm you."

"Don't pay no attention to that bloody Indian lover! Why, the very idea!"

"Won't harm nothing if we give her a hand," a man's hesitant voice said. "Ain't as though the savages are armed."

A shriek of outrage came from a short, rotund woman. Her face red with anger, she thrust herself before the speaker. "I'm your wife, and I say you don't lift a finger. You help that loose-living, Indian-loving woman to take them Indians to her shack, and you sleep outside tonight. You understand me?"

The man's eyes shifted. "No need to get so excited, missus. You don't want me to help, I won't." He shrugged. "Ain't nothing to me."

Triumphant, the woman stepped back and addressed the others. "Are we going to let her get away with this?" she demanded. "Are we going to let her take those lousy, evil-smelling Indians to her shack? We'll all be murdered in our beds, you mark my words! You saw the way that squaw handled the knife. How'd you like that done to you, eh? Only, next time she won't be aiming for the arm, but for the throat. I say we drive the Indians off!"

A roar of agreement came. The people surged forward, their faces ugly with aroused passion, their hands already reaching out.

"Wait!" A thickset blond young man jumped in front of them and began waving his arms for attention. "We'll drive 'em off, all right, but before we do, let's have some fun. Let's carve 'em up a bit first. Them that's got the guts for it, of course." He looked meaningfully at the group of men who had detached themselves from the crowd. "I can see that some ain't. Disgusts you, does it, you chickenhearted sods?"

he jeered. "Well, you go and hide yourselves away while we do your work for you. How about that, eh?"

"You're right," Jack Barker said, stepping forward, "it does disgust us. We'll have no hand in it. Those Indians are savages. They don't know any better. But if you go on with this, you'll be worse than savages, because you're supposed to know better."

"Shut your face! You'll be having a prayer meeting next!" Insolently, the blond man turned his back on him. "Let 'em go, the bloody cowards. We'll have our fun anyway."

Laughter came from the crowd. Encouraged, the blond man grinned widely and jerked his thumb at Caroline. "While we're about it, let's teach her a lesson, too."

"Leave her be," a man shouted. "I don't mind going along with you about the Indians, but I don't want to tangle with Lawrence. Got a nasty temper, he has."

"Him?" With a feeling that he was losing his audience, the blond man strutted before them. "I ain't afraid of Lawrence. If he says anything, or tries anything, I'll scrag him too. And that's a promise."

"Will you, Cassidy?" a quiet, cold voice said. "Why don't you show these people how well you intend to keep that promise."

Alarmed, Cassidy swung around to face Justin Lawrence. Buck Carey was standing beside him. Both men had come up so quietly that he had heard nothing until they were upon him. "Now, you look here, Lawrence," he blustered, "if you think I'm afraid of you, you've got it all bloody wrong!"

"I'm delighted to hear it. It will make what I have to do so much pleasanter." Justin's eyes went briefly to Caroline and the two with her. If he was surprised to see White Bird, he gave no sign. "Suppose you tell me, Cassidy, what delightful plans you had in mind for my friend and my wife?"

Cassidy noticed the stress he laid on the word "friend." His face flushed. Damned if Lawrence didn't have the look of a savage himself. It would be interesting to find out if the bastard was part-Indian. It wouldn't surprise him any to find that he was. Unthinkingly, Cassidy moved back a step. He found himself chilled by the dangerous look in the dark eyes regarding him. He would have given a great deal to back down. But how could he? There were too many watching him and waiting to see how he would handle himself. Whether he liked it or not, he had to stand up to Lawrence. Losing his head, he shouted, "I don't doubt them savages are friends of yours. Why not? I'd expect anything from a man who's got a whore living with him and calling herself wife!"

Justin smiled. "Ah! Do you know, Cassidy, I fear you have made me quite angry." The cold, glittering smile widened. "I shall have to do something about that. Don't you agree?"

Cassidy glared at Justin. Binding him up with words! Smiling at him! And that smile, like a bloody sword thrust in the face. Goddamn him to hell, the arrogant swine! "You better get on with it, then, Lawrence!"

"Patience, Cassidy. Buck, oblige me by keeping these people back."

"Sure thing." Buck brought his musket up and leveled it. "It's primed and ready," he said cheerfully. "And this is just in the interest of fair play, my bunch of bloodthirsty friends."

Cassidy swung a punch. His hard knuckles opened a cut just below Justin's eye. It was first blood to him. Grinning, he began dancing around just out of reach, his fists jabbing and feinting at the air.

Staggering, Justin shook his head to clear it. Then, collecting himself, he launched himself at the other man. The unnatural calm that had so disturbed Cassidy was quite gone now. Justin's fists were like hammers, smashing into his face, his body, his head. Cassidy fought back and managed to get in one or two telling blows, but he knew he was no match for this dark giant of a man. Blood and sweat dripped into his eyes. He felt his nose go, and his lungs burned as he fought to draw his breath.

Justin grabbed him by his shirtfront and pulled him up from the ground. "Had enough, Cassidy?"

Cassidy glared at him, longing to say yes, but his pride would not allow it. Turning his head, he spat the blood from his mouth. Then, raising his heavy arm, he smashed his fist into Justin's face. "That's my answer," he panted, "you Indian-loving bastard!"

Caroline felt cold and sick as the sodden thud of blows went on and on. Cassidy was a pitiful sight. Both his eyes were almost closed, and his nose was mashed. He continued to fight, but his aim was wild. Justin himself was not unscathed. Blood from the cut below his right eye smeared his face. There was another cut beside his mouth, and a swelling beneath his left eye. Caroline clasped her shaking hands together. She longed to cry out: For God's sake, finish it, Justin! Either that, or let him go. What do I care about the names they call me? Nothing is worth this massacre. I don't want vengeance. And I don't believe White Bird would have it this way!

Convinced that she was right, Caroline turned her head and glanced at the Indian boy. He and Lianne were as still as statues, faces impassive, but their eyes betrayed them. She knew then that she had been mistaken. White Bird would indeed have it so. The glow of excitement in his eyes told her that. But it was Lianne's eyes that caught and held her attention. They blazed from her still face in avid response to the bloody battle. Biting her lip, Caroline looked away. She is enjoying this, she thought. That little savage is actually enjoying it!

Lianne, however, was not concerned with the fight. She was unaware of anyone but Justin, and the blaze in her eyes was for him. Heat flushed her body, and there was a tingling in her breasts. Surely he is a god, she thought. Never before have I seen such a man! Not even Jack Langley could be compared to Lawrence. Looking at him now, Lianne did not see the marks of battle on his face; she saw him as he had been when he first came into her sight. Tall, broad-shouldered, lean of waist and hips. His skin was burned a deep brown by the strong Virginia sun, his black hair with those slight touches of winter in it curled thickly over his forehead, and his eyes were as dark as the night sky.

Still held by that throbbing excitement, Lianne turned her eyes to White Bird. Did he know what was in her mind? There would be a great anger in him when she told him that he must never touch her again. But his anger must cool itself, for one did not quarrel with the gods. White Bird would know, even as she did, that Lawrence was the white mate they had destined for her. It had to be that way. It *would* be that way! Once more her hand stole to the knife in her belt. Her fingers gripped the hilt convulsively. She would take what she wanted. Lawrence would feel the weight of the Great Spirit's hand upon his heart, and he would look at her with love and desire. She and she alone would be Lawrence's woman. There was an unveiled threat in Lianne's eyes as she looked at Caroline. If that one attempted to interfere, she would kill her!

The fight was finished. Lawrence was the victor. Without compassion for the vanquished, White Bird watched Cassidy sag to his knees. The man wavered there for a moment, and then fell forward and lay still. Lawrence has avenged us, White Bird thought. He is my true friend.

As though the defeat of Cassidy had marked an end, the people began to drift away. Watching them go, White Bird saw the glances they made over their shoulders. There was still anger in them. They would not forget or forgive, but somehow he knew that they would accept the presence of Lianne and himself. Lawrence was only one man, but he was the strong one, and his will would prevail. There would be other strong ones to mingle their will with Lawrence's, for strength gravitated to strength. Lawrence was a leader, and those people were followers. In time they would come to see that the Indians they hated today meant them no harm, and a true peace would return to the settlement.

Justin wiped the blood from his face with his shirt sleeve. Buck was grinning at him, and his battered face broke into a responsive smile. "Cassidy's some fighter, eh, Justin?" Buck said. "He sure as hell stood up to you, and you got a punch like a mule."

"You're right." Wincing, Justin touched his face. "He damn near broke my jaw. I wouldn't like to tangle with him too often." Justin looked down at the prone Cassidy. "Won't hurt him to lie there for a bit. We'll attend to him in a minute. Come over here, Buck. I'd like you to meet White Bird. I told you about him. Remember?"

"Sure do." Buck spoke lightly, but there was something wary in his expression. "You best be on your guard, Justin, lad. That li'l squaw there, she's looking at you like she could eat you."

Justin nodded, not taking in Buck's words. The expression on his face had struck him. So he must take notice whenever he came in contact with a strange Indian.

White Bird got to his feet as Justin approached. He rose easily now, for the victory had seemed to bring a new strength to him. He inclined his head. "Lawrence. It pleases my eyes to see you once more."

Justin gripped his hand warmly. "We have much talking to

do, White Bird." He indicated Buck. "This is another friend, Buck Carey."

"Buck Carey." Again White Bird inclined his head, and there was no recognition in his eyes. In the way Justin had taught him, he extended his hand. "If you are a friend of Lawrence, you are a friend of mine."

"I'm his friend, all right." Buck clasped the Indian's hand briefly.

White Bird turned to Lianne. "This is my woman. Her name is Lianne."

Justin smiled at her and nodded. He did not exclaim over her name, as most did. He was polite, but his attention was on the woman who shared his lodge.

"Carrie." Justin reached down and helped her to her feet. "Are you all right, love?"

"Of course I am." Caroline smiled at him. "I should be asking you that question. Your face is not exactly pretty at this moment."

Justin smiled at her. "The scars of honorable warfare. Do you like them?"

"I do not," Caroline said firmly.

Again heat flushed Lianne's body, but this time it was the heat of anger. With smoldering eyes she watched Caroline lay her cheek against Lawrence's arm. She saw the smile they exchanged. Buck Carey was staring at her, and now Lawrence too glanced her way. Lianne bowed her head. The thoughts of the heart flew to the eyes, and Lawrence must not see her hatred of the woman mirrored there.

"Lianne ..." White Bird spoke softly. "Lawrence is the victor. Why do you not give him proper greeting?"

Buck smiled as Lianne fell to her knees and lowered herself on her stomach. He was wondering what Justin would make of it.

Justin watched with startled eyes as the Indian girl inched along on her stomach. He stared as she laid her lips reverently against his dusty boots. "What the devil! Get up, girl. Get up!"

"It's all right, Justin," Buck said in a low voice. "It their custom. This is the way squaws always greet a victor."

"But don't expect it from me," Caroline whispered.

"We'll see. I could develop a taste for it, Carrie, love."

Lianne heard their low voices, but she could not make out what they were saying. She rose gracefully to her feet and stood with bowed head before Justin. This man was hers. Very soon, he would know that he belonged to her.

Chapter 9

He had climbed the tree when dawn had traced the sky with
its fiery beauty. Perched high, hidden from sight by the thick,
leaf-laden branches, the brave waited for a sound that would
tell him his quarry was near. He shifted his knife from his
right hand to his left and wiped his sweating palm on his
buckskin breeches. His name was Black Cloud. He was fifteen years old, and Chief Little Wolf had entrusted him with
a very important mission.

Black Cloud peered through the screening leaves. Only the
innocent earth met his narrowed, intent gaze. The only sound
was the rustle and slither of awakening life. A bird swooped
into view. It came to rest and dug its beak into the thick
layer of leaf mold that coated the earth. Black Cloud, glad of
something to take his mind off the task before him, studied
the bird's white-speckled blue plumage with an almost exaggerated interest. His mother had been named for this bird.
He knew the story well. As his grandmother had sweated and
strained to bear the child who was to become his mother, a
bird of this particular plumage had fluttered for a brief moment within the opening of her lodge. And so his mother had
been named Speckled Bird.

Black Cloud drew back. He had no interest in birds. It was
because he was afraid that he allowed his mind to dwell on
such trivialities, he told himself sternly. Fear? The word rose
up in his mind, lingering there, making his stomach lurch.
Forgetting for a moment the need for silence, he spat the
taste of fear from his mouth.

He thought of last night with his mother. She had showed
her fear by her rare tears. She knew well that it was wrong
for a woman to cry when a brave went forth on a mission,
but even so she allowed herself that indulgence. Hidden away
in her lodge so that others might not glimpse her shame,

Speckled Bird had clutched him in her thin, strong arms and held him fiercely close. "You are so young," she mourned, and her usually still face was broken with weeping. "You are my only son, the child of my old age, and I fear for you. What is this mission on which you go?"

Almost, he had answered her: My mission is to kill Lawrence. He who stands in the way of Little Wolf. But he could not discuss his mission, which was to be conducted in the greatest secrecy. He had been forbidden by Little Wolf even to discuss it with the other braves, so certainly he could not do so with a mere woman.

He had withdrawn himself from her clinging arms. Ignoring the latter part of her speech, he had spoken to her in harsh rebuke. "I am not so very young, my mother. I have reached fifteen summers." Knowing the thing that was always foremost in her mind, he had added, "One day I will take a woman to my lodge. I will plant my seed within her body, and you will have that which you most desire. Grandchildren."

"You have found the woman of your choice, my son?"

"No. There is no one for whom I feel desire. But it will happen, my mother."

Once more Speckled Bird reverted to her previous question. "Why are you painted as if for war? I find this strange, for I know you go alone. Tell me of this mission?"

Again he had allowed the harshness to enter his voice. "You forget yourself! If you were meant to know, you would know. It is not for a woman to question."

Black Cloud caught a bright glint from the little stream that threaded its way through the trees. He was suddenly alert. If the sun had managed to penetrate, the hour must be advanced. Every morning, Lawrence walked this way, Little Wolf had told him. Would he come soon?

With his half-closed eyes on the stream, gazing mistily through the leaves, Black Cloud began to consider his mission, and as he thought, his chest swelled with pride. Of all the braves in the village, Little Wolf had chosen him. He had been entirely truthful with him, which showed that he had the utmost trust in him. "With Lawrence's death," Little Wolf had said, "there will be no further need to consider the word of Running Fox, my father, for Lawrence will no longer be there. You understand me, Black Cloud?"

"I understand." Privately, Black Cloud thought, he had been both proud and dismayed. Proud because he was trusted, and dismayed because it seemed to him that the course Little Wolf intended to follow was treacherous and dishonorable. For a few moments these two emotions had battled within him. Pride had won.

Little Wolf had leaned forward and looked intently into his eyes. "With Lawrence dead, it will be war. We will drive them from our lands!" His voice rose in shaken passion. "War on the pale-skins—it is the only way."

Caught up by Little Wolf's words, Black Cloud had felt a fierce excitement blaze in him. "War!" he had shouted.

"You will take this. You will leave it beside the body of Lawrence," Little Wolf had said, handing him an amulet.

Holding the amulet in his hand, Black Cloud had recognized it immediately. The amulet was always worn by his brothers who dwelt beyond the waterfall, and by it they were known. He recognized the significance of it, and again he was disturbed.

"Black Cloud, hear me well. It must not be thought that we had any part in the murder of Lawrence. You understand?"

Stamping down the disturbed feeling, he had nodded. Looking up, he met Little Wolf's glittering eyes. "Understand this, too, Black Cloud. If you betray me, if you allow one word of this to leave your lips, you will die in a most unpleasant way. Those I trust must serve me without thought or question."

He had sat up straight, very conscious of the importance Little Wolf's trust had given to him. "I will not betray you, O Chief."

Little Wolf had nodded. "If you are successful, I will entrust you with another mission. I want Buck Carey. But I want him alive."

"Buck Carey? The man for whom the western tribes hunt?"

"It is so. But those who hunt him will never find him. I intend him to die, but slowly, and at my hands. But that is for another time."

His heart beating very fast, he had said, "And if I fail to kill Lawrence?"

"You will not fail."

He could not leave it alone, for the shameful fear was twisting his stomach. "But if I do?" he had insisted.

Little Wolf's eyes had half-closed, as though he were considering the matter. "If you do," he said at last, "you will return again and again until you are successful."

Then his failure would not bring death. Again he was ashamed, this time of the relief that flooded through him.

It might have been that Little Wolf had understood something of his feelings, although he cringed inside at the thought, for he had leaned forward and placed his hand on his. "I do not like failure, Black Cloud, but I do not punish those who have failed through no fault of their own."

He should have been reassured by these words, Black Cloud thought, but somehow he was not.

The stout branch beneath him creaked slightly as he sat up straighter and took the amulet from the pouch at his belt. He stared at it for a long moment; then he replaced it in the pouch. Again the struggle raged inside him. Little Wolf wanted Lawrence dead so that he need no longer heed his father's given word. But it was not honorable. It was not the way Running Fox would have acted.

Black Cloud's clenched hand touched the pouch. It was not for him to disobey the chief. He would do what he had come to do. With this decision, an uneasy peace came to him.

It was the rustle of leaves below him that disturbed him. Footsteps! Somebody was coming. Was it Lawrence? Although he had never seen this man he had come to kill, he was confident that he would know him. "You cannot mistake him," Little Wolf had said, tapping his finger against his palm to emphasize each point. "He is a man of great height, with skin that is burned brown. His hair is black, like the plumage seen on the bird who plunders our cornfields. His hair is worn long, and in looks he resembles a man of our people. He has somewhat the same cast of features as Tall Grass, my lamented brother."

Black Cloud smiled to himself, for he remembered the dead warrior well. Of all the sons Sweet Water had borne to Running Fox, Tall Grass had been the most beloved. Surely Black Cloud could not fail to recognize Lawrence, not with the image of Tall Grass in his mind.

Listening to the footsteps coming nearer, he wondered why Little Wolf had sent someone who was not familiar with

Lawrence's appearance. As a possible explanation came to him, he felt a cold feeling at his heart. Was it because he was young and untried? If disaster came, and he was killed, was it because he would not be missed as much as a seasoned warrior? He did not like the thought, and he closed his mind firmly against it. He must keep telling himself that Little Wolf had sent him because he trusted him above all the other warriors. After all, had not Little Wolf revealed to him those dark and secret places in his mind?

Lianne came through the trees. She paused in the patch of sunlight and shadow, her expression dreaming, and then, as she thought of Caroline Fane, her expression turned sullen. She hated the woman, and even though she had spent only one night there, she did not like the life at the settlement. If it had not been for Lawrence, she would have taken this opportunity to run away. Later, she supposed, when Caroline Fane awoke, she would do as she had promised. She would clothe her in one of those ugly gowns she wore. Lianne thrust out a pouting lower lip. Even though she was half-white, she did not wish to envelop her body in folds of cloth as the white women did. She shrugged. Later, if she wished to stay near Lawrence, she would be forced to wear a gown, but for the moment it did not matter.

Lianne's soft mouth took on a hard line as she thought of White Bird. He had threatened to beat her again if her manner toward Lawrence's woman did not improve. It was because of White Bird and his threat that she had been forced to sleep in that airless wooden place that Caroline Fane called a shack. She could not go elsewhere, for although there were three women without men, they had refused to take in "the Indian," as they called her. And so Caroline had strung a cloth across, dividing the small room into two. It had made her very restless to know that Lawrence slept on the other side of that cloth with the woman at his side. She shuddered. That terrible room! Even though Lawrence was present, she would much rather have slept outside under the stars, as White Bird did. She could not breathe in that stuffy place. But when she had suggested that she sleep outside, Caroline had shaken her head. With so many men about, she had told her, she feared for her safety. Bah! As if she could not take care of herself.

Lianne scowled. Once again, because White Bird was

watching her, she had been forced to suffer Caroline's hands upon her as she smoothed salve into her skin. She had wanted to snatch the little pot from her hand and hurl it at her head. She would have done so, if White Bird had not been there. But she would not think of that woman now. She would think instead of Lawrence.

Lianne's sullen expression lifted, and she became conscious of a great excitement. She had heard Caroline tell White Bird that Lawrence walked this way every morning. Perhaps, as she herself intended to do, he bathed in the stream. Like she had done, he had awakened very early. She had watched him from that square hole they called a window. He had been headed in this direction. He would have been here before her if Buck Carey had not stopped and spoken to him. As it was, she had managed to slip past without either man observing her. When Lawrence finally arrived, she would pretend to be greatly surprised. By that time she would be in the stream. She would rise from the water, and he would see her full beauty. She touched her breasts, some of her pleasure leaving her. If only she were not scarred!

She took a step forward, and then paused again as her eyes were caught by a glint of blue. Stooping, she picked up a little blue feather. She examined it, and then looked upward, as though seeking the bird who had shed it. Losing interest, she let the feather flutter from her hand. Smiling, she walked on in the direction of the stream.

Black Cloud's eyes were opened very wide. The face that had looked upward was bruised, but it was the most beautiful face he had ever seen. He thought of the words he had spoken to his mother. "One day I will take a woman to my lodge. I will plant my seed within her body." There, in the person of that maiden who walked like a swaying flower, were all his secret dreams. For her, he knew, he could feel the most urgent and burning desire. He had but fifteen summers, and it heartened him now to remember that his father had taken Speckled Bird to his lodge before he had achieved his fifteenth summer. But who was she? To what tribe did she belong? Somehow he must find out.

Black Cloud's heart hammered, and his breathing grew ragged as the maiden, pausing on the edge of the stream, removed her little jacket. She undid the strings of her leather apron and let it fall to her feet. Naked, she turned about, posing there, as though expecting somebody to appear. Her breasts were round and full, and from this distance her nipples looked like dark buds.

Black Cloud saw the girl start as the sound of footsteps scuffling through the undergrowth came to her. Recalled by this to his duty, he tensed, his fingers tightening about the hilt of his knife. But even then he could not prevent his eyes from straying in her direction. Her startled expression had changed to one of glowing expectancy. She slid downward into the stream, hiding herself from his hungry eyes.

Lianne had decided to abandon any pretense at surprise. She would call to him. It was a pity she could not see his first expression, for he was hidden from her by the trees. But he would follow her voice. When he came to the edge of the stream, perhaps she would rise from the water and go into his arms. She would kiss him upon the lips in that strange, sweet way that White Bird had taught her, and she would tell him that she had been waiting for him. She smiled. Or perhaps she would make a game of it. She would dive below the water, and only her hair would be floating on the top. He would find her. He would clasp her to him, and there would be only the rising bubbles to mark their presence. "Lawrence!" she called, her voice clear and gay. "Lawrence!" Laughing, she slid beneath the icy water.

Black Cloud felt a spurt of furious anger. He knew the tones of desire when he heard them. The girl wanted this man who had just appeared between the opening in the trees. Hearing a woman's voice, the man paused and looked about him. Black Cloud stared down at him, his jealousy fading and uncertainty taking its place. Was this Lawrence? He was certainly tall, but he was not of the height he had expected. Black hair that was worn long, skin that was burned brown, but still, there was something that did not quite fit.

Black Cloud moved uneasily. Picking up the slight sound, the man looked upward, his eyes narrowing against the thin bars of sunlight that filtered through the trees.

Black Cloud held himself perfectly still. If he did not move, the man could not possibly see him. His bewilderment grew. It must be Lawrence who stood there. The girl had obviously been expecting him. She had called his name. And yet, this man, save for his coloring, did not in any way resemble Tall Grass. Tall Grass had been handsome beyond the average, but when the man had looked upward, his features had been blunt, almost ugly. He would wait, Black Cloud thought, making up his mind. The girl would call again, and he would mark the man's response. It would not do to make a mistake.

Black Cloud heard the splashing of water. Glancing swiftly in that direction, he saw the girl's head emerge. Her fingers gripping the bank, she raised her voice once more, impatiently this time. "Come to me, Lawrence!"

The man's shoulders straightened, and he was grinning now, his teeth a flash of white against the sunburned darkness of his face. "I'm coming!" he shouted.

The man had responded. It was Lawrence! One step the man took, now another. He was looking about him again, as though he were not very familiar with this part of the forest.

Black Cloud drew in a sharp breath. Gripping the knife tightly in his right hand, his flesh tingling in anticipation, he crawled forward. He had killed animals, many of them, but never before had he thrust his blade into a human creature, but he would not let himself think of that. The pale-skins were the enemy. And this one in particular, this Lawrence, was the worst enemy of all, for he stood in the way of Little Wolf. Why didn't the man move? Why did he just stand there looking about him? Praying that the gods would not allow the branch on which he was balanced to break, Black Cloud caught his lower lip between his teeth. Through the painted circles surrounding them, his eyes held a ferocious, impatient glare. Take another step, Black Cloud silently instructed the man. Just one more step, and you will be in position.

Lianne's laughing face had changed. Like an animal who scents danger, she knew that something was about to happen. Her ears caught a faint whinny, followed by an impatient stamping, and her sense of danger increased. She knew well that the wild horses did not roam this part of the forest: they preferred the great open stretches. Who sat astride that horse, carefully hidden from sight? Why, hearing her voice had he not come forward? Sounds carried in the forest, and the rider would be aware of her presence. Was he watching her, waiting? Another possibility occurred to her, and she felt her flesh creep. Perhaps the horse waited for a rider who would never return. Perhaps the dead body of the rider was very near to her now. If so, she did not wish to see it. It was bad luck to look upon the face of a dead man.

The great tree near the forest clearing swayed, and Lianne looked up sharply. Her mouth opened to scream a warning as she caught a flashing glimpse of the figure that went hurtling downward. The scream did not come. It emerged instead as a whimper. The figure had been painted for war! She heard a startled shout, a thudding sound, and then a spine-chilling scream. She knew what that scream meant. It was victory. The warrior's knife had found its target! Lawrence!

Lianne's fingers gripped the edge as she tried to haul herself from the water. There was no strength in her limbs, she could not move. Even when the red-and-white-striped figure ran past her, she still could not move. She heard the thunder of hooves receding into the distance. Then another sound came to her. A moaning, followed by a dragging sound. Lawrence was dragging himself toward her. He was not yet dead, and he was trying to reach her. She shrank within herself, her cold limbs shaking violently. He must not come near her, the voice in her head screamed. She must not look upon his face, for if she did, disaster would follow. The gods must look first. She knew they had not yet done so—for did he not still live? She did not ask herself if there were any way in which she could help him. She knew it was too late for him. She was wise in the ways of warriors. A warrior did not raise his voice in the sound of victory unless he knew beyond any doubt that his knife had pierced the heart of his victim.

Lianne's eyes dilated with horror as Lawrence crawled nearer to her, the knife still quivering in his back.

The crawling figure made a thick sound, as though he were trying to say something. Her name, on the lips of a dying man! The scream trapped in her throat burst forth at last. The shrill, ugly sound sent a flock of startled birds whirring upward. They separated, flying off in small clouds.

Terror gave Lianne a sudden strength. The tears raining down her face, the screams still issuing from her, she managed to pull herself from the water. Her clothes forgotten, her arm pressed hard across her eyes so that she need not look at him, her naked body dripping water, she attempted to rush past him. She was almost level with him when a raised tree root tripped her and sent her crashing down in his path. Although she would not look at him, she knew that he was

almost on top of her. Her heart jerked as the painful
crawling ceased. There was a darkening against the lids of
her firmly closed eyes, and she knew that he was looming
over her. She wanted to scramble away, but she was too par-
alyzed with fear to move.

"H-h-help me!" Lianne's flinching ears heard the thick, labored voice of the dying man. There was still sight in his
eyes, for a hand sticky with blood came out and grasped her
arm with a surprising strength. "D-dying. Help me-me!"

"I can't help you!" Lianne tried to pull her arm free, but
the fingers gripping her clung with a last burst of tenacious
life. "Let me go!" She tried to raise herself, but fell back exhausted with the effort. This was no longer the handsome, vital Lawrence whom the gods had decreed should be her mate,
she thought despairingly. They had changed their minds, and
Lawrence, although a spark of life still lingered, was already
a ghost.

The dying man made a choking sound. Blood spewed from
his mouth, dyeing her body and spattering her face, and he
fell heavily across her body, pinning her to the ground. She
began to scream again. Mindless with terror, still screaming
helplessly, she went hurtling downward into the darkness and
peace of unconsciousness.

Justin Lawrence heard the screaming from far off. He began to run, pulling his pistol from his belt as he went.
Trailing vines scratched at his face. Once he fell headlong,
the pistol flying from his hand. Getting to his feet again, he
took a few moments to find the weapon. Recovering it at last,
he ran on, impelled by a sense of urgency.

He was breathing hard when he finally reached the clearing. Forgetting the need for caution that Buck had so pain-
stakingly instilled in him, he burst through the opening in the
trees. Holding the pistol steady, he stood there looking about
him. Nothing. Even the screaming had stopped. The only
sounds were the calling of birds, the chirping of the cicadas,
and the rustling of the busy life in the undergrowth.

Dragging his handkerchief from his pocket, Justin wiped
his sweating face. His eyes were caught by the glint of metal.
Automatically he stooped and picked up the object. An amulet of some sort, he thought, examining it without curiosity.

Probably Indian work. He thrust it into his pocket together
with the handkerchief.

Indian! A warning bell rang in his brain. He went on,
more cautiously this time. Passing the fringe of screening
trees, he stepped out into the open space that led down to the
stream. "Holy Christ!" He stopped short, staring. A naked Indian
girl lay there. Her face was bloody; the other parts of
her body that he could see were dyed with blood. Slumped
over her was a man.

Blood! Justin thought, going forward. It seemed to be everywhere.
Standing over the man, he stared at the knife protruding
from his back, his mind subconsciously noting the
curious design on the hilt. He shook his head. He did not
need to examine the victim for signs of life. He was dead, all
right. Justin looked at the girl. Despite the grotesque smearing
of blood on her face, he recognized her as White Bird's
woman. Her head was beginning to turn restlessly. She would
be coming out of her faint in a little while, so he must work
swiftly. The knift had entered very deeply, he noted, so
deeply that none of the blade was visible. Grimly, refusing to
allow himself to feel anything in particular, he pulled at the
knife. Failing to dislodge it, he put down the pistol and used
both hands. After a brief struggle, he managed to wrench it
free. It came out with a sucking sound. The blood on the
blade looked jelled, almost black. He dug it into the earth
several times to clean it, and then thrust it into his belt. The
design on the hilt meant nothing to him, but it might mean
something to Buck.

Kneeling, he managed to pull the man off the girl. Turning
him over, he stared at the distorted face. Tom Bedford! He
looked at the girl again. For the first time, he considered the
possibility that she might have struck the blow. He frowned,
and then rejected the idea. No, such a blow would require
tremendous strength, much more strength than she possessed.
White Bird, then? He had not seen him this morning. Had he
followed Lianne and found Tom Bedford making love to her?

Lianne moaned. Lying there with her eyes tightly closed,
she was aware that the weight had gone from her body. Had
the gods taken Lawrence? Or had human hands removed
him? Her heart began to beat very fast. She could hear the
sound of soft breathing. Cautiously she half-opened her eyes.

"Lawrence!" Her eyes flew wide with shock. He was leaning over the body of a man. "That man! I thought he was you!"

Justin's dark eyes turned to her. "No," he said in a measured voice. "It is Tom Bedford." The girl's eyes were wide, the fear still burning in them. He remembered something he had once heard. Madness can give to a person the strength of ten. Could it have been the girl? "Did you do this thing, Lianne?" He watched her closely, waiting for her reaction.

Abruptly she sat up straight and she drew up her knees, clasping her hands about them. "No!" she said. He noticed that she did not glance at the dead man, and she seemed to be oblivious of the blood upon her body.

He took the knife from his belt, holding it out for her inspection. "This is the knife that killed him."

She looked at it, and then turned her eyes away. He waited for her to speak. When she said nothing, he went on. "If you did not do it, do you know who did?"

She thought of the figure hurtling from the trees. The figure that had been painted for war. The man who had been killed was not Lawrence, and so he meant nothing to her. Some instinct of loyalty stirred, sealing her lips. She shook her head. "I do not know."

"Was it White Bird? Did he follow you to the clearing?"

White Bird! It might be an opportunity to rid herself of him once and for all. "Yes," she said eagerly. "Yes, it was White Bird."

He had seen her quick, skimming glance. Almost, he had seen the decision forming in her mind. He did not believe her. His voice harsh, he said, "It was not White Bird, was it? Why are you lying?"

He was about to rise. He did not believe her. He was angry, and he was going to leave her alone with the dead man! He was on his feet now, his judging eyes upon her. With a choked cry she jumped to her feet and hurled herself into his arms. "Do not leave me, Lawrence!"

Instinctively his arms closed about her. He felt the shivering of her body against his. It was so small and slender. A child's body. "Why did you lie?" he said in a gentler voice.

She raised her face to his. "I did not mean to lie. I did not, Lawrence. It was because I was afraid. There is much confusion in my head, and I thought ... I thought you wanted me to say that it was White Bird."

"No more lies, Lianne."

Without answering, she pressed closer to him. His shirt was open, and the pressure of her full breasts with their aroused nipples seemed to burn against his flesh. Had he said a child's body? No, this was no child he held in his arms, but a woman. He was suddenly ashamed that, even with Bedford's blood smearing her, he should feel a spurt of hot desire. He let his arms drop away. "Go down to the stream and wash yourself," he said curtly. He removed his shirt. "When you have washed, put this on."

"I have my own clothes."

"They will not do. You will wear the shirt."

"Yes, Lawrence," she said meekly. She took the shirt from his hand. Like the child he had likened her to, she touched his broad chest with her hand, her fingers lingering against the dark hair that grew there.

He stepped back. "I said go!"

She was laughing as she fled toward the stream. That look in his eyes! The dark smoldering of desire! He was very much aware of her. "You will not leave me here?" she called to him.

"No. I will take you back to the settlement. Hurry!"

Justin heard the splashing of water, her voice raised in a gay little song. He looked down at the dead man. Violent death! It would seem that it meant nothing to her. He thought of the terror-filled screams that had brought him running to this spot. Her fear too had passed. Frowning, he turned away, forgetting Lianne. The killing of Bedford had been done by an Indian—he was almost sure of it. He took out the knife again. Weighing it on his palm, he studied it thoughtfully, his conviction growing. Bedford, along with Buck and Jock, who must be counted as seasoned veterans, had been in these parts longer than most. Before coming to the settlement, he had hunted the buffalo, selling the meat and the hides of the huge animals at a considerable profit. To hear Bedford tell it, he had done many things. He had roamed the high country in search of adventure. He had several times been the prisoner of hostile Indians, and had barely managed to escape with his life.

Justin replaced the knife in his belt. He himself was inclined to discredit most of Bedford's stories, but now he could not help wondering if the story of his marriage to an Indian squaw had any truth in it. After less than two years Bedford had tired of the squaw. Without a word of farewell to her, he had got up one morning, packed his gear, and left. He had left behind him not only a wife but also a small son. If that particular story was true, it opened up the possibility that his killing had been an act of vengeance. Or perhaps it was a senseless killing, without thought or motive behind it.

Justin's thoughts went to Little Wolf, and he remembered the hatred in his eyes. The Indian girl Bedford had supposedly married was not of the same tribe as Little Wolf, but all the same it would not do to count Little Wolf out. It would not surprise Justin to find that Little Wolf was mixed up somewhere in this business. He thought of the amulet he had found. That too might have a connection with the killing.

"Lawrence." Lianne's voice startled Justin. She had approached so silently that he had heard nothing. He turned slowly and looked at her.

Lianne smiled shyly. "I have washed the blood away," she said in a soft voice. "Do you like me now?"

Justin's eyes narrowed as he took in her appearance. Her hair shedding water, pearls of moisture on her face, eyes wide and shining as if with some inner joy. Dark-blue eyes. The eyes of Eve. Her full red mouth looked soft, inviting, faintly tremulous. Lips made for kissing, he thought. Her pose appeared to him to be calculating, brazenly seductive, for she had pulled back the folds of the shirt and was holding it tautly behind her with one hand. The thin material clung to her damp body, faithfully following every curve. His eyes dropped to her thrusting breasts and lingered there.

"Lawrence . . ." She came closer to him. Her body swayed forward, almost touching his. "I asked you if you liked me now."

Justin's hands clenched at his sides. I have all the instincts of a rutting animal, he thought with contempt. Bedford lies there dead, but my mind is centered on this child with her ripe mouth and her woman's breasts. Carrie was right about me. In such a situation as this I will always react like Rogue Lawrence. He looked at Lianne, who was breathlessly awaiting his answer. "Yes," he said coldly, "I prefer you clean."

Cold voice. Cold eyes that could not quite disguise the

flame behind the coldness. Lianne smiled her secret smile.
Without bothering to undo the buttons, she pulled the shirt
over her head and threw it from her. Slim, beautiful in her
nakedness, her skin smelling of the outdoors, she wound her
arms about his neck and pressed herself against him. She felt
the hard bulge of his response against her, and her limbs felt
suddenly weak. This dark giant of a man was her gift from
the gods, and she could not wait to feel him inside her. Suddenly afraid that she would fall, she tightened her arms. "I
belong to you. The gods have guided you to me!"

He wanted to crush that moist red mouth beneath his own.
He wanted to touch her breasts with his lips. He wanted to
throw her to the ground and take the body so freely offered.
Instead, he pulled her arms downward. "You bloody witch!"
he said, his fingers biting into her flesh. "What are you trying
to do? What do you want from me?"

She almost laughed aloud. What did she want! Why must
he play with words? Quite suddenly her amusement gave way
to an uneasy feeling. Now she was not so sure that he wanted
her. "Is it because my breasts are disfigured, Lawrence?" Her
voice rose, high and shrill, like that of a petulant child. "Is
that why you fight me?"

"Don't be foolish. I had not noticed the scarring until you
mentioned it."

"Then you want me?"

"No. You are White Bird's woman. As for me, I have a
woman of my own."

"Bah! She is nothing. White Bird is nothing! I want you,
Lawrence. You belong to me!"

He could make nothing of her words. He did not even try
to understand; he was concerned only with ending these dangerous moments. "Nonsense!" he said curtly.

He was treating her like a child! She felt such a furious anger that she wanted to strike him. "It was meant to be!" she
shouted. "The gods have ordained it!"

"Your gods are nothing to me, Lianne." For a moment he
played with the notion of kissing her. One kiss. What harm
would it do? If it came to that, who would know if he took
her body? She was very willing. He bent his head toward her,
and it was then he saw the tiny spot of blood on her chin.
Bedford's blood! Coming back to his senses, he thrust her
from him violently. With his eyes on Bedford's sprawled

body, he said in an icy voice, "Pick up that shirt and put it on. We must get back to the settlement to report Bedford's death."

She obeyed him sullenly, her lowered lids masking the glitter of frustration and anger in her eyes as she followed after him. He had thrust her away as though she were of little account, she thought, nursing her anger. As though she had suddenly become loathsome to him. She drew in a deep, steadying breath, refusing to allow her anger to cloud her brain. No matter what he said or how he acted, she knew that the desire for her was there. In the end he would belong to her. But first, because he had rejected her, she must find a way to punish him for his disregard of the gods and for his arrogant disbelief.

Lianne put a finger to her lips thinking deeply. How best to punish him? She thought suddenly of Buck Carey, who was Lawrence's friend. Buck had not been like those other people who had touched her with violent hands and had wanted to drive her away. He had been kind to her, almost gentle. Why, instead of her own name, had he called her Small Flower? After calling her by that name, he had seemed confused. His face had flushed, and there had been a line of pain about his mouth. His eyes, too, had looked strange, overbright, as hers sometimes looked when she was about to cry.

Thinking of that incident, Lianne felt a stirring of unaccountable jealousy. Who was this Small Flower? What had she meant to Buck Carey? She must have been important to him to make him look so very unhappy. Lawrence must know of the part Small Flower had played in his life, for his quick glance at his friend had been full of concern. He had placed his hand on Buck's shoulder and given it a comforting squeeze. "Easy, Buck, easy," he had said. "Her name is Lianne."

Buck had closed his eyes and then opened them quickly. He had answered Lawrence in that strangely accented voice of his. "I know her name, all right, Justin." His voice, that voice that so intrigued her, had dropped so low that she had had to strain to hear it. "Never noticed the likeness at first, her face kinda bruised up. It was when the light struck her full that it hit me. She is so like to . . . to . . ." Shrugging, he had broken off. Turning about, he walked away. She had hoped he would turn his head and look at her again, but he had not.

Lianne thought over the puzzling question of Buck Carey. It confused her that he should be so much in her thoughts. Why should his unhappiness matter to her? Uneasily she thought of the impulse she had had to touch him, to speak to him gently.

Lianne's winged black brows drew together. She had always believed that men were meant to serve her. She had white blood, which meant that she was no humble squaw to run after a man and serve his needs, as the other maidens did. Why, then, had she wanted to serve and to comfort Buck Carey?

Lianne's heart began to beat uncomfortably fast, and she felt stifled. She felt that the gods were angry with her, that they were reminding her that Buck was not important. Only Justin Lawrence was important, and she must remember that. Acknowledging this, she felt easier. Her mouth turned upward in a smile as an idea came to her. How would Lawrence like it, she wondered, if she gave herself to his soft-spoken friend?

Lianne hastened her footsteps. No, Lawrence would not like that, she felt sure, but she would do it just the same. Because the thought gave her pleasure, she allowed her mind to revert to Buck Carey. The gods would not mind if she used him to gain her own ends. It would teach Lawrence a lesson, and it would humble him. Buck Carey should be part of her plan. She did not doubt for a moment that she could draw him to her. She had been only a few moments in his company, yet she had had the strangest feeling that she had always known him. He would come to her willingly, gladly. He was a man who had suffered, who had much inner sadness. She had seen the reflection of it in his eyes. He might hide it from others with his easy smile and his carefree manner, but he could not deceive her. It would be a challenge to use her lips and her body to drive that sadness away. For a little while she would bring him love and warmth and joy. Her flesh tingled at the thought, and she felt a mounting excitement. It would not be such a hard thing to do. Buck Carey attracted her strongly, and she admitted it freely. So strongly, in fact, that she could almost wish it were he whom the gods intended for her.

Her mouth drooped, and she was filled with melancholy. It hurt her to think of Buck's sadness when Justin claimed her. Confused, she put a hand to her throat. The thoughts, feelings, emotions of others, had never mattered to her before. She had always found that the most comfortable thing to do was to think only of herself. So why should Buck's feelings matter to her so much? She and Justin Lawrence were meant for each other, and she must make him understand that. He would, of course. He would eventually realize that he was a means to an end. That he was nothing to her. That he must remain nothing.

Lianne raised her eyes and looked at Justin. He was so handsome! An exciting black eagle of a man! There was kindness in him, as well as harshness, for she had experienced it when he had lifted her trembling body into his arms and carried her to the shack. But his kindness did not make her glow, as Buck Carey's had done. It did not make her feel secure and wanted. You must stop thinking of him, she bade herself sternly. Think only of Lawrence, of his jealousy when he finds you in Buck Carey's arms.

Justin was smiling as he strode along. Lianne the beautiful, he thought. Lianne, of the moist red lips; the full, thrusting breasts; the body that was made for love, and with all that beauty, the unheeding brain of a child. Yes, beautiful she was, and he could not deny that he had been tempted. Now, in the light of clearer thinking, he could laugh at those moments of temptation. That posturing child! After having known Carrie! He must have been insane. Despite her beauty, Lianne was in many ways rather pathetic. There was her supreme confidence in her attractions, for instance. Her evident belief that she could have any man for the asking. No one could possibly be as irresistible as Lianne apparently believed herself to be, and in time life would teach her that rude lesson.

Justin's smile vanished. Buck understood the Indian mind. He should—he had dealings enough with them, and he was part-Indian himself. Perhaps he would understand the meaning of Lianne's rambling talk of gods and destiny. Last night when White Bird had addressed Lianne as "half-breed woman," there had been a most unusual flash in Buck's eyes. Could it be that he, with his minute portion of Indian blood, thought of himself as a half-breed? Justin's thoughts turned to White Bird. Where did he figure in this matter? He claimed Lianne as his woman, and yet her actions tended to deny this.

Justin's frown deepened. Lianne. It all came back to her. If he were at all superstitious, he would be inclined to the belief that the Indian girl had brought bad luck with her. There was an uneasiness in the atmosphere that seemed to have its center in her. There was White Bird's hostility, the hot jealousy in his eyes, his curt answers to the questions he was asked. White Bird had always been reserved and remote, but never hostile. Then, there was Carrie's attitude. Almost as hostile in her manner as White Bird, she had nonetheless tended to Lianne's many cuts and bruises. But she did it with the air of one who is forced to do her duty. It was almost as though she could not bear to touch the girl. Had her woman's intuition given her warning? What went on in her mind? Why had she lain so stiffly by his side, barely responding to his touch, his voice? And then, Buck. The change in him had been even more marked. There was the look in his eyes when they rested upon Lianne, his slip of the tongue that had caused him to call the girl by his murdered wife's name. Was Lianne really so like Small Flower? It would seem so, if one were to go by his general attitude. Quite suddenly, Buck was no longer himself. He did not smile, he did not make his small jokes, and above all, he did not look at Lianne again, and that in itself seemed significant. Shortly after that, he had taken his leave.

Justin thought of another disturbing incident. It had been the turn of himself and Jock McPherson to maintain the night vigilance over the settlement. It was when he had gone with Jock to make a last inspection of the gates that he had seen Buck standing in the shadows, opposite the shack he had left an hour or more ago. There had been a rigidity in his attitude, and he seemed to be listening to the sound of Lianne's voice as it rose and fell in stilted conversation with Carrie.

Justin had called to Buck, inviting him to join them, but Buck had not answered. Instead, he had walked quickly away. Perhaps he had not heard.

Jock McPherson was not of this opinion. "The laddie heard us, all right," he had said in his blunt way. "I am thinking 'tis the Indian lassie who is ailing him, and I am no liking it. She isna good for him, I can tell. I saw the way he looked at her."

"Is Lianne like Small Flower?"

"I dinna know. I never met the lassie." McPherson had looked grim. "But if this Lianne is going to cause him more suffering, I'm for sending her on her way. I dinna mind telling ye that Buck has had more than enough of that in his life, and I am not wanting more for the poor laddie."

White Bird, Caroline, Buck—all of them reacting in their different ways to the girl. All acting like stiff and unfriendly strangers. And now, Bedford, lying dead in the forest in a pool of his own congealing blood. Justin fingered the amulet in his pocket, his uneasiness increasing. The murder of Bedford might be the prelude to an outbreak of violence. But on the other hand, it might be an isolated incident, with no particular significance. Only time would tell. But in the meantime, it was better to be on the safe side. They must set up stronger barricades, and double the guard.

Shaking his mind free from anxiety, Justin stopped walking. Turning his head, he looked at Lianne. She was walking slowly, with head bent, and she appeared to be deep in thought. With the folds of the shirt flapping about her slender legs, she looked like a child in an oversized nightshirt. He felt a stab of compunction. He need not have spoken to her so harshly. "Lianne." Smiling, he held out his hand to her. "Friends."

She ran to him. "Friends, Lawrence," she said, placing her hand in his.

He put his arm lightly about her shoulders. They walked for a while in companionable silence. It was Lianne who broke it. Looking up at him, she said in a low voice, "How many years has Buck Carey?"

"Why?"

She jumped, startled by his abruptness. "It is simply that I wish to know, Lawrence."

Justin hesitated. "I believe he has passed his fiftieth year."

She nodded. "It is not young, Lawrence. But on him the years do not matter. He is a man of much attraction."

"He is. But he is also a man who would not take kindly to having his emotions tampered with."

"Are you warning me, Lawrence?"

"I am." Again he stopped walking. Turning her about to

face him, he looked at her searchingly. "What is in that mind of yours, Lianne?"

She smiled a small secret smile he had noted before. Her eyes looked innocent as she answered him. "There is nothing in my mind but curiosity. You believe this, Lawrence?"

"I'm not sure," he said, still studying her. "But in any case, your curiosity has now been satisfied."

She shook her head. "No, Lawrence, not quite. Why did he call me Small Flower? Is it the name of someone he loves?"

"You must ask him that."

"Why? He is your friend. You must know."

"If Buck wishes you to know, he will tell you."

She pouted. "Then I will go to him."

"You should beware of opening up old scars, Lianne."

For a moment she did not understand his words; then, as his meaning came to her, she smiled. "He has been hurt in some way. I know this. But it may be that I can cure that hurt."

Justin did not answer. He began to walk on. After a moment she followed him. Her interest in Buck had not aroused his jealousy, she thought angrily. His only concern seemed to be for his friend. He did not want him to be hurt again. She started as his arm settled about her shoulders again. All would be well, she thought. She had but to wait. Perhaps at this moment it would not be wise to arouse suspicion or jealousy in him. That must come later. To please and divert him, she began to tell him of small incidents in her life.

Justin listened with interest, amazed at the subtleties of the Indian mind. When she grew silent, he countered with stories of his own. He could tell from her blank expression that she did not always grasp the point of the stories. But when she realized that the story was meant to be amusing, she laughed obligingly.

When they came in sight of the settlement, his arm was still about her shoulders. Lianne was laughing her high-pitched laughter. Looking at her delicately flushed face, the sound of her laughter in his ears, Justin was able to tell himself that he had exaggerated the danger she represented, just as he had dreamed up all those complexities in her nature. She was egotistical, vain, too sure of her own beauty and attractions, but were not those the faults of most young girls? Rather uneasily, he remembered her naked body pressed to his, her clinging arms. Again he found an excuse for her. She was a savage. He could not expect her to behave as a civilized girl. Although, if it came to that, many so-called civilized girls from his past were only too happy to behave as savages. In the future he would remember that Lianne was little more than a child. He would treat her as such.

Ben Cressy opened the gates for them. He greeted Justin respectfully enough, but his eyes were brooding when he looked at Lianne. "Is them Indians going to stay permanent at the settlement?" he asked Justin.

"The decision is not mine, Ben," Justin answered him curtly. "It will be the will of the majority, I daresay."

Ben Cressy stared after them. The will of the majority? He turned the words over in his mind and thought rather sourly of the three who, in his opinion, ran the settlement. Justin Lawrence, Buck Carey, and Jock McPherson. It would no doubt be their will that prevailed. They were fair enough, of course, and he had nothing but liking and respect for them, but he would be easier in his mind if they sent the Indians off. It made him feel queer to have them walking among white people, as though they had every right. Nothing good would come of it.

Chapter 10

Caroline stood just within the open door, her eyes on Justin and Buck. They were deep in discussion, their arms propped on the stockade rail. What were they talking about? she wondered.

Frowning, she brushed away the fly that had settled on her heated flesh. Flies, heat, sometimes bone-piercing cold, constant anxiety, and added to that, the heavy burden of the child dragging her down. What had happened to her bright dreams, to her spirit of adventure? It was strange, she thought, that she should be more despairing now than she had been when she had stepped off the convict ship the *Merryventure*. At Montrose Plantation, she and Justin had been the slaves of Tobias Markham, but even then she had retained her dreams. Tobias Markham. She remembered the strange light eyes in the dark face, and she wondered if he still searched for his runaway slaves. In his own way, Markham had been kind, and he had prided himself on being strictly just. The life at Montrose had not been too unendurable. It was the indignity of being a slave that had rankled. Perhaps they might have been at Montrose still, had it not been for Miss Biddy, Markham's drink-sodden, half-insane wife.

Caroline thought of the flogging she had received at Miss Biddy's instruction, and she shuddered. Tobias Markham had been away at that time. Intoxicated by her temporary freedom from her husband, Miss Biddy had gone on a rampage, her madness rising to new heights. Her word was law. It was that flogging, Caroline thought, that had broken her, and so she had run from her bondage. She had run desperately, blindly, praying that Justin would find her somehow. Praying that she would not be discovered and taken back to Montrose.

It was later, after he had witnessed the killing of Moon, the big gentle black man, and Eliza, the frail little white girl who had loved Moon, that Justin had made his own bid for freedom. Knowing nothing of the dangers, not really caring, he had plunged into the forest in search of her. If it had not been for White Bird, it might have ended in tragedy for them both. But suddenly, like a miracle, White Bird was there.

Caroline smiled. Not that she had known much about the miracle at that time. White Bird had found her. She had been half out of her mind with delirium, he had told her in his grave way. For a time he had feared she would die. It was also he who had led Justin to her.

Caroline pushed back her hair with nervous fingers. She owed so much to White Bird. Then why, knowing this, could she not bring herself to trust Lianne, who was White Bird's woman? Lianne, the child called woman. Caroline wanted to laugh at the inept description, but whenever she thought of the Indian girl, there was no laughter in her. Yes, White Bird called Lianne his woman. But why were Lianne's eyes constantly on Justin? Why, whenever she passed him, did she find some excuse to touch him? And it was not only Justin. Buck rarely spoke to Lianne, and whenever possible, he avoided her, but whenever he came into Lianne's sight, she would follow him about like a little puppy at the heels of its master. White Bird looked on, saying nothing, but she could not help wondering what his thoughts might be. Sometimes, because she felt this deep hostility toward Lianne, she would feel ashamed. Was she really so lacking in gratitude to White Bird, so petty that she must read a sinister meaning into everything that Lianne did? Lately, Lianne's sullen manner had lifted. She had become friendly. The girl had given her every reason to trust her, and she worked hard to please her. Why, then, did Caroline feel threatened whenever Lianne was near?

Caroline's thoughts broke off as she saw Justin turn and rest his back against the stockade rail. She saw the quick flash of his smile as he said something to Buck. Her eyes softened. She was a fool! As long as she had Justin, what did anything matter? Flies, heat, her fear of Indians—all her anxieties faded when he smiled at her and looked at her with love in his eyes. He was her dream, her adventure! He always would be. Rogue Lawrence, the man who should have been hanged, and herself, Caroline Fane, accused of murder and adultery.

They had loved, hated, and then loved again. England had rejected them, and in that convict ship they had been forced to come halfway across the world. But they were still together, as they were meant to be.

Looking at Justin now, Caroline felt such a welling of love that she trembled with the force of it. She remembered him as he had once been. The Rogue. The fascinating challenge to so many women. Long, slender fingers loaded with rings, lace at his throat, his wrists, dressed in the height of fashion. A man who lived for adventure, who thrived on danger. He was garbed in stained buckskins now, and there were no rings on his fingers. His hands were callused with hard work, but he was still the most handsome man she had ever seen.

Caroline's hand rested on the bulge of her stomach. And she? She was Caroline Fane, Rogue's mistress, who hoped one day to become his wife. She carried his child. And that child would grow tall and strong in this vast, nature-scented, wonderful land. Somehow, she was sure that she carried a son. But if the child proved to be a daughter, she would be welcomed with love. The child was part of Justin, part of herself, but more important, part of the exciting future of this country.

Caroline's smile faded, and the dreams in her eyes vanished as she heard a rustle behind her. She did not need to turn; she knew that Lianne was making herself useful again.

Lianne straightened up from her task and turned her eyes on Caroline. If only the child would kill her! she thought venomously. Why did the woman just stand there in the doorway staring outside? What was she thinking about?

Lianne crept nearer, silent-footed as always. She saw Caroline half-turn and rest her hand against the rough edge of the door. She waited, thinking that the woman meant to say something. When she did not, Lianne continued with her critical inspection. Her eyes dropped to the great pregnant belly. The gray cloth of Caroline's gown strained over the mound, and she could see the fluttering movements of the child within, the sudden and startling bulge of tiny limb. The child was impatient to be born. Surely the woman would soon drop the child. While she carried it in her belly, Lawrence would not drive Caroline from his lodge. But afterward! She could hardly wait for afterward!

Biting her lip, Lianne turned away and halfheartedly

resumed her task of dusting the roughly built furniture. Lawrence gave her no encouragement. She could not tell what he was thinking. His mind seemed to be centered on the woman. He touched her with love. And although Lianne had found that he could sometimes be brusque and impatient, he was never so with Caroline. No doubt he was sorry for her because she was so heavy and lumbering. The brusqueness and the impatience were reserved for her, Lianne thought resentfully. Why could he not be gentle with her, as he was with Caroline?

Gentle? The word conjured up Buck Carey. He was gentle with animals, with children, and for a short time he had been gentle with her. It was no longer so. She had found, after all, that it was not so easy to draw Buck to her. It seemed to her that he avoided her. And when circumstances forced him to be where she was, he was stiff, unfriendly, his eyes sliding away as though he could not bear the sight of her.

Lianne put both hands on the rickety table, leaning on it heavily as the pain welled up inside her. The thought of him made her want to cry. Somehow, whenever she caught sight of him, it always became harder to remember the will of the gods. She was often frightened, caught between longings she did not understand and her fear of divine anger. Once, distressed by the turmoil inside her, she had even asked herself if Lawrence was really meant for her.

The gods had made quick answer. No sooner had the thought left her mind than the sky had darkened. Lightning split the sky. The thunder crashed in her ears with a sound of doom. The heavens had opened. The heavy gray sheet of the rain had battered at her; the violence of the downpour almost bruising her skin.

Soaked, terrified, she had turned her face toward the mountains, the great craggy mountains, where, it was said, many of the gods resided. "I will obey!" she had cried aloud. She had stretched out her arms, asking for mercy. "I will not think of Buck Carey!"

Running for shelter, her head down, she had cannoned into Justin. He had caught her and held her steady, and for a brief moment she had been clasped in his arms. Rain from his hair dripped onto her upturned face. Lightning lit his rain-wet face, the deep dark eyes that looked at her inquiringly, wondering at her terror. Panting, she had clung to him.

He was not as one with the gods as she was, and so he had not understood the cause of her terror. He had smiled at her, and kissed her cheek. A light salute that meant nothing. "Silly child," he had said, a hint of laughter in his voice. "There is nothing to be afraid of. The storm will soon pass."

The storm had passed, but the storm within her remained. She found that she could not stop thinking of Buck. Sometimes she did not even try. Mingling with her fear these days was a defiance, and that defiance set her wandering after him whenever she could. She knew now that she was fated to belong to Lawrence; nothing could change that. And because she acknowledged it, she told herself, anger would not fall upon her if she thought of Buck, spoke to him, was in his presence. No, not even if he desired her body and she submitted to him. In the end, it would be Justin, for had not the gods given her an answer?

Lianne looked at Caroline again. The woman was very pale. There were shadows beneath her eyes, and her bright hair looked dull. She did not bear the child well. It might be that the birth would kill her. Lianne's breathing quickened at the thought. If she did not die, she must be helped out of this life.

Struck by Lianne's agitated breathing, Caroline turned and looked at her. "What is it?" she said quietly. "Are you feeling ill?"

Lianne shook her head. "I am well," she said in a grave voice. Her face was always still when she looked at Caroline. Lately, though, there were times when she had to conquer a sudden desire to smile at this white woman who stood in her way toward Lawrence. Other times, too, when she felt a flash of something that was not hatred. She would not analyze the feeling. She had closed her mind against it.

"I am glad to hear it," Caroline said. Almost, she thought, that wooden face had smiled. The girl was so beautiful, she should smile more. On those occasions when she had seen her smile at others, that beauty had been quite breathtaking. But the wooden expression, purposely donned for her, she suspected, dulled her beauty, so that one was sometimes unaware of it.

Lianne had made no answer. Flushing, Caroline turned away from the door. Moving over to a chair, she sat down carefully. She was aware that there had been an edge of sarcasm in her voice, and she was annoyed with herself. What did it matter if Lianne refused to smile at her? The girl was polite enough. She worked hard, and she did her best to please. Perhaps that was it, Caroline thought. Lianne tried too hard. So much so that Caroline could not help suspecting that there was another motive behind all the industry. A motive that was not good.

Lianne was still rubbing at the splintered table. A useless task, but apparently she liked to keep busy. Caroline smiled to herself. Justin was not skilled in the art of furniture making, and the ugly old table had been his first effort. Only last night he had said to her, "Wait, Carrie. One of these days you will live in a big, shining, gracious house. I promise you. You will have beautiful furniture all about you." Laughing, he had brought down a clenched fist on the table, almost overturning it. "This rubbish that surrounds you now will seem like a bad dream."

Through half-closed eyes—she was always so tired these days—Caroline watched Lianne. The girl was wearing an old yellow gown of hers. It was one that Tobias Markham had bought for her, for he had believed in clothing his slaves neatly and well. The gown had shrunk from frequent washings, and the color was slightly faded, but it suited Lianne well. Although Lianne had retained her fringe, knowing that it was well-suited to her particular style of looks, she no longer did her hair in the fashion of an unmarried Indian maiden. The short sides were already growing longer, and she had released the back hair from its tight braid. Long and shining, it flowed down her slender back like a black waterfall.

Lianne was not aware of Caroline's eyes upon her. She continued to rub at the table, but her mind was not on the task. She was listening to the murmur of voices outside. Straightening up, she put down the cloth. Pushing back a lock of hair that had fallen forward, she sauntered unhurriedly to the door. Leaning out, her hands on either side of the frame, she looked across at the two men. Buck was smiling, and Justin was leaning close to him, looking at something Buck held in his hand. Lianne sighed, and she did not know why she did so.

Caroline studied the droop of Lianne's shoulders. There was something about her pose that suggested unhappiness. It was wrong of her to be so stiff and formal with the girl, so unfriendly, she thought guiltily. She should be kinder, more understanding. "Lianne . . ." She spoke quickly, before she could change her mind. "I noticed yesterday that the berries are ready for picking. They are growing near the edge of the forest, so we won't have to go in very far. How would you like to go berry-picking with me?" She paused. "It will be a nice surprise for Justin. He likes berry pies."

Lianne dragged her eyes away from Buck. "What did you say, Caroline?" She said the name unwillingly, as though she did not care for the sound of it on her tongue.

Perhaps, Caroline thought with a flash of sarcasm, Lianne would prefer to call her "Lawrence's woman," as she had done at first. Mildly, determined to be friendly, Caroline repeated her question.

Lianne's eyes returned to Buck. "Today?" she said absently. "May we go tomorrow instead? Today I have something else I wish to do."

Something else? Caroline thought. Did that something else she had to do concern Justin? "Yes, of course," she answered, the coldness back in her voice. "Tomorrow will do very well."

From the corner of his eye Buck saw the Indian girl standing in the doorway. Casually, as though he had not noticed her, he turned his back. She was so young, he thought, so fresh and beautiful, so very like Small Flower! Whenever he looked at Lianne, he felt the pain of longing for something that once had been and could never be again. He, who had never been conscious of the passing of the years, mourned now for his lost youth. The girl was constantly on his mind; she had lodged there, and he could not shake her loose. Sometimes, when he had had a little too much of the strong, clear liquor that Maggie Tate was constantly making up from the secret recipe she had brought with her from England, he would get Lianne muddled up with Small Flower. Even when he was sober, the two were inclined to merge into one. To hold Lianne in his arms would be as if he held Small Flower once again.

Buck's hands tightened on the rail before him, his knuckles whitening. He asked himself why she followed him about. To her, he must seem like an old man, so what did she want of him? At first, flattered because she followed so constantly at his heels, he had been foolish enough to believe that the girl was attracted to him. Later, pondering on the matter, he had laughed bitterly at this absurd belief. Old fool! he had raged at himself. You goddamned old fool! Later, when he had grown calmer, he had taken out the liquor from the place where he had hidden, it and he had drunk himself insensible. A fool thing to do, he realized, when he had awakened the next morning with a throbbing head and feeling sick and sorry for himself. He was not a man who normally enjoyed drinking to excess, and he had told himself that he would drink no more. But of course he had.

Justin too had seen Lianne. Studying Buck's averted face, he felt the slow burn of anger. Why in the name of Christ wouldn't the girl leave Buck alone? She was always staring at him, always following him. He looked down at the amulet Buck had passed back to him. "You were saying?" he said, breaking the tension.

Buck started, and then rushed into words to cover the involuntary movement. "It's like I told you, Justin, that amulet has nothing to do with Little Wolf's tribe."

Justin smiled. "I should know that by now. You have told me several times."

"I have?" Buck seemed about to argue the point. "Maybe I have," he conceded. "I don't know where my head is these days." He shrugged. "Anyway, it's been four weeks since you found Bedford's body, and ain't nothing happened. I guess it was a stray Injun who dropped that amulet, and he who killed Bedford. Might be he had his reasons for sticking Bedford, and then again, maybe not. It's just as likely there wasn't no reason. Maybe that Injun made himself a promise to kill all the white folk he come across."

"I keep thinking of that Indian we glimpsed a couple of weeks back," Justin said, frowning. "Would he have had anything to do with Bedford's murder?"

Buck shook his head. "If you're asking me that question seriously, then I say it ain't likely. He's a young 'un all right, and he's one of Little Wolf's warriors. Ain't scarcely been tried yet, I'd say, even though he's painted up so fine. Don't know what he could have been doing alone and so close in to us. You happen to notice anything 'bout that Injun before he ran off?"

Justin shook his head. "I had only a flashing glimpse of

him. He was gone so quickly that I thought for a moment I'd dreamed him up."

"Weren't no dream. All Injuns move fast. One minute they're there, and the next they ain't. I saw his face when Lianne came along and called your name. That Injun looked like he'd seen a ghost." Buck pulled thoughtfully at his lower lip. "I cain't help wondering why."

Justin was silent for a moment; then he said slowly, "As to that, I've got no answers for you. I've been expecting more raids from Little Wolf. . . . We all have. But everything has remained so quiet that it makes me uneasy."

Buck gave him a quick, unsmiling glance. "You stay uneasy and on the alert," he said, in what was for him an unusually serious voice. "That's the best way to keep your hair fastened to your head."

"While we're on the question of uneasiness, Buck . . . do you mind if I say something?"

"That depends on what it is."

"It's just that you make me uneasy, Buck. Look at you! Your hands are shaky, and you can't seem to concentrate. What's going on? What are you doing to yourself?"

Justin was treading on delicate ground, and he was prepared for Buck's anger, even his resentment, but he was not prepared for the quiet, unemotional answering voice. "That's a good question. What am I doing to myself? You'd be surprised at how many times I've asked myself that same thing."

"And what's the answer?"

"Ain't one."

"It is Lianne, isn't it?"

Again Buck surprised him. He made no attempt to deny it. "It's her, all right." He sighed. "Cain't seem to settle nohow. So I reckon it's time for me to be moving on, Justin."

"No!" Justin spoke sharply, hoping to convince. "You belong here. We need you. We'll send Lianne on her way, instead."

"No, leave her be." Buck sounded suddenly very weary. "Ain't no one needing me, and I don't belong nowhere. Never have. I'm a saddle tramp and cain't stay too long in one place."

"Buck, listen to—"

"Time for listening is over," Buck said, turning away.

"Ain't no more to be said. Come time, I'll get my gear ready and be heading on out."

Justin watched him as he walked away. The abrupt leave-taking had startled him, but he made no effort to call his friend back. He had the feeling that Buck was best left on his own for a time. There was a tautness about him, as though one extra push would send him over the edge, and he would be lost in dangerous emotions that he would have no way of managing.

A flicker of yellow brought Justin's attention to Lianne. He was not surprised when he saw that she was preparing to follow after Buck's retreating figure. He called to her. "Wait, Lianne."

Lianne heard the anger in his voice. She moved forward quickly. "Yes, Lawrence?" she said in a low voice, stopping before him.

"Were you going after Buck?" he demanded.

So he was jealous! Lianne should have felt triumph, but somehow she did not. She dropped her head meekly. "No, Lawrence," she lied. She was afraid that he would stop her, and she would not be stopped. Not today of all days. It had become, without her quite realizing it, the day that would decide something in her life. What that something was, she did not know, and for the present she was content not to cudgel her brains.

Her meekness did not deceive him, for he knew that there was nothing meek about her. She was lying to him, of course. There was something she wanted from Buck, and he wanted to find out what it might be. Buck, he knew, would doubtless appeal to most mature women. He was handsome, attractive in his gentle simplicity, and he looked younger than his years. But Lianne was not a mature woman. To her, Buck must seem old. He himself, though many years Buck's junior, would no doubt appear old in her eyes. Therefore, he argued, there had to be another reason for her pursuit. "What do you want from Buck?" He made his voice harsh, hoping to frighten her into an admission.

She confounded him. "Why do you ask me that, Lawrence? There is nothing I want."

Another lie! Did she perhaps see Buck as a Jack Langley, the white father of whom she had spoken so proudly? But even if that were so, Buck's feelings toward her were far from fatherly. "Listen to me, Lianne." Justin placed his hand on her shoulder. "I want you to leave Buck alone. There are things you do not understand. You will only stir up trouble, and that would be dangerous for you as well as Buck. You see, Buck is . . ." Justin broke off, suddenly at a loss.

She had heard the softer note in his voice, and she took quick advantage of it. She raised her eyes to his face. "What are these things about Buck I do not understand?"

His hand dropped from her shoulder. With that expression in her eyes, there was nothing he need tell her, he felt. Nothing that she did not know. Confused, he evaded her question. "Do you think of Buck as a father? Is that it?"

A father? Her mouth dropped open in genuine surprise. Didn't he know? Couldn't he guess? She wanted to laugh aloud. She wanted to say to him: "I will be yours, Lawrence, for the gods have decided this. But never would I see Buck Carey as a father. Even to see him pass by starts a heat in my body. Once, by accident, he touched me, and I grew weak with my longing for him." But she could not say that to Justin. Bad luck would follow if she admitted such a thing aloud. She said in a low voice, "Yes, Lawrence. That is how I think of him." She gave him a swift look. The thought came to her that she no longer had to make him jealous. He could not escape the destiny the gods had planned for him.

She turned away from him. "I may go now, Lawrence?"

He hesitated, aware of uneasiness. "If you'll give me your promise not to go near Buck."

She nodded. "If that pleases you, Lawrence." Without another word, she walked away, her head held high.

"She will go straight to Buck, of course," Caroline's voice said from the doorway. "She is determined to have her own way, and she finds it easier to lie." Caroline turned away from the door.

"What makes you think she is lying?" Justin was still conscious of the uneasiness as he followed her inside. "Why do you dislike her so much, Carrie?"

Caroline's face flushed. "If I tell you, you'll laugh. You'll say I am imagining things."

"No, Carrie, I won't." He went to her and put his arms about her. "Tell me, love."

Caroline's lips trembled. "It sounds foolish, I know. But I have this feeling that she means me harm."

He stared at her, half-alarmed for the influence the Indian girl seemed to be exerting over Carrie's mind, and half-impatient with such fantasies. The impatience won. "Carrie. For God's sake, talk sense!"

"I can't help it, I tell you!" Her voice rose, and he heard the edge of hysteria in it. "Perhaps I am mad, or perhaps it is the child affecting me, but I do feel it. She wants you, and she wants Buck. Both of you! And she wants me out of the way."

"She is a child, but you make her sound like an evil, scheming woman."

"I'm sick of hearing that she is only a child!" She pushed against him, trying to free herself. "In years she is a child, but that is all. She has a dark mind, and there is something brewing in it."

"Then you do think of her as an evil, scheming woman?"

"Yes!" she shouted, infuriated by the smile in his eyes. "Yes, I do. And on top of that, she is a savage. I will tell you something. What Lianne wants, she will have."

Justin smiled at her, refusing to take her seriously. The baby was late in coming. Her nerves were on edge. She could not really believe the things she was saying! "Carrie, love!" He kissed her long and lingeringly. Thankful to feel the relaxing of her tense body, he said gently, "I can't speak for Buck, but I can speak for myself. If, as you so flatteringly say, she wants me, she is out of luck. I belong to you, and that's the way it will remain."

"Rogue Lawrence, the ever-faithful." She wound her arms about his neck. "Is that what you are saying to me?"

"Certainly. You believe me, don't you?"

"Hmm!" She smiled at him. "Ask me in another fifty years. I might then be able to give you an answer."

"Is there no pleasing you, trollop?"

She laughed, her fears for the moment forgotten. "And who made me a trollop?"

"I did. I am sure you will appreciate the fact that I had to live up to my reputation?"

"Fool! Oh, Justin, I do love you so much!"

"There! I have pleased you."

"But I would be better pleased if you would find some way of placing a wedding ring on my finger."

"Carrie Fane wishes to be respectable?"

"And why not? It will be for the first time in my life."

"So it will. We must certainly do something about that."

She was silent for a moment. "Carrie Fane wishes to be respectable." Justin's words sounded in her ears. "It will be for the first time in my life," she had answered him. But that was not quite true. Once she had been known as Mistress Fane, the wife of Thomas Fane, the old man her father had married her to. Thomas, impotent, violating her body with the unspeakable humiliations he had visited upon it! She thought of him dead, his face twisted and blue, and a shudder shook her. How she had hated him. For a time, because of him, she had hated all men!

Justin's hands stroked her gently. "Don't think about him, Carrie, love," he said quietly.

"Do you always know what I am thinking?"

"Almost always. But there are twists and turns to your mind that I have yet to learn."

She pressed closer to him. Mindful of the child, he held her loosely, his lips against her hair. His mind drifted, taking him back to England, to Bewley Grange, the house that had witnessed the birth of the Lawrences for several generations. It had also witnessed the rebirth of Mistress Caroline Fane. It was there that she had become the woman he had always known she could be. The house was empty now. Paul was dead. And he, the last of the Lawrences, was on the other side of the world.

The child in Caroline's body moved. The last of the Lawrences? Justin thought. No, the child kicking in its mother's body had just reminded him that he was mistaken. One day his son, or perhaps his daughter, might return to England. The old house would resound once more with Lawrence voices, with their loves, their joys, their tragedies.

Bewley Grange! Justin smiled. He could see Carrie now, seated by the fire in that small anteroom. She had battled so hard against him, hating men, hating sex. He had often wondered what it had cost her to say the words he had waited so long to hear. "I love you, Justin. I want you!"

And he had wanted her. At that moment he had wanted her more than he had ever wanted any woman. He had carried her up the stairs and laid her upon his wide bed. Looking at her, he had known that the sickness and the revulsion inspired by Thomas Fane, her elderly husband, had finally been laid to rest. In his arms she had come alive, gloriously alive. She had flamed into such passion that he had been shaken by the force of it. He could remember his own words to her. "My God, Carrie, you are a flame! A beautiful, searing flame! I knew it. I knew how you would be!"

"What are you thinking about, Justin?" He started at the sound of Caroline's soft voice. Her hand touched his face gently. "You look so serious."

"I was dreaming, love. I was thinking of Bewley Grange, of you. Of how much I wanted you. Do you remember that time?"

"What a question! How could I possibly forget?" Caroline hesitated, feeling almost shy. "Do you still want me, Justin?"

He laughed. "It's my turn to say 'What a question!' "

"Yes. But—but, do you?"

"Carrie, love, I not only want you, I need you."

"But I look so ugly these days, with the baby and . . . and everything."

"Ugly!" Justin exclaimed. "How can you say that? I have often heard it said that a woman is more beautiful when she is carrying a child. Looking at you, I know that it's true."

Caroline rested her cheek against him. She felt completely happy. Lianne was forgotten. The menace of the Indians was forgotten. Only this man, her world, was important.

Chapter 11

Belle set down the two big buckets of steaming water, keeping her wary eyes on the Indian girl as she did so. "What you want?" she said, straightening up. Her voice was truculent, but her eyes showed fear. Indians, she had heard, could make bad magic against those who displeased them. Wiping her hand over her sweat-glazed black face, she repeated her question. "Well, what you want? Why you staring at me that way?"

"I want the water," Lianne said, pointing at the buckets.

The flat demand sent a chill through Belle. "You ain't getting it," she blustered. "I work hard to heat that water. It take me more'n an hour."

Lianne smiled. "All the same, black girl, I will have it."

"No!" Belle stepped back a pace as Lianne made a threatening move toward her. "That water, it's for Mr. Fordyce. He wanting to take himself a hot bath. Cain't use the stream. Cold water make him a misery in his bones."

"Then he must wait until you heat some more."

Belle tried again. "You wrong. Ain't likely I'll be handing them buckets over to you, Injun."

"I think you will. If you don't, I will make you very sorry."

"What you mean, Injun? What you saying to me?"

"You know." Lianne fingered the charm at her throat. She was not unaware of the black girl's fear, and she guessed accurately at the thoughts that moved through her brain. "You do know, don't you, Belle?"

Belle's mouth quivered. In that moment Lianne reminded her of a snake, a beautiful, deadly snake. "Don't want me no bad luck," she muttered. "Ain't wanting that none at all."

"Well, then?"

Belle's eyes avoided Lianne's. "Why you wanting this water?"

"It is for Buck Carey. Soon he will be in from the fields. The work is hard, and he will be weary. He will welcome the hot water."

"Buck?" Belle gave a shaky laugh. "If it for him, you wasting your time. Buck, he ain't none at all like Mr. Fordyce. He like to bathe in the stream. That old cold water don't make him no never-mind."

"He will welcome the hot water," Lianne said again. She looked down at the wooden tub. "I will carry that. You bring the water to his shack."

Again Belle felt moved to protest. "I about to tote that tub to Mr. Fordyce. It his property, and he ain't liking no one else to use it."

Lianne bent and lifted the tub. It had been lined with some kind of smooth material, and she thought of the pleasure Buck would take in a real white man's bath. "Bring the water," she said curtly.

Sighing, Belle obeyed. Trudging behind Lianne, her arms straining with the weight of the buckets, she hoped fervently that Mr. Fordyce would understand her reluctance to bring down a hex on her head.

Buck walked slowly, his head bent, in the direction of his shack. A man hailed him, and another called out a good-natured remark concerning the work they had done that day, but he pretended not to hear. He felt tired and depressed and disinclined for conversation. Listening to the women greeting their men, he felt lonely, too. He had no need to be lonely, he knew. He would be welcome to sit down with any one of the families and partake of the evening meal. Tonight, though, he preferred to be alone. Smiling faces and cheerful conversation would not cure him of this particular loneliness.

Buck's smile was wry as he came in sight of the shack. No doubt he was a fool to bother with field work, but he had to keep busy. There was no future for him here, and as he had told Justin, he would soon be moving on. He had promised his land to Abe Morrison. He would do better to turn it over to Abe immediately and have done with it. Buck frowned. For the first time in his adult life, he found himself reluctant to saddle up and head on out to nowhere. "Adventure-bound," he had once called his roamings. But now, having set eyes on Lianne, he felt that he would be riding out into a vast and desolate nowhere.

Lianne drew back as Buck came nearer. She did not want him to see her yet. He did not know he was being watched, and his face without its smile looked grim. Her eyes were tender as she saw him thrust his dusty black hat with its snakeskin band to the back of his head. She had noticed that this particular gesture was habitual with him when he was thinking deeply. She rose on her toes to get a better view. He entered the shack. She heard the door creak shut behind him.

Buck stopped short, staring with blank surprise at the tub in the center of the room. Steam rose from it. "What the blue blazes!" Squatting down beside it, he dabbled his hand in the water. It was Fordyce's tub, and Belle must have put it there. She would have had to sneak it past Fordyce, for the man usually refused to let anyone use it. Rising, he thought of Belle with gratitude. It was hard work to heat the water and then to lug the heavy buckets to the shack. "I don't know what I done to deserve it, Miss Belle," he said aloud, "but thank you kindly. That there is just what I'm needing."

He hurled his hat across the room, then stripped out of his sweat-stained clothing. He noticed the clean cloth and the small tub of soft soap beside the tub, and some of his misery lifted. Settling into the water, he felt something that was almost a sense of well-being. He did not ask himself why Belle had done this for him; he was just grateful that she had. Leaning back, he closed his eyes. "You a right nice lass, Belle," he murmured. "Right nice."

He was almost asleep when the door opened. "That you, Justin?"

"No."

Buck froze at the sound of Lianne's voice. "What are you doing here?" he demanded.

Lianne stared at the back of his head, waiting for him to turn it. When he did not, she said in a soft voice, "Will you not look at me?"

The hard beating of his heart, the trembling of his hands, annoyed him. He, Buck Carey, to tremble at the sound of a woman's voice! He gripped the sides of the tub, cursing himself for a fool. "Ain't got no interest in looking at you," he said roughly. "I asked what you're doing here."

He heard the rustle of her gown as she moved toward him, and he made a futile attempt to slide farther under the water.

She stood over him. "You are pleased to see me?"

Was she asking him or telling him? "I ain't," he said curtly. "You going to answer my question?"

"I will answer. I came to see you."

Just like that. As though she had every right. "You seen me. If that's all, you can just get right on out of here, little gal."

"But of course I will not go." She knelt beside the tub. "I am here, where I wish to be."

That voice of hers, the tone of it! Almost, he felt himself to be reproved. He could not help it—he had to look at her. His fascinated eyes took in the delicately flushed face, the yellow gown, the hair that flowed over her shoulders and down her back. It might have been Small Flower kneeling there. She was smiling at him, and her eyes were soft. Damn the half-breed bitch to hell! It was as though she enjoyed seeing him suffer. "Get out!" His voice rose to a shout. "God damn you, will you leave me alone? I don't want you here, don't you understand that?"

Her hand touched his forehead, gently smoothing back his damp curling hair. "Why are you angry with me?" She spoke calmly, as though she did not believe in his anger. "What have I done?" She leaned close. "Tell me."

A little closer, he thought, and she would be in the tub with him. "What ain't you done? That's the question." He stared at her half-revealed breasts. A strand of her hair had fallen forward. It was touching his shoulder. "Lianne!" His voice was hoarse and unsteady. "Lianne, don't do this!"

She pressed her lips to his. "Do you like me? Say that you do!"

Like her! There was a fire inside him! His wet arms grabbed for her, crushing her close against him. He kissed her again and again, long-awaited kisses that had in them all of his hopelessness, all of his pain. Then, just as suddenly as he had grabbed her, he thrust her from him.

She gave a little cry as she lost her balance. She remained where she had fallen, unmoving. Water slopped over her skirts as he rose from the tub, and still she did not move. Wide-eyed, she watched him dress.

"Now, then." Buck turned and looked at her. The ends of

her hair were wet. Her mouth looked bruised, he thought. "Get up," he bade her. "We got some talking to do."

He waited until she had got to her feet. Taking her hand, he led her over to a long bench. Pushing her down, he seated himself beside her. "Why do you keep after me?" His voice was gentle now. "I have nothing you want."

She stared at him. She wanted him to hold her in his arms. She wanted to say to him, "I love you!" But she did not dare to utter the words aloud. It was Lawrence whom she must love. Lawrence who was destined for her, and she would do whatever she had to do to obtain him. It was the way it must be. There was nothing she could do about it. She thought of Justin's great height, the heart-stirring look of him. But she found that her heart did not stir, and she was not comforted.

Buck was looking at her. There was something in those amber-brown eyes of his that betrayed him. Something that was more than desire. She had wanted him to love her, but now she felt crushed by a burden of sorrow. It was as though, inside, she was breaking apart. Tears filled her eyes and rolled down her cheeks. Her tears were for both of them. Because the thing she had suspected was true. She loved him. And because, since she could not fight the will of the gods, he must remain in the secret part of her life. She could not give him up, not entirely.

"Darling!" Buck could not stop the words that sprang to his lips. He was destroyed by her tears. Tenderly, he put his arms about her and held her close. "Don't cry, Lianne."

In her own driving need, she became oblivious of his. "Love me! Please love me!"

He stiffened. Beneath her cheek she could feel the hard racing of his heart. She heard his voice, shaken, incredulous. "Do you know what you're saying?"

She raised her head and looked at him. "Yes . . . I know."

"You cain't know!" Her eyes! Surely it was love he saw in them. He was afraid to believe. Afraid of the suffering that would be his if he should be mistaken.

Now it was his eyes that were wet. She wanted to comfort him. She thought of the word he had said—"darling." She had never heard the word before. She did not know what it meant. But he had said it so tenderly. On his tongue it had had such beauty that she felt that it must be something very nice indeed. She lifted her hand, her fingers touching his wet eyes gently. Hesitating before trying the strange word, she let her fingers trail down his face as she said it to herself.

"Lianne!" His eyes held hers. "There's so many years between us." He took her face between his hands, gently kissing her cheeks, her soft mouth. "I had a wife once. Her name was Small Flower. She was like you, little and sweet and soft to hold. You're so like her."

"I am not Small Flower!" Her jealousy rose like a hot tide. "I am Lianne. Love me!"

He saw the flash in her eyes. She was jealous! He looked at her in wonder. "You are Lianne, and I do love you."

"Only me?" she insisted.

He thought of Small Flower with love and tenderness. But that love was from another part of his life. "Only you, Lianne," he said softly. He did not think of it as a betrayal. He would love Small Flower always. She would understand. Had she not always understood?

"Come and kiss me!"

He was happy in a way he had never thought to be again. He thought fleetingly of the many years between them. But it would seem that, to Lianne, they did not matter. He did not pursue the thought, and he asked himself if he were afraid to do so. Yes, he admitted, he was afraid. Stop thinking, Buck Carey! What did anything matter if Lianne loved him? And she did, he could no longer doubt it. This young girl, so fresh, so lovely. That was the wonder. How long would she love him . . . for an hour, a day, a year? She loved him now. For the moment it was enough. He kissed her softly, cherishingly, hungrily. And he did not notice or remember that she had not actually said the words.

Lianne drew herself from his arms. Laughing, she stood up, unconsciously posing for him, inviting his admiration. She drew the yellow gown over her head and flung it carelessly to one side. Beneath the gown she wore nothing. Seeing the hunger in Buck's eyes, she was glad that Caroline had not been able to persuade her to wear those uncomfortably stiff undergarments. She no longer thought of the scars on her breasts. She knew that she would have no flaw in Buck's eyes.

Buck stood up. He touched her breasts gently. Then he bent his head and kissed them. She touched his hair, feeling its thick, springy warmth beneath her fingers.

Her head fell back as he lifted her. Her black hair

streamed over his arm as he carried her to the bed on which he would make love to her.

Afterward, lying in his arms, his face against hers, she wondered how she could ever have believed that she had found fulfillment with White Bird. Buck had lifted her to glorious heights that she would not have believed possible. White Bird, by comparison, had been crude and clumsy.

Her mood checked. She moved her head slightly. Buck was sleeping. Quietly, as he did most things. It was not fair to compare White Bird with him. He was a man, White Bird a boy.

Lianne smiled, pleased with the generosity of the thought. Already Buck was leaving his mark upon her.

As though he felt her eyes upon him, Buck moved restlessly. "Lianne!" He said her name on a sighing breath.

"I am here." Lianne touched his hair caressingly. She thought of the strange word that had been so sweet on his tongue. When he awakened, she would ask him to explain its meaning. She said it now, slowly, experimentally. "Darling, darling!"

Chapter 12

Caroline's eyes were uneasy as she glanced at White Bird. There was something about him that frightened her. He stood by the door, his posture stiff and straight. His face, lit by the flickering candlelight, was impassive, and yet it seemed to her that he exuded an air of menace. Since entering the shack some moments ago, he had volunteered only one remark. "Lawrence asked me to come," he had said. "There is a meeting of the white men that he must attend."

The meeting had been called, Caroline knew, to decide what was to be done about the two Indians in their midst. Since the coming of the Indians, there had been no overt actions against them, no hostile remarks. Yet, for all that, the bitter hostility, the opposition to their presence at the settlement, had not died down. Feelings, held in check, simmered dangerously below the surface, waiting to erupt. Looking at White Bird now, she felt sure that he knew the temper of the people. It had always seemed to her that he knew everything. He knew the thoughts of the mind before ever they were uttered. Once, when she had said this to Justin, he had laughed at her and looked at her with amused eyes. "White Bird does not have the wisdom of the ages," he had answered lightly, "it just seems that way. It is the impression he gives. The impression, I would imagine, that most Indians give."

Behind the blank mask of his face, White Bird's thoughts were chaotic. There was anger in him as well as misery. He had seen Lianne enter the shack of Buck Carey. He had stood outside a long time, waiting for her to emerge, but she had not done so. He would be there yet, had not Lawrence asked him to deliver the message to the white woman. The meeting tonight was to decide the fate of himself and Lianne. But only he, if she had betrayed him, could decide Lianne's fate. Had she betrayed him? That was the question that gnawed ceaselessly at his mind. He had seen the way she looked at Justin. He had seen the way she looked at Buck. He felt suddenly bewildered and uncertain. There was a difference in her eyes when she looked at Buck. A look such as he had never seen before. What was she doing in that shack? Did she lie in Buck's arms inviting him to enter her body and take that which should be White Bird's alone?

Caroline saw the slight change in his face. A flicker of expression, quickly gone. "White Bird," she began, "is there something you wish to say to me?" Annoyed with the nervous color that flooded her face, she ventured a smile. "There is something wrong, I know." She hesitated, then added quickly, "Are you worried about the outcome of the meeting?"

"No." White Bird's eyes turned to her. "Whatever the white people decide, I know that Lawrence will not add the voice of hatred to theirs. I am content in that knowledge. If we are fated to move on, we will do so."

Caroline leaned forward in her chair. "I hope that it will not happen. I don't have to tell you how I feel about the matter, do I?"

"No, lady. You are always kind."

Caroline noticed that he did not use her name, as he had been wont to do, and she felt chilled by the omission. "I am your friend, White Bird. I hope that you are mine?"

"Do you doubt it, lady?"

"No."

But in that moment, she did doubt it, he knew, and the thought pained him. White Bird's eyes softened as he looked at Caroline. Her body was heavy with the child soon to be born, but it did not detract from her shining beauty. Her hair, which he had always likened to sunlight, gleaming in the light of the candles. The brown eyes regarding him with such sympathy had the sheen and the softness of the tiny flowers that unfurled their velvety brown petals in the springtime. She was troubled because he no longer used her name. He wanted to say to her: "Do not think I have turned enemy. I do not use your name because the sound of it on my tongue is resented by the white men. And so, knowing this, I have the wish to protect you from their doubts of you and Lawrence. From their petty fears." But he could not say this to her. Were he to do so, her anger would rise against her own kind.

Caroline found herself confused by the steady regard of his black eyes. She said quickly, "What is it, White Bird? Something else is troubling you."

White Bird inclined his head. "Yes, lady. I await the half-breed woman. There is something I must say to her." His hand touched the knife at his belt. "I think perhaps that there is something that I must do."

"What?" The word, shrill with her renewed fear, came out before she could stop it. "What are you going to do, White Bird?"

He was sorry that he had been the one to put the fear in her eyes, but she had asked him a question. He must answer it. "Do you know what we do with faithless women, lady?"

"No." Caroline touched her throat with nervous fingers.

"We scar their faces."

"White Bird!"

"It is true." White Bird pulled the knife from his belt. Candlelight struck the blade, causing it to glitter. "They become hideous to the sight. A man may not look upon them without shuddering."

Caroline drew back as White Bird advanced upon her, the knife still gripped in his hand. "Have you proof that Lianne has been faithless?"

White Bird halted. "No, lady. My eyes have not seen this proof." He touched his forehead and the region of his heart. "The proof is here. In my heart, my mind. The eyes do not always need to see."

Caroline stared at him, trying to conceal the horror she was feeling. "The white man's law does not accept the proof of the senses."

"I am not a white man, lady."

Caroline rose slowly to her feet. It seemed strange to her that she had now been put into a position where she must defend Lianne, if she could. "White Bird, you must not do this thing. Promise me that you will not."

White Bird restored the knife to his belt. "Why do you plead for her? You dislike Lianne. I know, for I have seen your dislike mirrored in your eyes."

It was useless to deny it, and she made no attempt to do so. "Yes, you are right," she said quickly. "I do dislike her. But I would not want her to be harmed, and this thing you would do is cruel and savage. And you are not a savage, White Bird."

"The people here have called me so."

Beneath his suddenly inimical eyes, Caroline flushed. "What does it matter what they say?" she cried. "I know that you are not. You are sensitive and kind. Above all others, surely I should know that?"

Her hand was on his arm. The light touch reminded him of another day, another time, when he had believed that he had first claim on this white woman. He knew that he was not proof against her, and so he glared sullenly, hoping to hide his treacherous softening.

"White Bird! Tell me that you will not do this thing to Lianne?"

He shrugged. "If it pleases you, I will wait for the proof of the eyes." He did not look at her as he said it. He had allowed a woman to persuade him, and he was ashamed.

"Thank you." Now that she had won, Caroline's voice trembled with strain. "But it would please me better if you . . ." She broke off, her ears caught by an uproar from outside. "What is it?" she said, startled. "What is happening?"

"Help!" a voice screamed. "Help me!"

"It is the half-breed woman who calls!" White Bird leaped toward the door. Flinging it open, he ran outside.

Lianne lay on the ground. She was struggling to rise and her face was contorted with terror. On his knees, looming over her, was Jack Fordyce. "Indian bitch!" Fordyce roared. "I saw you sneaking out of the shack! Been lying with a white man, ain't you? And another thing, Belle told me what you done to her." His heavy hand cracked across her face. "You think you can come among us white folk and work your bloody spells on us." He slapped her again. "Bitch! Filthy Indian bitch!"

Caroline, running after White Bird, almost collided with him as he stopped abruptly.

"Fordyce!" Justin pushed his way through the crowd that had gathered. "Get your hands off that girl. What the hell do you think you're doing!"

Fordyce rose to his feet. "You keep out of this, Indian-lover!" he snarled, his small blue eyes glaring from his congested face. "Ain't only a whore, this one, she's a thief, too. Stole my tub, she did."

A silence fell. Fordyce was not popular. He was a mean, tight-fisted man. Justin Lawrence did not take kindly to insults, and Fordyce had called him an "Indian-lover." The crowd waited in an almost pleasurable excitement for Justin to pick up the challenge.

"Fordyce." Buck's quiet voice diverted their attention. "Turn around, Fordyce."

Fordyce stiffened; then he swung round to face Buck. His eyes widened with dismay as he saw the pistol in his hand. "What's all this?" he shouted. "You another one of them Indian-lovers, are you?"

"Well, now," Buck drawled, "I just could be, at that." He smiled. "That upset you, does it?"

Fordyce stared into the hard eyes that did not match the smile. Frightened, he backed a step. "You've gone mad, that's what! Now, you look here, Buck, there ain't no need to be pointing that pistol at me. I'm not going to quarrel with you over a lousy, poxy Indian squaw."

Buck pushed his hat to the back of his head, his smile widening. "Now, that there is right mean-mouthed of you, Fordyce. You're going to make killing you a real pleasure. 'Nother thing. You put your hands on that little gal, and you hurt her. That wasn't nice. Not nice at all. Old Buck Carey, he don't like that. You hearing me, Fordyce?"

"Buck!" Justin's voice rose, sharply urgent. "Put that pistol away. This is not a killing matter."

"This ain't your affair, Justin. It's mine. I'm gonna fix this skunk good."

Lianne saw Justin's expression, and she was frightened for Buck. She wanted Fordyce to be hurt, as he had hurt her. But she did not want vengeance at this high price. Lianne made no attempt to rise. She edged herself forward. "You must not do it. He did not hurt me very much. If you kill him, men will come to hunt you down and take you away! Please!"

White Bird stared. He heard the tears in Lianne's voice, he saw her look. She, who thought only of her own needs, had put someone before herself. Agony moved inside him. She was in love with Buck Carey! Now he knew why there was a difference in her eyes whenever she looked at him.

Caroline heard the muffled sound the Indian boy made.

Frightened, she took a step toward him. "White Bird, what . . . ?"

White Bird turned on her. She saw his eyes, glittering and dangerous in his strained face. "Keep back, Caroline!" He pushed her from him.

Caroline screamed as she went stumbling backward. Recovering her balance, she stared at the knife in White Bird's hand.

"Put it away. Don't do it, White Bird, don't!"

Without answering, he turned his back on her. His arm lifted. The knife flew from his hand.

Fordyce staggered as the sharp blade buried itself in his arm. "My God!" he said in a thick voice. He stared stupidly at the still-quivering hilt of the knife. "That red devil's d-done for me!"

Buck lowered the pistol. "Don't worry, Fordyce, you ain't going to die. Would, if I had my way. Reckon that Injun saved you from my bullet."

A man standing near Fordyce raised an excited yell. "The Indian's knifed Fordyce! He's getting away. Look at that savage run!"

"Get him! Spread out. We'll cut him off!"

Justin pushed his way through the milling men. "Buck, you get Lianne to the shack. One of you women attend to Fordyce."

Running toward Caroline, Justin caught a flash from the copper ornaments about White Bird's neck. Then the boy was gone, swallowed up in the darkness of the forest. "Carrie!" Reaching her, he pulled her into his arms. "Are you all right, love?"

"Yes, yes!" Caroline clung to him. "Justin, did you see? It was White Bird who threw that knife! Why did he do it?"

"Revenge for Lianne, I suppose."

Caroline listened to the yelling of the men who were pursuing White Bird. She shuddered. "If they catch him, what will they do to him?"

"Ain't likely they'll catch him, Caroline." Holding Lianne tightly in his arms, Buck had paused beside them. "White Bird will be right at home in the forest. Don't you worry—he'll be long gone."

"But if they do catch him?" Caroline persisted.

"They'll hang him."

Caroline's expression was distraught. "Justin, you must find White Bird. You must help him!"

"I'll do what I can, Carrie."

"Justin and I, we'll both search," Buck chimed in. He hesitated. "Lianne will be needing your help, Caroline."

Caroline stared at the girl. Her head was resting against Buck's shoulder, and she was smiling, showing no concern for White Bird. "Of course, Buck," she answered coldly. "Bring her into the shack."

Lianne knew what Caroline was thinking. What did the woman expect from her? Tears? Hysteria? Of course, she hoped White Bird would get away, but she did not see the need to say so. Buck would have murdered Fordyce, and White Bird had saved him from that. For that alone she wished him well. Her head rose from its resting place. "I need no help," she said, giving Caroline a haughty look. "You will please put me down, Buck Carey. I can walk."

Buck held her for a moment longer, his eyes smiling into hers. "You sure you ain't hurt?" he whispered.

Lianne fought an impulse to put her arms about his neck. She wanted to stay in his arms, safe and content. Instead, she said quickly, "No. I am not hurt."

Buck set her on her feet so carefully that she might have been a doll that would break at the first rough touch. Her eyes misted. She loved this man so very much, that she was afraid that the gods would look into her heart and see the love resting there. But she had not spoken that love aloud, she thought, trying to reason her fear away; therefore, the gods could not be angry with her. They would not punish her.

Following them to the shack, Justin was struck by the expression he had glimpsed on Buck's face. He looked happy. A very different man from the one who had spoken so morosely of moving on. What did his expression of happiness and quiet contentment mean? The answer came to him at once. He could not look like that unless something good had happened between Lianne and himself. He thought of Buck's eyes above the pistol. The man in possession. The man in love, defending that which was his. If White Bird had not flung that knife, he might well have killed Fordyce.

Pausing by the door, he did not enter at once. He was remembering Lianne's voice pleading with Buck. "You must

not do it. . . . If you kill him, men will come to hunt you
down. . . . Please!"

Justin smiled. It had been love for Buck that he had heard
in Lianne's voice. He had believed that the difference in ages
made an impassable barrier. He had been wrong, and he was
glad. Lianne and her gods! Her belief that they spoke to her,
directed her. She believed that she must bow down to their
will and obey them in all things. She had spoken to him at
great length of her gods and of many other things. She had
even told him that the gods had chosen a man for her. A
white man. Was that man Buck? Lianne saw signs in many
things. In trees, in flowers, in the way a twig fell. She was full
of superstitions. Full of so many things that were alien to the
white mind. Buck, on the other hand, despite his trace of Indian blood, was white. He thought, believed, and acted like a
white man, having nothing to do with pagan beliefs. If he
and Lianne were to have any kind of life together, he must
do battle with these things that were in Lianne. If Justin
knew anything of Buck, he would win the battle. He would
turn that beautiful but shallow girl into a warm, loving
woman. If he had the chance.

If he had the chance? Justin's smile faded as White Bird
came into his mind. White Bird claimed Lianne as his
woman, and he too must have heard the love in Lianne's
voice. Had his knife been meant for Buck? Justin frowned
thoughtfully. If he were not mistaken, Fordyce had moved
his position just a second before White Bird had flung the
knife. Which one had it been meant for? Buck? Fordyce? He
thought of something Buck had once said to him. "Injuns are
real good with knives and arrows. Once they pick a target, it
ain't often they miss." Had White Bird missed, or had he
meant that knife for Fordyce?

Seated in her chair, with Buck standing beside her, Lianne
was uneasy. When she had left Buck's shack, she had picked
up a leaf that was brown at the edges and pierced with holes.
Was it a sign of death, and were the gods telling her that
Buck would die unless she gave him up entirely? When Buck
set her on her feet and led her into Lawrence's shack, she argued with herself that the gods would stay their hand because
she had not spoken her love aloud. But she had the cold

feeling that they knew everything and they were waiting to see what she would do.

Lianne's eyes darted to Justin. He was standing by the door, and he seemed to be lost in thought. Caroline had her back to them. She was stooping over the cupboard where she kept her salves and her rolls of clean linen. It was safe to speak with Buck. If she kept her voice low, she would not be overheard.

With the idea of protecting him strong in her mind, she looked up at him. "There is something that I must say to you."

"Oh?" Buck smiled at her. "But why the hell are we whispering?" he said, matching his tone to hers. Stooping over the chair, he placed his hand gently on her shoulder. "What is it you have to say, my darling?"

She wanted to tell him: "It is over, there is no longer love in my heart for you"—but she could not bring herself to utter such a terrible lie. She tried then to compromise. "You ... you must not call me that. And you must say nothing of what happened between us."

"Why?"

The word came out hard, full of suspicion. There was hurt there, too. She could see it in his eyes. Looking at his changed expression, she found herself remembering his uncertainty, his many references to the years between them. The story he had told her of his Indian wife, Small Flower, and of the son who had not been allowed to live, was still fresh in her mind. He had been hurt so much in the past. How, then, could she bring herself to add to that hurt? She could not tell him, as she had meant to do, that the gods intended another man for her. Were she to do so, he would go away, and she would never see him again.

Lianne struggled with her tears. If she could not see Buck, she would die! She put her hand to her head. The painful throbbing in her temples had begun when she had seen that look in his eyes. She was so confused and miserable!

Lianne's thoughts on the gods who ruled her life had always been contradictory. At one moment they were blind gods, with the secrets of the heart hidden from them, knowing only those things that were uttered aloud. At other times they were all-powerful. Seeing and knowing everything. Although she did not realize it, she had always shaped her beliefs to suit the purpose of the moment. She did so now. It might be that she had misunderstood the message of the gods.

Her mind moved on in confused circles. She glanced at Justin, who was still standing by the door. It did not occur to her that Justin Lawrence might be her savior.

Lianne's face brightened as an idea came to her. There was a way in which she could find out for sure if she had misunderstood the message of the gods. Why had she not thought of it before? When she could manage to slip away undetected, she would go again to the stream in the forest. In the way that she had seen her mother do many times, she would find two twigs and float them upon the water. If the twigs came together and crossed, she would know that the gods intended Lawrence for her. If the twigs drifted, not touching at any point, it would be a sign that she was free to follow her heart.

Buck stared into her absorbed face. He did not understand the look in her eyes. What was she thinking about? He had been a fool to believe that she could love him. He should have understood that she was only a young girl intent on trying out her power over men. He felt sick, and there was a trembling inside him. She had played a game with him, and she did not understand how such games could wound. But for all that, she should answer to him now. "Tell me why?" His hand tightened on her shoulder.

Tomorrow, Lianne thought, the god of the waters will tell me what I want to know. With the burden of anxiety weighing her down, it was difficult to smile at him, difficult to answer. She managed both. "T-tomorrow," she said in a shaken voice.

Buck was not aware that Justin had entered the room, or that Caroline had turned about and was watching him with anxious eyes. He was aware only of Lianne. Her smile was only a movement of the lips, Buck thought. It meant nothing. Now he understood the look in her eyes. She had retreated from him. Already, after only a few hours, she had tired of the game. Words of explanation from her would only wound him further, but he would have them. Maybe it was the cure he needed. "Tell me now, Lianne."

Lianne shook her head. "It must be tomorrow. I will talk to you then."

Buck withdrew his hand slowly. "When you've got some-

thing you want to say to me, you'll know where to find me."
He turned on his heel. Without looking at Justin, still only
half-aware that there were others in the room, he made for
the door.

"No!" Lianne started up from the chair. "Wait!" her voice
rose to a scream. "I think you do not understand."

Buck turned to look at her. "Maybe I don't, but I've got a
mighty uneasy feeling that I understand all too well. Ain't
your fault, it's mine. I'm old enough to know better."

"Buck," Justin's quiet voice cut in, "what's going on? Is
there anything I can do?"

Buck looked at Justin for the first time. "Ain't important.
Thought it was, but it turns out it ain't."

"Buck, wait a minute."

"Cain't. I just remembered that I've got things to do."
Buck nodded at Caroline. "Ma'am," he said politely, "sorry
for causing a ruckus."

Justin waited until the door had closed behind him, then
moved over to Lianne. "What did you say to Buck to make
him look like that?"

"I think, Justin," Caroline said, "it was more what she did
not say."

"What do you mean?"

"How do I know what I mean?" Caroline said crossly. "It's
a feeling I have. Buck wanted an answer. She didn't give it to
him. For some reason, he's hurt. If you know what it's about,
I wish you'd tell me."

Justin did not answer. He turned back to the girl. She was
still standing motionless, her eyes fixed on the closed door.
He had the feeling that she had not heard anything they had
said. "Lianne . . ." He touched her shoulder. "Do you want to
tell me about it?"

She came to life at his touch. "Lawrence!" Sobbing wildly,
she threw herself into his arms. "What shall I do?"

Justin's arms closed about her. "Are you in love with
Buck? Is that it?"

Lianne stiffened. "No, no!" Her rising voice was terrified.
"You must not say that!" She clutched at his arms. "Harm
will come to him. There are those who listen. Don't you understand?"

Justin held her away from him and looked into her frantic
face. "No, I don't understand."

"The gods—"

"Ah, the gods again." Justin's tone was dry. "Lianne, listen to me. There is only one God, and he—"

"Don't!" Lianne struggled out of his arms. "I do not believe in this God of yours. I have never seen him."

"And have you seen your gods?"

"Yes. They are in the wind, the sky, the trees. They are everywhere."

"But have you actually seen them?"

For some reason that she was unable to define, Caroline's dislike of the girl faded. Pity took its place. She looked trapped, terrified. "Justin," Caroline said gently, "if Lianne believes in her gods, it is better to leave it alone."

"I can't, Carrie." Justin gave her a frowning look that said as plainly as if he had spoken the words aloud: "Keep out of this." He turned back to Lianne. "If, as I believe, Lianne, you are in love with Buck, you must not let anything stand in the way. Do you understand me?"

Lianne stared at him, her eyes wide and fever-bright. "I won't listen to you! I dare not!"

"Lianne." Caroline put out her hand. "You are upset. Things will look better in the morning."

Lianne shrunk away from her hand. "Don't touch me, white woman!" Moaning, she sank to the ground. With her hands over her eyes, her hair falling forward, she rocked herself to and fro. Words emerged from her. "You must not interfere. You must let me find my own way. There is a thing that I must do. When it is done, I shall know the direction my life must take."

Caroline stooped over her. "We won't interfere, Lianne. No one will." She put her hand on the girl's shoulder, patting it gently. "You must do as you think best."

Lianne shrank from her touch. She heard the pity in Caroline's voice. The patting hand was almost affectionate. But she did not want pity or affection from this white woman. She wanted hard, cold dislike. If she should be forced to kill her, it would make the task so much easier. It was as though Caroline knew the thoughts in her mind, for now her hand was stroking her hair. Lianne's head lifted. "Don't!" she shrieked. "I have told you not to touch me!"

"Leave her alone, Carrie," Justin said. He looked at Lianne coldly. "She is hysterical. She will get over it in a while."

Flushing, Caroline turned away. "I think, Justin, that it is a little more than hysteria." In an effort to change the subject, she said in a low voice, "What were the results of the meeting?"

Justin shrugged. "None. We did not finish it." He glanced quickly at Lianne. "The meeting broke up when Fordyce caught sight of Lianne through the window. But after what happened with White Bird, I think you will be able to guess the verdict."

"Is there nothing you can do?"

"I doubt it. The will of the majority will prevail."

"But—"

"Carrie." Justin took her hand and led her over to the far side of the room. "Everyone is bound to be stirred up. It will be better if you keep Lianne out of sight as much as possible. Find things for her to do. Anything to keep her out of the way. And stay with her."

Caroline nodded. "I will. What about White Bird?"

Justin ran a distracted hand through his hair. "Damn! Why the devil did he have to throw that knife!"

"Justin, you won't let him be hurt?"

"Not if I can help it. . . . I don't think the men will find him. Not, that is, unless he wants to be found. If Buck and I should come across him, we'll send him on his way, and no harm done."

"He'll need a horse. Food and water."

"I've already thought of that. I'll see to it." Justin looked across at Lianne. She was still crouched on the floor, her hands over her face. "If we should find White Bird," he said, turning back to Caroline, "I'll ask him which direction he intends to take. I think he trusts me enough to tell me. We'll send Lianne after him." He hesitated. "If Buck wants to follow, that will be up to him."

Caroline remembered the knife in White Bird's hand when he had said, "Do you know what we do with faithless women, lady? We scar their faces." She remembered the look in his eye. . . . "Justin, White Bird is angry with Lianne. He feels that she has betrayed him." Hastily she began to tell him of White Bird's attitude. Of his implied threat.

Justin listened in silence. "That does rather alter things," he said after a moment. He saw the troubled expression in her eyes. "I'll think of something," he added. "Don't worry, Carrie, love."

From his hiding place, White Bird watched Lianne. She had been kneeling by the stream for a long time. When first she had approached, passing quite near to the place where he was hidden, he had seen the little bundle of twigs in her hand. He knew from this that she wished for a message or a sign from the god of the water. The god of the water was very powerful, and all who sought him knew that he gave immediate answer. Therefore, why did Lianne continue to kneel there? Could it be that she was not satisfied with the answer she had been given? White Bird trembled for her temerity. It was not for mortals to question the gods. But Lianne might. She was a bold and foolish maiden.

White Bird's hands clenched. His fear for her was forgotten as his anger came rushing back. She had betrayed him! He did not need the proof of the eyes to know that. She was in love with Buck Carey. That love had been plain in her voice. Why, then, knowing that she had betrayed him, had he helped her? She was afraid for Buck Carey. Afraid that, if he murdered Fordyce, the men would come to hunt him down. And so, to prevent the murder, White Bird had flung his knife at Fordyce. Why had he done it? Was he the weak fool that Lianne had so often called him? Perhaps he was, he thought bitterly. But if he had his knife now, he would take the half-breed woman by her flowing hair and throw her to the ground and slash her lying, deceitful face!

Four times! Lianne thought. Four times had she floated the twigs upon the water. They had not drifted apart, as she had hoped. Each time, they had come together and crossed. The will of the water god, of all the gods, was plain. It was Justin Lawrence. Buck Carey was lost to her!

Lianne threw the rest of the twigs into the water. Not waiting to see how they would float, she rose to her feet and turned about. Kneeling there at the edge of the stream, she had had the strangest feeling that she had died. Her legs trembled beneath her as she walked.

White Bird stared at the advancing girl. She looked different to his eyes, older, as though she had left youth behind. What trouble had she taken to the water god? What answer had she received to make her look like that? Crushing down a feeling of pity, he rose slowly to his feet.

Lianne stopped short as White Bird advanced toward her. If she was surprised or afraid, she did not show it. She simply stood there looking at him, her face expressionless.

White Bird halted before her. "You are not surprised to see me, Lianne?"

"No."

"You knew I would come?"

"Yes. I felt you near."

White Bird was uneasy. It was like talking to someone he did not know. She was lifeless. There was nothing there for him. "You know why I flung my knife at Fordyce?"

"Yes. You did it for me. To protect Buck Carey from the hunters. I have betrayed you, White Bird. The knowledge of this is in your eyes."

"And what do you think I should do about it, Lianne?"

"Whatever you will. I will not fight you, White Bird."

Now that she had said it, he felt confused. He had desired Lianne, but not this one who stood before him. He had the certain feeling that she would not care if he punished her, even attempted to kill her. No, she would not care, because she was already dead. Of what use, then, was it to hold on to his anger and his desire for vengeance upon a faithless woman? The dead were sacred. One does not visit punishment upon them.

White Bird backed away from her. "Go, woman. You are no longer of interest to me."

She passed him by without a word or a look. He stood there stiffly, watching her walk away from him. When she was out of sight, he went slowly back to his hiding place. He would rest there for a while, and then he would move on. The men would come again to search for him, he knew. One more day, two perhaps, until they tired of the hunt. They would not find him.

Chapter 13

The weather had taken another turn. It was hot and sultry, enervating. The slight wind that now and again stirred the leaves on the trees did nothing to relieve either the heat or tightly strung nerves. It served only to carry the sound of the drums beyond the hills, increasing the heat-induced tension that hung over the settlement.

To Caroline, lying on her pallet, her body shivering beneath a quilt, it might have been winter. She had felt chilled ever since Justin and Buck had left the settlement two days ago to search for White Bird. Justin had told her that they would make camp somewhere rather than waste time by returning to the settlement when night fell. Buck, who knew what he was about, had attempted to reassure her. "If we haven't found White Bird after two days of searching," he had said, smiling at her, "you can expect to see us back on the third day. Take more than Indians to trap Buck Carey."

Clutching the quilt to her, Caroline turned over on her back. "Take more than Indians to trap Buck Carey." His words kept on repeating themselves in her mind. She could not shake herself free of the feeling of dread that had weighed her down ever since their departure. Justin was rash, as he had always been, inclined to take too many chances. He would ignore danger until it was upon him, for this light, almost careless disregard of personal safety was part of his nature. Whatever the situation of the moment, Justin would believe that he was fully capable of extricating himself. But this was not England, and he could no longer be as he once had been, the daring, amusingly impudent, charming Rogue Lawrence who had laughed his way through life. This America, for all its beauty and its never-ending wonders, was a savage and dangerous land. It gave much, and in return it claimed all of a man. One's nature must be adapted to fit such a life. All of the challenges America offered, its open and its hidden dangers, could be turned to advantage. But if one wanted to live, one could not ignore them. Suffering, it was true had put its mark upon Justin. He was grimly determined to succeed, and to a certain extent he had adapted.

But had he adapted enough to this land? That was the question that haunted her now.

Caroline's mind turned back to Buck. The change in him had come about within a matter of hours, or so it seemed to her. Certainly he was not the man he had been. There was a strangely uncaring quality about him now, and he had the look of one who has tired of life. It was Lianne, she knew, that had brought about the change in him.

The pallet rustled as Caroline moved restlessly. Lianne was different, too. Although her eyes were unhappy and there was a listlessness in her movements, she seemed, oddly enough, more inclined to be friendly. And yet, Caroline thought, she could not quite bring herself to believe in this new attitude.

Recalling her hesitation to question Buck, Caroline frowned. For all Buck's surface amiability, his easy, friendly grin, she had always known that there was a deep inner reserve in him that forbade questions, and more especially at this time. Buck was Justin's friend, and she herself was extremely fond of him, and she feared this change in him. The worry this caused her was perhaps exaggerated by her condition, but it was very real to her. From Buck she had turned to Lianne, and with her she had had no restraining delicacy. Lianne, however, had evaded all her questions. She had smiled that new, hard, bright smile of hers that caused Caroline to wince inwardly. "Do not ask me about him," she had said. "There is nothing that I can tell you, Caroline. You must know that our lives are not our own. They are shaped for us. But I will tell you this. The ways of the gods are not to be questioned."

Are our lives shaped for us? Caroline thought. If they are, it is certainly not by Lianne's gods. But to her, of course, they were very real, and certainly not to be disputed. But what command could these gods have given her that had caused her to hurt Buck so cruelly?

Caroline's thoughts broke off as she felt the niggling pain again. She had been feeling it all night. The pain was not intense enough to mean that the baby was coming. Almost fearfully she put her hands on the mound of her stomach. Beneath her fingers she felt the fluttering of agitated life. If only she were not so stupid. If only she knew more about birth, and what exactly she must expect.

Her mind roved over the various women of the settlement. With the exception of one or two, they were unfriendly toward her. To them, she was apparently unashamed that she lived in open sin with a man who was not her husband, and it would seem that they could not forgive her for this lack of shame, for the delight that she took in her lover. Those who had been disposed to offer her friendship found themselves ostracized by the others. Now they were not quite so friendly, and it seemed to her that they went out of their way to avoid her. If the baby came now, what would she do? Justin might not return in time to aid her, and there was no one else on whom she could rely. She could not count on Lianne, for despite the recent show of friendship, she felt that nothing had really altered between them. Lianne, for reasons of her own, hated her. She was convinced of that.

The pain came again, and with it an almost overwhelming nausea. Swallowing against the sickness, Caroline sat up straight, pressing her fingers hard into her stomach. She must not lose her head. The pain was nothing. As for the nausea, that was probably caused by the fish she had eaten last night.

"Caroline! Is something wrong?"

Caroline started. "Lianne. I did not hear the door open."

Carrying a bucket of water, Lianne came into the room. "I thought you were sleeping," she said, closing the door behind her. "So I was very quiet."

Despite her suspicions, Caroline felt a wave of relief. "I'm glad you're here," she said hesitantly. "I . . . I have been having some pain."

Lianne set the bucket of water down. Wiping her hands on the skirt of her print gown, she turned her head and looked intently at Caroline. "Tell me about these pains. Are they very severe?"

"No. They come and they go, but they are not . . . not severe."

Lianne moved over to the pallet. "Where are you having this pain?" she said, looking down at Caroline.

"Here." Caroline pointed to her stomach. "And in my

back." Now, with the nausea receding, she was anxious to make light of it. "But I'm sure that it's nothing."

The woman was pretending to be indifferent, Lianne thought, but she was not. The eyes did not lie, and Caroline's plainly showed the fear she was trying to hide. The pain she was experiencing now might well mean that the child was on the way. On the other hand, it might mean nothing at all. How could she be expected to know? In any case, it would soon be over for Caroline. Once the child was born, she would find the means to get rid of this woman who stood in her way. She thought of these things calmly, and it surprised her to find that she no longer felt any particular hatred toward this woman of Lawrence's. It was quite simply a thing that had to be. She was the instrument of the gods, and she was determined to set in motion their plan for her. Only in this way, by showing them that she was obedient, could she hope to atone for her wayward thoughts. Refusing to think of Buck Carey, for that way lay pain, Lianne smiled her bright smile. "It is nothing," she said in a steady voice. "You are right about that. If the child were due to be born, you would cry out with the severity of the pain." She hesitated. "I know of these things," she lied, "for I have been present at many births. It is the heat affecting you, that is all."

Looking into Lianne's wide, dark-blue eyes, Caroline could detect nothing but friendliness. Suddenly ashamed of her previous thoughts and suspicions, she refrained from mentioning the chill she had been feeling all morning. "Perhaps you're right," she said, returning the smile. "But there's nothing we can do about the heat."

"There is a thing we can do." Lianne held out her hand. "Come, get up. It is cool in the forest. We will walk there. We can pick the berries you wanted. We were going to get them a few days ago. Remember?"

Berries, Caroline thought. An unimportant reason for taking a walk. Her smile was wry as she took Lianne's hand and struggled to her feet. There was no pain now, but all the same, she had never felt less like walking. But Lianne was obviously restless, and Caroline had done her best to reassure her a few moments ago. Perhaps Lianne needed to walk to work off that restlessness. Indians, she knew, were not used to being confined. The least she could do was to acquiesce with good grace. "So much has happened that I had forgotten all about the berries." She smiled. "They are probably overripe by now."

Lianne shook her head. "No. I saw them this morning. They are just right for gathering. But I think it will be better if we go a little farther in. The berries are a better size, and there are more of them."

"Farther in?" Caroline frowned uneasily. "Do you think we should do that?"

"It will be perfectly safe. Do you think I would lead you into danger?"

"No, Lianne, of course not. It is just that—"

"I know the forest. There is nothing to fear." Lianne turned away. "I will get the baskets," she finished in a muffled voice.

Outside, the air seemed to shimmer with the heat. After the chill she had been experiencing, it struck Caroline like a blow in the face. Gasping, the perspiration already prickling along her hairline, she would have given much to turn back. A glance at Lianne's face decided her against it. No doubt she thought of white women as being soft and weak. She would show her that she was mistaken.

Following Caroline through the blazing heat, Lianne did not notice the other woman's discomfort. Her thoughts were centered on the words Caroline had spoken. "So much has happened," she had said. Yes, Lianne thought, unable to help a surge of bitterness, much had happened. So much that, lying in bed at nights, she could scarcely comprehend it or understand the difference within herself. That she had changed, she knew. It might be only where Buck was concerned, but she had changed. When she thought of him, there was a softness, a gentleness that was mixed up with her constant bitter yearning for him.

Lianne's hand clenched convulsively about the handle of the basket. Buck! Why couldn't she forget him, as she had so easily forgotten others in the past? His soft, husky, drawling voice haunted her dreams, waking and sleeping. "My darling!" he had said, and he had touched her with a tenderness, a reverence such as she had never known before. She loved him. She would love him forever, and she could no longer cover that love or seek to ignore it by lying to herself or to the gods who ruled her destiny.

On this last thought, Lianne's heart quivered with fear, but her head lifted defiantly, almost arrogantly. Let the gods listen. She had given them the assurance that she would obey their will. It was all that mattered. She had put Buck Carey from her life, as had been demanded of her. Once he left the settlement and traveled on, she would never see him again. Sh cried out to him in silent anguish. How can I endure this pain? With every wind that blows, with every rustle of the leaves, I shall hear your voice saying to me: "My darling!"

A sob caught in Lianne's throat, and she stumbled. "Steady," Caroline said, giving her an anxious look. The sight of the girl's drawn face alarmed her, but she felt a reluctance to pry into the cause of her distress. Lianne, she felt, would only withdraw further into herself, were she to do so. In a voice she strove to keep light, she said, "I thought you were supposed to be supporting me."

Lianne did not answer. Caroline was not surprised; she had not expected an answer. She had grown used to Lianne's long, brooding silences. The tears rolling down the girl's cheeks brought quick, comforting words to her lips, but she suppressed them. As though she could see into Lianne's mind, she knew that Lianne was thinking of Buck. Her brows drew together in a frown. She did not understand this bitter unhappiness. She had thought that it had been Lianne who hurt Buck, but now she was not so sure. Could it be that Lianne was in love with him, and he had rejected her? But Justin had said that he believed Buck was in love with the girl. It was all very puzzling. Caroline sighed heavily. She did not understand the situation at all, and at the moment she was much too hot and tired to make the attempt to work it out in her mind.

They reached the edge of the forest, and Caroline sighed again, this time with relief. She must be getting soft and lazy, she thought, thankfully entering into the dim greenness of the forest. The contrast to the heat gave her the feeling that cool fingers were stroking her heated flesh. Worry nibbled at her mind. It must be more than the child. She should not feel quite so exhausted. These days, she felt lifeless. Completely drained. She touched the protuberance of her belly with tentative fingers. This child she carried must surely be a boy. He was so big, such a heavy, dragging weight, and so active. Her fingers lingered there, and now her touch was protective. Justin's son! She loved him already, and she could hardly wait to greet him. Until she had met Justin, there had been little love in her life. She had given that stored love to Justin, and it would spill over and embrace the boy. "I love you ... my son? My daughter? Come soon, please." The worry returned, and she added words that were almost like a prayer: "Be healthy, my child!"

Lianne looked at Caroline sharply. What was she whispering about? Was she praying to her God? "What did you say?" she demanded in a loud, impatient voice.

In the silence of the forest, Lianne's voice sounded overloud. It came to Caroline's ears almost like a shout. Wincing a little, she said hastily, "It was nothing of importance." She changed the subject. "It is pleasant here. I'm glad we came." With Lianne's suddenly hard eyes upon her, she did not wish to discuss her child.

Lianne shrugged. "Yes, it is pleasant." Her eyes were dry now, her expression stony, giving no hint of the turmoil inside her. "But it is better farther in. The berries are bigger." She turned away. "Come this way."

The words were curtly delivered, admitting of no argument, and Caroline made no attempt to do so. But although she followed Lianne without protest, she was aware of a growing feeling of uneasiness. In her heart she had never really trusted Lianne, so why was she trusting her now? Why was she following her so meekly? "A lamb to the slaughter." The words came into her mind, lingering there. She was being a fool, of course, she told herself impatiently. There was nothing to fear. To erase the words in her mind, she let herself dwell on the enigma of Lianne. It was true that the girl had white blood, but she was also half-Indian, a member of a cruel and savage people, and it was not wise to forget that. With the exception of Justin and Buck, she had shown no particular liking for the people among whom fate had cast her. And to Caroline, at times, she had shown a hatred that she had not troubled to disguise. She boasted often of her mixed blood, and she seemed to be inordinately proud of the side of her that was white.

Thinking deeply, Caroline stumbled. Recovering her balance, she frowned thoughtfully. That was the vital question. Did Lianne act a part? Or was she as proud as she professed to be? It seemed to her that the girl was Indian in all her thoughts and emotions, in her praying and bowing down to her gods. Was it not, then, inevitable that her heart would turn more to those with whom she had the greater affinity?

Lianne stopped abruptly, and Caroline, immersed in her thoughts, almost cannoned into her. She drew back with a start as Lianne pointed triumphantly. "See," she said. "I told you the berries were better here."

Caroline felt foolish, and although she was relieved to find her suspicions unjustified, she did not like the feeling. She felt mean and petty, too. How stupid of her to credit the girl with such sinister intentions, and how ungenerous. They were not so very far into the forest, after all. The berries, growing there in heavy purplish-black clusters, were a silent reproach to her. Mute evidence of Lianne's innocence and her good intentions. Trying to make up for her obviously unworthy suspicions, Caroline managed to muster a bright smile. "You were quite right, Lianne. They look luscious." She took a firmer grip on the handle of the basket. "Shall we get busy?"

Lianne did not move at once. "You look strange, Caroline," she said, staring at her. "Is anything wrong?"

Caroline jumped nervously, almost dropping the basket. "N-no," she blurted, coloring guiltily. "Nothing is wrong."

"No?" Lianne's eyes narrowed. "You are afraid, Caroline," she accused, her voice overloud again. "You are afraid of me."

The girl was deliberately taunting her. Why? Anger overcame Caroline's feeling of guilt. "Ridiculous!" she said curtly. Her eyes flashed with a fire that Justin would have recognized. "You are talking nonsense, Lianne!"

"Am I? What do you mean by that?" Lianne took a step toward her, her hand lifting as though she meant to strike. "Why do you call it nonsense? Why don't you admit that you are afraid of me?"

Caroline stared at the raised hand. "Do you wish to strike me, Lianne? Do you really hate me that much?"

"I did hate you." Lianne slowly lowered her hand, dull color flushing her face. "I did." She took a step back.

"And now?" Caroline pursued.

Lianne's eyes turned away from Caroline's challenging brown ones. "There is no reason to hate you now. But for all that, there are things that I must do. Perhaps I do not wish to do these things, but they will be done, for it is beyond my control."

Despite her anger, Caroline felt a return of her fear. "Tell me what you mean."

Lianne shook her head. As though she had lost interest in the conversation, her face went blank. "We will pick the berries," was all she answered.

She would get no more from her, Caroline knew. It had been the strangest conversation. What could it mean? Her heart beating uncomfortably fast, her teeth biting into her lower lip, Caroline turned her back and busied herself with picking the berries. She was beginning to feel nauseated again, and the pains had returned. They were stronger this time. She wanted to say, "Let us go back." She opened her mouth to speak; then, pride stiffening her, she pressed her lips firmly together. She would say or do nothing to bring that malicious, taunting look back to Lianne's eyes.

Lianne had forgotten Caroline and the conversation they had just had. Her mind had returned to Buck Carey. Thinking of him, she picked listlessly at the berries, not noticing if they landed in the basket or fell to the ground. She moved her basket to her other arm and wiped her stained hand on the bodice of her gown. Her eyes were attracted to the large smear left behind. She stared at it dully. It was the color of blood. Symbolic, she thought, for she felt as though her heart was bleeding. The last time she had seen Buck alone had been when she had left the forest after making her pleas to the god of the waters to tell her which way her heart should turn. The answer had been that she must put him from her! Turning away from the stream, she had seen White Bird standing there. He had spoken to her, and she had seen his anger in his eyes. Strange, but she still could not remember what he had said to her, or how or even whether she had replied to him. After a while she had walked on, leaving him standing there. Approaching the shack, where she knew Buck would be waiting for her, had been the unhappiest moment of her life.

"Lianne!" He had stood up as she pushed open the door and walked into the room. Saying no more, he had waited for her to speak. But if his tongue was still, those expressive amber-brown eyes spoke for him. There was no smile in them now. There was a wariness, a waiting. A kind of dread that matched her own.

She had clasped her hands before her and prayed for the

strength to tell him. When at last she managed to force her tongue to speak, her words came hard, draggingly. "I have come to give you the answers to your questions."

A muscle twitched beside his mouth. His eyes turned away as if he could not bear to look at her. Then, drawn against his will, they returned to her. "Yes?"

"I . . . I . . ." She was only conscious of his eyes. It was as though the rest of his face had been blanked out. The expression in them had changed. They were aware, suffering, knowing what she would say. "I do not love you." Her words dropped between them with the heaviness of stones. "It . . . it is over."

His eyes! Would she ever forget how they looked in that moment, before they dulled over and became expressionless? What had she expected from him. Anger? Had she thought he would beg her to change her mind? Not Buck Carey! Not with his fierce pride. Trying to protect herself from the pain, she had allowed her mind to wander. They called him "drifter," she thought. "Saddle tramp." "Man without a home." When he rode out from the settlement and left her behind, would people add a new name? Would they call him "Buck Carey, the man without love"? But it would not be true! Her throat ached with the tears she wanted to shed. To call him so would be a lie. Never was man more loved!

Now his face became clear to her. Its craggily handsome lines tightened in the only sign of emotion he had allowed himself to show. "Yes," he said at last. "I expected it. Ain't surprised, and ain't blaming you none. You're too young to know what you're doing." He turned away from her. "You've said what you came to say. Now, I think you better go."

She stared at his back. She was not aware of having moved, but suddenly she was across the room. Her arms were about his waist. Her cheek was pressed against his shirt, her tears dampening the fabric.

She had felt his hands touching hers, forcing them apart, and then he was facing her again. He had looked at her with his blank eyes. "No need for all this carrying-on," he had said in a toneless voice. "It's all right."

Why was he so gentle? In her anguish, she had cried out to him. "Punish me! It is your right!" Dropping to her knees before him, she had bowed her head in submission to whatever he chose to do to her. "Punish me!" she had begged him.

Lifting her to her feet, he had guided her over to the door. "Go now, Lianne."

There had been a break in his voice. She had known then that she could not stay. A warrior is shamed if a woman looks upon his tears.

So she had walked away. She knew he was watching her, for it seemed a long time before her straining ears heard the creak of the closing door.

She had seen him after that, but never alone. If he could, he avoided looking at her. She watched him when she believed that he was unaware of her. There were new lines about his mouth. He looked older, but to her he had never seemed more dear.

If she watched Buck, there were other eyes that watched her. Justin's eyes. Caroline's, and always with a question in them. Buck would not speak, and therefore they were at a loss to know what had happened. Often she would feel the wish to tell them. It would have been a relief to pour out her anguish. But of what use would it be for her to speak? They did not understand her gods, nor believe in their power. They believed only in their own white God, who controlled the winds, the rain, the seasons, and who caused flowers to bloom and crops to grow. He, who punished sin, but mourned for the sinners. Who gave infinite love and compassion. It could not be true, Lianne told herself passionately. If it were, then she bowed to false gods, and she had lost Buck for nothing. How could there be only one God to control all?

Lianne's eyes turned to Caroline. Caroline's back was to her. She was making gasping sounds as though she could not bear the heat, and yet it was quite cool here among the arching trees and the damp undergrowth. She seemed to be moving very slowly, too, as though every movement pained her. And yet, Lianne thought, her winged brows drawing together uneasily, it could not be the child. White women made a great fuss when a child was coming. She knew, for she had heard Betsy Cooper, the wife of the blacksmith, screaming like a thousand wildcats when her child was about to be born. Indian women, unless the gods had put death in their bodies, did not cry out. They endured.

Lianne's hand went to the knife in the pocket of her gown. It was a great pity, she thought, that she could no longer think of Caroline as her enemy. The woman did not like her.

It was plain in her eyes, but in her own way she had tried to be kind. But her kindness altered nothing. The gods meant Lianne to be Lawrence's woman, and Caroline was an obstacle that must be removed.

Caroline sensed Lianne's eyes upon her, but she did not turn. Her mind whirled in confused circles. She had been a fool! She should have spoken when the pains became strong. Now they were almost more than she could bear. Pride! Cold comfort now. The child was coming. There could not be such pain if he were not. Impossible to get back to the settlement in time. She would have the child here, in the forest, with only the Indian girl to attend her. If, indeed, Lianne would attend her. If she did not run away and leave her to die. Caroline thought of the hidden perils in the undergrowth. Only last week Meg Forester had been bitten by a snake. She had died. Why did she have to think of that now? Caroline bit down hard on her quivering lip. God give me courage! she prayed silently. Protect my child!

Lianne stared as a quivering moan broke from Caroline's lips. "Caroline?" She put an uncertain hand on the hunched shoulder and felt the dampness of the fabric beneath her fingers. "Is the child coming?"

Caroline did not answer at once. She bent farther forward, hunching in on herself as though trying to find the breath to speak.

Lianne's fingers tightened on Caroline's shoulder. "You will answer me, please."

Caroline straightened up. She turned, and Lianne saw her white, sweating face and desperation in her brown eyes. "Yes!" she gasped. "I ... I have left it too long." She clutched at her stomach. "The pain is v-very bad now." The cords in her throat were prominent as she fought to hold back a scream. "Oh, God! There is no time left! The ... the child is coming!" She sagged to her knees, and now she was unable to hold back the scream. "Help me, Lianne! Help me!"

Lianne stared at the writhing figure on the ground. She had been present at many births, but she had taken no part in them. She had not wanted to. Even had she been willing, she knew well that the squaws would have scorned the help of the half-breed. It was as though they thought her white blood made her less intelligent, less capable than they.

Caroline's water, breaking, gushed from her, and for a moment Lianne was frozen. Then a thought prodded insistently at her mind. While it was true that she could leave the woman to die, for the gods would applaud rather than blame her if she did, yet they would frown on the deliberate murder of a male child. And if she ran off, what else would it be but murdering the child? Besides, this child fighting to be born must be saved. He was Lawrence's son. And with Caroline out of the way, he would become her son, too.

Lianne moved fast. Falling to her knees, she turned the struggling, moaning Caroline on her back. Roughly she jerked up the hampering skirts and exposed the great pale mound of her stomach.

"Don't!" In a purely automatic gesture, Caroline clutched at her skirts and tried to pull them down again. "Please!"

Lianne bent over and thrust her face close to Caroline's. "You want this child of Lawrence's?" she said in a harsh voice.

"Yes, yes!"

Lianne jerked up her skirts again. "Then, if he is to drop into my hands and not into your petticoats, you will obey me. Do you understand?"

Caroline did not answer. She seemed unaware of Lianne now. She was gasping like someone who had been running for a long time. Her eyes were wild, and sweat slid down her face in great drops. She screamed, her knees jerking up and her legs falling apart.

Lianne was not concerned with her pain. Her eyes were on the straining stomach. As another contraction seized Caroline, she touched her stomach. Bending low, she placed her face against it. She could feel no struggle within. It was undoubtedly the child's time to be born, but he was making no effort.

"It will not be yet, Caroline," she said loudly. "The child rests from its labors."

Like a tortured animal, Caroline's head turned from side to side. There was something wrong. She knew it. "I . . . I can endure the pain," she gasped. "But . . . but I am afraid. It is . . . is as though the child is not trying to be born. As . . . as though I am struggling to eject some d-dead thing."

A thrill of horror went through Lianne. For the first time she regretted that she had only looked on at the laboring women and not tried to learn. Because Caroline's words had frightened her, she said harshly, "I know that women have many hours of pain before a child is born. Do you think you are so different, white woman?"

"You don't un-understand!" Caroline fumbled for Lianne's hand. Finding it, she clutched it tightly. "The child has always been so ... so active." She faltered, trying hard to explain. "But now there is ... is such a heaviness inside me." Her nails bit into Lianne's flesh. "Lianne! Is the child dead? Tell me he is not dead."

Caroline did not hear Lianne's answer. She screamed as a strong contraction seized her. Her screaming died, and she made a helpless grunting sound as she tried to bear downward. "Oh, God!" she sobbed. "I can't!"

"You can, white woman!" Lianne shouted. "You will!" As she had seen the old squaws do, she pushed down hard on Caroline's quivering stomach. Caroline screamed again, a raw, agonized sound, but Lianne did not heed her. "I tell you that Lawrence's child lives! He lives!" She pushed again.

"Don't!" Caroline shrieked. "Don't do that!"

"I am trying to help you, you fool white woman!" Suddenly making up her mind, Lianne inserted her hand into Caroline. Pushing upward, she touched something. The child? She could not be sure. She only knew there was no movement, no faintest quiver of life. Withdrawing her bloodied hand, she wiped it on the hem of her skirt, trying not to meet Caroline's eyes.

"The ... the baby?" Caroline's panting voice sounded weaker, hoarse. "Is he dead?"

"I have felt Lawrence's son." Lianne's loud voice attempted to cover fear. "He lies still. But it may be that a child is always inert until the moment he is ready to be born."

Agony was rending her body apart, but Caroline had caught the note of uncertainty in Lianne's voice. "You are lying. You do not really know."

Not caring if she inflicted pain, knowing only that she had seen the old squaws do it many times, Lianne began to knead and push at Caroline's straining stomach. Caroline's mouth opened, and she began to shout the words aloud. "I can't bear it! Help me. Somebody help me!" Her legs jerked spasmodically. Her body strained as she struggled to push the child out.

Lianne ceased her labors, glaring at the helpless woman. If

the child was not born soon, she thought grimly, the woman would die. Never before had she seen such agony! She tried to tell herself that she did not care for the pain Caroline was enduring. But she did, and she knew it. This time it was not the hands of the gods upon her, but the hands of the two white men. The one whom she loved. The other who drew her, fascinated her, whose woman she was to become. They were bidding her to care, to have compassion. In a voice strangely unlike her own, she said gently, "I am with you, Caroline. You must not give in." She leaned closer, her hair spilling forward. "The child sleeps, that is all. He sleeps!" Now her hand stroked the tortured belly, and she did not ask herself what she would do when the child was born. For the first time in her life she was trying to give comfort and support to another woman. How she would kill the white woman did not enter her mind at that moment. That would come later.

Chapter 14

Tall Tree heard the high, frenzied screaming, and he cringed inwardly. There were many stories of the specter that walked the forest uttering wild, inhuman cries. Supposedly the specter was that of the long-dead Swaying Flower, she who had taken such a valiant part in the uprising of 1622. In warrior's garb, she had fought beside the great chief who had led the uprising. And until she lay dying, the chief had not known she was his woman. When he had found out, he had held her in his arms, and his tears had fallen on her dying face, for he had loved Swaying Flower well. How was he to know that hidden behind the mask of war paint was the face of his beloved? In stories that were told of the uprising, her dying words were repeated many times so that eager ears might hear and absorb, so that they might never forget. Clinging to the chief, who was to have been united to her, Swaying Flower had said, "My spirit will know no rest until the pale-skins are driven from our land. You will hear my voice in the wind, in the silence of the night, and in the bright gold of the day, still mourning for our fallen warriors, still crying of my hatred for the invaders."

Tall Tree had never heard these words in reality, but only in the oft-repeated tale. It seemed to him that a dying woman would not have the breath to make such a long speech. He did not say so, however, having no wish to be scorned and spit upon by those who strutted proudly and bragged of hearing the voice of the dead Swaying Flower. To protect himself, Tall Tree told his own tales, and such was his power and his magnetism that he soon collected an enthralled audience. At nights, seated by the fire, he would tell them of the misty figure that formed in the rainbow spray of the waterfall and who came to him alone. The figure was that of a woman with long, flowing hair. She would stretch out her arms to him, as though begging him to embrace her. Above the rush and tumble of the water, her voice would rise high and pure—the voice of one who has been purged of earthly sin. "Kill!" the voice would cry. Sometimes, Tall Tree would continue, warming to his story and almost believing it himself, the voice of Swaying Flower would become the sighing wind, for the Castle of the Wind was her home. The flower-scented breeze was the perfume of her body.

Tall Tree shivered, hoping that the two warriors behind him had not noticed. He enjoyed the tales he told of Swaying Flower, and although he almost believed, he could not wholly do so. Nevertheless, he told himself firmly, he must not think of the specter of Swaying Flower now. The screaming he was hearing did not come from a specter. It was real. A woman, perhaps? Or could it be a trapped animal?

Tall Tree turned to the warriors. As a teller of tales he had achieved a certain fame, and he knew what was expected of him. His face suitably grave, he said in a low voice, "Death walks here, my brothers. Even now the sound of death echoes in our ears. May the gods seal the eyes and stop the mouth of the agonized one."

Bright Feather's mouth fell open as Tall Tree spoke these words. He loved life, and he hated death. The only hatred he had that was vaster than death was his hatred of the pale-skins. If death did indeed walk here, was it wise to linger? He was a proud man, and not wishing his fear to show, he said in a steady voice, "My brothers, let us go from here. To outdistance death is to defeat it."

"Defeat it?" Tall Tree gave him a scornful look. "The warrior does not live who can outdistance death. All our lives, the hand of death hovers at our shoulder. If you do not know this, Bright Feather, then truly the hyena has entered your lodge and feasted upon your brains."

Bright Feather drew himself up. The look he turned upon Tall Tree was arrogant. It was not wise for Tall Tree to speak to him so. He should remember that, if the gods flew away with the spirit of Little Wolf, he, Bright Feather, became chief. He said coldly, "It may be that the hyena has entered my lodge, but not before he first gorged himself in yours."

Black Cloud looked from one warrior to the other. What was this talk of death? His eyes apprehensive, his young face strained, he moved nearer to Tall Tree. He chose his words carefully. Since his failure to kill Lawrence, he had been in disgrace. Feeling this disgrace deeply, he often hesitated to speak, but this time, he felt, he must. "Why do you talk of death, Tall Tree?" he said in a low voice. "I believe that the sounds we are hearing come from the throat of one who struggles to bring forth life."

Tall Tree looked at him. He was a strange one, this young warrior. It was not for him to instruct his elders. An inclination came to him to rebuke Black Cloud, but he decided against it. It might be wiser to listen. This one, who spoke with the voice of untried youth, had many times been known to speak with the wisdom of age. He had failed in his mission to kill Lawrence, for the thing he had been given to do was now well known to the other warriors. It was because of this that his head was bowed in shame whenever he approached Little Wolf. But if Tall Tree heeded the voice of the disgraced one now, it was not necessary that Little Wolf should come to know of it. With a swift, suspicious look at Bright Feather, whom he had never been able to bring himself to trust, Tall Tree spoke lightly and indulgently to Black Cloud. It was just the right tone, he thought, for he did not want the youth to start to imagine that he was important. "Then lead us to this giver of life, Black Cloud," he said.

With the proper degree of humbleness, though he fumed inwardly at the half-amused look on Tall Tree's face, Black Cloud bowed his head. Lifting it again, he pointed a finger. "Then, if you permit, we will go this way."

Bright Feather was determined to establish himself and his own importance, and he spoke first. "You have my permission, Black Cloud," he said, with a triumphant sidelong look at Tall Tree. "We will follow after you."

They moved after the tall, slender youth. And although they did not know it, at this moment both Bright Feather and Tall Tree were in accord. The youth might be wrong, was the thought in both their minds. It might well be that death did indeed stalk the forest, waiting to claim fresh victims. Because of this hidden fear, they moved as silently as the grim specter.

Black Cloud made an opening in the crowding bushes. He looked without surprise at the struggling figure of the one who labored to bring forth a new life. It was a white woman, and that did surprise him a little. Never before had he seen a woman of that race so exposed. Something within him felt sorry for her, but for all that, he was determined to look his fill. It was not at the prompting of lewdness, but of curiosity. The white women he had seen, always from a safe distance, had been swaddled in folds of material that had made them look a very odd shape indeed. It was apparent to him that they did not worship the god of the sun, and that they would have been ashamed to take off the cloth so that his golden fingers might caress their bodies with love. He had always wondered how they would look without the swaddling, and many times he had asked himself if, beneath the cloth, they could possibly be shaped as an Indian maiden.

Black Cloud's brows drew together, and he puffed out his lips in consideration. It was perhaps not fair to make judgment at a moment like this, he decided. This white woman, with her breasts tumbling from her low-cut bodice, her pale stomach still swollen with the unborn warrior, and her legs flung wide to accommodate his passage into life, was certainly not as she would be under more favorable circumstances. But as far as he could see, she would normally be the same shape as an Indian maiden.

Black Cloud looked at her breasts for a long moment, and he wondered if they would taste the same to lips that were used to kissing darker, sun-kissed flesh. Dismissing the idea, he turned his eyes to the one who was stooped over the woman. Her hair had fallen forward. It was touching the distended stomach like a spill of rich black earth. The maiden looked up at that moment. Recognizing her instantly, Black Cloud drew in his breath sharply. It was she, the golden-skinned maiden who had bathed in the stream. He had dreamed of her so many times. He would hear her voice, heavy and throaty with desire, calling to Lawrence. To the white man! The enemy! Yes, she had called to him. To the false Lawrence, as it had turned out. But she had not known that then. Had it been the real Lawrence, and if his blade had not found him first and felled him, she would have opened her body to him. The intention had been plain in her voice.

Black Cloud thought of the dream he was always having of this maiden with the mouth that was like a ripe red fruit. He saw her lying on the soft skins of his bedding. Her legs were

opened wide, as were the white woman's now, but they were
opened to accommodate him. Naked, his loins hot and throbbing, he would stand over her, letting her admire the huge,
swollen length of his masculinity. She would lift her arms,
crying out to him to enter her. Her fingers would reach hungrily, already curling as though she held the object of her
desire between them. Then, seeing her wild eyes, the rigidity
of her thrusting nipples, he would go down on his knees
between her wide-flung legs and plunge into her, thrusting
himself up high. He would feel her legs, like velvet snakes,
inching up to clasp his waist, and then, not quite satisfied,
going higher until at last they encircled his neck. He thought of
her as a wild mare beneath him, and he the triumphant stallion
riding her. Plunging deeper, savoring all of her, he would bite
her breasts very gently, and when he took her hardened nipple
into his mouth and sucked it, he would hear her loud scream
of joy. Her body would buck and rear beneath his, like the
wild mare to which he had likened her.

Coming back to himself, Black Cloud sighed. Although
they were only dreams, they were very real to him.

Bright Feather did not notice Black Cloud's absorbed face.
Even if he had, the face or the rigidity of the youth's body
would have meant nothing to him. He was absorbed, as he
invariably was, in the sick desires that rode him. Looking at
the laboring white woman, he was bemused, delighted, and
terribly excited by the scene before him. He moistened his
dry lips and swallowed, hoping to ease his racing heart.

Tall Tree, who had found himself a place between the two
men, turned his head and looked sharply at Bright Feather. It
seemed to him that he had heard a moan escape the man's
lips. He could not be sure, however, for the woman had
begun screaming again. Certainly Bright Feather looked
strange, like someone in the grip of a spell, and the eyes that
turned to him now for a brief unseeing moment had a bright,
hot, sick glitter. Bright Feather did not look horrified, as he
himself felt. If anything, he appeared pleased and excited.

Puzzled, made vaguely uncomfortable by the man beside
him, Tall Tree turned his eyes back to the woman. Birth was
a sacred thing, and the woman who bore the child was to be
revered, but there was no denying that the birth itself was an
uneasy sight to watch. For himself, he would not have looked
at all, had he not feared that the others, seeing his discom-

fiture, would have laughed at him and chided him for being a coward. Birth! The mystery of it, the pain of the expulsion, frightened him. If only the woman would not scream so! She had bitten through her lip; he could see the beads of blood on her chin. She was straining so, her fingers digging into the earth. Surely the effort she was making would kill her?

"Push!" Lianne shouted. "Push, woman, push!"

"No more!" Tears ran from the corners of Caroline's eyes. "Oh, God, no more!"

"Yes, more! Push, I tell you! I can see the child's head!"

Tall Tree winced at the scream that came from the woman then. Her heels were drumming as though she sought to drive them into the earth. She looked crazed and at the end of her endurance. She was surely possessed, he thought. The evil ones must have lodged in her throat, for only they, sending forth their unholy chorus, could make those terrible sounds that now issued from her.

Black Cloud stiffened as the Indian maiden began to shout to the woman. "Just one more push! One more!"

"Lianne! Please, Lianne!"

Lianne? Black Cloud thought. So that was the name of the beautiful maiden. It was a strange name. Haunting. He could not remember hearing the name before. Silently, he repeated it. Lianne. It suited her well, and it made a chiming, beautiful sound in his mind.

Tall Tree felt very odd. He could see the head of the child. Things seemed to be receding, and he had the alarmed feeling that his senses were trying to leave him. Sweat broke out on his forehead. He could feel the wet prickling of it as it ran down his face in tiny streams. He must hold on! Without thinking, he put his hand on Black Cloud's shoulder, his fingers gripping fiercely. The child was coming. It burst forth from the womb and now lay in the young squaw's hands. Great Spirit, be merciful! If this is birth, let me not look upon it again!

Lianne looked at the new born flesh in her hands. A male child and the birth cord was wound tightly about the neck! Her heart racing with fear, she bent her head. Her sharp teeth chewed through the cord, releasing the child's neck from the stranglehold. No change. He was unmoving, no breath of life animating his body. When a child was born, there was something that the old squaws did. She fought the confusion and the fear, and memory, sharp and clear, came back to her. They would grip the child by its tiny ankles, and dangling it, they would slap it sharply on the bottom. She knew well that this was done so that the devils who tried to ride man from his birth to his death would be forced to release their seal of evil from the mouth. The gods listened happily to the first cry the child sent forth. The blessed sound drew them, and they gathered about the child to endow it with strength, beauty, courage, and love. So, too, would they do for this man-child she held in her hands.

Lianne did not look at Caroline. She had forgotten her. Only the child was important. Smiling, she held it aloft. "Gods of wisdom, truth, and beauty, look upon the son of Lawrence!" She slapped the child, and there was a wincing all through her that she must be the first one to put pain upon its body. "Hear me, O blessed ones. Drive the devils away!" Again she slapped the inert flesh. "Let the voice of this male-child, the son of Lawrence, the white chief, issue forth. Give him your love. Give him all of your precious gifts, especially the gift of courage, so that he may fight his enemies and stand tall and strong upon this earth. A true warrior. A warrior who knows no fear!"

The fear was back in Caroline's eyes. The child did not move or cry. He was dead! But she would hold him once, before he was lost to her forever. A male child, Lianne had said. Justin's son! Her boy! "Give him to me!" she cried. "Give me my son, Lianne!"

Black Cloud looked at the exhausted white woman, who was reaching out hungry arms for her dead child. His eyes turned to Lianne, and he saw the knowledge dawning in her expression. What she had tried to deny was heavy upon her. She knew that the child was dead. Black Cloud felt a tenderness for her. It was no fault of hers. She should not look so distraught. She had cried out to the gods. She had done all that she could.

Lianne looked up, and Caroline saw the tears shining on her cheeks. "He is dead!" Lianne's voice was loud, defiant. She knew where Caroline would place the blame.

Caroline's hands clenched against the pain of loss. "I . . . I know," she said in a shaking voice. "You did all you could, Lianne. I know that, too."

Lianne rose slowly to her feet. She placed the child carefully on the ground. Pulling Caroline away, she arranged her limbs decently and pulled down her skirts and tenderly placed the child in her arms.

Bright Feather's eyes narrowed with hatred as the Indian girl picked up the child and put it into the woman's arms. He turned fiercely commanding eyes on the other two warriors. "We will take them back to the village," he said in a low, harsh voice.

"It is not necessary," Tall Tree said. "They are only women. What harm can they do?"

Bright Feather's teeth showed in a mirthless grin. "If you had used your ears, you would know that the white one is the woman of Lawrence. Little Wolf will be happy to see her."

Black Cloud's head whirled. If only he were not so young. If only he knew what to say. "And ... and the maiden?" He faltered.

"She is friend to the white one, and therefore the enemy."

Caroline looked in alarm at Lianne's stiffening figure. "What is it?" she cried. "What is wrong?"

"Someone is there," Lianne whispered, "hiding behind the bushes."

Caroline screamed as Bright Feather burst forth from cover. Behind him came two others. Her arms tightened about the child. "Lianne. Speak to them. Ask them to let us go in peace."

"I speak your language, white woman." Bright Feather bent over Caroline, his braided hair falling forward.

Caroline stared up into the fierce, hawklike face. She tried not to flinch as she met the narrowed black eyes. "What do you want of us?" Unconsciously, an imperious note had entered her voice. Her head lifted as she added, "Go away. We have done you no harm."

"You are white. That is harm enough. And you are the woman of Lawrence. There in your arms you hold the child that sprang from his loins." His hands reached toward the child.

The color drained from Caroline's face. "Don't dare to touch my child!"

Bright Feather's teeth gritted together. He would break this proud and arrogant white woman, and would humble her. Before he was done with her, she would crawl to him, kiss his feet. His rough hands wrenched the child from her arms. He held the child aloft for a moment, and something seemed to snap in Caroline's brain. Horror, grief, rage, gave her a burst of strength. She jumped to her feet and hurled herself at Bright Feather. She did not hear Lianne's screams. She did not see her struggling in the grip of the other two warriors. Her nails stabbed at Bright Feather's face, tearing a long furrow down one cheek. "Filthy savage!" Her feet kicked viciously. "I'll kill you, Indian, I'll kill you! Bastard, may God strike you dead!" The tears were blinding her, but she saw his face in her mind. She would never forget his narrow, glittering eyes, the thin, cruel curve of his lips, the green feathers blowing in his hair. There was no fear in her, only hatred so all-encompassing that she went on fighting.

Bright Feather held her struggling form away from him. His face was bleeding, and there was a great rage in him. This woman of Lawrence's was mad! Her teeth were bared, her face was the color of death, and through the tears he saw the insane glitter of her eyes. She would kill him if she could. His hard fingers gained a stranglehold on the woman's throat, momentarily stilling her from further action. He had meant to hurl the child from him like the trash he believed it to be, but now he was not sure what to do. He looked furtively about him, hoping that the others had not noted his indecision. He was considerably relieved to find that Tall Tree and Black Cloud were not looking at him. They were fully occupied in trying to subdue the struggling Indian maiden. Bright Feather's lip curled in contempt as he glared at Lianne.

A croaking sound came from the white woman's throat. Bright Feather started. He must not kill her. Little Wolf must decide the fate of this madwoman. He cautiously relaxed his grip on Caroline's throat. She slumped but did not fall, and he heard the gasping sounds she made as she fought to draw air into her tortured lungs. After a few moments he heard her distorted voice. "M-my child. Give him to . . . to me."

Bright Feather stared at her. Even now, though she was obviously in great distress, she still demanded that he return to her the body of her dead son. It was fear rather than pity that dictated his next action, the fear of becoming tainted with her madness. Slowly he lowered the arm that held the child aloft, and looked at the little form for a long moment. Then, abruptly, he thrust it into her quivering, outstretched arms. "Take it," he muttered. "Bury it, before I change my mind!"

Caroline's expression changed as she cradled her son in her arms. Her lips moved, bringing out difficult words. "My son!" she whispered, as her tears fell on the still white face, on the tiny curled fists that lay each side of his head. Sleeping, she thought. He looks as though he is only sleeping. Her pain-filled eyes saw the perfect nails, the fine down of black hair on the round head, and her heart broke afresh. Blindly she turned away. "Help me, Lianne," she appealed. "Help me to bury my son."

Lianne had stopped her struggling. Her nerves must be playing tricks on her, she thought, for it seemed to her that a stillness had fallen over everything. The hands holding her had fallen away. Her two Indian captors were standing so still that they might have been carvings of stone. Just across from her, the tall Indian with the green feathers in his hair was just as still. Only his terrible eyes seemed to be alive. Eyes that told of the suffering he had in store for them. Li-anne dragged her gaze from him. Fear was swamped by pity, and she felt a great burning lump in her throat as she watched Caroline making her unsteady way toward her, her arms still tightly holding her precious burden. "Help me!" Li-anne winced at the sound of Caroline's strained voice. "My son must have a decent burial. Please, Lianne, please. You must!"

"I must." Lianne repeated the words softly. Then, in a louder voice, "I must, I must!" She looked entreatingly into the face of the young Indian. "Please," she whispered. "She has not the strength to do it by herself."

Black Cloud cleared his throat. He wanted to accede to her request. Fearing he would see denial in Bright Feather's face, he did not even glance in his direction. Avoiding Tall Tree's fixed stare, he made a motion with his hand. "Help the white woman, then," he said gruffly. "But hurry."

Lianne threw aside the flat stone with which she had scooped out the earth. Looking down into the narrow grave she had made, she said, "It is done, Caroline. Give him to me."

Caroline shrank back, her eyes wild. For a moment it seemed that she would turn and run away with her burden.

"Caroline!" Lianne's voice took on a note of sharp command. "I said give him to me." Impatient and bewildered by her surging emotion, Lianne glared at her. "Come, woman, you know it must be."

Caroline's eyes dulled over. "Yes," she said in a toneless voice. "Yes, it must be." She made to hand the small bundle to the girl, then sharply drew back. "I will do it, Lianne." Her raised hand checked Lianne's impetuous forward movement. "No, don't you see? It is the only thing I can do for him."

Lianne's head drooped, her black hair falling forward to hide her face as Caroline placed the little body into the grave. How gently she handles him, she thought. It was almost as though she was placing a sleeping child into its cradle.

"Lianne!" The choked note in Caroline's voice brought Lianne's head sharply upward. "I can't drop the earth on him. I can't do that!"

Lianne sprang forward and pushed her roughly aside. "Get away. I will do it." She stole a quick glance at Caroline's blanched face. "Don't look, you fool woman, don't look!"

"Oh, God!" Caroline sank down beside the open grave and covered her face with her hands.

After a moment, Bright Feather saw the white woman's hands fall away from her face. Her eyes were closed, and her lips were moving. Was she praying to her God? Well, her God could not help her now. Bright Feather waited until the grave had been filled in; then he moved toward Caroline, his eyes triumphant. His hands reached down. Grasping her beneath the armpits, he pulled her to her feet. "Now, woman."

Caroline stared at him. "Leave me alone." Her voice was dull, uncaring.

"Leave you alone, you white filth?" Bright Feather roared the words. "You dare to say that to me!" Once again he was feeling his power. His fear was gone now. He was conscious only of a desire to hurt and punish her. Lifting his arm, he shoved her to the ground.

Seeing Caroline fall, Lianne scarcely felt the hands that had grasped her once more. The white woman lay there like one dead, crumpled at the feet of the huge warrior with the green feathers in his hair. Staring at her, so white and so unmoving, Lianne began to shake. She was convinced that the blow had killed her. Everything was over. Caroline was dead, but she had not died by her hand. Buck Carey was lost to her. And for some reason that she could not hope to guess, the gods had turned their faces from her. It would seem that she was not fated to become the woman of Lawrence. She did not mind that. But she did mind dying without first having known the warmth and wonder of Buck Carey's love. She would die, she knew, unless a warrior chose her to be his squaw. She had been seen in the company of a white woman. She had helped her to bear her child, and to the eyes that looked on, it must have seemed the sign of the greatest friendship. Even worse, she lived among the enemy. Although these hill Indians kept themselves well out of sight, moving as stealthily and as silently as snakes, yet she had always known that the settlement's every movement was watched. She lived among the white people, and she could not delude herself that this fact was not known to them.

Black Cloud saw Lianne's despairing expression. Impetuous, as always, not even caring if he should be heard, he whispered to her, "Do not fear. I will try to help you."

"Why?" Lianne turned her head and looked into Black Cloud's eyes. She had seen the same expression of the eyes of many other men when they looked at her. She knew what it meant. He wanted her. Uncaring, not even trying to use this male weakness to gain her own ends, she said in a dull voice, "Why should you wish to help me? I have nothing to give to you. Nothing that I want to give."

Black Cloud flushed. He told himself that she did not mean it. She was meant to belong to him, and deep inside her, she must know that. She was afraid—that was why she spoke to him so uncaringly. Trembling with the longing that came to him to throw her to the ground and enter her body with all his stored-up passion and violence, he answered her stiffly, "I will try to help you because it is in my heart to do so." He hesitated, knowing that it was not wise to speak further, but the words clamored to be said, and he could not deny them utterance. "I have seen you before," he went on. "In the forest. You were bathing in the stream. You ... you were expecting the white man. You called to him."

Lianne had a flashing memory of that day. Again she saw the figure running past her. His body had been painted in

broad red and white stripes, as though for war. There had
been white circles about his eyes. It was he, this boy, who
had hurtled from the tree. In memory, she heard the white
man shout. She heard the warrior's scream of victory. The
whinny of the horse hidden deep in the forest. She saw the
dying man dragging himself toward her, the knife buried
deep in his back. The man she had thought was Lawrence.
"You!" she whispered, a spark of life awakening in her eyes.
"It was you who killed Bedford!"

Black Cloud inclined his head. "My knife was meant for
Lawrence."

Lianne's lip curled. "Was it at the behest of your great
chief?"

Black Cloud's fist clenched into a hard knot with the temptation that came to him then. She was taunting him. She was
defying him to strike her down. With this realization, his fingers uncurled slowly. He looked at her with a puzzled frown.
Why did she wish for his anger rather than his tenderness?
He could kill her where she stood. No one would blame him
if he plunged his knife into her throat. She was his prisoner.
He wanted to speak to her harshly, but again the words he
did not wish to utter came from his lips. "I want you!" he
said. "I will kill anyone who tries to harm you!"

Tall Tree had heard Black Cloud's impetuous words—"I
will kill anyone who tries to harm you!" Tall Tree smiled to
himself.

He had a fondness for Black Cloud, who, it would seem,
sighed for this haughty maiden. After all, he had no wish to
bring fresh trouble down on the youth's unfortunately rash
head. And although there were only a dozen years between
them, had he not always looked upon Black Cloud almost as
a son? But did the youth mean it? Would he really kill anyone who tried to harm the girl?

His thick brows drawing together in an uneasy frown, Tall
Tree covertly studied the girl. Her hair was tumbled, and her
face was dirty; blood spotted her gown and her arms, and she
did not look too attractive at this moment; but for all that, he
could tell that in the ordinary way she would be very lovely.
Yet there was something different about her. Something that
was not quite . . . Tall Tree drew in his breath sharply. The
girl was a half-breed! Surely he could not be mistaken. Experimentally, keeping his wary eyes on Black Cloud, Tall

Tree jerked at the girl's arm. "Get along, half-breed!" he shouted.

Startled, the girl stumbled. Instantly, even before she had recovered her balance, Black Cloud's knife was in his hand. "Touch her again, Tall Tree," he snarled, "and I will cut out your heart!"

Tall Tree drew back. He was not offended; he was sad for the youth. This strange and intense Black Cloud really would kill anyone who harmed her. With such murderous thoughts in his heart and mind, how could he expect to live to a venerable age? Tall Tree looked at the girl again. Her eyes were upon him, mocking, scornful, daring him to touch her again. He would not touch her. He had no wish to feel the blade of one who was almost a son to him pierce his body. There were other ways of showing one's disgust. He hawked loudly, and deliberately spit the gob of spittle near the girl's feet. Wiping his arm across his mouth, he looked up and encountered the dangerous flame in Black Cloud's eyes. Tall Tree shuffled his feet and looked back at him imperiously.

His expression sullen, Black Cloud mounted his horse. Tall Tree watched him stretch out reluctant arms to take the woman from Bright Feather. No doubt he was suspicious of Bright Feather, who obviously meant to carry the girl before him. Again the heavy and saddening thought came to him that it would not be a good thing to take the youth lightly. After a moment, he shrugged the heaviness from him. It would be a marvelously romantic tale he would have to spin when the others gathered about the fire.

Tall Tree mounted his horse, his self-satisfaction somewhat shattered when he found that he was expected to take the girl up before him. He thought of refusing, but, meeting the narrowed black eyes fixed upon him with menace in their depths, he remembered that Bright Feather would be chief if anything should happen to Little Wolf. Tall Tree puffed out his lips so that Bright Feather would know that he was not entirely intimidated. Frowning heavily, for the benefit of the girl, he stretched out his hand to aid her to mount.

Lianne felt very tired. She would have liked to rest her head against the warrior's broad chest, but he was distasteful to her. He smelled of stale bear grease and urine. She moved restlessly, and the smell of her own body was wafted to her. Exhausted tears gathered in her eyes and spilled down her cheeks. It was a small thing, this smell that came from her body, and soon remedied, but somehow, in that moment, it seemed to her like an overwhelming disaster. She pressed her lips tightly together, but still she could not stop the sob that broke from her.

"Be silent!" Tall Tree's arm tightened cruelly about her waist. "Do not waste your tears, you stinking half-breed! Save them for the pain and trouble that will surely come to you."

Red rage exploded in Lianne's brain, and she forgot caution. She spat on his arm. Her long nails raked at his flesh. "You foul hyena!"

Swearing, Tall Tree jerked his arm away. Grasping her hair, he wound the strands tightly about her throat. "I could kill you now!" he hissed.

She was choking. The trees, the flowering bushes, the patch of blue sky she could see through the branches—all swam together in a dizzying whirl. Let him kill her! The thought darted through her fading senses. She would die anyway, and this was better than the torture. Willing herself to die quickly, she went limp against him.

Tall Tree felt the difference in her. The spitting, raging wildcat was drained of strength. If he unwound the hair from her throat, she would cry out and alert Black Cloud. He did not fear the youth, but it would kill the loving heart within him if he had to fight him. Thinking quickly, he released the stranglehold very slightly, just enough to allow her to breathe but not enough to enable her to cry out. He heard the quick gasping intake of her breath. Impelled by urgency, he raised his other hand and chopped at the back of her neck. She slumped forward heavily, almost tumbling from the horse. He grabbed for her. Unwinding the hair, he settled her against him. It was true that he should have killed her for her impudence, but he was a merciful man. He would settle for her silence for the rest of the way. If she stirred, he would hit her again. Almost, he hoped that her senses would swim back from the deep unconsciousness that claimed her. The thought of striking her again and seeing the angry flash of her eyes gave him a feeling of intense pleasure that was akin to the feeling he always had when relating tales to an enthralled audience.

White Bird drew back into the shadow of the trees as the

three horsemen passed along the narrow trail in single file.
The recent rains had not penetrated too well the heavy barri-
ers of the leaf-laden branches, and it was dusty upon the
trail. A thicker dust, eddying from the horse's hooves,
brought with it a strong inclination to sneeze. He pressed his
hand hard over his nose and mouth, suppressing the sneeze.
His eyes wide above his hand, he stared at the horsemen.

The first riding a white horse, was a big warrior with green
feathers blowing in his hair. He wore heavy chains of copper
about his neck, and set within each loop of the chain was a
large, rough-looking blue stone. Both his cheeks were decorated with three deep symmetrical slashes, and the slashes
had been artistically filled in with scarlet paint. He looked
imposing, White Bird thought, as though he might be a great
chief.

The second horseman was a youth. He would be about
White Bird's own age, he imagined. His features were
hawklike and handsome, and the single braid of his hair hung
down his back, reaching almost to his waist. The hair above
his ears was loose, stuck through with a black feather and a
red. His cheeks were smooth, unmarred by slashes. White
Bird's eyes went to the woman crumpled in front of the
youth. His heart jumped in alarm, and he swallowed against
a sudden dryness in his throat. A white woman! Was it Caroline! Her long, pale hair spilled forward, hiding her face,
and he could not be sure. But surely he recognized that gray
gown with the little blue dancing figures printed on it? The
gown was hitched up, and its hem was soaked with blood.
There was blood on her legs, too, and more blood staining
the dappled side of the horse.

The third horseman lagged slightly behind the other two.
White Bird's eyes turned to him with a dreadful fascination.
Somehow, he knew what he would find. Lianne lay against
the warrior, but her head sagged forward as though her neck
was broken. Her hair, too, covered her face. But he did not
need to see her face. Did he not know every line and curve
of Lianne's body? Blood spotted her gown. It stained her
trailing hand and arm. Great Spirit! What had happened
here? The gray gown with the printed blue dancing figures
hung loosely on the white woman's body. The child had been
born, but where was it?

White Bird's arms clenched about the trunk of the tree, but he did not feel the gnarled roughness of the bark pressing into his flesh. His head swam with a swirl of thoughts and ideas to aid the two women. But of them all, only one emerged clearly. Find Lawrence and Buck Carey.

White Bird drew in a deep, shuddering breath. They searched for him—he knew that. He had seen them. He had heard their voices calling his name again and again.

He had nothing to fear from these two men who hunted him so zealously, their faces shiny with sweat and their damp buckskins clinging uncomfortably. But for all that, even though the wish had been in him to do so, he had not shown himself. There had been a sullenness, a hatred in his heart for Buck Carey, the man whom Lianne loved. The feeling within him had been made much worse by the thought that he could have liked and admired Buck Carey under different circumstances. White Bird had studied him, and he believed that he, like Lawrence, had the mark of the great warrior upon him.

Thinking back to his feelings then, stunted now by his jealousy, White Bird scowled. It was because of his liking for the man, as well as his love for Lianne, that he had flung the knife to protect Buck Carey from those who would hunt him down for the crime of murder.

So, brooding, allowing his heart to harden, he had thought: Let them call until they have no voices left, and still I will return to them no answer. Let them be filled with the venom of the snake. Let them lie in the undergrowth until the worms eat their guts. I will not answer. He had remained still. Flitting before them like a shadow, but always keeping them in sight. Not so much by the rustle of a leaf had he betrayed his presence, and they had had no idea they were being watched. He had derived from this elaborate game of hide-and-seek a perverse and morose satisfaction. Time and again, his lips tightening, he had stared at Buck's broad back, and he had wished that he had his knife with him. This time he would have thrown it to some purpose, burying it deep in the flesh of his rival. Then he would have shown himself. Triumphant, he would have stood over Buck and smiled as the lifeblood gushed from him. But he did not have his knife. He had lost it in defense of this same man whom he now wished to kill.

Fighting the liking he still had for Buck, obstinately refusing to allow it to come to the surface of his mind, he had deliberately hardened his heart still further against the pale-skins, even against Lawrence, who, he believed, was his true friend. Justin was one of them—he was like Buck, smiling, holding out the hand of friendship, but treacherous beneath. Had not Buck proved his treachery by taking Lianne, his woman? And Justin Lawrence? Did he not still smile upon Buck and call him "friend"? White Bird would not like them. They were his enemies. He would sever his life from all connection with theirs.

Now, White Bird drew farther back as the warriors passed out of sight. For a moment it had seemed to him that he knew the warrior with the green feathers in his hair. A memory had stirred, showing him a picture of two boys, one young, the other much older. The older boy had been kind to the younger, befriending him, bringing to his life a warmth and comradeship that had been sadly lacking. The older boy, almost a man really, had been named Bright Feather. He had said to the younger boy, who had been himself, "White Bird, if ever I can aid you, I will be happy to do so. We are of a different tribe. The paths of our lives lie in different directions, but I am your friend. I will always remember that. Your problem is that you are weak and lame, and until I came, friendless. My problem is something deep within me. It is something that I will never speak of."

White Bird shook his head in bewilderment. No, that warrior could not be Bright Feather. There had been a kindness in Bright Feather's eyes, a smiling generosity to his lips. The warrior with the green feathers showed none of these qualities. He looked hard, merciless. A man whom his enemies must greatly fear. There was no kindness in him, no generosity. The grim lines of his face showed that. Therefore, it could not be Bright Feather, the youth who was almost a man, who had once, for a brief and wonderful time, accidentally crossed the path of his life.

Annoyed at his foolishness, White Bird waited for the dust to settle and the sound of the plodding hooves to fade into the distance. A wind rustled through the leaves, dispersing the strong odor of heated animal flesh. Above his head, a small brown bird, perched on the highest branch of the tree, broke into song.

White Bird's eyes followed the flight of a white-and-orange

butterfly, but he did not really see it. His mind was still on the warriors and their captives. He knew the tribe. He knew where the warriors were headed now. And he knew what would happen to the women. If they were not immediately tortured and killed, they would both be offered to Little Wolf, the chief. If the chief did not want them, they would then be passed among the warriors, who would spill their seed into them. Afterward, it might be that their worn-out bodies would be allowed to live, but only as beasts of burden to fetch and carry for the warriors and to be kicked and spit upon by the women. Tortured, even, if the mood moved them. He had seen other miserable female prisoners, a leather strap about their heads, the other end of the strap fastened to a laden sled. He had seen their terrible struggle to drag the wooden runners over the uneven ground. It had never seemed to him to be wrong, when he had looked at these women. They were the enemy. It was right that they should suffer. But this fate must not happen to Lianne and Caroline. Better death.

White Bird's hands clenched into fists. Because of Lianne and Caroline, his life could not be as he had planned. He must break the vow he had made to have nothing further to do with the pale-skins. He must find Justin Lawrence and Buck Carey.

Running through the green gloom of the forest, careless now of betraying sounds, White Bird blundered like a tenderfoot as he thought of the two women, who, in their varying ways, had made such a strong impact on his life. Caroline Fane, the first white woman he had ever seen, with her spill of sun bright hair, her huge brown eyes, and her white skin. When, as she lay in unconsciousness, he had touched that skin, he had found it to be as soft as the wings of a butterfly. She was so strong, so bold, and so beautiful that she had fascinated him to the point where he had believed that he must be in love with her. He had found her wandering in the forest, and because she was white and he had found her, he had believed that she belonged to him alone. It had taken Lianne, with her lithe golden body, that body that he had entered again and again, each time seeming like the first time, to show him the difference between fascination and love. Lianne, as beautiful as Caroline, though different, with her dark-blue eyes, her ripe, moist mouth, and her hair that was like the spread of the night. She was so selfish, so cruel and wanton. But when she had met Buck, she had changed. He had seen the light in her eyes when she looked at the white man. The soft music in her voice that should have been for him was for Buck Carey.

White Bird stumbled, almost falling. Righting himself, he ran on, the breath laboring in his lungs, his body dripping sweat. Let both be safe. If this could be so, then for Lianne's sake he would acknowledge and respect Buck as the man she loved. If the gods would but range themselves on the side of these two so very different women, he would, for the rest of his life, give allegiance not only to his gods but also to Justin Lawrence and Buck Carey. Allegiance to the two men, but never servitude. This he swore.

Panting, White Bird stopped for a moment to catch his breath. His chest heaving, he wiped the sweat from his eyes, cursing himself for a fool. All day he had kept the white men within his sight. Why now, when he needed them, had he taken his eyes from them? He must come upon them soon. If he did not, it might be too late.

Gritting his teeth together, ignoring the stabbing pain in his side, White Bird went plunging on. He must not go too deep into the forest, he told himself, for to do so would be to waste precious time. If he did not find them, he must go alone to the village of the hill Indians. He must try a rescue on his own. It might be that he would die with these two women who were so important to him, but at least he would die knowing that he had tried. Courage—and it would take that—gave you an immediate entry into the Heavenly Hunting Grounds. He was scorned for his lameness, and because of it his brothers thought that he lacked courage. Before the sun deserted the sky, he would prove that it was not true.

Chapter 15

Buck cursed loudly as a thorn bush sprang back and whipped at the side of his face, leaving a long bloody track. "That's it, as far as I'm concerned," he ended.

Seated on a fallen tree truck, Justin looked up at him in mock reproof. "You know something, Buck, I've mingled with the riffraff of the London slums, and I bedded down with convicts, thieves, and murderers, but damned if I've ever heard such a flow of rich and original curses as those you've just come out with." His tired face, dark with a two-day growth of beard, broke into a grin. "I compliment you on your repertoire."

Looking slightly shamefaced, Buck returned the grin. "Danged if you don't make it sound like you never heard cursing before," he said, seating himself beside Justin. "Of course, you ain't telling me that, are you?"

Justin's brows rose in amusement. "No, my friend, I'm not telling you that. But I've never heard your particular brand of cursing before."

"That so?" Buck shrugged. "Reckon you'll hear it many times 'fore you die, especially if you get yourself in with drifters and backwoodsmen. Ain't nothing too special 'bout it." He turned an aggrieved face to Justin. "Be mighty fine if we flushed out this White Bird, but it seems like we ain't going to. I've had about enough of this hunt, so how about we head back to the settlement? I've got my gear to pack, and plans to make."

"Plans?" Justin frowned down at the ground. "You're still determined to leave, then?"

Buck nodded. "You know that."

"Yes, I know." Justin turned his head and looked at Buck. "Maybe I hoped you'd change your mind."

"I won't. Not now."

"It's not my business, I know. But you never did tell me what happened between you and Lianne."

"Reason I ain't told you is 'cause I was wanting you to go on having some respect for me. Didn't want you to know what a fool I made of myself." He glanced quickly at Justin. "If you want to hear, I'll tell you."

"It doesn't matter. I think I can guess." Justin looked away. "I'll be sorry to lose you, Buck."

"You'll be seeing me from time to time. Might be a few years in between, but you'll be seeing me."

"I hope so. Well, Buck, what now?"

"Well, if we're banged up, bruised up, scratched up enough to suit you, let's get back."

"All right." Justin rose to his feet. "I suppose, if White Bird wanted to be found, we'd have come across him." He looked inquiringly at Buck. "It strike you that way?"

"Told you it'd be that way, didn't I? White Bird's been near to us several times. I've felt his eyes watching me. Ain't you?"

"Yes, I've had that feeling. White Bird's around somewhere quite near. You can bet on it."

"Ain't needing to take no bet on that. It's like I told you before—Injuns is strange in their thinking. Smart, too. He doesn't want to be found."

"I hoped he'd still consider us to be his friends."

Buck rose. "He'd have maybe come out of hiding if you'd been alone. Won't come out with me around. I've been giving it some thought, and White Bird, he's maybe thinking I took his woman."

Justin looked at him sharply. "Did you, Buck?"

"Nope. Would have, if I could. Lianne ain't mine, so if he's thinking that, that's one mistaken Injun." Buck shook his head. "Ain't mine," he repeated. "But then, I reckon she ain't his, neither." He smiled faintly. "So that makes two mistaken Injuns, doesn't it."

"Two? White Bird calls you a pale-skin."

"Know he does. Don't know I've got Injun blood. Even if he did, he wouldn't consider it enough to make me no Injun. It's what I think myself that counts."

"And you think of yourself as an Indian?"

"Sometimes." Buck grinned.

"I wouldn't have known you were anything else but a

white man, if you hadn't told me differently. The way I think of it is—" Justin broke off as Buck grabbed his arm. "What is it?"

"Somebody's coming."

"Lawrence!" White Bird's voice came to them.

"It's him!" Justin raised his voice. "Over here, White Bird. This way!"

White Bird burst from cover and reeled drunkenly toward them.

"What's wrong?" Justin took White Bird's arm. "I think you'd better sit down and recover your breath."

Impatiently White Bird pulled his arm free. "There is no time for sitting." He looked at Justin. "The hill Indians have taken your woman."

"Carrie?" Justin's first reaction was one of disbelief. "Impossible! Carrie wouldn't stir from the settlement. She ..." He paused, his expression changing. "Oh, dear Christ! Are you telling me there's been a raid on the settlement?"

"I cannot tell you that, Lawrence. I have been far from that place. But there is no mistake. They have Caroline. I know what I saw." White Bird's head turned to Buck, and with his next words he relinquished his claim on Lianne. "And yours. The hill Indians have taken your woman, too."

Buck flinched, as though he had been struck. Then he said in an expressionless voice, "I think you'd better tell us about it, what you've seen. Everything."

"You do not question me. You believe me?"

"I do. If you say you've seen them carrying off the women, then you've seen it." Buck's voice quivered on the last word.

White Bird, his breathing easier now, launched at once into an explanation. When his voice faded, there was a tense silence.

Buck looked into Justin's drained face. "He's telling the truth," he said in a low voice.

"I believe him." Justin's fists clenched. "My God, we've got to get them out of that village." He turned to White Bird. "Do you know the way? Can you lead us?"

"I can. You have but to follow me."

Though Buck's shock was great, he took pity on the stark horror that was apparent in Justin's expression. "We'll get 'em out, Justin. Ain't nothing going to happen to them."

Abruptly, Justin lost his temper. "For Christ's sake, Buck," he snapped, "don't treat me like a child. Nothing's going to happen to them, you say? Do you think I believe that?"

"Ain't treating you like a child." Buck tried to smile, but the effort did not quite come off. "It's just that you come from a different world, and it's harder on you. You're right. Ain't gonna be easy, but me and White Bird'll manage it."

"You and White Bird?" Justin said in a dangerous voice.

"That's right. That's the way it's gotta be. White Bird knows what he's doing. As for me, I ain't got nothing to lose."

"Only your life! Buck, will you—"

"I know Injuns," Buck hurried on. "I know their ways, how they think. You don't. It'd be better if you stay behind."

"Shut your mouth, Buck, and listen to me. I won't—"

"It'd be better if you stay," Buck interrupted again. "Besides, Miss Caroline is likely to be grateful to see you all in one piece when she gets free. That makes sense, don't it?"

"Not to me. I'm coming."

"I just got through telling you that you don't know nothing about Injuns."

"And so I get my woman back through the courtesy of Buck Carey?" Justin looked at Buck with smoldering eyes. "No, thanks. I'm coming. What I don't know about Indians, you can bloody well teach me!"

"Ain't no time."

"All right. But my mind is made up. There is no more to be said." Seeing Buck's mouth opening to bring out further argument, he went on harshly, "First you treat me like a child, and now like a damned sniveling coward!"

"God damn you! You know it ain't that."

"You listen to me for a change, Buck. If anyone should stay behind, it's you. Little Wolf has sworn to kill you."

"Don't matter. I'll take my chances. They got Lianne, and you ain't leaving me behind."

"And they have Carrie. So the matter is settled."

"If there must be arguments," White Bird said impatiently, "let it be on the way. There is no more time for such foolishness."

Buck nodded. "You're right." He put his hand on his musket. "Lead on."

Copying his action, Justin touched the pistol at his belt. "Let's hope this kind of persuasion will win the day for us."

"Two guns against a bunch of Injuns don't bring too much comfort, not to my way of thinking," Buck said, his expression grim. "Anyway, cain't rightly say what'll happen till we get there." Nodding to Justin, he followed after White Bird.

Forging his way through the hot, breathless gloom of the forest, Justin was reminded of another time when he had searched for Caroline. He had been almost at the end of his resources when White Bird had entered his life for the first time. The Indian boy, grateful to him for saving him from a savage mauling, had led him to Caroline. Now he was leading him to her again. But this time the outcome might well be tragically different. Despite the moist heat, Justin felt icy cold with apprehension. What if Carrie should be already dead, and the child with her? His hand clenched tightly over the butt of the pistol. No, he would not think that way! She had to be alive. He was going to get Carrie and their child out of that Indian village.

White Bird, glancing from time to time at Justin, thought he saw the further questions that lay unasked in the man's eyes. He felt a touch of pity. Perhaps, he thought, Lawrence was afraid of the answers he would receive to those questions. He was suddenly glad that he had not told him of the flowing of Caroline's blood that had stained the side of the young warrior's horse. Justin's child was lost to him, and perhaps his woman, too. Why speak? When they arrived at their destination, Justin would see all that there was to see. He was a man who, regardless of the consequences, would take his own action. Now White Bird felt admiration mingling with pity. This Lawrence, this dark giant of a man, who, as Buck Carey had said, came from another world, was prepared to fight the hill Indians for his woman. As clearly as if it were happening now before his eyes, he knew what Justin would do, if not restrained from a hasty action. Knowing nothing of the people, he would walk into their village, his weapon leveled, and he would demand that they surrender Caroline. His was the kind of courage that demanded direct action. But that kind of courage had no place in this situation. They must think, plan, try in some way to outsmart the hill Indians. Only when Justin had as many years and as much wisdom upon him as Buck, would he know how to deal with those who were different from himself.

From the corner of his eye, White Bird studied Buck. He saw the grayness of his face and the tight line of his mouth. This man, too, though in a different way from Lawrence, had a blindness to danger. Little Wolf had vowed to kill him, but only Lianne was important to him. Even if he died for it, he would somehow manage to set her free and send her back to life. Even if that life must be lived without him.

White Bird was startled to find that his hatred and enmity for Buck had died. There was nothing now in his heart but a feeling of warmth and comradeship. If he had ever loved Lianne, he asked himself, how could he feel comradeship for Buck Carey?

Disturbed, White Bird lengthened his stride. Searching within himself, he found the answer. He did love Lianne. But not as Buck Carey loved her. Not with all of himself. He could never give her that kind of love. Perhaps it was not there to give to any woman.

Chapter 16

They abandoned the horses at the foot of the narrow trail that led into the village. The young warrior, dismounting, gathered the reins in his hand and departed with the animals.

Caroline turned her head and looked after him. Tall, his head erect, his shoulders proudly squared, he walked with long strides as he led the skittish horses away.

Caroline put a hand to her head, her fingers rubbing at her temples as she tried to ease the throbbing ache. Her pain-dulled brain had registered the names of her captors as they called backward and forward to each other on that long, tortuous way. Black Cloud, the youth was called. Perhaps because he was so young, and he had held her on the horse not ungently, he seemed to her to be less brutal than Bright Feather and Tall Tree.

She averted her eyes, trying not to think of what might await her in the Indian village, where Little Wolf was the chief. Little Wolf, who hated Justin, and would therefore extend that hatred to the woman of Justin Lawrence. She had heard the warriors talking between themselves, and it was not hard to guess at her fate and Lianne's.

Trying to close her mind to terror, Caroline began to take notice of the scenery about her. With the desperate eyes of one who might never see such beauty again, she noted the grandeur of the mountains, with their purple-hazed peaks, which reared upward as if in a straining effort to touch the hot blue of the sky. The dense masses of foliage that, starting at the foot of the mountains, tumbled like a thick green waterfall into the ravine. The gleaming of the lake in the distance, the swift overhead flight of a red-winged bird. Great trees, so lofty that she had to crane her neck to see the tops of them, threw a shade over the trail and patterned Lianne's distraught face with dancing, leafy shadows. And below the trail, looking to her like sun-bleached skeletons, were sharp-edged rocks. She shuddered. Perhaps there really were skeletons among the rocks, she thought. The bones of other victims, who, like themselves, had been captured and brought to this village to die. Had they been tortured, screaming in their death agony?

Bright Feather looked away from the still-struggling Indian girl. His narrow black eyes turned to the white woman, studying her closely. She had made a strong appeal to his senses when she had labored to bring forth the child, but he did not find her appealing now. Her bright hair was dank with sweat, and stray wisps clung to her thin, colorless face. There were dark shadows beneath her eyes, and where her teeth had bitten into her lower lip there was a crust of dried blood. The skirt of her gray gown was torn, stained with the blood that still came from her body, and she was trembling like someone in the grip of a fever. She did not, he thought with an inner sneer, look like a member of the arrogant white race who were attempting to take the land from his people.

Bright Feather's nostrils flared in disgust as he caught the odor that came from her body. His hatred of the pale-skins made a burning inside of him. You white woman, he thought triumphantly, now you are not so proud. Now your arrogance is gone, for you are brought lower than the lowest!

Lianne cried out as Tall Tree took a stronger grip on her arm. Bright Feather heard the outcry she made, but he did not look at her. Ignoring Tall Tree, who was politely waiting for him to start first up the trail, he continued to stare at Caroline.

Caroline felt his eyes upon her, and her own turned to meet his. A grunt of anger escaped Bright Feather. Her brown eyes were full of hatred, but the fear he had hoped to see was absent. He wanted her to be afraid. He wanted her to cringe before him. And so she should, he vowed. Before he was done with her, she would have good cause to fear him.

Letting his anger grow, almost enjoying the strength of it, he put his hand to his gouged cheek. This woman had called him a filthy savage. And then she had cried out to her white God to strike him dead. There was another name she had flung at him—"Bastard!" He did not know what bastard meant, but then, he thought, he did not need to know what it meant. The insult had been in the way she had said it.

Bright Feather's eyes gleamed. An impulse came to him to degrade her further. He saw her startled look as he reached his hand toward her.

Caroline stepped back a pace. "Don't touch me!"

Bright Feather's breathing came faster. He could see the shadow of fear in her haunted eyes. She hid her fear well, but he knew now that it was there beneath the hatred. Slowly, drawing out the moment, enjoying her desperation, he advanced his hand nearer. "Do not tell me not to touch you, white woman. I will do with you as I wish." He hooked his fingers into the low neckline of her bodice. Ripping savagely at the thin material, he exposed her to the waist. Grinning, he stared at Caroline's breasts. Breasts that were heavy and swollen with the nourishment for the child who had not lived. As he watched the woman's futile efforts to cover herself with the torn halves of the bodice, another memory came to him. Once again he saw her stomach straining as she strove to eject the child from her womb. Anger flared as he felt his instant swelling erection. Even the memory of those moments could start the heat in his loins again. With a snarling sound of fury, he struck her hands away. Gripping her breasts in his hands, he bent his head and began to suckle her nipples.

Caroline screamed aloud in agony and lost all control. Her shrill, piercing cries went on and on. Tears gushed from her eyes. She wept for herself, for her dead child, for Justin, whom she would never see again. That it should end here, like this, after all that they had been through together. Words began to mingle with the screams.

Lianne stared, her eyes opening wide. Feeling awoke in her. She did not recognize it for what it was, compassion for the white woman. "Don't touch her again!" she shouted. Lianne tore her arm from Tall Tree's grip. Like a small, furious animal, she flung herself at Bright Feather's back. "You yellow dog!" She battered at him with clenched fists. "You foul, slinking hyena!"

Bright Feather released his hold on Caroline's breasts. His face tight with fury and outrage, he swung around on Lianne. Lifting his hand, he struck her hard in the face, sending her reeling against Tall Tree. Contemptuously, he made a hawking sound. "Half-breed!" he exclaimed, spitting upon the ground. "Put your hands on me again, and I will have them lopped from your wrists!" He turned a furious face to Tall

Tree. "Why do you just stand there? Have your limbs been stricken? Take the half-breed to the village. I will follow in a few moments."

Caroline gave a strangled cry. "No!" Lunging forward, she caught at Lianne's arm. "Don't leave me alone with him!"

Lianne pulled herself free of Caroline's feverish grip. Already she was regretting her impetuous defense. She expected to be tortured before she died; almost, she was resigned to that, but now, because of the insult she had put upon him, Bright Feather, if he had his way, would see to it that she died slow and hard. She looked at Caroline almost with hatred. "I cannot stay. I can do nothing for you." Her voice rose as Tall Tree began to drag her along the trail. "We will both die!"

"Lianne!" Caroline started up the trail, her hand extended in appeal.

Bright Feather seized her by the hair and dragged her back. He had forgotten his belief that he dealt with one who was mad. She must be punished. She must crawl on her knees to him, this woman of Lawrence's, who had robbed him of his inner dignity, who had made him swell with desire for her laboring body. Before she died, she must know his punishment! "White filth!" He swung her around to face him. "Get down on your knees." He put his hands on her shoulders. "Kneel to me, I say!"

God help me! God have mercy! Justin, Justin, where are you? I need you! Prayers, entreaties, jumbled in crazy confusion in Caroline's brain as she struggled to resist the pressure on her shoulders. Her lungs burned with the effort she was putting forth, and it was becoming increasingly hard to breathe, but her defiance and her hatred were greater than her failing strength. Somehow she managed to gasp out words. "I'll . . . I'll see you in hell, I-Indian, before I'll kneel to you." Her white face lifted, and she spat full in his face. "May God damn you!" Her nails raked viciously at his arms. Bright Feather drew back from the sting of her nails. His eyes blazing, he held her with one hand. Lifting the other, he wiped the spittle from his face. "Your God can do nothing to me," he shouted. "You will die!" he said, thrusting his face close to hers. "I promise you that. And you will not like the manner of your dying. That, too, I promise you!"

Caroline drew in a deep, shaky breath. She would fight

again. And she would go on fighting until the death the Indian had promised her put an end to her struggles.

Bright Feather released his grip on her wrists. The woman was quiet enough now. Bright spots of color burned in her cheeks, but she was obviously cowed. "You will kneel to me now, pale-skin," he said triumphantly.

"No!" With a tremendous effort, Caroline lifted her hand again and struck for his face.

"Daughter of a bitch!" Bright Feather hurled her from him.

Caroline struck the ground heavily. Dazed, unable to move for the moment, she lay there. Her fingers twitched feebly as she remembered the lifting of the Indian's arm, the look on his face as he had held her child aloft. He had meant to hurl that tiny body from him; she had seen his intention in his eyes. Caroline bit her lips against the agony of memory. Tears for the child she had left buried in the earth, the grave unmarked, were cold on her cheeks. There was a wild weeping inside her as she looked at Bright Feather. I will get up, she told herself. I will fight him. It will be better if he kills me now. Anything, rather than that I should just lie here.

Bright Feather watched her frantic efforts to raise herself. She should not rise. She was there on the ground where he wanted her to be. It was true that she had not yet knelt to him, but he would see to it that she did. "Stay where you are, woman," he shouted, launching himself at her.

Caroline screamed as his heavy body landed. Hoping that he would kill her now, she forced herself to lie still. She had heard of the tortures the Indians inflicted upon the captives, and she did not think she was brave enough to endure such agony. She found herself remembering Jock McPherson. He, not knowing that she stood near, listening, had been telling Justin of the fate of a white woman who had been captured by the Indians. Her breasts had been pierced through with sharpened sticks, and she had been forced to look on as her husband died in indescribable agony. When the tortured man drew his last breath, the Indians had renewed their attentions to her. Her teeth had been smashed from her head with rocks, and her tongue cut out. Last, although the woman was already dying, she had been laid on the ground and her vagina filled with small red-hot stones. Two squaws had held

her legs tightly together as she struggled madly in her final
death agony.

Bright Feather was alarmed by the tremors shaking her
body. If the woman died before she could be brought to
Little Wolf for final judgment, he would be punished. Cursing
Little Wolf beneath his breath, he reluctantly rolled clear. He
scowled down at her. He saw that her eyes were closed, and
for the moment she seemed oblivious of his presence. Yes,
perhaps it was discreet not to put his weight on her again.
She was already so weak that it might well kill her. But for
all that, he was not yet done with her.

Bright Feather's scowl lifted as an idea came to him. His
fingers touched the hem of her gray gown. He smiled as he
saw the tightening of her mouth. She was aware of him. With
a sudden movement, he lifted her skirt and flung it over her
head.

"No!" Caroline screamed, her voice muffled by the folds of
cloth. The Indian was holding her arms down and she could
not free her head. Death she could accept, because she must,
she thought wildly. But not this final indignity. "Don't touch
me. Don't!"

Bright Feather stared as her body reared madly. So she
had some strength left, even if it was only a false strength.
He shrugged. No matter, it would spend itself. Looking at
her, he was again reminded of the birth. He saw the blood
clotted on her legs, and he shuddered.

"Please!" Caroline's struggles were growing weaker. There
was a drumming in her head and a tightness in her throat,
but still she continued to cry out. "Please show some mercy!"

For the first time, her words penetrated. Bright Feather
drew in his breath sharply as the insult implied in those
words registered in his brain. This white woman dared to
think that he would touch her when she was in this condition!
The angry blood pounded in his temples. "You!" he shouted,
slapping roughly at her legs. "Do you think I would touch
you now, you white filth? You are impure. You would sully
me!" Beside himself, he slapped at her legs again.

Caroline lay very still, not believing this nightmare, hardly
daring to breathe with the fresh terror that his raging, cursing
voice brought to her.

Bright Feather looked down at the woman. Bending, he
grabbed her skirt and pulled it down. Wide blank eyes looked

into his, eyes that seemed to hold no recognition of either him or her surroundings. Bright Feather thought of Little Wolf's wrath should he be balked now, and he shivered. Had he driven her too far? Had her reason left her for all time? Straightening up again, Bright Feather poked her with his foot. His voice hoarse with his suppressed fear, he shouted at her, "Get up, woman! Get up, I say!"

Caroline stared up at him with those blank, overbright eyes. She could remember being very afraid. She could remember her voice screaming defiance, but after that, nothing. What had happened to her, where was she now? Her eyes became fixed and intent on the dark face bending over her. "Indian!" The word jumped into her dazed and reeling mind. Had she been captured? She looked away, unwilling to surrender the small oasis of peace her shocked mind had granted her. She mustn't think too deeply. If she did, the horror would return. She would become afraid again. Justin. She would think of him instead. He was somewhere near. He would protect her. "Justin?" She spoke his name questioningly, as though expecting him to appear, to explain.

Bright Feather poked her again. "Get up!"

Caroline's eyes turned back to him. Green feathers! An arm lifting to throw something from him. My baby! My son! Terror came then in an overwhelming flood. "Justin!" She screamed his name despairingly. "Justin, help me, help me!"

Swearing, Bright Feather dragged her to her feet. For a moment he stared into her frenzied eyes; then he turned her about and began to prod her along. "Move, woman!" he shouted. "Move!"

Reality faded again for Caroline as she stumbled along the trail. She only knew that she was going somewhere, but she could not quite remember where. It lurked on the edge of her consciousness, just out of reach. She had been afraid; she could remember that. But what was it she had feared? Her body felt very cold, and yet, at the same time, her face burned as if with a fever.

"Hurry!" Bright Feather barked.

Caroline gave a little sob as sharp stones cut into her bare feet. Where are my shoes? Why have I come out without them? It was not like her to be so careless. Tears leaked from her eyes, and she rubbed at them angrily with the back of her hand. Her feet hurt. It was a great tragedy, this loss of her shoes. Someone had stolen them. Of course, that was the explanation. There were so many thieves on the *Merryventure*. She did not like being on this convict ship. She did not want to come to the New World. She was afraid of the Indians. Feathers in their hair. Their faces painted for war. Please, God, let me not think of that! Green feathers. Green sleeves. My lovely Lady Greensleeves! The little boy in the corner of the carriage—he was playing the melody. Justin! Blood on his face! The judge, with his merciless eyes. Newgate. They were being taken back to Newgate Prison!

A wail broke from Caroline as something hard stabbed into her back. The flogger! Had she had her trial? Yes, she remembered now. She had been tried for her life. She had been found guilty. She was to be flogged along the streets of London. Afterward, she was to be taken to Tyburn to be hanged. But she wasn't guilty. She had not murdered Thomas Fane. She had told the cold-faced judge that she was innocent, and he would not listen. No one would listen to her.

She cringed as the hard something stabbed at her back again. Was it the handle of the whip? Was the flogging about to begin? But that heavy whip with its leaded tip would cut her to ribbons! How could she bear such agony without crying out? The heat of defiance and hatred stiffened her spine. Damn them all to hell! Though they killed her, she would not cry out!

Her head turned, in wild searching, from side to side. Justin would save her. Quite suddenly she saw him. Rogue Lawrence, outlined against the sky. Wind ruffled his dark hair, the laces at his throat; it blew his black cloak back from his shoulders. He was coming for her.

She smiled brilliantly as he came nearer. "Carrie, love!" He held out slender, jeweled hands to her.

"I knew you would come, Justin. I knew."

Bright Feather glared at the lurching white woman. What was she mumbling about? It seemed to him that she was almost at the end of her strength. Perhaps she would die. The thought brought fear again. If she must die, let it be in Little Wolf's presence. If he brought the living woman before Little Wolf, he could scarcely be blamed if she died. The woman stumbled. "Hurry!" he shouted, grasping her by the arm.

Caroline turned her head and looked at him. Her eyes widened with horror. The man looming over her was very tall. He looked fierce and terrible to her eyes. The feathers in his long black hair were green! The veil of unreality lifted a little. Thought, reasoning power, stirred, bringing with it terror and an intolerable anguish. She looked down at the hand holding her arm. His spread fingers were very dark against her white skin. She shuddered. He was so alien to her, with his barbaric jewelry, his long, coarse hair, the paint-filled slashes on his cheeks, and the strange smell that emanated from his body. "Don't touch me!" She heard the thick mumble of her voice almost with surprise. It might have been a stranger speaking. Useless, she thought despairingly, to beg him not to touch her. She had done so many times before, and he had not heeded her. Looking into his eyes, she knew that it was foolish to persist, but still she forced out the words, driven on by something she felt deeply inside herself. "You have no need to hold me. Are . . . are you afraid that I w-will run?"

Afraid that she would run? As if she could, in her condition. No, there was nowhere she could run from him. Had he not been so angry, he would have laughed at the arrogance that prompted her words. That same arrogance he had noted in other pale-skins with whom he had come in contact. Would they never learn, these invaders of the red man's land? His fingers tightened on her arm. "Come, woman." He spoke the words contemptuously.

"T-take your hand away."

Bright Feather felt a coldness creeping over him as he met her gaze, but, unwillingly, he felt too a touch of respect. She had courage, this one. But for all that, he must remember that she was mad. Hastily he averted his eyes. He must not look at her directly. If he did, she would put an evil spell upon him. He would be robbed of his wits. Retaining his clutch on her arm, he dragged her the few remaining yards to the village.

Entering the village, Bright Feather stood still, the better to exhibit his captive. The three pale-skins he had captured before had been men. He was the first warrior to bring a white woman to the village. His shoulders proudly squared, he awaited the reaction to his prize.

Caroline's legs were trembling. If Bright Feather had not been holding her arm, she would have collapsed. Everything about her seemed to be far away, wavering. Shaking her head in an effort to clear it, she stared vaguely at the evenly spaced wigwams, with smoke issuing from narrow vents at the top. In the center of the cleared space around which the wigwams stood, a huge fire blazed. There were people, many of them, and small children, who shrieked joyfully as they ran in play.

Caroline drew back, her breath coming faster as she saw the children cease their running. When they had first entered the village, the adults had been engaged in various tasks. But now, like the children, they had stopped what they were doing and were looking in her direction. Perspiration broke out on her forehead. Why did they all stare so, as if she were some strange species?

The silence that had fallen was broken by a babble of voices. Bright Feather, releasing Caroline's arm, moved away a step. Now, in her terror, it was Caroline who clutched at him.

"White bitch!" Cursing, Bright Feather struck her in the face. Pulling his arm free, he strode away.

Her lips trembling, Caroline stared with haunted eyes at the women who were rushing toward her. Women with braided hair and dark-skinned faces. They were crowding in close now. So close that she could smell the odor of their bodies. They were touching her, pulling at her hair, clutching her gown, hurting her.

Screaming, Caroline tried to fight back. Her defiance seemed to enrage the women. Several of them began tugging at her gown. There was a sharp rending sound as they ripped it from her body. They pushed at her. They pinched her skin, and pulled viciously at her hair. The children did not join in. They stood by, watching with solemn dark eyes, as though wondering what game it was that their elders played.

She could fight no more. It was useless to try. She had no strength left. Moaning, Caroline sank to the ground. Let them do with her as they willed. She was beyond caring.

She did not notice when the women stopped tormenting her. Shivering violently, she lay where she had fallen, and wondered how long it would take her to die.

"Get up, woman," a voice commanded.

Starting, Caroline raised her head and looked up into the stern face of Black Cloud. "I can't." She shook her head. "I . . . I am too weak."

"You will either walk or you will be dragged." Black Cloud reached down and hauled her to her feet. "Little Wolf awaits you."

Little Wolf, Justin's sworn enemy! A spark of pride awoke in Caroline, strong enough to overcome her weakness momentarily. She raised her head. "I will walk."

Black Cloud nodded. "Then come, woman."

Chapter 17

Screened by the thickly growing bushes, the two men and the slender youth lay stretched out on the uneven ground.

With a quick glance at the other two, Justin edged forward on his stomach. With some damage to his hands, he parted the thorny bushes and looked downward. They were high above the Indian village. From his point of view, the Indians moving about below looked like small black dots. The hot wind had died, and the sound of the drums, muffled by distance, came to them.

Frowning, he drew back. How could he just lie here? Buck and White Bird had insisted that they wait for nightfall, when most of the braves would be sleeping, before attempting a rescue. Anxiety, impatience, a wish to be up and doing something, boiled inside him. Had he been alone, he did not think he could have waited out the time. But as things were, if he insisted upon going now, Buck and White Bird would follow, and he did not have the right to risk their lives. But what was happening to Carrie—was she already dead? The agonized questions went round and round in his mind. If they had killed her, he would somehow contrive to take a few of them with him before he, in his turn, died. Without Carrie, nothing was worthwhile. In those old carefree days in England, he had lived and been motivated only by excitement and the lure of danger. Then, when Carrie came into his life, he had dragged her into that dangerous whirlpool in which he existed. It had taken him a long time to realize how much she meant to him.

He moved his head restlessly as another terrifying thought came to him: What of the child? Carrie had been over full term, and it was due at any time. Without wishing to do so, he found his mind going back to the grisly story Buck had related to him of the fate of his Indian wife, Small Flower, and their unborn child. Once again he was hearing the words

220

spoken in Buck's soft, drawling, carefully unemotional voice, and they came now with the sound of doom. "At the time she got killed," Buck had said, "Small Flower was carrying my baby. After she died, they cut the baby from her stomach. Smothered it, and then buried it with my wife."

Why did he have to think of that now? Justin's hands clenched tightly together. Danger to himself, he could face, had faced. For even now it could still bring with it traces of the old thrill he had once known. But danger to Carrie, he could not face. If he managed to get her out of that village, and he must, he would see to it that she led a serene and peaceful life.

Justin turned his head and found that White Bird was watching him closely. "What is it, White Bird? What are you thinking about?"

"Of you, Lawrence, and of Caroline"

"What about us?"

"I am wondering if Buck Carey and I, between us, can restrain you from plunging into danger?"

"We better," Buck put in, "or all three of us we going to wind up dead."

White Bird nodded. "It is true. But I see signs in you, Lawrence, signs of impatience. I understand this. But if we are to recover Caroline and Lianne, then once again I must advise patience."

"I will listen," Justin answered. "But it does seem to me that we are too far away from the village. I think we should try to move nearer."

"No, Lawrence. In this one thing I must ask you to trust me. There is no other place where we may lie safely concealed. The hill Indians are not fools. They will not easily be taken by surprise. Everywhere, except in this one place, they have their lookouts."

Justin's face darkened. "I understand. But how are we going to get all the way down there, once it is dark? And what of the lookouts then?"

White Bird smiled faintly. "Darkness conceals many things. As for the distance, you have Buck Carey and me to lead you. We both know this country well."

"Better listen, Justin," Buck said quietly. "You're all for rushing in—me too, if it comes to that. But it won't work."

"And are you so sure it will work tonight?"

"Of course I ain't." Buck shrugged. "Never did know any plan to be foolproof. We gotta take a chance on sneaking Caroline and Lianne away while them Injuns are snoring."

"What if they're not sleeping?"

"Most of 'em will be. In case you haven't noticed, Injuns are human too."

Justin made an impatient sound. "I know that," he answered curtly. "I think you know what I mean."

"No need to get your feathers ruffled." Buck pulled his knife from the sheath at his belt. "Them Injuns that ain't sleeping," he said, holding up the knife, "are going to get theirselves silenced all nice and quiet like. I know a few Injun tricks myself. One of 'em is how to come up on the enemy without even stirring a blade of grass. Comes in right handy. Times like this, a knife's better than a pistol." He restored the knife to the sheath. "Well?" he continued, looking steadily at Justin. "You willing to wait out the time?"

"Hardly willing. In any case, I don't appear to have a choice."

"That's right, you don't. 'Less, of course, you ain't minding a lump on your head. Which, I don't mind telling you, I ain't unwilling to give, if you try stirring one goddamned foot from this place."

For the first time in a long while, Justin smiled. "You think you can take me on, Buck?"

"Cain't say. But you try anything, and I aim to have a good try."

Justin nodded. "I believe you. One thing, though. I wish you'd tell me your secret."

"My secret? What do you mean by that?"

"You always seem to be at ease. Always able to laugh at everything."

"That the impression you get?" Buck shrugged. "Ain't no secret. Just my way. Ain't never felt less like laughing in my life."

Before the look in Buck's eyes, Justin flushed darkly and cursed himself for a fool. He was letting nerves guide his tongue, and it would be better if he pulled himself together and saw things as they really were. Again he remembered Buck speaking of the murder of his wife, and of his revenge upon Swift River, his great-grandfather, who had ordered the murder. "Swift River ordered her death, so I killed him.

Wound his goddamned braid 'bout his throat and choked him to death."

Justin, remembering how he had looked then, said quickly, "Sorry, Buck, that was a damn fool thing I said."

"Don't matter. Most folks think that way 'bout me. I'm used to it."

"But I should have known better. In fact, I do know better."

Buck smiled. "I know you do, Justin. So there ain't no need to go lashing yourself. This ain't exactly a normal time for you and me, is it?"

"No." Justin hesitated. "Here's another foolish question for you. Do you think that Carrie and Lianne are still alive?"

"Cain't say about Lianne." Buck answered in a difficult voice. "Could be she's dead. Them Injuns don't know about my feelings for her, so they ain't got no reason to keep her alive. It's a different matter with Caroline. She'll likely be the bait to bring you in, so it wouldn't surprise me none to find her alive. Little Wolf ain't stupid, and he'll have thought of using her as bait."

Before the agony of mind that Buck must be undergoing, Justin felt almost ashamed of the relief he felt. "Lianne too," he said hastily. "I'm sure we'll find her alive."

"Yes," White Bird said in a soft voice. "I too am sure. Lianne would wish to save her life." He looked at Buck. "She will remember that Little Wolf hunts you."

Buck turned somber eyes to the Indian. "You think Lianne will tell them 'bout me?"

"Yes, I think that she might. If she believed the telling was a way of saving her life."

Buck shook his head. "No. I don't believe that."

"It may be that I am deceived. I hope it is so."

"Ain't thinking 'bout myself being used for bait. It's just that I think you're wrong 'bout Lianne."

White Bird inclined his head. "Where Lianne is concerned," he said in a grave voice, "I have been wrong many times. I allowed her to deceive me, and even worse, I deceived myself." He looked at Buck consideringly. "When Lianne saw you, she seemed to change. Yes, it may well be that you are right about her. It may be that she will not speak."

Again Buck's eyes met White Bird's. "There's something I

have to say to you, and it don't come easy. You've got a right to hate me. I knew she was your woman when I took her. And even now, I cain't really say that I'm sorry it happened."

"It is true that I did hate you," White Bird answered. "To say differently would be to lie. But that was because I did not really understand what I was thinking and feeling about Lianne. I thought of Lianne as my woman. I know now that she was never really mine. Therefore, my feelings concerning you have undergone a change. I wish you well. Both you and Lianne."

"If it comes to that," Buck said grimly, "Lianne was never mine. So it looks like we're both in the same canoe." Buck's smile did not hide the pain in his eyes. "It's way too late now, White Bird. Whatever was between me and Lianne is over and done with."

"Nothing is ever over unless the gods decree that it should be so."

Buck's shrug was eloquent. "You think not? Well, now, it seems to me that them gods of yours have been lying down on the job. Either that, or else Lianne ain't been listening too good to what they've got to say."

White Bird hid his shock at these sacrilegious words. "I think that the reason for the hurt you suffer now is because Lianne listens very well to the gods, but it may be that she has not understood them." He looked meaningly at Justin.

Buck's eyes sharpened. "Are you saying that Justin's got something to do with it, White Bird?"

"What do you mean?" Justin said in an astonished voice. "I don't know what went on between you and Lianne, so what could I have to do with it?"

"I saw the way White Bird looked at you," Buck answered. "As though he knew something, or you did. Well, White Bird?"

"No, if you are thinking that Lawrence used you badly, you are mistaken. He has not offered you the hand of friendship while deceiving you behind your back."

"My thanks, White Bird," Justin put in, dryly sarcastic. "I hope I have your vote of confidence too, Buck?"

Buck did not answer. His eyes were still fixed upon White Bird. "What was the meaning of that look, then?"

"You are very perceptive. I should have remembered that. Yes, Lawrence is involved, or he was. But this involvement was not known to him. I say to you again that he is your true friend. He has not deceived you."

Buck met Justin's wrathful eyes. "Cain't say that I really thought you had, Justin," he said in an apologetic voice. "All right, White Bird, I've accepted that. What's the rest of it?"

"At this moment, I would rather not say." White Bird gave him a long, serious look. "But this much I will say. Lawrence's unknowing involvement concerns Lianne's belief in the gods and her own destiny."

"Tell me now," Buck said impatiently.

White Bird shook his head. "No, that is for Lianne to do. All will be revealed to you at the proper time and in the proper place." Folding his lips tightly together as a sign that he would speak no more on the subject, he looked away.

"A proper time and in the proper place?" Buck repeated in a faintly weary voice. "If Little Wolf has his way, there likely won't be a time or a place." He sighed. "All right, White Bird. If you've made up your mind, I won't badger you. I know you won't speak if you don't want to."

"But I think you must speak, White Bird, if you know anything that will set Buck's mind at ease," Justin said quietly. "We don't know what we might find in that village, and it seems to me that there will never be a better time and place than right here. How about it?"

Buck looked at White Bird's expressionless face. "It ain't no use, Justin," he said in a resigned voice. "You're just wasting your breath. Leave him be. You cain't make an Injun speak, not unless he's a mind to." Seeing Justin's expression, he added in a lighter voice, "Come a few years' experience, and you'll be knowing them and their ways."

"Perhaps." Frowning, Justin looked as though he might speak again. Then, thinking better of it, he nodded.

Buck turned his head away. His thoughts, never far these days from Lianne, returned to her at once. He remembered her ardent body lying beneath his, the wildflower smell that arose from her skin. The softness of her breasts and the way she had responded to him, as though he was everything to her. The only man her eyes would ever see. It had turned out to be a lie. But it was something he could remember.

Buck put his knuckles against his mouth. He had taken many women in his time, but only two had had magic for him. His wife, timid, modest, beautiful Small Flower. And

Lianne. Lianne was a child in years, but she was all fire. All woman. Even Small Flower, whom he had loved with a young boy's eager passion and wonder, had not been so wildly and generously giving as Lianne. No, Small Flower had not loved him without restraint, but in her own curiously dear and haunting way.

He remembered the first time he had seen Small Flower. Standing before him, her eyes downcast, she had been so lovely in her doeskin tunic. Her thick black braids were bound with strips of colored leather. The beads with which the tunic was decorated had glittered brightly in the sun. But when she looked at him, it had seemed to him that her large, soft, dark eyes were even brighter.

Small Flower had not come to him out of love. She came to his bed out of duty to her father, who had arranged the marriage. At first she had been afraid of "the white man," as he was called. But it had not been long before she learned to love him. And if it had never been with Lianne's abandoned passion, it was nonetheless a sweet and true love.

Surprised to find that his eyes were wet, Buck rubbed at them impatiently. Always, after he had made love to Small Flower, she would cling to him with something like desperation. With the tears shining on her cheeks, she would say in a choked voice, "I love you, Buck, but it may be that I will die. Or that you will tire of me, as my father tired of my mother. Sooner than have you go back to your white world, where I may not follow, I would have you take another woman into your lodge. Promise me!"

"It may be that I will die." Long afterward, he had thought that Small Flower must have had a premonition of her violent death. But at that time, his only feeling was one of outrage. He loved her so much that another woman was unthinkable. "There will never be another woman for me, Small Flower. I will always love you!"

He had wondered then if she enjoyed tormenting him. He had not been mature enough to conceal his feelings, and he had cried out to her in anguish, "Don't talk like that. I cain't bear it!"

After one such time, Small Flower had drawn his head to her breast. Then, holding him close, she had spoken to him in a low, soothing voice, as though she sought to comfort a child whom she had hurt. "Hush, I am not worthy of your tears."

Even now he could remember her kiss on his hair, just as he would always remember her words to him that day. "You think like a white man. But I am all Indian, and there are visions that I have. Visions that trouble me greatly."

Reluctantly, he had given in. "I promise. But there ain't nothing going to happen to you, my love. I won't let it!"

Small Flower had seemed happier then. Afterward, when he held her in his arms, she was relaxed. So thoughtful of his happiness, in her own strange way. So much more loving than he had realized. And it was this loving woman who had been accused of adultery by a jealous old man who wanted her out of his great-grandson's life.

Buck felt the old familiar bitterness, and he hastily closed his mind against the memory of that last terrible day. No, it was not in Small Flower's nature to respond as passionately as Lianne, but for all that, she had loved him tenderly and truly. Swift River, who had kept to his lies even at the moment of his death, could not tell him otherwise. Small Flower had been his wife, his other self.

Buck closed his eyes tightly. His mind returned to Lianne, who was passion without love. The brief affair with her, during which he had allowed himself to dream again, was over. It was better so. If Lianne still lived, he would make the try to free her. Then, if he managed to come through with a whole skin, he would do as he had promised himself. He would travel on. So it would be the last time he would touch upon her life.

White Bird turned his head and looked at Justin. Lawrence is not with us, he thought. His spirit has flown ahead to Caroline. Justin moved, and White Bird saw his unsmiling eyes. Those eyes of Lawrence's, he thought. They were so intensely dark, so like unto his own eyes and those of his brothers. But they were solemn now, without light. What were the exact thoughts of this man whom Caroline often called "Rogue Lawrence"? he wondered. He felt the same curiosity that he had felt from the first moment of their meeting. Lawrence had committed crimes in his own country; this he knew. When White Bird had gone to Caroline and spoken of this, she had told him that it was true. Because of these crimes, both she and Justin had been sent away from their own country. She had never told him the nature of the crimes, and it was not his way to inquire too deeply. He respected her reserve, as he felt sure she respected his. Still, he had often thought that it must be something very grave indeed to cause a country to reject them.

White Bird frowned thoughtfully. England. That was the name of the country from which Justin Lawrence and Caroline Fane came. It was hard for him to picture England, even though Caroline had tried to describe it to him.

White Bird flicked an ant from his buckskin leggings. Caroline had told him that there was a city. It was full of people, and it was called London. He was not quite sure what a city was. He had wanted to ask her, but he was too proud to show ignorance. Listening to her, he did not think that this London could be like a garden. To him it sounded gray and dirty and overcrowded.

Puzzled, he had remarked on this to Caroline. She had laughed and said, "But London is different, White Bird. There is nowhere else like it in the world. Yes, it is dirty and overcrowded, yet it has a great fascination."

Once, White Bird remembered, he had said to Caroline, "Were you happy in this country across the sea?"

Her face had darkened, as though with some dreadful memory. "When I was a little girl," she had answered him, "I was very happy. It was later, as I grew older, that things began to change."

"Did you know Lawrence when you were a child?"

"No. My meeting with him came much later."

He had been consumed with curiosity, and he had wished to ask questions, but he had not done so. Instinctively he knew that she no longer wished to dwell upon those times in England. What part had Lawrence played in her life? he wondered. When had she met him, and how? Once, passing the open door of Lawrence's shack, he had heard Lawrence say in a laughing voice, "The thief and the lady, Carrie. We are a perfect combination."

"The thief and the lady." White Bird spoke his thoughts aloud.

Justin started. "What did you say, White Bird?"

"It is nothing. I was thinking aloud. It is a habit of mine when I am disturbed."

Justin's eyes held his. "You were thinking of Carrie and Lianne?"

"Of Caroline," White Bird answered truthfully. "Yes, Lawrence."

"I have done nothing else but think of them." Justin looked up at the sky. "It is darkening over there," he said, pointing.

White Bird heard the eagerness in his voice, and he frowned uneasily. Lawrence was hard to hold. But he must be held for quite some time yet. "Yes, Lawrence," he answered, "soon it will be dark. But we must still wait. We cannot leave this place at the moment the sun deserts the sky."

"He's right, Justin." Buck did not turn his head as he spoke. "Take it easy. We'll have to give them braves time to settle for the night."

A shadow crossed Justin's face. "Wait, wait," he said impatiently. "I don't think I can stand much more of it."

"You will stand it, Lawrence, because you must," White Bird said quietly. "And because, in your heart, you know that the waiting is necessary." He paused, and then added with a touch of admiration, "It is apparent to me that there is no fear in you. You are a true warrior."

Justin heard Buck's stifled laugh. He said quickly, "You are wrong, White Bird, there is plenty of fear in me. The man who knows no fear does not exist. Or, if he does, he is totally without imagination."

"But despite this fear, you will still try to rescue Caroline?"

"Yes. A man does what he must do."

White Bird was silent for a long time. "Your words bring me much comfort," he said at last. "I have often known fear. Because of this, I believed myself to be a coward. This is a hard confession for me to make, but it is true."

Justin looked at the crouched figure of the Indian boy, at the scarlet feathers stuck through his hair knot, the barbaric chains of copper about his neck, and suddenly the whole situation seemed unreal. Was it really he, Justin Lawrence, sitting here with a buckskin-clad drifter and an Indian? He had traveled far since those days in England, and he had undergone much suffering, but never, not in his wildest flights of imagination, could he have pictured himself lying here, waiting for the darkness to fall, so that he might steal into an Indian village and rescue his woman. He thought of the fate that would be theirs, should they be discovered, and he shuddered inwardly.

"You do not answer me, Lawrence."

Justin looked up and met White Bird's eyes. "Sorry. Tell me, White Bird, on those occasions when you knew fear, did you turn away from the object of your fear?"

"No, Lawrence."

"Then you are no coward."

Little Antelope stopped walking. It was growing dark, and he had wandered far from his village. He felt a touch of fear at the thought of facing his father's wrath. But surely today, on the occasion of his tenth birthday, his father would overlook it? To give himself confidence, Little Antelope touched the small bow slung over his shoulder. Then he touched the quiver of arrows, and last his hair, which had been freshly oiled and braided in honor of his tenth year on this earth. No, he did not believe that his father would be seriously angry with him. Not on this, his special day. All the same, it might be better to retrace his steps. But first he would rest for a while. He had walked for a long time, and his feet were sore.

Little Antelope sat down with a sigh of relief, and rested his back against the trunk of a tree. Near to him, closed in by trees and thornbushes, was the stretch of ground that lay above his village. Although it was near to him, he could not help being glad that it was not too near. The stretch of ground, left unguarded by his people, was sacred, for it was said that the gods congregated there at nights and laughed and danced together. When Little Wolf became chief, he had wanted to put a guard here, in case his enemies from beyond the waterfall should intrude upon this happy place of the gods. He had not done so, because the people had made a great fuss. He was the chief, and they were bound to obey him, they said, but in this one thing he went too far. The gods would be angry if they were spied upon.

Little Antelope turned his head away. "I am not spying," he said in a faint whisper. "Sacred gods, hear me. I am not spying!"

To demonstrate his good faith, Little Antelope pretended to be very busy with other things. Taking an arrow from the quiver, he poked its head into a small anthill. He had often wondered if ants slept at nights, as humans did. If only he had the magic to make himself very small, he would crawl into the anthill and see for himself what the ants were doing.

But since he could not go in and see the ants, they must come out and see him. Again he thrust the head of the arrow into the anthill. For a little while he watched the aimless scurrying of the tiny creatures who had erupted forth at his insistent prodding; then he lost interest.

Unwilling to move for the moment, Little Antelope closed his eyes and gave himself up to thoughts of the white woman who was Bright Feather's prisoner. When Bright Feather had first arrived in triumph with the woman, he had been about to set forth on his exploring expedition. He was anxious to inspect a certain cave, where, it was said, the spirits of health, humor, and worthy ambition lived. The squaws had been very excited when they had seen the woman standing beside Bright Feather. Far more excited then they had been when Tall Tree had delivered the half-breed woman to the village elders. The braves had not moved; they had been content to stare. But the squaws had rushed toward the woman, screaming angrily.

Little Antelope's lips drew in as he continued to ponder on the matter. His father often accused him of being dull-witted, but there were often times when he saw things very clearly. And it had seemed to him that the squaws, despite their show of almost hysterical anger, were really more frightened than angry. It was fear that had driven them into such a frenzy.

Little Antelope plucked a blade of grass. Putting it in his mouth, he sucked on it reflectively. Perhaps he would not have thought of fear in connection with the screaming squaws, had he not seen his mother's expression as she ran forward with the others. He always knew when she was afraid. Was it the pale-skin woman's oddly colored hair they feared, the big brown eyes set in the white face, the strangeness of her? Did they believe that she might be a demon sent to bring trouble and tragedy upon them all? He had watched as the squaws, his mother among them, punched with clenched fists at the woman's body, pulled at her hair, and pinched her skin. Finally, when they had torn her single garment from her body, he had turned away. It was not that he did not want to look at the woman, for indeed he was very interested. It was simply that the call of adventure was stronger than his curiosity. Anyway, unless Little Wolf had already had her put to death, there would be time enough for him to inspect the pale-skin.

Frowning, Little Antelope stirred uneasily. For a long time now, he suddenly realized, he had been hearing a soft murmuring sound. Occupied with thoughts of the woman, he had pushed the sound to the back of his mind. But now it had impinged upon his consciousness, bringing him fully alert. Sitting up straighter, he put his head to one side and listened intently. It could not be the wind sighing through the trees, he decided, for he knew well that the wind had long since died. The wind god rested from his labors, and even the leaves above his head were motionless. The murmuring sounded like voices talking together. And those voices, he felt sure, were coming from the sacred place!

Trying to stifle the fear that gripped him, he concentrated on a caterpillar that was inching along the large speckled leaf of a low-growing plant. He found that he could not concentrate. The caterpillar, though fascinating, did not hold his interest.

Hoping to steady himself and drive some of the fear away, Little Antelope drew in a deep breath as he got slowly and carefully to his feet. It could not be the gods who held conversation there, for everyone knew that they did not come until it was full dark. It must be humans in the sacred place.

Little Antelope would have liked to run away. Instead, calling upon his pride, he decided to investigate. After all, he was no longer a child. He was almost a man. He touched his oiled braids for reassurance. Full of fear, he placed his moccasined feet in the way that his painstaking father had taught him, and moved forward soundlessly. His father's voice, patient, instructive, sounded in the ears of his memory. "Not a twig must crack, my son. Not a leaf must rustle beneath your feet, or you will give warning to him whom you stalk."

Little Antelope's heart was pounding when he stopped before the trees that screened the sacred place. The voices, though pitched low, sounded very loud in his ears now. He was almost afraid to look, yet pride, honor to himself, demanded that he should. Careful not to be seen, he peered through a narrow opening in the trees. Then, his eyes widening, he saw them. Two pale-skins and an Indian. The Indian held a small stick in his hand, with which he was absently prodding at the ground. He was not one of the enemy who lived beyond the waterfall. Little Antelope studied the Indian's coiled hair, the special way in which the scarlet feathers decorating it were crossed, and he knew him for a member of a tribe who dwelt many miles from here. Little Antelope's lip curled slightly. The scarlet feathers were merely decoration: they were not coup feathers. The Indian seemed to him to be quite old. Having reached his advanced age, he should surely have earned many coup feathers.

Little Antelope's eyes turned to the dark-haired pale-skin and studied him long and carefully. The pale-skin was broad-shouldered, and although he was seated, it could readily be seen that he was very tall. His skin was burned to a deep-brown by the sun, though it did not have the distinctive coppery hue of the Indian beside him. His hair curled thickly over his head, and curling tendrils touched his broad forehead. Admiring him, Little Antelope could not help wondering if this dark hawk of a man might not be one of the white people's gods.

Little Antelope looked at the other pale-skin. He was handsome, too, though in a rugged way that was different from the godlike man. He also had dark hair. It was thick, and it curled just as vigorously, but it was shorter than that of the other pale-skin. Both men had touches of winter in their hair.

Caution came to Little Antelope. Although he knew that his buckskins blended in well with the trees and the earth, he was still fearful of being seen, and he drew back slowly.

"Curse this lingering daylight," Little Antelope heard one of the men say. "It seems to go on forever."

"It'll be dark soon, Justin," the other replied. "So you just hold your horses."

Little Antelope waited for no more. Withdrawing as soundlessly as he had approached, he reached a place that he considered to be beyond earshot of the intruders. Now he could no longer see the godlike man, anger took the place of awe. He must return with all speed to his village. The elders must be told of this outrage of the sacred ground. They would know what to do about it. The punishment, he was sure, would be very severe.

Little Antelope, regretting the lack of a horse, began to run. He could run very fast. Some of his comrades had said that he should have been named Swift as the Wind. Thinking of this, his chest swelling with pride, he redoubled his efforts.

He had run so well that it was still not quite dark when he came into the village. The first person he saw was Black Cloud. Black Cloud was scowling, and he was muttering angrily to himself. Seeing him like this, Little Antelope, although he was full of news, hesitated to approach him. It was well-known that Black Cloud, although he had not yet reached full maturity, had a very fierce temper indeed.

"Black Cloud . . ." Overcoming his hesitation, Little Antelope touched his arm and brought him to a halt. "There is a thing I must tell you."

The young warrior looked at Little Antelope, but he did not seem to see him. Little Antelope plunged into his story of the outrage, but before he had proceeded very far, he knew that Black Cloud had not been listening.

"I will kill him!" Black Cloud muttered, his hands clenching spasmodically. "Have I not sworn to kill any who lay hands upon the maiden? I have made this vow, and I will keep it. I will kill him!"

"Whom will you kill?" Little Antelope faltered, disturbed by his ferocity. "If you speak of the intruders, there are three of them."

Black Cloud did not answer. Without another glance at Little Antelope, he strode away.

Little Antelope stood there for a moment; then he hurried on. Someone must listen to him. The intruders must be captured and brought back to the village for punishment. Soon it would be too dark to capture an enemy. To do so would mean that one would be caught by the forces of darkness, and then one's soul would be doomed. It would be without hope of ever entering that glorious afterlife where one walked and talked and smoked the sacred pipe with the gods. Where all was grace, beauty, and peace, and the bountiful game awaited the warrior's arrow.

Shuddering, Little Antelope came to a halt. Hurry, hurry! said the frantic beat of his heart. There is still time, Little Atnelope said to himself. The horses will carry the warriors swiftly to the place that has been defiled. They will be back with the prisoners before darkness throws its final blanket over the earth.

Little Antelope looked wildly about him, wondering whom to approach. He gave a sob of relief as he saw the tall warrior emerging from Little Wolf's wigwam. "Bright Feather!" Forgetting the dignity of bearing his father had always impressed upon him, he rushed forward. "Bright Feather, there is a thing I must tell you!"

Chapter 18

The sturdy squaw exclaimed in amazement as the white woman struggled to her feet again. Turning to her companion, she said in a low voice, "Three times have I felled this one, and you have seen that my hand has not been light upon her, and three times has she picked herself up from the ground. Truly the demons have put great strength into this skinny pale-skin. I, Falling Snow, tell you this."

Bright Rainbow felt an unfamiliar pang as she stared at the swaying white woman. "Look closer, Falling Snow," she said, speaking out impulsively. "Do you not see that it is her pride that gives her this strength?" She laid tentative fingers on Falling Snow's brawny arm. "Tall Tree tells me that her child was born dead. It was a brave. It would seem to me that she has been through much. Should we not leave her in peace for a little while?"

Falling Snow turned her fierce black eyes on Bright Rainbow. "Your heart is made of mush!" she shouted. "I have always suspected it. This woman is the enemy. How can you feel pity for her?"

Bright Rainbow flushed as the laughter of the other squaws sounded in her ears. "It is not that I pity her," she flashed. Her eyes swept the ring of grinning faces. "We have all tormented her, have we not? I say that enough is enough!"

Falling Snow's lip curled into a sneer. "We all see through you, Rainbow. It is because your womb is barren and your breasts empty that you feel for this one." She laughed. "You envy me my son. Can you deny it?"

Again color swept over Bright Rainbow's wizened face. "I do envy you your son, Falling Snow," she answered quietly. "Little Antelope will grow into a brave warrior. But then, since my time of child bearing is long over, I envy all women their sons."

Falling Snow lost interest in the conversation. Looking up at the darkening sky, she wondered where Little Antelope was.

"Move aside." Falling Snow's question was answered by the impatient voice of her son. Unobserved, Little Antelope had approached the group of women, and was now pushing at them in order to make his way to his mother's side.

Falling Snow leaped forward and clutched at the boy. "Where have you been?" she shouted, shaking him.

Little Antelope pulled himself free of his mother's clutching hands. He would have her remember that he was almost a man. Lifting his braided head, he said coldly, "I have been keeping watch upon the intruders. Those three who have defiled the happy meeting place of the gods."

Blotchy color mounted in Falling Snow's cheeks. "If I find that it is a lie you tell me, I will take over the whip when your father has finished with it, and I will add to your punishment."

Little Antelope heard the snickering of the other squaws. His mother still insisted upon treating him as a child. He stared into his mother's eyes. Before his gaze, hers dropped. With a haughtiness of manner he had never dared to use with her before this day, he said, "You crow big, my mother. But it will be best if you remember that you are only a woman."

Falling Snow glared at him. "There is something that you must remember. I am your mother!"

"As my mother, I will give you respect. If you, in your turn, will remember that I have today reached my tenth birthday."

Falling Snow was silent. It was true, she thought, feeling a pain at her heart. He was almost a man. Soon he would have gone beyond a mother's domination. Truly the lot of a woman was hard. "My son," she said almost meekly, "if I have offended you, I ask your pardon. It is true that I am only a woman, but there is love in my heart for you."

"And in mine for you, my mother."

Falling Snow smiled. "Tell us about the intruders in the sacred place, my son."

Little Antelope glanced across at the white woman. She was on her feet, her back pressed for support against the trunk of a tree. Someone had supplied her with a buckskin tunic. It was much too big for her, and it hung baggily about

her slender form. Her light hair had been pulled back from
her face, braided tightly, and twined with strips of colored
leather. It was strange to see her dressed thus, he thought,
when the marks of evil treatment flared scarlet across her
white face. One eye was swollen shut, and her lips were
puffed to twice their size. He did not doubt that the lavishly
beaded tunic hid further signs of brutality. This did not trouble him. It was natural to punish the enemy. But he did wonder why such care had been taken with her outer appearance.
Puzzled, he looked at his mother.

Falling Snow saw the question in his eyes, and she hurried
to enlighten him. "The white woman is to be offered to the
warriors. They will use her body."

"And afterward, my mother, when they have tired of her,
what then?"

Falling Snow shrugged. He asked too many questions, this
son of hers. "She will be a slave."

Little Antelope frowned, refusing to allow himself to feel
sorry for the white woman. "And is the same thing to happen
to the half-breed?" he asked.

Falling Snow smiled at him. "Little Wolf plans to take the
half-breed into his lodge for his own use. For a time, until he
wearies of her, she will be favored. But when his weariness
grows too heavy to support, she will become a slave, even as
the white woman."

"Perhaps he will not weary of her."

"He will. I do not believe the woman exists who could
hold Little Wolf's interest for long." Little Antelope could
smell the stale bear grease on his mother's hair as she leaned
nearer to him. "Black Cloud dares not show it openly,"
Falling Snow went on in a whisper, "but he is very angry. We
all believe that he wanted the half-breed for himself."

"Why do you believe this?"

"Do you remember the mission upon which Little Wolf
sent him?" Little Antelope nodded, and Falling Snow,
pitching her voice so low that the others could not hear, went
on quickly. "As it turned out, Black Cloud did not kill
Lawrence. Instead, mistakenly, he buried his knife in someone of unimportance."

"Everyone knows that," Little Antelope said impatiently.

Ignoring his impatience, Falling Snow went on serenely,
"When Little Wolf found out that the mission had failed, he

was full of anger. But, if you remember, Black Cloud hardly noticed. He was too full of praises for a certain maiden."

Little Antelope stared at her, his eyes round with wonder. "The half-breed?"

Falling Snow nodded. "Yes. The same. Black Cloud has said it. She has a strange name. She is called Lianne. I tell you, my son, Black Cloud is rebellious and angry because Little Wolf has decided to take the maiden for his own. Yet, knowing the temper of Little Wolf, he will be wise to hide his feelings. It was only because the god of good fortune favored him that Little Wolf did not have him put to death for his failure to kill Lawrence."

Little Antelope felt a trembling inside him. He had an affection for Black Cloud, who had sometimes stooped from the great height of his manhood to play at hunting the buffalo with him. His mother had said that Black Cloud dared not show his anger openly. But he *was* showing it. "I will kill him!" he had said. Remembering the look in Black Cloud's eyes, the clenching and unclenching of his hands, Little Antelope shivered. He thought of Black Cloud as his friend, and he did not want him to be hurt. But if he showed his anger and resentment too plainly, he would be.

Falling Snow was disturbed by the expression on her son's face. "What is it?" she said softly. "You look troubled."

"It is nothing, my mother." Little Antelope did not think it would be wise to give voice to his concern. With a wish to change the subject, he glanced across at the white woman. "What is her name?"

"The half-breed has said that her name is Caroline. She is the woman of Lawrence."

Little Antelope gasped. The white warrior who was hated by Little Wolf. His mother had announced it as if it were quite unimportant. "My mother," he said faintly, wishing to be sure, "would this be the same Lawrence whom Little Wolf has sworn to torture to death?"

Falling Snow nodded. "It would."

"Then that is why Little Wolf lets her live? Lawrence will find out who has taken her, and he will come for her."

Falling Snow bowed her head. "You are so wise, my son. I, being only a woman, had not thought of that."

Little Antelope gave her a sharp look. Did she mock him? Suddenly convinced that she did, he was about to speak rebukingly, when Falling Snow, forestalling him, laid a tender hand on his plump shoulder. "My son, you were going to tell us about the intruders in the sacred place."

"There are three men," Little Antelope said, nodding. "One is an Indian, though of a different tribe from ours." He looked down at his moccasined feet for a moment. Then, bringing up his head again, he said in an important voice, "As for the other two men, they are pale-skins. Even now Bright Feather and his warriors ride to capture them." He could not help smiling at the concerted gasp that arose. "It is true," he went on. "I, Little Antelope, tell you this. Bright Feather and his warriors will return before it is full dark, for their animals are swift. The intruders will be with them."

Falling Snow looked at him with unfeigned admiration. "And to think it is you, my own son, who discovered them and brought back the news. You are indeed a man!"

"He is indeed a man!" the other women echoed. Crying out, they crowded closer, their hands reaching out to touch him. "Before many moons have passed," an old woman cried, "the coup feathers will be thick in his hair."

Falling Snow loved her son. She was proud of him. But now, seeing his complacent smile, the way he preened himself beneath the women's admiration, she remembered that he had humiliated her before them. Obeying a small spiteful impulse, she lifted her arm and pointed a finger at the white woman. "And you shall have the same sport as a man, for you have earned it," she said in a hearty voice. "There is the woman. Use her, if it pleases you to do so."

Little Antelope felt an inner shrinking. Why had his mother said this thing to him? It was true that he was almost a man, but he was not yet ready to take a woman. Quite suddenly, seeing the expectant faces turned his way, he wanted to weep. He swallowed hard, hoping that the flame of embarrassment mounting in his face was hidden by the half-dark. "The woman must wait until I have refreshed myself with sleep," he said in the haughtiest voice he could muster. "I have traveled far today, and I am weary."

Falling Snow was already regretting her spite. She wanted to catch the boy in her arms and hide his hot, embarrassed face against her breast, but she could not bring herself to climb down yet. Once she had taken up a certain position, it was always hard for her to abandon it, and even harder to apologize. Her husband, Brave Hawk, was often angered by this fault in her. She spoke again, her hard voice hiding the contrition she felt. "But I pray you to take her, my son. You will be the first to use her. If you take her before the other warriors, just think of the honor that will be yours."

Little Antelope did not want the woman. His only feeling toward her was one of curiosity. All he wanted was to go to his lodge, lie down, and pull the fur robe over him. Swallowing a yawn, he turned to his mother and looked fully into her eyes. "Do not pester me," he said coldly. "When a man is tired, a woman is unimportant. She will not run away. She will still be there when I am rested."

Falling Snow was silent for a moment. Then, nodding, she said in a gentle voice, "I should have remembered that you would be weary. You are right. The woman can wait."

Little Antelope was eager to be gone. But still, he thought, it might be best to make a small show. "Before I make my way to the lodge," he said, "I will examine this woman. She is the first pale-skin woman I have seen."

Caroline's heart jumped as a hand touched her arm. She opened her heavy eyes. A short, plump little boy was staring at her, his dark eyes bright with curiosity. Firelight glowed on his round face, on the thick oiled braids that were decorated with yellow feathers. He wore fringed buckskin trousers. His tunic, also fringed at the sleeves, was lavishly decorated with brilliantly dyed porcupine quills in various colors. About his short, thick neck was a necklace of rough red stones. His ears had been pierced, and the same red stones weighted down his earlobes.

When he did not speak, Caroline said in a thick, difficult voice, "Go away."

"I will go away when I am ready." He picked up her hand. His fingers tightened as she cried out and tried to snatch it away. Turning her hand over, he examined the palm. "Your hand is very white," he said at last. "Almost as white as the snow after which my mother was named. It is clear to me that the sun god does not love you." Losing interest, he dropped her hand. "My name is Little Antelope," he told her. "Today I have done two things. I have made celebration of the tenth year of my life, and I have sent Bright Feather to capture two pale-skins and an Indian who were intruding upon the sacred ground of the gods."

Caroline hardly heard him. Her head was throbbing, there was a fever in her body, and her tongue was swollen. But her brain had registered the facts that he was only a boy and that his eyes were not unkind. Perhaps she could appeal to him. Her puffed lips moved, bringing out mumbled, painful words. "W-water. Please b-bring me water!"

Little Antelope was sorry for her. He would have liked to bring her water, but with the squaws looking on, he did not dare. As he had said, he was almost a man, and they must not think him weak. "I will give you water," he said in a loud voice. "Here it is, pale-skin." Pursing his lips, he spat at her. "There! Is the water good?"

He walked away. With a little cry of despair, Caroline sagged to the ground. Her thoughts whirled in hot confusion. She did not know why she had been dressed in this way, or why her hair had been braided like an Indian squaw's. The women had worked over her in grim silence, refusing to answer her questions. But if she did not know, she could most certainly guess at the reason.

Caroline pressed both hands to the ground and tried to raise herself. It was no use, she thought, as she fell back again; she could not bring her body to obey her will. She was in too much pain. Soon the braves would come to surround her. They would use her body, and under their rough and merciless usage she would die.

Forgetting the women who were looking on, she put her hand to her trembling mouth. She was finished, beaten. She was going to die. The thought was terrible. She was young, and she had so much to live for. But even so, she could accept death, she could even accept whatever torture they chose to inflict upon her, if only she could see Justin once more before she died. She whispered, "Once more, my love," as weak tears seeped from her eyes.

Caroline stared up at the sky, but she did not really see it. Instead, she saw Justin's face. The dark eyes in his brown face were tender. She had the strange impression that he was there, trying to give her new strength. Almost, she could see him stooping over her. She put up a weak hand to smooth back the hair that fell curling over his forehead, but she encountered only air. He was not there, but in spirit he was near to her. She knew it. She was a fool to think he would forget her. They were two of a kind, she and Justin. From the very beginning, even though they had fought, they had been meant to love each other. Her swollen lips moved, forming words. "I love you, Justin. You can no more forget me, I know, than I could forget you."

Caroline started as the drums began again. Every so often they rose to a shattering crescendo, driving her mad. There was something she had to think about. Whatever it was, it had been nibbling at the back of her mind. It was time to bring it forth and examine it.

Her brow wrinkling in fierce concentration, Caroline turned her head and stared toward the blazing fire in the center of the compound. The drums died to a gentle murmur, and with their dying, the image of the boy with the yellow feathers in his hair rose up before her. It was something the boy had said to her—that was what she had to think about. Slowly the words he had spoken came back to her: "I have sent Bright Feather to capture two pale-skins and an Indian who were intruding upon the sacred ground of the gods."

Two pale-skins and an Indian! Caroline could not help the wild hope that surged through her. Then, as she began to think of the consequences to them, should Bright Feather capture them and herd them back to the village, the hope died. She could not bear to see them tortured and broken, as she had been. Heedless of the eyes upon her, she whispered a desperate prayer. "Dear God, let it not be them. There is nothing they can do. Let them get away."

Lianne's dark-blue eyes were blazing with hatred. The hatred set the blood pounding through her, driving out fear. Screaming, kicking, she struggled madly, trying to break the grip the two squaws had on her arms. The tall squaw on Lianne's left raised her hand and dealt her a stinging slap on the side of her head. She laughed as the girl gave a choked cry. Taking a tighter grip on her victim's arm, she signaled to her companion to do the same. Together, the two women rushed her over the uneven ground toward the little stream that lay at the foot of the village. With a mighty push they sent her flying forward.

The icy waters of the stream closed over Lianne's head cutting off her screams. The tall squaw began to laugh as the girl's head broke the surface. Watching her frantic efforts to flounder to the safety of the bank, she called out in a jeering voice, "You will stay where you are, half-breed, until I say you may come out. When Little Wolf sends for you, the stink must be gone from your body."

Lianne pushed her wet hair back from her eyes. Spitting water from her mouth, she shrieked her defiant answer, "I will never go to Little Wolf! Do you hear me, you daughter of a diseased bitch? I will die before I let him put his hands upon me!"

The shorter, round-faced squaw joined in the laughter as Lianne managed to get one knee on the bank. "Cease your weeping and wailing," she shouted, pushing her back into the water. "You will die soon enough, half-breed, once Little Wolf has tired of you and cast you from his lodge."

"May the gods strike down you and yours, you pig-faced bitch!" Lianne slapped her hands upon the water, spattering the squaw. "May demons lodge in your guts!"

From his position among the concealing trees, Black Cloud looked on with brooding eyes. He saw the shorter of the two squaws, Opening Rose, the wife of Young Deer, wade into the water, her hand raised to punish the insult. He saw Lianne duck beneath the water. Bubbles arose, and her long black hair floated on the surface.

"She has bitten my leg!" It was a shriek from Opening Rose. "Come here, you half-breed. I'll kill you for that! I will see to it that the worms will soon be feeding upon your filthy carcass!" In her eagerness to grab Lianne, Opening Rose lost her footing. Immediately Lianne's arms closed tightly about her, forcing her downward.

With Opening Rose's cry for help ringing in his ears, Black Cloud turned away from the struggle taking place in the water. He did not fear for Lianne. The squaws would not dare to harm her. If they did, they would have to answer to Little Wolf.

Black Cloud touched the knife at his belt. "And you, Little Wolf," he muttered, "you will answer to me. Lianne is mine. You knew I desired her, and you have done this thing deliberately. Even as you said you would take her into your lodge to be your woman, your eyes were upon me, your mouth sneering. Lianne was meant to be mine. I knew it from the first moment I saw her. You shall not have her!"

The burning in Black Cloud's brain increased as he drew nearer to Little Wolf's lodge. There was a way he could enter the wigwam undetected by the others, so, for the moment, he was safe enough. In his arrogance and his belief in his own omnipotence, Little Wolf posted no guards before his lodge. Also, at this particular hour of the day, he liked to be alone to think his thoughts undisturbed.

Black Cloud's mouth twisted in bitter hatred. Little Wolf, though he did not know it, had little time left to him. He would not, in any case, be thinking his deep thoughts now. His mind would be occupied with the coming of Lianne, and he would be preparing himself for her. Black Cloud's anger grew as he pictured Little Wolf unbraiding his long black hair and shaking it loose about his shoulders. He would rub into his hair the perfumed grease that was always used by the warriors to titillate a maiden's senses. He would be naked at the top, so that she might note and admire the scars of bravery and honor that seamed his broad chest. Later, just before Lianne was brought before him, he would paint the scarlet stripe of passion upon his forehead.

Seated cross-legged before the fire in the center of his lodge, Little Wolf was smiling to himself. Everything was going his way, he thought, running his hand down the greased length of his hair. He had Lawrence's woman, and if he knew anything of the man, Lawrence would come for her. When he did, he would be ready. It might even be that Buck Carey, who was Lawrence's friend, would be with him. He hoped very much that this would be so. But even if he were not with Lawrence, it made little difference. Sooner or later both would be in his hands. Not one of his enemies, or any that stood in his way, should escape him. In time he would annihilate them all.

Pleased with this thought, Little Wolf laughed aloud. His narrow eyes gleaming with amusement, he pondered on Black Cloud. Black Cloud, from being the devoted admirer who hung on his every word, had become his enemy. When he had announced his intention of taking the half-breed maiden with the strange name into his lodge, had he not seen the hatred looking plainly from the youth's eyes? Yes, Black Cloud was his enemy now, and he had also failed him. Therefore, he must be punished. Little Wolf had started that punishment by taking the maiden of Black Cloud's desire from him, but it was not enough. Later, when he had the time to sit in judgment, he would think of other things. Perhaps the crippling of those strong young limbs. Perhaps a lingering tortured death. He had the power to order whatever punishment he desired. He would be obeyed. He was Little Wolf, the chief.

Little Wolf frowned as a memory of Running Fox, his father, came to him. Running Fox would not approve. He would say that he acted without honor. A chief must not behave out of motives of spite. He must not let his anger overflow and cloud his judgment. The thought of his father's displeasure had shaken his nerves. To calm himself, Little Wolf picked up his pipe. He ran his finger down the smooth stem. Then, taking a rawhide pouch from his belt, he opened it and filled the bowl of the pipe with kinnikinnick. Lighting it, he drew the smoke from the mixture of dried leaves and bark into his lungs. The smoke sent out a pleasing aromatic odor, soothing him and banishing the memory of his father.

Little Wolf lay down on his bed of skins, his feet toward the fire. He began to think of Lianne. The pipe dropped unheeded from his hand as his body quickened with desire. Soon his body would be joined with hers. A pleasant lassitude stole over Little Wolf. He closed his eyes. It was a pity he could not make children to succeed him as chief. Instead, if he should be the first to die, Bright Feather would become chief.

Little Wolf moved restlessly. It was a displeasing thought, for he had long nourished a hatred for Bright Feather. He frowned. He would not think of him now. Deliberately, as he had long since accustomed himself to do, he made his mind a blank from earthly things. Instead, he allowed it to wander across the night sky. He ran in and out of the clustering stars and made his way toward the moon. For a moment he held the brilliant orb between his two hands. Then, releasing it gently, he turned about and began to travel down the misty hill that led toward the bright sky of day. He would have liked to hold the sun between his hands, but he feared that it would burn him. Little Wolf smiled. It was a pleasing fantasy. Whenever he was disturbed, he always allowed his mind to run away and roam those two skies.

Black Cloud looked through a chink in the curtain of woven grass that divided Little Wolf's wigwam, making it into two rooms. He was certain that no one had seen him, for he had entered the wigwam from the back. Careful to make no noise, he had lifted a corner of the hide covering and rolled his body beneath. Once inside the wigwam, he had got noiselessly to his feet and approached the curtain. For a long time he had simply stood there, his hand over his mouth so that his breathing should not be heard, but now he was ready to act. Little Wolf's eyes were closed now, and he appeared to be composing himself for slumber.

Frowning, Black Cloud looked at Little Wolf's relaxed limbs. He could steal upon Little Wolf and slit his throat. Or he could announce his presence and allow Little Wolf to see his executioner. He decided upon the latter. Kill him, he most certainly would, but there was something distasteful about stealing upon a man who was completely unaware of his presence.

Gripping his knife in his right hand, Black Cloud thrust the curtain to one side. "Little Wolf," he said in a harsh voice, "I am here."

With a start, Little Wolf opened his eyes. "What are you doing here?" he said haughtily. Sitting up, he stared coldly at Black Cloud. "I have not sent for you."

"No." Black Cloud lifted his hand and allowed Little Wolf to see the knife. "You have not sent for me, but nevertheless I am here. I have come to kill you."

"Kill me?" Little Wolf's jaw dropped. "Do you dare to say you will kill me, your chief!"

Black Cloud's face was expressionless, but his black eyes were fiery with the hatred consuming him. This man who lay now before him, his eyes darting swiftly about him, seeking help was no longer the object of his worship. He had thought Little Wolf to be larger than life, a warrior above all others, but now he seemed small and shriveled. Because of his arrogance in believing himself invincible, he had sent the guard away. He must know that no help was available to him.

Little Wolf did know. He also knew, unless Black Cloud came to his senses, that he was only a step away from death. "Why do you not answer me?" he shouted. "You will pay for this threat against my life, Black Cloud. I will have you staked out and tortured to death!"

"It is too late," Black Cloud said quietly. "You are going to die. A dead man cannot give orders."

Little Wolf stared at him. His death was written in Black Cloud's eyes. Little Wolf's thoughts flew in wild confusion. He had loosened his belt when he lay down, and the sheath containing his knife had somehow slipped beneath him. He jerked his body upward, feeling for the sheath. His hand closed about the hilt of his knife, and he clawed it from the sheath. Before his arm could lift and throw, Black Cloud's weapon arced toward him.

Little Wolf gave a strangled scream as the knife thudded into his breast. He fell back, the scream turning to a low gurgling sound in his throat as he fought for breath. A spreading fire in his chest was consuming his life. His eyes protruding with horror, he lifted his hand, his fingers scrabbling feebly at the hilt of the knife. Tears sprang into his eyes at the futility of the action. His strength was fast fading. He could not pull the blade free; it had entered too deeply. His life was ebbing away on a tide of scarlet, and with it his will to survive.

Black Cloud stood there motionless. He could not understand the expression on Little Wolf's dying face. He moved slowly forward. There was no guilt in him, no regret. Little Wolf had taken his woman. Black Cloud had done what had to be done. As he went to stand over Little Wolf, he found himself remembering the words of Little Eagle, who undetected, had once listened in on a prayer meeting given by a pale-skin woman. "The white squaw read aloud from a big black book," Little Eagle told him. "The words she read were these: 'Vengeance is mine, saith the Lord.' I do not know, but I believe these were the words of her great white God."

"Vengeance is mine," Black Cloud muttered, staring down at Little Wolf. He raised Little Wolf's head and looked into the wide-open, staring eyes. Shuddering, he let the head drop. Bending over, he pressed his ear against the motionless chest. Not a sound from within. Not the faintest whisper of life. Little Wolf was dead!

A pulse throbbed heavily in Black Cloud's temple, and now the full horror of what he had done overcame him. Hesitantly, he stretched out his hand toward the knife. Before he could touch the hilt, he snatched his hand back again.

Black Cloud rose to his feet. For the last time, he looked down at Little Wolf. He knew then that he had lost. He had killed the chief! His soul would forever be stained with the blood of Little Wolf. In killing him, he had enslaved himself. He must be punished for what he had done. His first inclination had been to steal away and leave the body of Little Wolf to be found by someone else. He could not do it. He was a murderer, his honor demanded that he turn himself over to justice. He had dreamed of eventual happiness with Lianne, but the dream was over.

As Black Cloud pushed aside the flap that guarded the entrance to the wigwam, he thought of his mother. When she knew what he had done, her heart would be broken. He had taken a life, and in return his brothers would take his.

Tall Tree, who was standing by the fire staring into the flames, looked up as Black Cloud approached him. "So there you are," he said in a peevish voice. "I have waited for a long time for the others to gather about the fire. I have many interesting tales to impart. Their slowness in gathering makes me think that they wish to avoid me."

Black Cloud said nothing. He stood before Tall Tree, his head bowed. Tall Tree gazed at him, his eyes sharpening with curiosity. "What is it?" he said. "What is wrong?"

Black Cloud raised his head and looked at him. "I seek Bright Feather," he said in a quiet, colorless voice. "Where is he?"

Tall Tree was annoyed by Black Cloud's evasion of his question. "I can tell you that he will soon be here. The lookout has reported that he is on his way back to the village." Relenting, Tall Tree ventured another question. "Your manner is strange, my brother. Why do you seek Bright Feather?"

Black Cloud's eyes went to the tall, slim squaw who was standing within earshot. It was Spring Rain. She could nearly always be found hovering in the vicinity of Little Wolf's wigwam. He felt a shuddering inside him as he thought of what he had to say. But Spring Rain would know soon enough that Little Wolf was dead. It was best that she heard it now. From him. Raising his voice, he said clearly, "I seek Bright Feather so that I may be the first to give my homage to the new chief."

Now Tall Tree noticed Spring Rain standing there. At Black Cloud's words, he saw her body stiffen and her eyes widen. He frowned. Spring Rain's open and unashamed love for Little Wolf was a disgrace to her dignity. It was not proper that a squaw should behave so. He wanted to tell her to go away and not to listen in on the private conversation of men. He found that he could not do it. Black Cloud's words and her stiff stance had filled him with a terrible sense of foreboding. "What are you talking about?" he said harshly. "Little Wolf is the chief."

Black Cloud shook his head. "No longer."

As Tall Tree drew back, startled, he noticed that the squaw had moved nearer. Standing there very still, she scarcely seemed to breathe. She might have been a statue. Vaguely sorry for her, Tall Tree did not rebuke her, as was his right. His eyes turned back to Black Cloud. "Explain yourself," he said, and the fear that was in the woman was plain in his voice.

Black Cloud could not look away from Spring Rain. They had played together as children, and now he was about to kill the heart in her. "Little Wolf is no longer the chief," he answered Tall Tree. "I have killed him."

The round earthenware bowl Spring Rain was holding fell from her nerveless hands and shattered, small pieces flying everywhere. The look in her eyes burned through Black Cloud, shriveling him. He knew that there was nothing he could say to her. Nothing that she would want to hear from him, and yet he wanted to try. His lips moved, but the words died unuttered as Spring Rain wheeled about and fled in the direction of Little Wolf's wigwam.

Black Cloud waited, and then Spring Rain's scream came, wild, piercing, heartbroken. It ripped into Black Cloud, shattering his unnatural composure. Sweat broke out on his forehead and ran down his face like dull pearls. Trembling violently, he looked about him. Spring Rain was running back. Black Cloud felt withered by the tears on her face, the wild blaze in her eyes. She was heading straight for him, her hands outstretched, her fingers crooked. There would never be another day in which to atone. His life had ended when he had stood over Little Wolf and watched him die.

"Murderer!" Spring Rain's lips skinned back from her teeth in a snarl of pure hatred. Her weight was slight, for she was a fragile woman, but such was the momentum of her leap that Black Cloud fell heavily beneath her. "Murderer!" Her teeth bit into his flesh, her nails clawed at his eyes, and he had the dazed illusion that it was a wildcat rather than a woman that had hurled itself upon him. He moaned faintly beneath the stinging pain of her assault, but he made no attempt to throw her off. Whatever came to him, he deserved.

Other hands were dragging Spring Rain from him. There was a babble of many voices. He made no protest when he was dragged along the ground. His head throbbed, his face blazed with pain, and he could see only dimly. Somebody screamed when he was staked out and left to await punishment. The scream had not come from Spring Rain. With a tremendous effort of will, Black Cloud managed to raise his head. Through the mist before his torn eyes he saw the crowd of braves and squaws who had gathered to stare at him. Some of the faces were wondering, others shocked, and some were twisted with hatred. Then he saw his mother. He knew then that the scream had come from her.

"My son!" Speckled Bird fought her way to his side. Falling to her knees, she laid a trembling blue-veined hand upon his head. "They are saying that you have killed Chief Little Wolf."

It hurt him to see her looking so old, her seamed face broken with weeping. He swallowed against the constriction in his throat. "It is true," he whispered.

Speckled Bird sat back upon her heels. She stared at his arms, which were stretched painfully up beyond his head. His wrists had been bound with rawhide thongs, the ends of the thongs twisted about small stakes that had been hastily hammered into the ground. His legs had been pulled wide, and his ankles were likewise bound and fastened to stakes. "Why did you do it, my son?"

"I was mad," he answered her. "I am sane now, and I know that only my death will atone."

Speckled Bird's head drooped. Black Cloud felt her braid touch his torn face. "They will kill you," she said in an anguished voice. "When that happens, I shall die too!"

"No!" He tried to make his voice harsh and commanding. "You are only a woman, and foolish. I forgive you, but you must not say that again."

Her head began an agitated shaking, and her braid moved against his face. "Bright Feather comes. He is almost here!"

"I know. When he comes, I shall be judged and punished."

Speckled Bird's tears fell upon his face, stinging in the

cuts. "They will tie you to a stake, my son!" Her voice quavered. "They will shoot the flaming arrows into your body."

"For this I am prepared. It is only what I deserve."

Speckled Bird raised her head, and Black Cloud saw the tremendous struggle she was making to achieve calm. "If I could prevent your death, I would. We both know that there is nothing I can do." She tried to smile at him. "I know you well, my son; therefore I know you will die like a warrior."

He had never felt less brave. His heart was thundering with terror of the moment that would soon be upon him. But, as she had said, he would die like a warrior. He would bring no further disgrace upon his name or hers. "I will, my mother," he answered her in a steady voice. "Have no fear."

"I do not fear. I know you." Her finger touched his lips, feather-light, tender. "I must go now, my son. I will prepare a parfleche of food. You must have food to take with you on your last journey." This time her smile was successful. "I have this day made many of your favorite foods. When you offer them to the gods, I pray they will be accepted with pleasure."

She stood up. He wanted to beg her not to go. Instead, he nodded to her, and stretched his lips into a painful answering smile. "Do not look on at my death. You must promise me that."

"I promise," she tried to whisper, and failing, turned away.

Black Cloud managed to raise his head again. He watched the small, stooped figure of his mother until she was out of sight. He wanted to make an impression of her on his mind and his heart, so that he might carry it with him on his last journey.

"The lookout is waving his arm," a man's voice roared. "He is telling us that Bright Feather comes along the path. Our chief has returned!"

Spring Rain pushed herself out of the crowd and ran up to Black Cloud. "Have you heard, you murderer?" she shouted. "Bright Feather comes." Her moccasined foot kicked viciously at his head. "Now you will die."

Chapter 19

They had been hearing the drums for some time now. The wind, rising again after its temporary lull, had drifted the sound. The beating pounded in Justin's head until it seemed to him that the world about him contained nothing else but that ceaseless primitive throbbing. It was enough to drive a man out of his mind, he thought, glancing at Buck and White Bird. He was surprised to find that their battered faces were expressionless. It was as though their minds were divorced both from the beating of the drums and from the situation in which they found themselves. He began to wonder if the warriors, who were herding them along like pigs to a market, read anything significant in the message of the drums? If so, it did not show in their faces. Only the tall warrior, whose name, he had learned, was Bright Feather, showed any emotion. Whenever his narrow black eyes rested on his three prisoners, they glittered with a ferocious hatred.

There was a pause in the order of marching. Bright Feather said something in his own language. Hands pushed them forward again, and they began to make their way up a steep, winding path. As they mounted higher, the beating changed in tone. There was now an almost savage frenzy in the sound, as though the drummers had gone mad.

Buck seemed to listen for the first time. "Ain't nothing particular in the message of them drums," he said, reading Justin's mind. "Them Injuns is having themselves a good time spelling out the names of their enemies." He listened again. "They say they got news that'll make their enemies think twice."

"What news?"

Buck shrugged. "They ain't saying as yet. Injuns are like that. They like to keep the enemy wondering. They'll tell in a minute, won't be able to keep it to themselves for long. I'll keep my ears open."

Trying to ignore the sound, Justin said abruptly, "Where are we, Buck? Do you know?"

"Yeah, I know right enough." Buck's gruff voice hid the pain he was feeling. "We're almost at the village. This path leads into it."

Bright Feather gave Buck a violent push. "No talking, pale-skin!"

A furious anger boiled in Justin as Buck stumbled and almost fell. God curse the damned savages! With their hands tied behind their backs, the way was made difficult enough without the constant jostling, pushing, and prodding of Bright Feather and his band of braves. Justin bit down hard on his lip. Pain throbbed through his head, his hair was matted with blood, and his wrists were bound so tightly that there was no feeling in his hands.

Buck seemed to sense the rebellion in Justin's mind. Ignoring Bright Feather's order, he said in a low, urgent voice, "You just take a hold on yourself, Justin. Don't you go getting any damn fool notion 'bout jumping them braves. You make one move, and they'll likely club you to death. Wouldn't think twice 'bout hurling you over the side."

Carrie! Justin thought in anguish. What have they done to you? Are you dead, my love? If you are, I don't want to go on living without you. Let them do their worst. Looking at Buck, he saw the grimness of his expression, and he knew Buck was thinking about Lianne. "Whatever happens, Buck," he said in a low voice, "we won't go under without a fight."

"Goddamn right!" Buck answered. "Ain't much we can do 'gainst 'em, but we'll give it a try." He paused. When he spoke again, his words echoed the thought that had been in Justin's mind. "If I should find that Lianne's dead, then I ain't much caring what they do to me."

Justin flinched from the raw pain in Buck's voice. Forcing a smile, he said quickly, "No matter what, friend, we'll give them a show."

"That's right." Buck blinked his eyes, trying to clear his vision. He was half-blinded by the blood that trickled into his eyes from the deep, ugly cut on his forehead. "But it ain't no manner of use starting something till we know what's happened to Lianne and Caroline."

"And if we find them alive, what then?"

"Don't know." Buck grimaced. "I cain't seem to think. My head feels as though it's about to bust wide open."

Justin fell silent. Buck couldn't think, because there was nothing to think about. The situation was hopeless. They both knew it. It was impossible to fight their way out. If Caroline and Lianne were still alive, it might be that they would be allowed to die together. There was little comfort in the thought of dying, but at least one would not be left behind to face life without the other. A new and frightening thought struck him. Would they be tortured? Could Carrie stand up to that? For the matter of that, could he? No man could know what he would do under such alien circumstances. But if one could call upon all one's courage and endurance to meet the test, it might be said by the Indians that the pale-skins had died bravely. Again, small comfort. Justin gritted his teeth together. There were many kinds of torture. The torture of the body passed, the torture of the heart did not, not until the last breath was drawn. To be alone in this world without Carrie—that was one torture he was not prepared to face.

A faint moan, quickly stifled, came from White Bird. Justin's eyes turned to him. He looked at the clotted blood on White Bird's face, the fresh blood that trickled down his neck from the cut at the back of his head. When they had been discovered by the Indians, they had fought to throw off their captors. They had all been clubbed, but White Bird, in addition to this, had had two fingers on his right hand smashed. He must be in excruciating agony. At one time, on the journey to the village, White Bird has lost his footing and fallen heavily. As a result, he had received another clubbing. The beating had been administered by a short, wild-eyed, ferocious-looking warrior who, from his general bearing and his constantly shouted orders to the others, seemed to be second-in-command to Bright Feather.

"My God!" The exclamation came from Buck. "Will you listen to them drums, Justin!"

The tempo of the drums had changed again. "Well, Buck? What are they saying?"

"They're saying that Little Wolf is dead." Buck's voice was incredulous. "Bright Feather is the new chief."

A howl of triumph came from Bright Feather. "Attend, warriors, attend. Listen to the message of the drums! I am now your chief. Black Cloud has taken the life of Little Wolf!"

White Bird gave a moan of protest as he was jostled faster up the path by the excited warriors. He felt sick with the pain in his head and his smashed fingers. He was not aware of the drums, or of the message they sent forth. Even if he had heard the message, it would have meant nothing to him. His dulled mind could only concentrate on his bitter remorse. He had wished to help Justin and Buck; instead, he had brought about their destruction and his own. When he had led them to that hiding place above the village, he had given no thought to the possibility of being discovered by a stray passerby. But so it had turned out. The tall warrior, who still seemed vaguely familiar to him, had taken much pleasure in telling them that their hiding place had been discovered by a small boy at his play. "Little Antelope came straight to me with the news of your intrusion upon this sacred place of the gods," he had said. Then, his lip curling in a sneer, he had added, "It would seem from this that our small boys, though they are not as yet entitled to call themselves men, are, every one of them, worth more than two pale-skins and one traitor Indian."

From sneering, the tall warrior's mood had turned threatening. His face distorted with rage, he had wheeled around on Lawrence. "You look like a man of my people," he shouted. "But I know well that you are only a cursed pale-skin. You will die! For this insult you have offered to the gods, you will all die! But first, before I bear you to the village, you will answer my question. Why are you hiding here?"

Lawrence had spoken up. Refusing to acknowledge defeat, he had looked straight into the eyes of his interrogator, and he had said in a hard voice, "You have my woman. I have come for her."

White Bird half-closed his eyes as he remembered his thoughts then: Now it will all come out. They wanted Lawrence, and they have got him. It is over, finished. Five will die this day!

Recovering from the audacity of the man who stood before him, the tall warrior had said in a harsh voice, "So you have come for your woman. Are you Lawrence?"

"Yes. I am Lawrence."

"Ah!" The tall warrior's eyes had flared wide with triumph. "By the sacred gods, this is indeed a divine day. I will bring the enemy of Little Wolf before him, and he will bless me." Wheeling his horse about, he had pointed at Buck. "Two birds in one trap! Warriors, you all have cause to know that man standing there. It is Buck Carey. Many times he has trapped our game, and always he has managed to elude us. This time he will not. Take them. Bind them tightly. And do not forget the traitor Indian!"

Justin and Buck were not men to submit tamely, White Bird thought, remembering the pride he had felt in these two whom he called friends. They were pale-skins, but the blood of warriors ran in their veins. Knowing that resistance was hopeless, they had nonetheless flung themselves upon the warriors. It had been a short fight, but memorable. He had aided them in their resistance. Before they had been over-come by the war clubs, they had managed to fell at least five of the warriors.

When order had been restored, the tall warrior had spoken up again. "Take the traitor Indian. Smash his fingers. He has fought on the side of the enemy. I order that this shall be done!"

White Bird's head lifted proudly, and the movement caused the pain in his head to flare higher. When the warriors had smashed his fingers, he had not cried out. They had done the job as slowly as possible, one finger at a time, hoping to wring a cry from him. But he had bitten back the sound of agony. His lips clamped tightly together, he had endured.

White Bird looked about him. For the first time, he took note. They were about to enter the village. Soon now, they would all die. Chief Little Wolf would no doubt order that they be tortured before being put to death. He could face his own death calmly. But for Justin and Buck it was a different matter. Astoundingly, they did not believe in his gods, and they had therefore not been trained to accept their will, as he had been, from the moment of his first understanding. He knew well that they would make no outcry, but they could not be expected to have the same calm acceptance.

Justin looked at White Bird again. The Indian boy seemed unaware of pain now. He was far removed from them, lost in deep thought. Hadn't he heard Bright Feather's triumphant howling, the panting excitement of the warriors, the message of the drums? "White Bird"—Justin nudged him with his shoulder—"did you hear the drums?"

White Bird's eyes turned to him. "I did not, Lawrence. What do they say?"

"Little Wolf is dead. Bright Feather is now the chief."

"Bright Feather?" White Bird said sharply. "Did you say Bright Feather?"

"I did." Justin jerked his head. "He's the tall warrior behind us, with the green feathers in his hair. The one who's doing the fiendish yelling."

"And you are quite certain that his name is Bright Feather, Lawrence?"

White Bird was obviously dazed, Justin thought. "I'm certain," he answered gently. "He told us his name. Don't you remember?"

White Bird shook his head. "I am sorry, Lawrence. I could not have been listening."

"Oh, well, it doesn't matter, does it?" Justin's tone was wry. "Whatever his name is, our end will be the same. That much is certain."

White Bird did not reply. His thoughts had turned inward again. It was no wonder that the tall warrior had seemed familiar to him. He was Bright Feather, the boy who had been almost a man, who had befriended him in those days when he had badly needed a friend. His breathing quickened as once again he remembered the words of Bright Feather, spoken to him on that last day. They had known they must part, each to go his own way, but there was sadness in the parting. Clasping his hand strongly, Bright Feather had said, "White Bird, if ever I can aid you, I will be happy to do so. We are of a different tribe. The paths of our lives lie in different directions, but I am your friend. I will always remember that."

The fingers of White Bird's uninjured hand clenched, and he winced as he felt the bite of the rawhide thongs. Had Bright Feather continued to remember, or had he put the memory from him? If reminded, would he care to acknowledge friendship with one whom he had designated "traitor"? White Bird frowned uneasily. He himself had always honored a friendship, and he believed the obligations imposed upon one in the name of that friendship to be binding. It was to be hoped that Bright Feather, even under these circumstances, would feel the same. Perhaps, because of the old tie between them, he might be satisfied to take his life alone, and let the others go free. He would remind Bright Feather of his promise. He would ask him for the lives of Justin and Buck and their women. It might come to nothing, but it was worth a try.

White Bird's hope of repaying his debt to Justin and Buck, and thus wiping out his mistake, was so great that he stumbled. He stiffened, trying to prevent himself from falling. "Walk, you cursed cripple!" Bright Feather's snarling voice sounded in his ears. "We are about to enter the village." Doubling his fist, he punched the boy in the back.

Sinkingly aware of the dying of his hope, White Bird answered him in an expressionless voice. "I hear you, Bright Feather." It seemed to him then that it would be useless to appeal to this man, so changed was he from the friend he had known. Bright Feather, in those days, had seemed to him to be gentle and compassionate. But now it was as if a new and alien being had stepped into his place. What should he do now? Should he still make the appeal, in the hope that if compassion was lost, honor would still prevail?

White Bird stole a quick look at Justin Lawrence's grim profile. Now that these sick doubts had come to him about Bright Feather, it would not be wise to speak to Lawrence, as he had planned to do. Lawrence, though obviously not a man who resigned himself easily, at least appeared to have accepted his fate. Why give him hope, when it might well be made into a lie by Bright Feather's rejection of himself? He craned his head to look at Buck Carey. Buck was walking very stiffly, his eyes staring straight ahead. Buck knew what to expect at the hands of their captors, while Justin, who was new to this land and to the ever-growing hatred that seethed between white man and red man, could only guess at his fate. But for all that, when the time came to die, White Bird knew that neither man would flinch or beg for mercy. He did not make the mistake of believing them to be without fear, as he would once have done, for the words Lawrence had spoken to him were still fresh in his ears: "The man who knows no fear does not exist." Because of these words, he felt that he could see inside them, and he knew there would be much fear in them, as there would be in himself. It would seem that a craven lay in wait inside every man. But Lawrence had made him understand that the only shame was in allowing that craven to emerge and take control. Therefore, because these men hid their fear and faced boldly what they must face, they would be known as brave men. White Bird, having made his judgment, lifted his head proudly. If die he must, he would do so in good company.

Herded from behind by the warriors, the three men entered the village. Braves and squaws were standing about in little groups. Some were congregated near the great leaping fire. Others stood outside their wigwams and called across to their neighbors. The atmosphere, which was one of great tension and excitement, was not usual, White Bird knew. It was the unexpected death of Little Wolf that had brought it about.

Buck's eyes were caught by the straining body of the boy who lay staked out just beyond the fire. He would be Black Cloud, Buck guessed, the young warrior who had put an end to Little Wolf's life. He wondered what had possessed him to do it. What dark thoughts had moved inside his head to bring him to murder? Had he been prompted by hatred of all that the man stood for? Little Wolf was not like the other sons of Running Fox. He was the odd one. From the stories Buck had heard, Little Wolf had no honor. He was known to be harsh and unjust, punishing mistakes ruthlessly. Buck's mouth folded into a grim line. When Little Wolf became chief, Running Fox must have turned over in his grave. Buck looked again at the staked-out body of the boy. Perhaps Black Cloud had nursed a resentment over something he considered unfair, a lowering of his dignity as a warrior. Or, then again, it might have been a case of jealousy. He might have desired a woman who belonged to Little Wolf.

"Carrie!" The choked exclamation came from Justin. "Buck, that's Carrie over there!"

Buck stared at the girl lying beneath the tree a little distance from them. Firelight touched the silvery braids of her hair, and flickering fitfully over her thin body, brought dancing sparks of light from the beads that decorated her buckskin tunic. Buck averted his eyes, not daring to look at Justin. He believed that he knew why she had been dressed like that. Had the warriors already raped her? Was that why she was lying so still, like one dead?

Caroline's utter stillness impressed itself upon Justin. She was dead. His agonized eyes dropped to her flat belly. What of the child—was it dead too, or was it lying somewhere neglected, at the mercy of these savages? "Buck! She's dead, isn't she? Carrie's dead!"

The agony in Justin's voice brought the hot tears stinging at the backs of Buck's eyes. He blinked them quickly away. "I don't know," he said in a difficult voice. "I pray not."

"Shouldn't you be telling me that she's better off dead?"

"We ain't knowing for sure that Caroline's dead."

"The child has been born, Buck." Justin's voice was tightly controlled now. "What can have happened to it?"

Buck's thoughts whirled wildly. There must be something that would help to ease Justin's agony of mind. "It ain't likely that they'd harm a babe."

Justin stared at him. Not likely, Buck had said. Did he forget the story he had told him about the cruel fate of his own child? He saw Buck's tightly compressed lips. Buck was suffering too.

White Bird noted the trembling of Justin Lawrence's powerful frame, and he was afraid for him. Perhaps Lawrence could not be broken down on his own account, but the effect on him of the death of his woman and his child was another matter. Sweat beaded Lawrence's face, and his eyes looked wild. White Bird looked across at Caroline. Was she really dead, the woman with the sunshine hair? His heart leaped as he saw the faint movement of her hand. "Lawrence!" White Bird's voice was harsh with excitement. "Caroline is alive. I saw her hand move!"

Bright Feather glared angrily as Justin started forward. "White carrion!" His vicious push sent Justin sprawling.

For a moment Justin was stunned by the force of the fall. Then, recovering, he rolled over on his back and managed to raise himself to a sitting position. "I would like to see Caroline, Bright Feather."

Bright Feather's smile was slow and taunting. But Lawrence's quiet voice was strangely at variance with the blaze of anger in his eyes. Reaching down, Bright Feather caught him beneath the elbows and dragged him to his feet. "You may not see your woman unless I grant you permission to do so. And you will not move unless I say you may. Do you understand me, Lawrence?"

"I understand. Perhaps, then, since I require your permission, you would be kind enough to grant it?"

Again Lawrence's voice was quiet, but there was a cutting edge of sarcasm to it that brought the hot blood of anger to Bright Feather's face. He did not understand the man before him, and because he did not understand, his anger grew. Lawrence was a fool to talk to him in such a fashion. Didn't he understand that, as his prisoner, he was completely at his mercy? Where was the fear he had hoped to see? It was not in Justin Lawrence or in Buck Carey. Bright Feather's glaring eyes swung to White Bird. There was no fear there, either. The Indian youth, the traitor to his own kind. There was something about him that puzzled Bright Feather and made him uneasy. The boy's face and his general appearance seemed to rouse strange feelings inside of him. There should be a name for those feelings, but he could not imagine what it might be. He had seen the boy before. A memory came to him in a quick flash. He saw a sunlit field. There were horses in the field. A mare who nuzzled the neck of a sobbing boy. Bright Feather frowned as he tried to catch and hold the memory. It was no use; it was too fleeting. Too much had happened in his life, and his memories were all confused and out of order. His life had been turned upside down when the pale-skins had butchered his father and his mother. He himself had counted coup on the enemy many times since their murder. He had been so well-steeped in hatred that he could scarcely be expected to remember everyone who crossed the path of his life. He stared at White Bird, still feeling that inner tug. Uncertainty came to mingle with anger, causing all that was cruel in his nature to surface.

"Chief Bright Feather"—the voice of Lawrence came to scatter his thoughts—"may I see Caroline?"

Bright Feather's taunting smile appeared again. "Do you beg me, Lawrence?"

"I do not beg anyone. Least of all you."

Bright Feather managed with some difficulty to smother his flare of anger. So the pale-skin was still arrogant. Even with his hands bound behind him and the sweat standing out on his face, he still stood like a chief. But he had seen the fear in Lawrence's eyes, fear for his woman. He had good cause to fear. Before the stars left the sky, he should see her body rent asunder by his warriors. Perhaps then Justin would beg.

Perhaps he would even show fear for himself. "You wish to see your woman before you die, Lawrence?"

"Yes. If I am to die, I would like to see her." On the surface, Justin's words were calm, almost casual, but there was nothing calm about the feelings that seethed inside him. A primitive rage and hatred mingled with a bitter grief for Caroline, and for his child, at whose fate he could only guess.

"*If*, Lawrence? You will die, you may be sure of that." Bright Feather's smile widened to a fixed grimace. "No, you may not see your woman. You may not see your child. He is dead." Savoring the enjoyment he had in the telling, he went on quickly. "I myself saw the woman laboring to bring forth life. Instead, she brought forth death."

Justin saw the triumph in the narrow, glittering eyes that were set high in the dark, savage face. In that moment nothing seemed real to him. His eyes roved, burning with a desperate light. Caroline, lying so still and silent beneath the tree. The village, with its clustering wigwams. The people, who had now fallen silent, the hostile eyes that watched him intently. The leaping fire that lit up the painted copper-skinned faces and cast dark hollows beneath high cheekbones. The tall warrior who stood before him, staring at him with such malice. His taunting smile, his oiled black braids, stuck through with green feathers, dangling to his shoulders; the decorative slashes on his cheeks, the barbaric chains about his neck. Even Buck and White Bird were like frozen figures in some grim tableau. And above everything there was the persistent mutter of the drums. The sound soaked into his brain, breeding a violence and a frenzy that would normally have been alien to him. All the people, everything about him, was unreal. It was like something out of a nightmare.

"Well, Lawrence?" Bright Feather's voice stabbed at him. "I have spoken. Have you more you wish to say?"

Justin felt himself tightening. This was no nightmare. It was bizarre, but it was shockingly real. Thoughts raced through his brain, of the life he had led, the risks he had taken. But all that had gone before had been only a prelude to this moment in time. There had been those rare times when he had hated, but the emotion he had felt then had been a poor pallid thing when compared to the hatred he felt for the painted savage before him. His eyes met Bright Feather's. "Yes, I have more to say." His voice was harsh with his hatred. "What has happened to my son? Where is his body?"

Bright Feather felt triumph as he saw the convulsive twitching of the muscles beside Justin's mouth. Bleed, white man! he thought. Bleed for your woman and your son and the life you are to lose. Bleed, as we, in our anguish over the loss of our lands and our ancient heritage, have bled. As we will go on bleeding at the hands of your kind! "The body of your son lies somewhere in the forest," he answered. "No doubt the animals have devoured it by now." He smiled as he saw the blanching of his enemy's face. Then, unable to resist the cruel lie, he went on in a loud voice, "I gave your child a fitting burial, Lawrence. I took him from his mother, and I threw him from me. Thus, had I my way, would die all pale-skins. I would use them to fertilize the earth they try so hard to steal from us."

"Dear Christ!" Buck exclaimed.

Justin did not hear him. He did not see White Bird's wincing, or the pity in his eyes. As he stared at Bright Feather, his first stunned reaction passed. Murder blazed from his dark eyes. His hands writhed against the bonds that cut into his wrists. If only he could snap them. If only he could get his hands about the man's throat and choke him to death! There was a reeling in his head. Through a bloodred haze he saw Bright Feather's sneering face. "You savage! You bloody, stinking savage! I'll smash you, trample you!" It was the raging bellow of primeval man. "I'll destroy you, you redskin bastard!" Lowering his head, he rushed forward.

Bright Feather gasped as Justin's hard head drove into his stomach with the force of a battering ram. He fell back before the onslaught.

"You filth! You swine!" Justin's eyes glowed red with hatred. He kicked upward, his foot smashing into Bright Feather's jaw.

Nobody moved. The people fumed at this insult to the chief. But they could do nothing unless he called upon them.

Little Antelope, who had drawn near, gaped with dropped jaw, wondering how Chief Bright Feather would avenge this insult upon his person. Watching, he felt suddenly cold and frightened. He had brought this capture about. He should have felt proud, but somehow he did not. Instead he was filled with horror.

Little Antelope's eyes filled with tears, and he found himself wishing that he were not almost a man. This day, the day of his tenth birthday, had been long and disastrous, and it was robbed of all joy. Little Wolf was dead. He did not grieve for Little Wolf, but for Black Cloud, who had killed him. Black Cloud, his friend, who lay staked out awaiting the torture.

His ears wincing away from the raw sounds of the white man's fury and grief, Little Antelope hastily blinked the tears from his eyes. Whether he liked it or not, he was almost a man, and he would be disgraced if others saw his tears. At this moment, he wished passionately for peace.

Despite this wish, Little Antelope found that he could not look away from the scene of violence before him. It was horrifying, but at the same time, fascinating. The white man was still kicking out wildly and doing his best to kill Bright Feather. But now Bright Feather, recovering himself, easily avoided him. He moved still farther out of reach, his face a twisted mask of hatred and pain.

"Pale-skin!" Bright Feather snarled, rushing in on Justin. Almost choking on his rage, he smashed his fist against his mouth.

Justin reeled back before the force of the blow, but he managed to keep his footing. Blood from his mashed lip trickled into his mouth. Turning his head, he spat the blood in Bright Feather's direction. "I'm going to kill you, Bright Feather! Somehow, I'll manage it!"

Bright Feather laughed outright. "How grandly the cock crows." His hand lashed out again. "That is my answer to you, Lawrence." Bright Feather pushed him to one side. Moving away again, he raised his hand.

Bright Feather's signal brought the braves rushing forward. They were closely followed by the squaws and the children. Only Little Antelope hung back, and he did not know why he did so. His absence was not noted, not even by his mother. She, with the others, surrounded Bright Feather, the new chief. Little Wolf was forgotten. Later he would be buried with full honors, but this moment belonged to Bright Feather alone.

Still not understanding his reluctance to mingle, Little Antelope turned away. He stopped short as an old squaw on the edge of the crowd began trying to squeeze her way through the press of bodies. "Kill Justin Lawrence!" Her voice rose, wavering and shrill. "Kill Buck Carey and the traitor red brother!" She pounded at the backs that impeded her. "Kill them!"

Little Antelope gasped. He had heard Lawrence's name on Bright Feather's lips, but not until this moment had he really connected him with the Lawrence of Little Wolf's virulent hatred. He turned his head and looked at the white woman, who still lay motionless beneath the tree. He took one step forward, then another. Once again he stopped short. The half-breed was running toward Lawrence's woman. There was a crazed look on her face. Reaching her, she fell to her knees beside her. Little Antelope saw her lips moving rapidly as she began to shake the woman.

"Caroline!" Lianne's fingers dug into Caroline's shoulders. "You must listen to me! Open your eyes. Bright Feather has captured Justin and Buck. Do you hear me? They have been taken!"

Dribbles of water from Lianne's wet hair fell onto Caroline's face. She moaned, reluctant to let go of the peaceful blankness. The water that fell on her face and the voice that cried her name were too insistent. She opened her eyes slowly and looked into Lianne's distraught face. Lianne gripped her harder, managing to raise her a little. Caroline's blond braids swung as she was shaken to and fro. "Don't, Lianne," she pleaded. "Please don't!"

"Don't!" Lianne screamed. "Haven't you been listening to me, woman? Justin and Buck are here. They have been taken!" Abruptly she released Caroline's shoulders. Covering her face with her hands, she rocked in anguish. "Gods defend them!" she sobbed. "They will be put to the torture. They will die!"

Caroline's expression grew radiant, as though she was lit from within. Justin was here. He was here! She must go to him. Her breath rattled harshly in her lungs as she raised herself.

Lianne's hands dropped. Her frenzied sobbing broke off as she stared in amazement. Caroline was on her hands and knees, already crawling toward the place where she believed her man to be. Lianne put her hand to her mouth to stifle a cry. She could have sworn that Caroline's strength was gone.

"Justin, I'm coming!" Caroline's voice was a thin cry.

Stones cut into her knees, and clumps of tough grass scratched at her hands. She did not feel the new pain. Nothing mattered to her now save that Justin was near. She crawled painfully onward, impelled by her driving need to be with him. To be held, comforted, and loved. The scene before her wavered and spun, but she would not give up. He was somewhere in the heart of that crowd of people. He must be. Unconsciousness tried to claim her again, but she fought it back with that same doggedness that she had applied to every tense situation in her troubled life. Strangely, she did not connect Justin's presence with danger to himself. She only knew that he was her love, the light that beckoned her on, her safe haven.

"Lawrence, Lawrence!" The high excited scream of many voices pierced Caroline's ears. "Kill Lawrence! Kill the pale-skins!"

Horror turned Caroline cold. Now, at last, she understood his danger. He was to die at the hands of these Indians. Her lips moved in silent prayer, for Justin, for all of them. "It is too late for me, but help them! As for myself, I ask only one thing, that I be allowed to die at his side."

Panting, she stopped for a moment. Then, her fingers digging into the earth, she forced herself onward. Her eyes wild, she listened to the drums. They were pounding out a message of death. Words came into her mind and would not be dismissed. Their death chant!

Lianne stared after Caroline's crawling figure, and understanding came to her. The knowledge that Lawrence was near had given his woman a new strength. Lianne looked up at the star-pricked sky. Had the God, he whom the white people worshiped, given Caroline this strength? God was love, the white people said, and Caroline loved both Justin and her God, so perhaps it was one and the same. If they were spared she would renounce her own gods and worship only the white man's God.

Lianne closed her eyes in sudden fear that her gods would punish her. After a moment, she shook her head and put the fear from her. There was only one terror for her now. The terror of being without Buck. Beside that, nothing else, no one else mattered.

Opening her eyes, Lianne rose to her feet. Caroline had almost reached the edge of the crowd. Tears misted her eyes as

she followed quickly after her. Buck, if you die, I die. I beg
that my spirit will leave me at the moment yours departs
your body. Now she no longer knew to whom she prayed,
whether it be to Buck's God, to her own gods, or simply to
Buck himself.

Little Antelope saw the half-breed woman catch up to the
crawling figure of Lawrence's woman. Now she had taken a
few steps past her. She was battering at the people who stood
in her way, even as the old squaw had done. "Let me
through!" her voice was loud and demanding. Little Antelope
ran forward. He no longer wished to hold himself apart. He
wanted to see if the half-breed's arrogance would be punished.

"Look!" a woman's voice shrieked. "Here is the half-breed
demanding to be let through. The white woman is with her!"

The crowd parted like a wave, and a silence fell over them.
Caroline was aware only of Justin. His strained face softened
as he saw her, and his dark eyes turned to tenderness. "Justin!" She held up a quivering hand.

"Carrie!" Justin fell to his knees beside her. "Oh, my Carrie! What have they done to you?"

Caroline could not bear the pain in his voice, the tears that
glittered in his eyes. "Don't cry for me," she whispered.
"Hold me, just hold me!"

Buck stared at Lianne, dazed by the shining look of love
she gave him. He had taken a step toward her, when Caroline's words penetrated. He turned his head sharply and
looked at Bright Feather.

"Yes, Buck Carey?" Bright Feather said in a flat voice. "Is
there something you wish to say?"

"Yes." Buck nodded toward Justin and Caroline. When he
looked back at the Indian chief and saw his stony expression,
he burst out roughly, "For Christ's sake, show them a little
mercy. Free his wrists. You got us now, ain't no way we can
escape. Cain't you release his hands for a few moments and
let him hold his woman?"

Bright Feather's coldly glittering eyes went to Justin. "Will
the pale-skin beg me to do this?" He kicked Justin with his
foot. "Do you beg me, Lawrence?"

The hatred in Justin's eyes was undisguised as he looked
up at him.

Caroline saw the change in Justin's expression. For her, he

would beg Bright Feather. But she could not bear to see him humiliated. She must stop him. "No, love," she whispered urgently. "No, my darling. Not for me!"

Justin bent closer to her, his warm breath fanning her cheek. "Not for you, but for me. I want to hold you in my arms."

"Lawrence!" Bright Feather's voice was loud and demanding. "What is your answer? Will you beg me?"

"Yes." Justin looked into Bright Feather's eyes. "I am begging you."

Bright Feather hesitated. Buck Carey was watching him. The Indian boy, too. But more important, his people watched and waited. For them, he was untried. Perhaps it would be as well to show them that he could be merciful. He would show them all that he was a great chief. He drew his knife from his belt. "Since you have begged me, Lawrence, I will show you my mercy." Stooping, he cut through the rawhide thongs.

"Carrie!" Justin's arms gathered her to him and held her tightly. "My darling, my Carrie!" He kissed her hair, her cold face. "I love you, sweetheart," he whispered in her ear.

She smiled. "We are together again, as we were always meant to be."

The pain he felt was almost more than he could bear. She was dying, and there was nothing he could do to comfort her. "We will always be together, Carrie. Nothing will ever part us again. I promise you."

"Justin, the baby. He is . . . is . . ."

"Hush, love." He saw the shadows of terror and grief in her eyes, and he held her even tighter. "We will not speak of the child now." He kissed her again, stilling the words on her lips.

Caroline's eyes were intent upon Justin's face, but now she saw him through a mist. Justin. He was two men in one. The man he had been, laughing, audacious, the smooth and charming thief. The man he was now, who held her so closely, so tenderly. Once, she had believed him to be incapable of love. There had been so many women in his life, so many light affairs. For him, then, a woman was an amusing pastime, not to be taken seriously. Untroubled in his conscience, he had gone on relieving foolishly infatuated women of their jewels and their virginity, taking his pleasures in his own reckless way. The way that had finally led him to the gallows. And then, with his miraculous escape from that same gallows, fate had brought them together. Rogue Lawrence, the man who refused to be tied to any one woman, had been tied to her by an unbreakable bond.

"Carrie!" Thinking, remembering, she was deaf to Justin's concerned exclamation. Her mind was drifting, and for the moment she was content to hide in the past. A smile welled up inside her as she recalled the first time she had seen Rogue Lawrence. He had been lying on the floor, his eyes closed, his lips blue-tinged in his deathly pale face. Bending over him was his brother, Paul, and two other men. At first, in her dazed and terrified state, she had thought that he must be Thomas, her husband, come back from the dead to try to revenge himself upon her. For the murder of Thomas, of which she was guiltless, she had been flogged. She had been told that she was to die upon the gallows. She would not be here now if the three men had not rescued her. Surely Thomas must know her agony? Surely he would be satisfied? Later, when they lifted the unconscious man up and settled him beside her on the wide bed, she had known he was not Thomas. He was somebody called Rogue. Or was it Justin? At that time she had not really cared, for her mind was closed to everything but her own pain. When the pain lifted a little, she found herself remembering voices that had cried out words she had not then understood. A young boy's voice, high and excited. "He's alive! I tell you that Justin is alive." A man's deep-toned answering voice. "Aye, lad, you're right. Rogue's alive."

Justin? Rogue? Frowning, she had turned her head and really looked at the man lying beside her. It was then that the excited voices resounding in her brain came together and made sense. Of course, she knew now who he was. He was Rogue Lawrence. Somehow he had escaped the gallows. The thief and the so-called murderess lay side by side, flesh touching flesh. It would have been funny, had not their situation been so tragic. It was in the desperate times that followed, that, without her really being aware of it, the bond between them had been forged. It had grown and strengthened, turning finally into love. That love, which had upheld them through all the evil and perilous times, was still with them now. Justin, her own dear love! How incredible to think that she had once hated and feared him.

"Why, Carrie, you are smiling." Justin's voice broke the dream that bound her.

"Yes." Caroline answered him with an effort. "It is because you are here with me." All the life that remained in her was in the glowing look she gave him. She sighed. "I am so glad you are holding me. I will always love you, Rogue Lawrence." Her eyes closed.

"Carrie!" In his fear and desperation, Justin shook her. "Open your eyes and look at me, hold me tighter."

Catching some of his fear, Buck called out sharply, "Justin, what is it? Don't tell me that she's ... she's ..." Seeing the look on Justin's face, he became quiet. He wanted to speak, to say something consoling, but the words would not come.

Justin vaguely heard Buck calling him in the background. For the moment he had forgotten where he was. Only the woman lying in his arms was real to him. She was so terribly still! He saw the slight rising and falling of her breast, and his breath caught in a gasp of relief. Some of the agony in him eased. God be thanked, his Caroline was not dead. He kept his eyes fixed on her face. He was shaken by a superstitious dread that, if he looked away, if he relaxed even slightly, she would slip the fragile hold she still retained upon life. "Carrie," he muttered, but though his voice was low, it might well have been a shout, for all his fear was in the words. "You can't leave me, Carrie. How do you expect me to go on without you? Open your eyes. Look at me. For Christ's sake, Carrie, hear me! You can't die, you can't!"

As though the agony in his voice had penetrated to those secret places that still clung tenaciously to life, Caroline moved slightly in his tight embrace. "Justin, don't ..." Her voice had a dragging, weary sound, as though even now she was eager to hurry back to the peace of nothingness. "Don't cry, my darling."

Justin's arms tightened about her as he blinked away his tears. In defiance of the terrible present, knowing that he dared not allow his mind to dwell on a life without her, Justin let his mind travel backward to the Carrie who was so afraid of him. She had looked at him with eyes that had blazed with anger. But behind the facade she had presented, he had seen her fear. Thomas Fane had a lot to answer for. His old man's lust had reduced her inwardly to a frightened child. Justin had wanted her more than he had ever wanted any other woman, and so he had beckoned the child on with sweet words, with the lure of smiles. When all he had really wanted to do was to hold her in his arms and kiss the fear from her trembling mouth. And afterward, very gently, to make love to her. More frequently, though, he had forgotten to smile. Instead he had lost his temper with her and had allowed his anger and his frustration to blaze forth. Carrie understood anger; it was not part of that mysterious relationship between a man and a woman, and so there was nothing to fear. Her eyes flashing defiance, she had given him back as good as he gave.

Justin's arms tightened about Caroline's limp form. His breath caught in his throat as he remembered the moment of her surrender. It was at Bewley Grange that the miracle had happened. She had admitted at last that she wanted him. Lifting her in his arms, he had carried her up the stairs. Yet, even with his arms about her trembling body, he still could not bring himself to believe that the child had turned into an ardent woman. Trying to ignore the hardening of his desire, he had placed her on the bed. Before he took her, he had to be sure she knew what she was doing. Managing to keep his voice low and soft, he had said, "You are quite sure, Carrie?"

For a moment she had hesitated. To him that moment had stretched out, and it was as though his heart had skipped several beats. Cursing himself for a fool, he was forced to admit that he had never felt quite like this before. He had to suppress a desire to shout, "Answer me, damn you!"

In the stillness of the room, her answering voice had sounded very loud, and, yes, almost triumphant. "I want you." Her arms stretched out to him in entreaty. "Teach me to love, Justin. Teach me to be a woman!"

And so he had taken her. Not once, but several times. He had never known anyone quite like her. She was fire in his arms, a flame that consumed and brought incredible delight. She was made to love and to be loved. He swallowed, as, in imagination, he once more felt the tight grip of her legs about his waist, the crushed softness of her breasts, the warmth of her sheathing him, the violent shuddering of her desire that met and matched with his own. "Teach me to be a woman," she had said. But that was one lesson she had not needed to learn. Because, unwillingly, she had grown to love him, it had needed only a touch to bring the woman forth.

Justin looked up blindly. His vision clearing, he saw the dark, fierce faces that ringed him about. They seemed to him to be not quite real; they were simply part of his nightmare. Then, as Bright Feather's face stood out from the rest, the expression in his eyes one of gloating triumph, reality rushed back. Staring at the Indian, Justin was conscious of the bitter, driving violence of his hatred. His inclination was to leap to his feet and hurl himself at Bright Feather, but he did not move. Instead, crouching forward, he tried to shield Caroline from those malignant eyes.

Buck had seen the look on Justin's face. He winced, for it was as though he absorbed the pain of his friend, could feel it all through him. "She cain't be dead," he muttered.

Lianne drew nearer to him. "No, Buck, do not look so stricken. Caroline is not yet dead."

Buck looked at her, and what he was feeling showed plainly in his eyes. "It . . . it might have been you lying there!"

"But it is not." She put her hand on his rigid arm. "At this moment, the only thing that matters to me is that we are together."

"They will kill us, Lianne." He looked deeply into her eyes. "Ain't you afraid?"

Lianne's nails drove deeply into her palms. Of course she was afraid. The force of her fear was a cold, ceaseless shuddering inside her. But if they were to die, they would not be parted for long. Afterward, they would be together forever. Such was her belief that her face brightened. She looked up again and saw the love in his eyes, and she was filled with wonder and delight. "Yes, Buck. Yes, I am afraid. But it is as I have said. Now that you are here, nothing else matters."

Nothing else matters? He could not believe she was saying such things to him. He was afraid to believe again. But it did not matter what he believed or did not believe, he thought, suddenly struck by the enormity of their situation. Only she was important. "Lianne, I cain't stand this for you!"

"I know. Or I for you. Foolish words, for there is nothing we can do about it." She smiled at him. "I love you, Buck. I ask you to believe me, for now there must be only truth between us. I lied when I said I did not love you. Tell me, white man, do you recognize the truth when you hear it?"

It was the truth. Now, when it was too late for them, he

knew it. It did not matter why she had lied before, and it was
unimportant. "Yes," he said simply. "I believe you, Lianne."
He smiled faintly. "I wish my hands weren't tied. I could
hold you and show you how very much I believe you."

Forgetful of the eyes upon her, Lianne slid her arms about
him. "But I can hold you, Buck!"

Bright Feather was enraged. "Half-breed!" he snarled. Seizing her, he hurled her to one side. His face contorted with
fury, he shouted above the excited shrieking of the squaws,
"Take the half-breed. Take them all. Bind the men securely
to posts!"

Chapter 20

Seated before his wigwam, the firelight flickering over his dark, intent face, Bright Feather gazed with an inner satisfaction at the two pale-skin men and the Indian boy. They had been lashed to posts, and, at his command, cords had been passed about their throats and knotted behind. The cords were tied in such a way that the prisoners, if they did not keep their heads rigidly upright, would find that the cord cut agonizingly into their windpipes. One moon had waned and another risen, which was the length of time they had been tied. He hoped they were feeling the strain and wondering what was to be their fate. Especially Lawrence, with his arrogant expression and the defiance that still blazed from his dark eyes. Although, now he came to think of it, it was not only Lawrence who angered him and deprived him of the satisfaction that should rightfully be his. Buck Carey, too, was wooden-faced, giving nothing away. The Indian boy seemed to be indifferent to his fate. At this very moment he was gazing straight ahead with his blank eyes. But they would show fear. Once they were broken, they would show it.

Bright Feather smothered his spurt of anger. Yawning, he concentrated instead on the series of impressions he had been at great pains to give to his warriors. In order to show them that he upheld justice, no matter the laceration to his own feelings, he had stood stony-faced before Speckled Bird while she pleaded for the life of her son, Black Cloud. He had heard her out in silence. Then, the sacred pipe held in his left hand, he had delivered a short but fiery speech. In it, he had told Speckled Bird exactly what was to happen to the traitor who had dyed his hands with the blood of a chief. Even as he spoke, his face suitably grave, he had felt the secret laughter welling up inside him. He had thought to himself that he should be rewarding Black Cloud rather than punishing him,

for had not the boy removed Little Wolf, the one obstacle
that had stood in his way to greatness? But eyes watched him,
weighing him, just as they would watch his every move from
now on. So, ignoring the secret laughter and his light-headed
feeling of joy, he had pronounced his dread judgment upon
Black Cloud. Speckled Bird had wailed loudly, keening for
the son she was shortly to lose. The strength leaving her
limbs, she had sunk to the ground. Then, her head hanging
low, she had crawled from his presence. Watching her go, he
had remained unmoved by her grief.

Bright Feather settled himself more comfortably on the
pile of skins. Later, after he had met with the elders and they
had smoked the sacred pipe together, he had likewise shown
his warriors the firm side of his nature. The Indian prisoner,
White Bird, had asked to speak with him. He had refused. It
was not for a chief to hold conversation with a miserable
prisoner. White Bird? Why did that name trouble him? It was
not really the name that troubled him, but the boy himself.
Whenever he looked at him, he would have the feeling that
there was something that eluded him, something that he
should remember.

Bright Feather's frown lifted. He would not think of White
Bird now. There were other, pleasanter things to occupy his
mind. Lawrence, for instance, no doubt thought that his
woman was beyond help. Perhaps he believed her to be already dead. But he would find that this was not so. A smile
touched Bright Feather's lips. He had arranged for the ceremony of healing. Lawrence would be able to look on while
the medicine-man restored the white woman to health.
Lawrence would be happy for a little while, but that happiness would soon vanish. Before he died, he should witness
his restored woman being given to the warriors. Before
Lawrence's eyes, she should die from the continual rape of
her body. Then, there was Buck Carey, who had betrayed his
love for the half-breed. He too would suffer as he watched
her come to the same fate as the white woman.

A muffled sound from the direction of the prisoners drew
Bright Feather's attention. He turned his head quickly, just in
time to catch Lawrence's look of pain. He had moved his
head without the proper caution, and the cord had bitten into
his throat. Almost immediately his face had smoothed itself
out. Bright Feather understood from this that Lawrence had

no intention of letting him see that he suffered. He was that kind of man. Justin Lawrence and Buck Carey, he thought, experiencing an unwelcome touch of admiration—they were both brave men. It would be hard to break them, but somehow it should be done. As for White Bird, he was Indian. He had been trained to stoicism.

A thought came to Bright Feather, and almost he laughed outright. The cords about the necks of the prisoners served a good purpose, in that they would be forced to look upon the torture of Black Cloud. The pale-skins, he had heard, were squeamish when it came to torture. It might be, when the punishment of Black Cloud began, that they would attempt to close their eyes and shut out the sight of Black Cloud's agony. But in this too he would defeat them. Those warriors who stood guard over the prisoners had been ordered to prick their eyelids with the point of a knife. They would be forced to look.

Bright Feather's pleasant thoughts came to an abrupt halt as he saw the tall figure of Fighting Bear pause before the prisoners. Scowling, he leaned forward, his hard gaze going over the warrior. He thought, as he had often thought before, of how much everything about the man offended him. He was tall himself, but Fighting Bear stood a good four inches taller. He resented this fact bitterly, for, proud of his own height, he had hoped to become the tallest of the warriors.

Still glowering, Bright Feather stroked his hairless chin. One of his virtues was that he had never blinded himself to the truth, and so he acknowledged now that it was not only this he resented about the warrior, but also many other things. For instance, it galled him unbearably that Fighting Bear had been beloved of Running Fox, and the confidant of Little Wolf. The man seemed to inspire trust in others, even though he had never managed to do so in himself. Over the years, Bright Feather's dislike of Fighting Bear, his childhood companion, had grown, until now it had mounted almost to an obsession. Another thing that rankled constantly inside him was the knowledge that Fighting Bear, with his handsome face and his regal bearing, would be the next chief after himself, should he die without issue. Bright Feather ground his teeth together in impotent rage. Taller, handsomer, stronger than he, popular with the warriors, a superior hunter—that was his rival, and he hated him for it! Another thing was that he could not help knowing that the hearts and the loyalties of the warriors were with Fighting Bear, as they were not with him, their new chief.

Bright Feather found that he could not turn his eyes from the man. There was a fascination in hatred, too. Although he knew that his action would be noted and commented upon by the warriors, he could not forbear. He hawked, and then spat upon the ground. Since his eyes were fixed upon Fighting Bear, it would be rightly construed by all that passed that this was meant to show his hatred and his enduring distrust of Fighting Bear. Perhaps, too, it would help to foster the idea in their minds that he looked with profound suspicion upon Fighting Bear's many activities that were not, as far as he was concerned, for the good of the tribe.

Although he had not seen Bright Feather's contemptuous action, Fighting Bear was fully aware of his blazing eyes upon him. He was not disturbed by this, for his conscience was clear. Also, as always, he was indifferent to the jealousy and anger of a man he heartily despised. Bright Feather was a jackal. A warrior without honor, even as Little Wolf had been.

Fighting Bear turned his frowning gaze upon the prisoners. He was wondering why he had chosen to stop before them. It had been an impulse, he admitted, and yet it was unlike him to give way to impulse. Curiosity, perhaps? A wish to know why the Indian prisoner was so insistent that he speak with Bright Feather. Encountering White Bird's solemn eyes, he said coldly, "You, traitor, I have heard that you wish to speak with Bright Feather. Although you do not deserve consideration, I will tell you that he might be influenced to see you." Fighting Bear heard his own words with surprise, and as a consequence, his voice grew even colder and his expression more forbidding. "This speech you wish to have with Chief Bright Feather—is it important?"

"It is important." A faint gleam of hope showed in White Bird's eyes. "How are you called, warrior?"

Fighting Bear gave him an austere look. "I am Fighting Bear. But I can think of no reason why my name should be of interest to you. It would seem to me that you are uncommonly curious for one who is about to die."

"It is for that very reason that I am interested," White Bird replied. He knew that the eyes of Justin and Buck were turned his way, but he did not look at them. He concentrated instead upon Fighting Bear. "If you can get me before Chief Bright Feather, you will have done me a kindness. Therefore, when my soul departs my body, I will mention this kindly act to the gods. It will store up rewards for you."

Fighting Bear was much impressed by this, but he chose not to show it. His dark brows rose mockingly. "You are the enemy. A traitor to your people. Why should I do you a kindness?"

"I am no traitor, Fighting Bear. I am not the enemy. I repay kindness with loyalty, and these men have been kind to me."

"They are pale-skins! They seek to steal from us the land of our ancestors!"

"All this I know. Yet all pale-skins are not alike. Some, like Justin Lawrence and Buck Carey, are good and honorable men."

Fighting Bear waved an impatient hand. "Even if this be so, which I am not inclined to believe, why should I do you a kindness?"

White Bird looked deeply into his eyes. "I see into you, Fighting Bear, and what I see tells me that you are a hard man, but just. If I am to die anyway, them my request is reasonable. You cannot deny it."

Fighting Bear felt strange sensations rising in him. The boy's glance was straight, and there was honesty breathing in his voice. All his life he had prided himself on being able to read character, and it seemed to him that White Bird had been much misjudged. Even so, he knew there was nothing he could really do, save perhaps one thing. If Bright Feather was determined that these three should die, then die they would. But it might be, through the means of judicious speech, a subtle tickling of the new chief's many vanities, and because of his obvious desire to stand well with his people, that he could prevail upon him to at least give the boy a hearing. Making up his mind, Fighting Bear assumed a lofty manner, for even now, with the doubts riding him, it was not in him to lower his dignity, or to have it believed that he was weak-willed and easy to deal with. "I will do what I can," he said in a purposely harsh voice. "More you cannot expect."

White Bird looked at him long and deeply. As he had said, he had taken the measure of Fighting Bear. There was no weakness there, but there was justice. He was a good man. "More than that I do not expect," he said simply. "I thank you, Fighting Bear."

Fighting Bear bowed his head as an indication that he had heard. The eyes of Justin and Buck drew him. He looked, giving them glance for glance. He felt a great pull of comradeship, which, instantly, he ignored. The enemy, he reminded himself—they were the enemy. Why should he care if the glances of both men were as straight as the Indian boy's? "You are the enemy of my people." He spoke to them as though he defended himself against a charge.

Fighting Bear waited for Lawrence to speak. When he said nothing, he spoke to him in an even voice. "You, Lawrence. What have you to say?"

Justin's eyes were still defiant, their expression daring him to do what he would. I will endure, his eyes said, and damn you all to hell!

So convinced was Fighting Bear that he had read correctly the message in those deep, dark eyes that he was startled when the man added words. "Caroline, my woman. Does she still live?"

"She lives." Fighting Bear was glad to give him this assurance, though why he was glad, he did not pause to analyze. "Soon she will be restored to full health. Chief Bright Feather has ordered that the ceremony of the healing is to take place after Black Cloud has been gathered to the gods."

The dark eyes regarding him took on a wariness that effectively smothered the light of joy that had momentarily flickered in them. Justin's voice smote on his ears, raw and demanding. "And when she is restored to health, what happens then?"

Fighting Bear stared back at him. He was no fool; he knew that Bright Feather would not give his woman the gift of health if there were not another purpose behind it. He felt a dryness in his throat, and for the first time that he could remember, he lied. "I do not know."

"You know." Justin's voice was sharp, insistent. "Tell me!"

Fighting Bear's face took on a wooden expression. "I do not know, Lawrence," he repeated.

"Do not force him to answer, Lawrence." White Bird's quiet voice cut across the tense moment. "You will not like the answer. I think, when I have spoken to Bright Feather, that things will take on a different aspect."

Abruptly Justin lost his hold on his hard-won control. "What do you mean, White Bird?" he snapped. "As usual, you talk in cursed riddles. Explain yourself!"

Mindful of the constricting cord, White Bird turned his head carefully in Justin's direction, trying, with his eyes, to send him a message of caution. Sighing, he saw from the white man's expression that he had not understood. "No, Lawrence," he said aloud, "I cannot explain yet. It may be that I have judged wrongly. If that is so, then my silence is a kindness."

"For God's sake, White Bird, I'll be damned if I understand you! There has always been truth between us before. Let there be truth now. Explain!"

"No, Lawrence."

Buck knew, from the stubborn folding of White Bird's lips, that there was no more to be got out of him for the moment. What was the matter with Justin, anyway? Did he expect White Bird to reveal all that was in his mind while Fighting Bear was present? "Leave him be, Justin," he said quickly. "He'll tell us in his own good time."

Fighting Bear tried to make his mind a blank. He had already said too much; the prisoners had said too much. He would have no more to do with the conversation, for he did not care for the drift of it. They should not speak so openly before him; it made him uneasy, almost as if he conspired with them against his own. The drums rose to a new height of thundering sound. Looking at Lawrence, Fighting Bear saw the convulsive jumping of a muscle beside his mouth. Like most white men, he thought, Lawrence appeared to have a low tolerance for the sound of the war drums. Justin Lawrence was undoubtedly a brave man, as was Buck Carey, but Fighting Bear had known other brave men, their nerves shredded by the drums, to lose all control. For some reason that he could not explain to himself, as he strode away from them, he found himself hoping that it would not happen to these men.

Justin stared after the tall, commanding figure. If only he understood the Indian mind. If only he knew what Fighting Bear was thinking. Although he had not been told so, he sensed that the man held a position of importance with the tribe. It was too late for Buck, White Bird, and himself, but maybe, if Fighting Bear willed, he could save Carrie and Lianne from harm. His eyes burned with this last thought, and without looking at Buck, he knew that he was thinking along the same lines. Their lives, for Carrie's and Lianne's. He tried to make the thoughts in his mind reach out to the retreating warrior. The women have done you no harm. Nor will they. Save them, Fighting Bear. Save them!

Bright Feather's stare became harder as Fighting Bear approached. "Well," he said as the warrior stopped before him, "I note that you have had conversation with the prisoners. Have you sated your curiosity?"

Fighting Bear heard the sneer in Bright Feather's voice, but he pretended not to notice. Without asking permission, he lowered himself. Crossing his legs comfortably, he stared intently into Bright Feather's face. "A pale-skin is a pale-skin," he said lightly. "My curiosity concerning them has long since died."

"Yet you appear to enjoy the company of the enemy."

"If it appeared so to you, my chief, I greatly regret it." He leaned forward slightly. "There is a thing that White Bird has told me. A thing that I cannot believe."

White Bird again! Bright Feather glared at him, his eyes reddening with his chronic suspicion of the man before him. "What is this thing that the traitor has told you? Speak, Fighting Bear!"

"Do you command it?"

"By the sacred gods, I do!" Bright Feather's voice rose slightly. He regretted almost immediately his lack of control, but Fighting Bear always had this unfortunate effect upon him. "I have told you to speak!"

Fighting Bear lowered his eyes, so that Bright Feather might not see the embarrassment caused by what he had to say next. Unwillingly, and for the second time in his rigidly truthful life, he lied. "White Bird says that you are afraid to meet with him. He says there is something you do not wish to face." Fighting Bear paused, and then, unwittingly, he hit upon the truth. "He says that there are ghosts in your past, and that he is one of those ghosts."

Something stirred in Bright Feather's mind. Almost, he caught a glimpse of that memory that eluded him. He groped after it eagerly, but once again it vanished into the mist of long-forgotten things. "He lies!" he said in an anger-choked voice. "The traitor lies. I am afraid of nothing."

Fighting Bear nodded. "It is even so. He lies. I know well that you are a great and noble man. Why should you fear to meet with him?"

"I do not fear. I have said it."

"Of course," Fighting Bear murmured politely. "It is a matter of scornful laughter, should anyone think differently."

"Who does?" A vein throbbed heavily in Bright Feather's temple. "Tell me, Fighting Bear, who does?"

Fighting Bear shrugged. "I do not know, great one. It is simply that sometimes lying words get around, and perhaps take root in the minds of those who know no better. I would not presume to advise you. Only you can know the right thing to do."

Bright Feather's eyes narrowed. Fighting Bear had said that he was a great and noble man, but he knew that Fighting Bear did not really think so. In the past he had shown his contempt all too clearly. No, he Bright Feather, was no fool, and he did not believe a word of the man's flattery. There was something behind all his oily words, and in time he would find out what it was. For the moment, however, Fighting Bear's purpose was unimportant. The thing was to show him, to show them all, that he feared nothing. "Fighting Bear," he said harshly, "you will bring White Bird to my lodge after the ceremony of the healing. But mark this. If I should find that his only purpose is to beg for his cowardly life, I will slit his throat where he stands. Tell him that."

"It shall be done." Fighting Bear's shoulders slumped. Now that he had done what he had set out to do, he was full of puzzled disgust. Why should he set his hand to helping a traitor brother? A great hot anger rose in him. He had grown weak and soft. His behavior was that of a woman rather than a man. A woman who had not yet been blooded by disillusionment and despair. He thought then of those women who had been blooded, the fierce squaws who knew only hatred, whose cruelty to prisoners in the past had become a byword. His hands clenched in resolve. No, he had not grown weak and soft. To prove it, he would ask that the prisoners be given into the hands of these women. He looked up and saw that Bright Feather was staring at him, but this time more in curiosity than hatred.

"What is it?" Bright Feather asked. "You look like somebody who dwells upon an evil thing."

Fighting Bear drew in a deep breath. "I ask this of you. Until you order the death of the prisoners, let them be delivered into the hands of the warrior women."

Bright Feather's eyes opened wide with surprise. The warrior women? Those screaming shrews who struck terror into the hearts of captives. Why did Fighting Bear, who prided himself upon his moderation in all things, and who had been known to loudly express his disgust of the practice of unnecessary cruelty, ask this thing of him? He hated to give Fighting Bear his way in anything, but he would consent to this, for the idea was much to his own liking. He sat up straighter and gave the warrior a piercing look. "Very well," he grunted, "it shall be so. Why do you wish for this?"

Fighting Bear flushed, and he knew that the flush was not lost on Bright Feather. He did this thing for himself, to prove that he could be as hard and unrelenting, as merciless as the next man, and if it took cruelty to prove it, so be it. He groped in his mind for words that would satisfy, and would not provoke Bright Feather's contemptuous laughter. He found them. "Is it not obvious?" he said in an even voice. "The prisoners have shown great pride and arrogance. Even though they have been tied to the stakes for many hours, still they show no signs of breaking. They are our enemies. I would like to see them humbled."

Humbled. Bright Feather turned the word over in his mind. This, too, he found to his liking. He looked into Fighting Bear's eyes. "You have but echoed my own idea, but I will allow you to take the credit. You may arrange it." He gestured imperiously. "Leave me, now. There is much that I must think upon."

Chapter 21

"Heya—a—a—heya!" The shrill scream, rising above the thunder of the war drums, tore simultaneously from the throats of the warriors. In the leaping firelight, dark, vividly painted bodies gleamed with perspiration. Faces that had grown almost vacant from the soporific effects of the chanting and monotonous shuffling dance were sharpened now to a predatory cruelty.

"Heya—a—a—heya!" the scream came again as a short, muscular warrior leaped into the circle of firelight, brandishing a bow. Muscles twitched under the glistening skins as the other warriors drew back to watch him.

The short warrior, his body striped in green and red paint, yellow circles about his eyes, took a firmer grip on the bow. His feathered anklets fluttered as he leaped high in the air. Coming down lightly on the balls of his feet, he whirled about for a few intricate steps, and then, abruptly, grew still. In the firelight, his eyes glittered with a fierce light. He glared about him, his eyes going from one face to another. Nobody moved or spoke. Even the drums were muted, to await the warrior's words. His lips working, he drew himself up, and once again the fierce glance swept the circle of warriors. "I, Dead Tree, claim the honor of shooting the first arrow at the traitor brother!" he shouted. And then, as if he had been challenged: "Who is there here who dares to dispute my right?"

Only the sound of heavy, excited breathing answered him. Satisfied, Dead Tree nodded. Opening a pouch at his belt, he drew forth a handful of brown powder. Some of it trickled from between his fingers as he hesitated for a dramatic moment. With a quick movement, he flung the powder into the heart of the fire. The flames roared up dangerously high, their ruddy light changing to an eerie green. In the green light, the intently watching warriors had the look of so many corpses.

The green glow touched the faces of Buck and White Bird. Looking at them, Justin felt a shudder inside him. Corpses! Creatures out of hell! It was a foretaste of what was to come. The drums began again, rising to a crescendo, pounding into his head, driving him mad. Stop! he wanted to shout. Stop those bloody drums! He moved his head sharply, choking as the cord bit into his throat.

He turned his eyes as a muffled exclamation came from Buck. Buck was staring at the warriors grouped about the fire. The warriors moved at that moment, fanning out, giving him a clear view of Dead Tree.

Dead Tree, grinning now, drew an arrow from the full quiver at his side. Thrusting the tip of the arrow into the fire, he drew back, readying his bow. Withdrawing the flaming arrow, he held it up for the others to see, and then notched it into the bow.

"Hold on tight, Justin." Buck sounded sick. "It's beginning." His pitying eyes went to Black Cloud, whose naked body was bound to a post on the other side of the fire. "They're going to shoot their goddamned flaming arrows right into his body!" Buck's voice had a heavy, dragging sound, like one who was desperately tired. "Dear Christ, it just ain't human!"

The warriors guarding the prisoners moved in close, the knives in their hands catching a bright gleam from the fire. "You will keep your eyes open, pale-skins," the sullen-faced warrior nearest to Justin growled. "Chief Bright Feather has ordered that you watch the punishment of Black Cloud. He wishes you to know that we punish our own as savagely as we do the enemy." His face menacing now, he held up the knife. "If you do not watch, I will carve out your eyes."

Justin did not answer. His teeth dug hard into his underlip as the flaming arrow arced through the air toward the boy. The fiery tip of the arrow entered the fleshy part of his arm. Justin's throat constricted with the scream of pain that came from Black Cloud.

"Gods have mercy!" Unable to watch stoically the torture of her son, Speckled Bird broke from the rank of squaws. Her mouth wide-open in a scream she rushed toward Black Cloud. Reaching him, she tried frantically to pull the arrow from his blistering flesh. "Have mercy! He is my son!" The ears streaming from her eyes, she looked into Black Cloud's agonized face.

Another arrow, aimed deliberately low, felled Speckled Bird. Flames licked upward from her clothing, setting her hair alight. Screaming, she rolled over and over, trying to put out the flames. Still screaming, the sound high-pitched, inhuman, she died.

The flaming arrows were thick and fast now, tracing their flaring passage toward the victim. They entered Black Cloud's stomach, his legs, his straining arms. One lodged in his cheek, just below his wide-open, staring eyes. He was blind now, his reason gone. His screams turned to blood-chilling, snarling animal sounds. In the way a tortured animal would have done, he moved his head frantically, blindly, trying to snap at the arrows with his teeth.

The smell of burned hair and cooking flesh was thick in Justin's nostrils. His ears rang with the sounds of agony, the excited screams of the squaws, the helpless retching sound that came from Buck, his own stifled moans. God! he prayed silently, forcing words from a mind that reeled with horror. If you have mercy, let the boy die quickly! His mouth opened and words erupted from him, "Kill him, you bloody swines! Put an end to it."

"He's dead, Justin." Buck's shaken voice came to him. "Do you hear me, lad? He ain't suffering no more."

"Thank God!" Justin turned his eyes from the ghastly sight. Buck's haggard eyes stared into his. There was a white line about his mouth, and where his teeth had bitten into his lip, blood oozed forth in bright beads. Beyond him, White Bird stared straight ahead. Justin would have thought him unmoved had it not been for the trembling of his body and the thick coating of sweat that glazed his face.

Justin thought of Black Cloud, the flaming arrows that had thudded into his body, the agony that had seared his guts and cooked his flesh, and, finally, had broken his reason. Once again, in his mind's eye, he saw him driven into the semblance of a mad dog, his teeth vainly snapping at the torturing arrows. Was that how they would die, as mindless creatures, humans turned into snarling animals? He shuddered. Yes, he was afraid. So afraid that his flesh crawled with fear. Carrie! he thought. I pray to God, if you must die, that you will die without pain!

Justin blinked his eyes against the thick smoke that drifted their way. He watched as the sinking fire was replenished with great chunks of wood. Braves and squaws were running here and there, and there seemed to be a definite purpose in their movements, as though they were preparing for something.

Justin's attention was drawn back to Black Cloud. The body was still held to the post by the rawhide thongs, a blackened, shapeless thing that bore no resemblance to a man. Several squaws were standing before him, their heads together as though they conferred. Their high-pitched, twittering voices drifted across the intervening space. Justin winced as they began throwing water over the still-smoking remains of the young warrior. They ceased their activity as two warriors approached them, one carrying a blanket. They conversed for a moment; then, on a burst of laughter, the squaws scattered. The two warriors did not speak to each other. Working together, they cut down the charred corpse, wrapped it in the blanket, and took it away.

Noticing the direction of Justin's eyes, White Bird spoke for the first time. "Tomorrow," he said in a solemn voice, "the bones of Black Cloud will be scattered. He has killed a chief, which is the greatest crime a warrior can commit. Therefore, he will not be given an honorable burial. There will be no food provided to take with him on his last journey. He will wander forever in darkness, for the gods will despise him and turn their faces from him. Even the dogs will scorn his remains."

There was no horror in White Bird's voice, not the smallest grain of compassion. He was unmoved by the fate of Black Cloud. He had given them a simple statement of fact. "Do you agree that such punishment was right?" Justin asked sharply.

"Yes, Lawrence, it was right. It was fitting. Tribal law is just."

"Just! I can't believe you really think that. Not you, White Bird!"

"He's Injun," Buck said. "Ain't a smidgen of use trying to change him. It cain't be done. He's got his beliefs, his own creed, just as you've got yours."

"And you, Buck? You're part-Indian."

Buck smiled his faint, tired smile. "I've got too much white blood in me, I reckon. Cain't think like an Injun. Still, Injun or not, we've all got a bit of the savage in us, ain't we?"

Justin was silent. Buck was right. A savage lurked in everyone. It needed only the right circumstances to bring it out. He thought of himself in Newgate Prison, and later on the convict ship. Loaded down with fetters, beaten, driven, he had finally turned like a savage and had tried to kill his persecutors. In Buck, the streak of savagery had come to the fore when he had killed Swift River, his great-grandfather. Justin glanced at the Indian boy. Of the three, White Bird was the innocent. He acted as he believed right, and always with honor. He saw no wrong in anything he did, for he thought in the way he had been reared to think. Cruelty played no part in his thinking. It was simply justice, as he knew it. A child of the wilderness, and just as untamed. A savage, but still an innocent.

A high shriek startled them. The shriek came from a fat squaw. She was waddling rapidly toward the group about the fire, her flabby arms waving in excitement. "It is the halfbreed," she shouted. "She has turned a knife upon herself. She bleeds! She dies!"

A strangled sound came from Buck. In the light of the fire his face seemed drained of all life. "Lianne ... no!" His voice was uncontrolled.

"Stop!" White Bird's voice was sharp and commanding. "You are my friend, a man of honor. It is my wish to protect you from the eyes of the warriors. Do not let them see your grief. They wish to break you. It is what they have been waiting for. Do you understand?"

"Sure I understand," Buck said fiercely. "Don't show a goddamned thing. Keep your face like a wooden mask. That's the way of you Injuns, ain't it?" Hot, helpless tears welled into his eyes. "I ain't Injun enough, not to suit you, for I cain't think your way. And why the hell should I care anyway? Don't matter no more. If my little gal's dead, then nothing don't matter!"

"Listen to me, Buck." Justin spoke urgently, impelled by a dread of seeing the strength of Buck Carey broken. "We don't know for certain that Lianne is dead. Or, for that matter, Carrie. Until we do, try to hold on."

White Bird's attention was on the renewed thunder of the drums. "The ceremony of the healing is about to begin," he announced. "It is for the white woman." He listened again, then turned to Buck. "And for the half-breed woman."

Buck drew a shuddering breath. "Then Lianne is alive."

"Yes." White Bird's eyes were troubled. "It would have been better had she died. Better for the white woman, too."

Justin was not listening. He had seen Caroline. Two braves were carrying her toward the fire. Two other braves followed, carrying Lianne. Both were placed on the ground. Firelight flickered over Caroline's white face, gilding her hair, which had been loosened again. Beside her, Lianne lay very still.

The drumbeat grew louder as a strange figure emerged from the wigwam that stood nearest to the fire. Justin's heart pounded. Sweat broke out thickly on his forehead and rolled down his face as the figure approached the recumbent women.

Buck tore his eyes from Lianne. "Who the hell is that?"

"Listen," White Bird said sternly. "Do you not hear the warriors shouting his name? He is Red Sky, the medicine man. Few white eyes have ever looked upon this ceremony. Magic will flow from him."

Red Sky was the same height as Fighting Bear, and in every way gigantic. He was naked except for a beaded breechclout that strained over the great mound of his belly. His face, his legs, and his upper body had been painted in brilliant whorls of scarlet, green, and blue. About his eyes had been painted two circles, the inner circle red, the outer circle white. On his head he wore a bonnet made of snakeskins. The skins, which dangled to his shoulders, had been stuffed, and they had a frighteningly lifelike appearance. In his left hand he carried a rattle.

Justin drew in a sharp breath as Red Sky went on his knees between the two women. As he peered first into Caroline's unconscious face, and then into Lianne's, the skins that composed his bonnet appeared to be writhing.

Red Sky's intent scrutiny continued for a few moments. Then, lifting his head, he said something in a low voice. The hand holding the rattle motioned to two braves who were standing nearby.

The men came forward. One man lifted Caroline, turning her onto her stomach. The other did the same with Lianne. Stepping away again, the two men disappeared into the wigwam from which Red Sky had recently emerged. When they appeared again, one man was carefully carrying a large bark bowl filled with water. His companion held a long stick on which was fixed a square rough stone. The bowl of water was set down before Red Sky. Another motion of the rattle, and the man carrying the stick jumped forward and placed the stone head into the glowing heart of the fire.

Buck's voice was loud and frightened. "They're going to burn them with that stone!"

"It is to draw the poisons from their bodies." White Bird's calm voice sought to reassure him.

Justin did not hear Buck's frantic voice. Full of his own fear, he shouted curses and insults. If he could attract their attention, perhaps he could put an end to this grim farce they called healing. Straining against his bonds, he choked against the cord that bound his throat. In his mind he saw Caroline's soft skin blistering beneath the heated stone. He began to shout again.

Nobody moved or even glanced his way. For all the attention they paid, his cries might have been the buzzing of a fly, and as unimportant.

Red Sky, too, was undisturbed by the outburst. He remained motionless, his eyes looking upward as though in prayer. Then, with a quick movement, his big hands picked up the bowl and held it to his lips. Even the drums fell silent, the drummers intent upon the movements of the medicine man. Red Sky drew water into his mouth. The noisy sucking sound came plainly to Justin's ears. His cheeks bulging with fluid, the man replaced the bowl. Shaking his rattle violently and thumping his breast with his right hand, he pursed his lips and sprayed the water over himself. Then, with a curiously graceful movement for so large a man, he rose to his feet and began a furious shaking of the rattle over the prone bodies.

Sweat stung blindingly in Justin's eyes, and he blinked them furiously in an effort to clear his vision. Red Sky swam into focus as he approached the fire. Grasping the stick, he drew the stone head from the fire.

Nausea rose in Justin as he stared at the glowing head that was about to sear Caroline. "Stop this!" he shouted.

Red Sky turned his bonneted head, and the fierce eyes circled in white and red glared in Justin's direction. Other than that, it was as before, with the attention of the people concentrated entirely on the medicine man. Justin could hear Buck's agitated breathing, but he did not turn to look at him. With stark horror he watched Red Sky place the white-hot stone on Caroline's back. Her body jumped beneath the pressure. Turning, he did the same to Lianne. A strong smell of singeing flesh came to them.

"They ain't moving!" Buck said on a sobbing breath. "God curse that painted-up swine. He's killed them!"

Red Sky continued to touch the stone to both backs. He did this until the stone dulled from its first fierce glow. Then, satisfied, he flung the instrument to one side. Again he motioned to the two braves. Once more they disappeared inside the wigwam. When they emerged, they were carrying small bowls made of colored bark.

Grunting, Red Sky took the first bowl. Tipping it, he poured a scarlet stream over Caroline's back. Squatting down on his heels, he held out his hand for the second bowl. It contained a colorless paste, which he proceeded to smear lavishly over Lianne's chest. The job done, he held up his hand so that all might see the rusty red smear on his fingers.

"Blood!" Buck breathed. "That's her blood on his fingers!"

"The bleeding will stop soon," White Bird said in the same calm voice. "The red fluid is to draw out the poisons in Caroline's body, and to soothe her fever. I know, because I have watched this treatment many times. The paste that is without color is for wounds. It will rapidly heal the wound that the half-breed inflicted on herself."

Justin said nothing. He looked on with bleak, hopeless eyes as four more braves came forward. Two of them picked up Caroline, and the other two lifted Lianne. Chanting, the braves began to circle the fire with their burdens. Watching, he was certain that Caroline was dead. His brave, fiery little Carrie! She had survived floggings, plague, and famine, only to come to this. Death at the hands of these murdering savages. "I am going to die too, Carrie," he whispered. "But before I die, I'm going to do my best to take some of them with me. If it can be done, I will do it. I swear this to you, Carrie, love!"

A sudden movement caught Justin's eyes. Turning his head slightly, he saw that Fighting Bear was watching him. He stared back at him, hatred in his eyes.

Once again the orderly and correct Fighting Bear found himself shaken out of his reserve by the look in the white man's eyes. Walking forward, he stopped before the prisoners. "Your women will live," he said.

Chapter 22

Days had passed. Justin had lost count of how many. Wearily he opened his swollen eyes and stared at the now familiar scene. The great fire in the center of the circle of wigwams, which was never allowed to die. Squaws, busy at their unending tasks, stirring the contents of cook pots, tending their children, softening pieces of hide with their spittle and their grinding teeth for the making of moccasins, pounding garments clean on the stones beside the lake. Children, undisturbed by the scolding of the women or the stern glances of the men, shrieking and laughing at their play, darting here and there, like children everywhere. Braves, seated cross-legged before their wigwams, boasting of their deeds and their prowess in hunting, each man seeking to outdo the other. Making fresh arrows, sharpening the blunted heads of old ones, smoking their strangely shaped pipes, conversing amicably together. Sometimes, tiring of conversation, a brave would raise a beckoning hand to the particular squaw who served his needs. The squaw would rush forward in instant obedience, and there was nothing in her demeanor to suggest that she resented the imperious demands of the male. He was the hunter. The master. If anything, the squaw seemed overeager to serve. At his request, she would bring him meat, a drink in a bark bowl. She would wash his tired feet. And always, as the day drew to a close, it was her duty to sponge down her man's body with the icy water drawn from the lake. Afterward, she would groom his long, oiled black hair, inspecting it carefully for signs of lice.

Justin drew in a deep, shuddering breath. The endless hours and days. His limbs felt dead, no longer a part of him. His throat burned, feeling raw from the chafing of the cord. Beside him, Buck and White Bird were in like condition. When they could no longer keep their eyes open, they would try for a snatched sleep, only to have the strangling cord jerk them awake again. Even when they were released from their bonds to relieve themselves, they were not free for long enough to bring back the proper circulation to arms and legs. They were assured each time by the braves who guarded them that these brief periods of release were obtained only at the mercy of Bright Feather.

Mercy! Justin's lips twisted bitterly. Was it mercy to keep them trussed up, tied in such a way that it allowed no movement to restore life to numbed limbs, with a cord about the throat to make sure that they could not sleep? In time, he knew Bright Feather would order their death. Why not now? What was he waiting for?

Buck began to cough. Justin, glancing at him, saw that he was shivering. "How are you feeling, Buck?"

"Middling, lad." He began to cough again.

"Try keeping your head back, Buck," Justin said sharply. "Do you want to strangle yourself?"

Buck gasped. "It'd be an unpleasant death, I grant you, but likely quicker than the one they've got in mind for us."

Averting his eyes from Buck's gaunt, flushed face, Justin thought of the earlier plans they had made to overpower their guards. Freedom or death—they did not care which. It was to be put into operation on one of their brief periods of release, when they had been conducted to that spot just beyond the center of the village. They had tried, and failed. Vain hope! Laughable! They could barely stand, let alone raise their stone-heavy arms to make a fight of it.

A smell from one of the cook pots interrupted Justin's train of thought, and he realized in astonished bitterness that he was actually hungry. The spicy smell came from the pot that was hanging over a smaller fire to the left of the central one. At least, he thought in grim amusement, even if it was a case of fattening the victim before the kill, they could not complain of being starved. They were not allowed to feed themselves, but at least they were fed. It was always the same squaw who spooned the food into their mouths. Old, hobbling rather than walking, she looked, with her snarled white hair and her heavy, seamed face, not unlike a witch. At first his stomach had rebelled against the smell and the look of the food, and he had been unable to keep it down. Buck, chewing on his own portion, had advised him not to think or to ask what it was that was being offered. For his peace of mind, Justin had taken that advice. Overcoming his squeamishness, he now ate whatever was offered. But why, he wondered now, did he bother to eat? To eat was to sustain life, and without Caroline he could see no purpose in it. Perhaps, he ate because of the lingering hope that was not entirely dead.

Justin closed his eyes. They had no hope. It was time he faced it. He could hear the drums. He frowned faintly at the sound, but they no longer bothered him. They were now simply a background irritant that he was capable of ignoring whenever he wished. Closing his mind against the muffled, monotonous sound, he thought of Caroline. He found himself haunted by the thought of her death, but equally haunted by the thought of her recovery. He could not think of her without feeling the grinding pain of loss, for whether she lived or died, she was lost to him. Who would have thought, in those far-off days when they had talked together, laughed and loved, and roamed the green English countryside, that they would come to death at the hands of savages, and a nameless burial in a savage and untamed country? The painted-up Indian savages of Carrie's nightmares. How she had feared them. Perhaps she had had some inner, not consciously recognized knowledge of her fate.

Standing stiffly erect in Bright Feather's wigwam, Fighting Bear asked the question that had been in his mind for the last few days. "Why did you delay the torture of the prisoners by the warrior squaws?"

Bright Feather's eyebrows rose mockingly. He would make all very clear to him. "Today the women will be brought from the healing lodge. It is my wish that the pale-skin and half-breed woman be present to watch the torture of their men." He paused, then added on a note of malice, "You have not forgotten that the torture of the men by the warrior squaws was your idea?"

Fighting Bear nodded, his hands clenching at his sides. It had been his idea. Even though, at that time, Bright Feather had sought to claim the idea as his own. When he had asked Bright Feather for the torture of the prisoners, he had been angry and disgusted with himself for what he believed to be a weakness, and he had wished to prove to himself that he could be strong and ruthless. Now, because he knew that he had no need to prove anything, he was wishing that he had never made the request.

"What are you thinking about, Fighting Bear?" The malicious note in Bright Feather's voice was very pronounced.

Fighting Bear flushed with anger. "I was thinking that I was wrong," he said stiffly. "The pale-skins have no knowledge that would be of value to us; therefore, since they are to die anyway, the torture of their bodies is not necessary."

Fighting Bear was soft. A hollow mockery of a man. He should be called woman rather than warrior. Bright Feather felt a thrill of triumph. At last he had found a chink in the man's seeming perfection. "The torture will proceed," he said harshly. "I have spoken. . . .Come, Fighting Bear, why do you look so gloomy. Is your heart so tender that it is lacerated by the thought of the pale-skins' agony?"

At the implied insult, Fighting Bear's muscles tightened with anger. For a mad moment he was tempted to fling his knife into the sneering face. Controlling himself with an effort, he reflected on the situation. He could do nothing. Raising his head, he looked deeply into Bright Feather's eyes. "You have spoken," he said quietly. "There is one other matter that I must bring to your notice."

Bright Feather felt his anger rising hot and strong. He knew what Fighting Bear was about to say. He had hoped to avoid the subject of White Bird altogether, trusting that, in time, it would be completely forgotten. He should have remembered that Fighting Bear was nothing if not tenacious. "Speak, then," he growled.

Fighting Bear smiled inwardly. He was well aware of the devious workings of Bright Feather's mind. The man had no honor. He was unfit to be a chief. "It is on the matter of White Bird that I would speak." He paused. "My words are scarcely necessary, I know, for you will not have forgotten that you gave your word that you would see him."

Bright Feather's eyes narrowed. If only Fighting Bear were not so popular with the braves, he would kill him where he stood. But perhaps, later, an accident might be arranged. Comforted by this, he answered curtly, "Since I have given my word, you have no need to remind me. After the torture, you may bring White Bird to my lodge." With a dismissing gesture, Bright Feather rose to his feet. "The warrior squaws are assembled. They await my signal to begin."

Lying stiffly on her bed of soft skins, the fire in the center of the lodge warming her toes, Lianne listened to the babble of voices outside. She could not make out words, but the voices sounded shrill and excited on the part of the squaws; and on the part of the men, deep, vibrating with the same excitement. Her heart plunged, and then commenced a rapid beating. Something cruel was going to happen. Even here, in the healing lodge, she could feel the excited tension of those outside. Her mind flew to Buck. Was it something to do with him alone, or all three of the male prisoners?

Restlessly Lianne turned her head to one side, her eyes staring toward the entrance of the lodge. She had tried to kill herself, she thought with a rush of bitterness. She had wanted so badly to die, but they would not let her. She was to be spared nothing! Turning her head again, she looked at Caroline, lying next to her. Caroline's fever had only recently broken, and she was still weak. Even so, Lianne wondered how she could possibly sleep. With a touch of resentment in her eyes, her gaze swept over the other woman's wasted figure, then came to rest on the twitching face. The white woman slept uneasily, as though she had taken her nightmares with her into sleep.

Lianne looked away again, her resentment dying. After all, she did not envy Caroline her sleep, not if nightmares stalked it. The nightmares of full consciousness were bad enough. Her lips moved. "Buck . . ." She said his name softly, yearningly. "I would willingly give up my life to save yours."

Lianne moved restlessly, without thought. Pain stabbed through the healing wound in her chest. Her lips pressed tightly together, she thought of yesterday, when she had dragged herself across the floor to the opening of the lodge. Many days had passed since she had gashed her chest with the knife, but for Buck and his fellow prisoners, time had stood still, or so it seemed to her. They were still lashed tightly to the posts, their heads held awkwardly in order to avoid strangulation. The difference was the terrible change in their appearance. They looked gaunt and worn and at the last stages of exhaustion. Staring at them, she heard the painful sound of Buck's coughing. One way or the other, he was going to die; she was sure of it. Gods of mercy, let him die easy, let them all die easy.

Thinking of her fervent prayers, Lianne felt bitter tears fill her eyes. Of what use her prayers? What was life worth if she could not spend it with Buck? That was why she had tried to kill herself, because she had not wanted to hear the groans of agony they would wring from him. She had not wanted her eyes to see the torture that would be inflicted upon him.

"Justin!" Caroline's scream of terror as she started up, the wild expression in her eyes, startled Lianne. "Justin! What are they doing to you?"

Her screams had been heard. Instantly the skin flap that guarded the entrance to the lodge was pushed to one side. Two squaws entered. One was tall and angular, the other short and inclined to plumpness. The tall squaw, after glaring with hard suspicion at the two prisoners, spoke in a loud, hectoring voice. "You are both to come with us." Reaching down, she grasped Caroline's arm and dragged her roughly to her feet. She looked at Lianne, at the short squaw who was standing over her. "Get the half-breed to her feet," she shouted angrily. "Why do you just stand there looking?"

"Where are you taking us?" Caroline tried to pull her arm free. "I demand to know!" Her voice was weak and unconsciously arrogant.

The tall squaw stared at Caroline with baleful black eyes. She noted the fine film of perspiration on the haggard, colorless face, the faint tremble of her lips. Enjoying her moments of power, she tightened her grip, her fingers digging painfully into Caroline's arm. She thought of her husband, who had died at the hands of the pale-skins. They had killed him with the long stick that spat fire. He had died in agony, a ball of hot iron in his stomach, tearing his insides apart. "Demand, do you, pale-skin?" she snarled. "Then I will tell you. You are to witness the torture of the pale-skin men and the traitor Indian."

The hard-packed dirt floor beneath Caroline's feet seemed to heave up. This was to be the end of the dream of happiness she and Justin had had. The grand and glorious adventure, which had led them to death. She must witness Justin's torture. Before her eyes, they would break the strong, lithe body that had so often covered hers.

The tall squaw stared at Caroline. Because she had heard so many tales of the weakness of the white women and the unseemly emotions they were not ashamed of showing, she waited expectantly for the tears and the hysteria. No sound came from the prisoner. Instead, the squaw found herself flushing before the strange look in the dry, feverishly bright eyes, which showed no fear. She felt no admiration for the prisoner's stoicism. She was full of disappointment and anger. She wanted to see her weep and tremble. She wanted to hear her beg for mercy for her man. Losing her temper completely, she dropped Caroline's arm. Her hand shot out, and her fingers twined in her hair instead, twisting viciously. "The warrior squaws await." The blood drained from Lianne's face as she followed after Caroline.

Caroline stared across the fire at Justin, and an agony of grief awoke in her. The sight of him had brought her back to life. She struggled fiercely with the squaw, who was attempting to force her to her knees. Her voice rose to a shriek. "Justin, I'm here! I'm coming to you!"

Justin stared. He had been so convinced that she had died beneath the brutal treatment of the medicine man that, for a moment, he could not believe she was really there. She was a pale ghost of herself, her face paper-white, her long, light, unbound hair streaming over her shoulders. "Carrie!" He shouted her name. "My darling, I see you!"

Caroline heard him above the crackling of the flames and the sound of many voices. Her heart leaped with a wild joy, for they had not broken him yet. Her struggles increased. She would get to him, even if she died in the attempt. Managing to wrench one arm free, she struck the squaw hard in the face. "You can't keep me from him! I won't let you!"

A blow from the squaw's clenched fist toppled her, sending her sprawling to her knees. She shook her head from side to side to clear it, her hair tossing with the motion; then she was on her feet again. She managed to run forward for a few paces before the squaw caught her and dragged her back.

The squaw stared at Caroline with hatred in her eyes. The white woman could barely stand, but even so, she was not finished yet. She was still prepared to fight. She raised her hand. She moved a pace nearer, her fist already doubled to strike, when a shrill scream diverted her attention. She turned her head, her mouth falling open with surprise as she saw Pale Flower dragging the shrieking half-breed.

"Enough!" a voice roared. A hand reached down and jerked Lianne to her feet.

Pale Flower arose shakily. Trembling, she stood meekly before Fighting Bear. In the sudden silence that had fallen, the sound of her agitated breathing was very loud. Pale Flower hung her head. "The prisoners were trying to ... to escape," she stammered.

"You lie!" Lianne pushed herself forward. She was trembling violently, but she managed to stand erect. She looked boldly into Fighting Bear's eyes. His eyes dropped to the stain on the front of her tunic. "You are bleeding," he said. "Your wound has opened up again."

Lianne shrugged. "I care nothing if I bleed to death, for such was my intention. But first, let me go to Buck Carey."

"You accept the thought of death calmly?" Fighting Bear's dark eyes studied her. "You are a half-breed, yet you have courage." He beckoned to the tall squaw. "Take the half-breed woman to the healing lodge. Pack the wound with fresh moss. It will stanch the bleeding. Afterward, she is to be brought back to watch the torture, for so Chief Bright Feather has commanded."

With Lianne's screams ringing in her ears, Caroline studied the tall warrior with the crossed scarlet coup feathers blowing in his long, loose hair. Firelight glinted on the heavy chains of copper about his neck and made a multicolored dazzle of the beads that decorated his fringed white tunic. Feeling her stare, he turned his head to look at her, the heavy loops of copper that weighted down his ears swaying with the movement. There was something about the warrior's dark eyes that vaguely reminded her of Justin's own. Not recognizing the absurdity of such a feeling, she found herself faintly encouraged by this. Caroline's eyes did not flinch from his. She had the strangest feeling he wished the prisoners well. Her legs were trembling beneath her. The scene was like something out of one of her worst nightmares. The tall, barbaric figure of Fighting Bear. The leaping fire, the wigwams, the fierce, painted dark faces, the glittering eyes that watched her. Jus-

tin, Buck, White Bird—the three who waited to die. A nightmare she would not awaken from. The shadows and the terror would not go away. The only end to her pain and fear
would be in the darkness of the grave. Her hands clenched.
Speak, she told herself. Do anything to stop the screams from
escaping and shattering you utterly. Fighting Bear's eyes were
upon her. A sob caught in Caroline's throat as she watched
Bright Feather approach. She remembered the rank smell of
his body, the blaze of lust in his eyes, and her skin crawled
with loathing. She could no longer keep the terror at bay. She
knew they were all going to die. She lifted her head, and
across the fire her eyes met Justin's. He was smiling at her.
She forced her trembling lips to return the smile, trying by
this means to convey her love to him. It was all that was left
to them.

Watching her, Justin instinctively knew what her open-
handed gesture signified. She was releasing her hold on his
life and on her own. He had wondered if she hoped for a
miracle of deliverance. It was obvious to him now that she
had resigned herself to death and waited only for the moment
of their release.

Justin's jaw set in a hard, grim line as the warrior squaws
assembled. In their outer appearance they were no different
from the other women. The difference lay mostly in their
stony expressions and their hard, fierce eyes. He detected another difference. Their broad shoulders and their heavily
muscled arms gave them the appearance of being men in
women's garb.

Caroline did not notice when Lianne came to sit beside
her, and her voice caused her to start violently. "Gods protect
them, Caroline! I did not wish to see this. I had hoped to die
first."

Caroline's heart was beating so rapidly that she feared she
might be sick. Her eyes widened in stark horror as a wild,
spiraling scream came from one of the warrior squaws.
"Heya—a—a—heya! Kill them! Torture the pale-skins. Kill!
Kill!" Leaping toward the roaring fire, the squaw withdrew a
flaming stick. She was immediately followed by the others,
who repeated her action.

Justin's muscles tensed. The women were circling them.
They had blown out the flame on the sticks they held, and to

Justin it seemed that their eyes glowed like wolves'. That was what they were, he thought, a pack of wolves in human form, circling their victims, waiting for an opening to rend and devour.

Wild screams came tearing from their throats as the first woman sprang. The hot end of the stick jabbed into Justin's cheek, the heat searing, the specially sharpened end gashing his flesh. Beside him, Buck gave a muffled cry of pain. First blood! The blood excited the women, for suddenly, like the ravening animals they resembled, they swarmed all over their victims. The sharpened, still-hot sticks thrust at faces, at bodies, stabbed dangerously near to eyes, never quite entering, prolonging the agony until it was time to deliver the blinding thrust.

The women came on again. This time, in place of the sticks, they held sharpened stones. Stones to gash and scrape at tortured flesh, to cut the soles of the feet, to hammer at faces and arms, to reduce the whole body to flaming pain.

Just before he closed his eyes to shut out the sight of the wild faces and the glowing eyes, Justin caught a fleeting glimpse of Buck and White Bird. Their faces reflected his own agony.

Standing beside Chief Bright Feather, Fighting Bear looked on with a set expression. The women had reduced the faces of their victims to masks of blood. There were cuts on arms, legs, and breasts. Blood dripped from torn feet. Despite the hammering of the stones, he did not think that any bones had been broken yet. The warrior squaws were too shrewd and skilled in the methods of torture to do this. The breaking of the bones would be left to the last.

Fighting Bear turned his head and looked at Bright Feather. "It is true that they are our enemies," he said, "yet it does seem to me that they have shown themselves to be true warriors. Not once have the squaws been able to wring a cry from their lips. Even the traitor, in my opinion, has proved himself to be worthy of mercy. My chief, may we not show them mercy? May they not be allowed to die with dignity?"

Bright Feather did not answer. His eyes were fixed on the contorted face of the Indian boy, White Bird. The question of the boy's identity loomed large on his mind. Once again the disconcerting flashes of memory troubled him. A sunlit field.

Horses. The glossy, stretching necks of the animals as they cropped placidly at the grass. A sobbing boy. A mare who stood over the boy, nuzzling at his neck as if in sympathy. And himself, going to that boy, pulling him upward into a sitting position, speaking to him consolingly. "White Bird, it is not manly to display such grief. Come, now, will you not cease these tears?"

The boy clinging to him, hiding his hot, wet face against his shoulder. "I am a cripple, Bright Feather! I am as weak and as delicate as a squaw. I am a nothing!"

He had held the boy, for he had felt differently about things then, and he had had much compassion. "Yes, you are a cripple. But you have strength, White Bird. When you have your full growth, you will be a fearless warrior."

White Bird's arms had clung tighter. "You are my friend, Bright Feather?"

"Yes. Always your friend, White Bird. I swear this to you."

"The others laugh at me, but you do not. Why is this, Bright Feather?"

"I have told you. Although we are of different tribes, although the paths of our lives lie in different directions, you are my brother and my friend. We are destined to be parted, for that is the way of life. But should we meet again, ask of me what you will, and if it is within my power, I will grant it. I shall never forget you, little warrior. My oath on this!"

Bright Feather drew in a sharp breath. But he had forgotten. Until this moment, it was as if the memory of White Bird had been washed from his mind. Remembering White Bird's fervent admiration, and his own sympathy, even love for the pathetic crippled boy, he felt strange and forgotten emotions warring inside him.

Fighting Bear looked at Bright Feather with curious eyes. The chief was a man of such overwhelming ambition that he would kill any who stood in the way of that ambition; yet, at this moment, those predatory qualities that made up his nature seemed absent. He looked strangely vulnerable. "My chief . . ." Fighting Bear stooped and spoke into his ear. "Is anything wrong?"

Bright Feather started. He looked at Fighting Bear, but his face was blank. "Call off the squaws," he snapped. "They are to do nothing more to the prisoners until I give them the word." He turned on his heel. "Cut the traitor loose. Bring him to me. I will speak with him."

He strode away. Fighting Bear stared after him in amazement. Then, recovering himself, he moved toward the prisoners.

Chapter 23

Scorning the help of Fighting Bear, White Bird hobbled painfully toward the lodge of Chief Bright Feather. His eyes were
swollen almost closed, yet he had vision enough to be aware
of the eyes that watched him. Even more was he aware of the
warrior squaws, who, having been drawn off from their
victims, now stood on the other side of the fire, glaring in
frustration and muttering among themselves. They did not
understand or like the startling interruption in their work.
They were animals, not women, White Bird thought contemptuously. Animals who were temporarily unable to get at their
prey.

White Bird darted a swift look at Fighting Bear, who
walked on his left, and he remembered that he had yet to
thank him. It was painful to talk, but he managed it. "My
thanks to you, Fighting Bear."

"Why do you thank me, traitor?"

White Bird winced. No matter how many times he was
called so, he could not think of himself as a traitor. He had
tried to explain that he was no traitor, that, despite appear-
ances, he was loyal to his own people. He knew well that
their minds were too steeped in hatred of the pale-skins to
understand that some were different. That it was possible to
be friends with those special ones and still keep honor. He
said stiffly, "I am no traitor, Fighting Bear, whatever you
may choose to think. And I thank you for influencing Chief
Bright Feather to see me."

Fighting Bear hesitated, and then spoke with his usual
blunt honesty. "I have no influence over Chief Bright
Feather, and therefore I failed. The decision to see you was
his own." It was true, Fighting Bear thought, glancing at
White Bird. It was not his influence that had persuaded

306

Bright Feather, but something deep within him. The same something that had put that vulnerable look on his face.

Entering the lodge, accompanied by Fighting Bear, White Bird found Chief Bright Feather seated cross-legged by the fire, his eyes gazing into the flames. He was not alone. Three braves were lying on wooden hurdles drawn close to the fire. The hard wood beneath them had been softened with woven reed mats. Over the mats was a bearskin. A second skin, rolled up neatly with the fur outward, formed a pillow. At their feet was a third rolled-up skin, to be drawn over them when the night air grew cold.

Without looking at White Bird, Bright Feather lifted his hand in a signal for the others to leave. Only when they had withdrawn did he look up. A further motion of his hand indicated to White Bird that he was to be seated. With some difficulty, White Bird forced his painful limbs to bend. His legs were too painful to draw them up in Bright Feather's easy position, so he compromised by half-sitting, half-sprawling. Outside, with the cool wind blowing on his burned and gashed skin, the pain had been bearable. But here, with the warmth of the fire reaching out to every corner of the lodge, it was agony. He tightened his lips to suppress a groan.

If Bright Feather noticed his discomfort, he paid it no attention. Picking up a sliver of pine wood from a large pile beside him, he examined it minutely, as though it were of absorbing interest. "Do you know why I have sent for you?" he said at last.

White Bird hesitated. He had no way of knowing if Bright Feather had recognized him, and he did not know what he was expected to say. "You were kind enough to listen to my request and to grant it, Chief Bright Feather," he said carefully. "I am grateful to you."

Bright Feather replaced the sliver of wood on the pile. Turning his narrow dark eyes on White Bird, he said in a harsh voice, "It was because I have remembered that we were once brothers and friends. Until a few moments ago, I had forgotten your very existence. For this I feel regret." He frowned, surprised at his own words. He had not meant to say this. He had meant to be aloof and stern, his dignified attitude reminding White Bird that he was a chief, and no longer that simple youth of long ago. But there was something in the boy's eyes, a warmth that he was not used to seeing in the

eyes of those who looked his way. It made him feel that he
was all that he had wished to be. It would be so easy to re-
kindle the admiration that White Bird had once had for him,
perhaps still had. Quite suddenly his desire was that this
should be so. The harsh note in his voice gentled. "What is it
you wish of me, White Bird?"

White Bird stared at him. There was a difference in this
man that dismayed him. He was not as he had dreamed he
would be, should they meet again. He looked hard and dissi-
pated, and the line of his mouth was cruel. Yet, the expression in the eyes regarding him was almost that of the
Bright Feather he had loved and admired. He wanted to
reach out to him, to place his hand over his wrist in the old
friendly clasp, but he did not dare. Taking up his courage, he
said quickly, "Bright Feather, do you really believe me to be
a traitor to my own people?"

"You have mingled freely with the pale-skins. It would
seem so to me."

"But it is not so. Justin Lawrence and Buck Carey are not
like those others who have shown only greed and cruelty.
They are good men." With Bright Feather's eyes upon him,
he stumbled through an explanation, telling him as clearly as
he could of the circumstances that had caused his life to run
with that of the two white men. Even when his voice trailed
into silence, he could not tell if he had made any impression
upon Bright Feather. "Do you believe me, Bright Feather?"

Bright Feather's answer surprised and delighted him. "I
watched you endure torture. It is as I said it would be. You
have turned into a brave warrior."

"Then you believe me?"

A faint smile touched Bright Feather's lips. "How can I
not believe you? A warrior does not lie." He leaned forward.
"You have not yet told me what it is you wish of me?"

White Bird took a deep breath. "I wish you to take my life
in exchange for the pale-skins' and their women's."

Rage rose in Bright Feather, mingled with jealousy. "I do
not want your life, for you have proved yourself to me. But
the pale-skins must die."

"And I do not want my life given back to me in this way.
If they die, I die."

Bright Feather saw the boy's admiration dying. It had been
a heady experience for him. He had always looked upon him-

self as a great warrior, but although he had proved himself
by many deeds of valor, he could not help knowing that
those he most wished to impress had a low opinion of him as
a man. Now, even though his need angered him, he was hungry for the admiration that White Bird had always given him,
and he was reluctant to let it go. "What is it?" he snapped.
"Why do you look at me like that?"

"Forgive me if I offend, great Bright Feather. I was
remembering the words you once spoke to me."

"What words?"

"You once told me that I could ask of you what I willed.
You said that if it was within your power, you would grant
it. This thing that I ask is within your power, for you are
now a great chief. The two white men came to rescue their
women. In their place, it is a thing that you or I would have
done. I tell you again that they are good and honest men.
They are innocent of crimes against our people."

"And how do I know that this is really so? Many of the
pale-skins plead innocence, even while their hands still drip
with the blood of our people. I ask you again. How do I
know that this is so?"

"Because I have said it." White Bird bit his lip against the
burning pain of his body. He was wondering how much
longer he could sit calmly before Bright Feather without betraying his agony. Forcing a smile, he went on, "You have
said yourself that a warrior does not lie. I know these men.
I know their hearts and their minds."

Caught in his own trap, Bright Feather glared at him. The
last thing he wanted was to let the pale-skins go. Yet this
desire in him to have and keep White Bird's admiration was
growing. In the old days of their friendship, that admiration
had amounted to something that was almost idolatry. With
the boy's eyes steady upon him, he moved restlessly. His long,
thin fingers plucked at his hair, tugging on it fiercely as he
gave himself up to thought. There were only two courses
open to him, he decided at last. His black brows drew together in a frown. He could give an outright refusal and surrender the admiration and love that he greatly coveted, or he
could acquiesce. No, he would not refuse. Most certainly he
would acquiesce, but there must be conditions attached. Only
in this way could he bring himself to grant freedom to the
pale-skins and their women. He smiled inwardly. He did not

think the pale-skins could meet the conditions. He looked up. "White Bird," he said in a deep, solemn voice, "this thing that you ask of me shall be granted, provided that the pale-skins can prove themselves to me."

White Bird's eyes narrowed. There was a feeling of great dread inside him, for he thought he knew what was in Bright Feather's mind. "How so?" he asked.

"They must run the gauntlet."

White Bird's feeling of dread increased. "Most white men who run the gauntlet have not been robbed of their strength," he ventured. "Bright Feather has always been just and merciful to me. Would he be less so to others, even those whom he mistakenly believes to be his enemies?"

Bright Feather smiled. He could afford to make concessions. To run the gauntlet would try even the strongest. "They will be given sufficient time to recover their strength."

"I thank you, Bright Feather." White Bird hesitated. "And will the warriors use clubs or bastinadoes?"

Bright Feather pretended to consider. "Both," he said at last. His smile widened. "We know, do we not, White Bird, that innocent men will not be allowed to die under the battering of the warriors? The gods would not allow it."

White Bird's eyes met his. "And if we live?"

Bright Feather was startled by the question. "Why do you speak of 'we'? I have said you have proved yourself to me. You have no need to run the gauntlet."

"I, too, have a need to prove my innocence before all of my brothers. I wish to run with the other two."

"But you are lame!" Bright Feather saw White Bird's involuntary flinch, and he added quickly, "Nonetheless, you are a warrior."

"Therefore, Bright Feather, I beg you to let me run. Because I am innocent of treachery, the gods will, for that time take my lameness from me."

"You believe this will be so?"

"I do, Bright Feather."

"Very well." Bright Feather spoke reluctantly. "Perhaps it is the will of the gods speaking to me through your lips. You may run with the pale-skins."

White Bird bent his head in acknowledgment. Looking up again, he spoke in a low voice. "If the pale-skins succeed, you will let them go free?"

"I will." Bright Feather rose to his feet. "Then it is finished," he said, looking down at White Bird. "Remember this. What I have said will be." Going to the entrance of the lodge, he paused there a moment. "You will wait here." Pushing the skin that covered the entrance to one side, he went out.

White Bird waited patiently, his dark, wary gaze fixed on the entrance. Could he really trust a man as changed as Bright Feather? He moved, and a groan escaped him. His pain seemed to be mounting to a new height. He had the dismayed feeling that, should he attempt to rise, his legs would not support him.

Bright Feather was gone for some time. When he returned, he was accompanied by the medicine man. "I keep my promise to you, White Bird," Bright Feather said. "Your injuries shall be attended. Very soon you will heal, and with the healing, your full strength will return. Thus you cannot say that Bright Feather is not just and merciful."

White Bird looked at him, a long, close look that made Bright Feather wonder at the thoughts that moved behind his somber eyes. "It is as you say, Bright Feather. You are just and merciful. And shall the same be done for the pale-skins? If they are to run the gauntlet, they will have need of their strength."

Again Bright Feather felt the fierce flaring of anger. It had not been his intention to give aid to the white men. If they died, so much the better. Looking into White Bird's eyes, he saw that their expression had changed. Despite everything, he saw trust there. Once again that strange weakness moved inside him, for thus he designated the emotion. What was it about the boy that stirred these unfamiliar feelings, that made him desire to stand tall and noble in his eyes, to be everything he wished and thought him to be? With a rare truthfulness he acknowledged that even for White Bird he could not be everything that was noble, for this was not in his nature. But this one thing he could do. "It shall be," he said, and for all his desire to be noble, he spoke the words with a bad grace.

White Bird did not seem to notice the inflection. With his smile, some of the pain left his eyes. "I am grateful to you. You are indeed a great chief."

The medicine man saw the visible swelling of Bright

Feather's chest. The words of the boy had pleased him. Knowing well his own importance, the medicine man grunted. The sound told them that he was ready to get on with the healing and the conversation must now cease. A silence fell.

White Bird studied the awe-inspiring figure of the medicine man. He was painted and dressed as he had been on the occasion when he had attended Caroline and Lianne, except that he was not carrying the rattle. He was holding a rough wooden tray on which were several pots made of barkwood. As he knelt and placed the tray on the floor, the boy noticed that each pot contained a different-colored salve, while a larger pot held a light-green powder.

Staring into White Bird's eyes, the medicine man removed his bonnet of snakeskins. Without breaking his stare, he placed the bonnet next to the tray. It was as though his deep-set, hypnotic eyes were attempting to pierce through flesh and bone and discover the thoughts inside his patient's mind. White Bird felt lassitude overcoming him. He did not attempt to fight it, for with its coming the pain receded.

At last the medicine man turned his disconcerting eyes away and looked up at Bright Feather. "It is good," he said in his rumbling voice. "He is now in a condition to receive the treatment."

Bright Feather nodded. "My trust is in you, O wise one."

The medicine man's hands moved swiftly and lightly as he smeared the gashed flesh with a red salve. The burns, he treated with a yellow salve; and, finally, the whole of the body, even the uninjured parts, with a salve that was the color of violets. Satisfied that his patient was well-coated, he scooped up a handful of the light-green powder and sprinkled it lavishly, leaving a thick coating adhering to the salves. He was still for a moment, his eyes going over the body; then, his task finished, he picked up the tray and the bonnet of snakeskins. Rising to his feet, he departed in silence.

All through the process of the anointing, White Bird had felt nothing. He knew that the medicine man had entered into the temple of his mind and had rendered him immune to pain. Now that the anointing was over, he was conscious of a great and devastating weariness. He must sleep, or he would die. The tall figure of Bright Feather blurred, and White Bird's heavy eyes closed. Just before the black-velvet darkness of utter peace enveloped him, he saw the pain-twisted faces of Justin Lawrence and Buck Carey. His swollen lips moved, forming words. "The strong ones of this earth will always endure!"

Bright Feather looked down at the boy. Satisfied that he slept, he lowered himself to a squatting position. The strong ones of this earth. White Bird's mumbled words sounded in his ears again, and he was suddenly torn by doubt. Was he strong, or had his remembered and renewed affection for the lame boy rendered him weak? Thinking of Justin and Buck, he narrowed his eyes to gleaming slits of hate. No, he was not weak. He had given his word to White Bird, and he was determined to honor it. He would allow the curing of the white men's wounds. But when they ran the gauntlet, he would show them no mercy. His heart quailed as he thought of White Bird likewise running for his life, but he would not allow his feelings for the boy to soften him, he determined. Justin Lawrence and Buck Carey were pale-skins.

Smiling, Bright Feather sank back, his feet to the fire, his hands clasped behind his head. "May the gods grant that a tortured death be the end of the white dogs," he said with soft and deadly vehemence.

Chapter 24

Justin gazed up at the sky. It looked, he thought, like a great black-velvet canopy thickly sewn with stars. The moon, a great silver ball, hung low in the sky. So low that he had the illusion that if one reached up, it could be touched.

Impatient with the whimsy, Justin looked away. A cool breeze, fragrant with the mingled perfumes of the earth, touched his rapidly healing face. Experimentally he moved his loosely bound hands, and the thought came again to plague him. What was behind this lavish show of mercy on the part of Chief Bright Feather? Their wounds had been tended, their bonds loosened, and in company with their Indian guards they were allowed to exercise twice daily. They were still tied to the posts, but the strangling cord had been removed, and they were able to sleep. Uncomfortably, it was true, but sleep was sleep. Justin's thoughts went to White Bird. On the same night that they had been tortured by the warrior squaws, Fighting Bear had released White Bird from his bonds and taken him away. That had been some days ago. White Bird had not returned. He had not even been seen. Was he dead, or had he been taken to another place and imprisoned?

"Look there, Justin." Buck's voice scattered his troubled thoughts. "Them braves sure look like they're warming up for some kind of important action. Likely they've got something real special in mind. Drums ain't saying nothing as yet, so I don't know what it could be."

Justin turned his head and looked at him, and he marveled at the resilience of the man. Only a comparatively short time ago, a matter of days, Buck had had the appearance of a dying man. Torn by a cough, unable to keep food down, he had been so gaunt and exhausted that his death had seemed inevitable. Now, under the treatment of the medicine man, and

because of the relaxed bonds, coupled with the exercise and
the ability to sleep, he was a changed man. His cough seemed
to have vanished, his wounds were all but invisible, and he
ate whatever was offered to him and kept it down. But Buck,
like Justin himself, was far from being lulled by the unusual
leniency; he was highly suspicious of the motive behind it.
The words he had just spoken had been light enough, but
there was a troubled undercurrent to them. "We'll find out in
time, I suppose," Justin answered him. "You got any idea
what they're up to?"

"Just said I ain't." Buck hesitated, then jerked his head in
the direction of Bright Feather's lodge. "Could be I imagined
it, Justin, but I thought I caught a glimpse of White Bird a
moment ago."

"Where?" Justin turned his head sharply.

"Don't go snapping your neck. If it was him, he's gone
now."

Justin frowned. "Damned if I understand any of this. Why
hasn't White Bird been brought back . . . why have we been
shown mercy, if you can call it that?"

"Guess you can call it Injun-style mercy."

Justin grunted. "What the hell's going on, Buck?"

"Right now I cain't answer," Buck said. "Maybe the less
we know, the better."

Justin frowned. "I was just thinking aloud. I know you
don't have the answers."

"No, I don't. But this much I can tell you. Them Injuns
ain't about to let us go free, so it ain't no use getting your
hopes up."

"It's just that I keep hoping for a glimpse of Carrie. It's
driving me out of my mind, wondering what is going to happen to her."

Buck nodded. "Same here. I reckon them Injuns is just
about ready to . . ." He broke off, his breath catching in excitement. "It looks like our thoughts done conjured 'em up,
Justin. There's Caroline and Lianne." He lapsed into silence.
When he spoke again, there was a heavy, despairing note in
his voice. "Them gals is looking right perky. Been took real
good care of, you can see that. I cain't help wondering why."

The same thought had occurred to Justin. Looking at Caroline, he felt again the heavy burden of grinding anxiety that
was with him night and day, and he felt a bitter grief and

frustration at his helplessness to aid her. He would willingly give up his life for her, but since it was already forfeit, there was nothing he could do. When the bonds that held them had first been loosened, he had believed that he might manage to work his way free. A night of trying had shown him that it was hopeless. The bonds, though loosened, had been tied in such a way that it was impossible to get free. His eyes softened at the sight of her. She was looking at him, smiling the brilliant smile that was meant to uphold him and to cover her own terror. She was clad in a white buckskin tunic embroidered with colored beads. Her shining hair had been loosened. A thin band of colored leather circled her forehead, holding in place the three white feathers at the back of her head. She looked like a bride! The thought brought nausea, and he could feel the furious beating of the pulse in his temple. Dear God! Was that why she had been cared for—was she to be offered to a brave?

Buck's eyes were on Lianne. She was so beautiful, he thought painfully. So beautiful and so lost to him! Like Caroline, she was wearing a fringed and embroidered white buckskin tunic. Her black hair hung loose and shining about her shoulders, framing her small strained face and her haunted eyes. More than ever now she looked like his dead wife, Small Flower. So like that he had the crazy notion that Small Flower had come back from that misty and mysterious land of death to take his hand and guide him on his way. He blinked hard, dismissing the notion. Now he saw Lianne as herself. The hovering shadow of Small Flower had disappeared. To his wife he had given the sincere love of one part of his life, the eager, youthful part. To Lianne, child though she was in many ways, he gave the love of a mature man. Too late for anything but regret for the years he had wasted in idle roaming, in brawling and roistering.

It was almost as if Lianne had heard his thoughts. She sat up straight, her yearning eyes fixed upon him. "Buck Carey," she whispered, "if I am to die, I pray to the gods that it will be in your arms!"

Caroline heard her. A useless prayer, she thought. Lianne and her gods! Forgetting to smile, her mouth in a bitter line, she had prayed to her own God, prayed that she might be allowed to go to Justin. Again, a useless prayer. Her hand touched her shoulder as she remembered the savage beating she had received as punishment for her frantic attempts to gain his side. She looked at Lianne. "You want to die in Buck's arms?" she said in a hard voice. "But don't you know by now that you may look but not touch? You may watch their torture, but you may not stretch out a hand to comfort them. That is to be part of the punishment, to watch them die before your eyes."

Lianne stared at her. This was a different Caroline. A woman who had turned hard and bitter with the force of the pain that drove her. Lianne was suddenly frightened by the change in her. She understood it, but she was still afraid. "Don't!" she said. She scrubbed at her wet cheeks with a trembling hand. "I wish that I could die here and now!"

"Be quiet!" Caroline said fiercely. As Lianne shrank back, she said in a softer voice, "Don't cry, Lianne. Smile. A smile is such a little thing, and so useless at a time like this, but it is all we can do for them now. Tears will only add to their burden."

"How can you talk of smiling when Lawrence and Buck are to die?"

"What else can we do?"

Lianne glared at her. "And when they are dead, what is left to us? What shall we do without them?"

Death! Caroline shuddered. If only she could make her mind a blank, but even in her haunted dreams the grief and the terror rode her. Justin! Those intense dark eyes of his closed in death. The firm mouth that had smiled at her, that had kissed her in passion, in tenderness, and, yes, in those days before they had found love, had even kissed her in contempt for what he had believed her to be—that mouth, to be cold and still! My God, I cannot bear this! It is too much to be borne.

"What shall we do without them?" Lianne said again.

Caroline looked at her, her eyes feverishly bright. "I'll tell you what we can do. We can die! If this is also your wish, Lianne, we can die!"

Hot, responsive feeling rose in Lianne. "Yes, it is my wish. I do not want to live on without Buck!" In the first caress she had ever given to her, she laid her hand over Caroline's and squeezed gently. "Your words are good. I will remember them."

From the shadows cast by the lodge, White Bird watched

the two male prisoners. For many days he had stood watching them. He had seen the change in their appearance. Bright Feather had kept his word. Soon, now, the trial of courage would begin. Bright Feather had said it. White Bird clasped his shaking hands together. Of the three, who would live? He would die, for he had the feeling that he would not survive the test. His eyes went to Lianne and Caroline. It did not matter about himself. He had faced the thought of death. He had conquered the fear, and he had accepted. But Justin and Buck must not die. Bowing his head, White Bird turned away. Of late, he had offered up many prayers, but they did not comfort him.

Bright Feather came forward to greet him as White Bird entered the lodge. He saw the shadow on the boy's face, and he believed he knew what was troubling him. "My brother, my friend," he said, touching the rigid arm. "You are of our blood. The trial of courage is not for you. You have proved yourself."

"Justin Lawrence and Buck Carey have also proved themselves." White Bird's voice was suddenly urgent. "They are courageous men, Bright Feather. You know this. I ask you to let them go in peace."

"No!" Bright Feather's mouth hardened. "They must undergo the trial, but you, my brother, I say to you again that you have no need to take part."

White Bird looked back at him with blank eyes. "I will take part, Bright Feather. I have said it. If I die, it will be in the company of good and courageous men. A warrior can ask for no more than this."

Inside Bright Feather, grief again warred with anger and jealousy. White Bird would die. His lame leg would not allow him to escape any of the punishment. He would be too slow, and the clubs and the bastinadoes would batter the life from his body. "You once told me I was your only friend," he shouted. "But now it is no longer so. You have found others to idolize. These white men. The enemies of your people!" He spat on the floor to show his contempt. "How dare you stand before me and call them your friends?"

"Let them go in peace, and you will remain my only friend. If it is your wish, I will stay here beside you. I will never return to my own tribe."

"Because you cannot return to your own tribe. They have

cast you out." Bright Feather lunged forward and gripped White Bird by the shoulders. "Shun the test," he said, shaking him. "I, Bright Feather, say you may do this and still keep honor."

"You will not let the pale-skins go?"

"If they prove themselves."

"Then there is no more to be said."

Bright Feather glared at him. Since the coming of White Bird and Bright Feather's recognition of him, love had grown in his heart. He had not wanted to feel this love, for he considered that a warrior was weakened by such an emotion. If he could do so without besmirching White Bird's honor, he would have refused to allow him to take part. But he knew that he could not do this to him. "Die, then!" he shouted, pushing him away. "You have made your choice. The gods have heard you." He turned away to hide his pain.

Buck listened to the steadily increasing tempo of the drums. He did not look at Justin, but he could feel his eyes upon him, waiting, wondering. He moistened his dry lips. "Well, Justin, lad, now we know. We are to undergo the trial of courage. Then," Buck said, attempting a smile, "we will be allowed to go free. We've got hope, lad, but not too much. The trial is a gruesome thing." Justin's eyes were still upon him, and he explained briefly just what was in store for them. "White Bird goes with us," he concluded.

"White Bird? But why? You have just said that only white men undergo the trial."

"Usually. But it seems to be White Bird's wish to suffer along with us."

"I see." Justin felt shame for the thoughts he had been harboring about White Bird. He had believed that the boy had, by some means, managed to return to the good graces of his people, and having made his peace, had abandoned them. "You say that this is White Bird's wish, Buck?"

Buck nodded. "Yes. He ain't needing to undergo it unless he's wishful. Seems he is. He's quite a warrior."

Buck's eyes sought Lianne's face, and then turned to Caroline. She looked cold and stricken. "Justin . . ." Buck's voice was hoarse with suppressed emotion. "Caroline knows. It looks like Lianne has given her the message of the drums."

Justin knew the expression that would be on Caroline's

face. He knew how she would be suffering. He found that he could not look at her. For the moment, he could not take that added pain.

"They're starting up, Justin," Buck said in a low voice.

Justin looked in the direction of the blazing fire. The warriors and the squaws, peaceful an instant ago, were now beginning to gyrate. A shriek came from one of the squaws, and instantly following, there was a pandemonium of yelling and screaming as some leaped and some pranced about the fire. The movements grew wilder and wilder, until the dancers were lost in utter abandonment. The drums thundered, increasing the frenzy. Eyes rolled wildly, breasts bounced, bodies were thrust forward suggestively. Great drops of sweat streaked savage painted faces, and firelight shone on loose mouths and madly glittering eyes.

Justin looked for White Bird. He was standing still and straight beside Bright Feather, who was seated cross-legged before his wigwam. Behind him was Fighting Bear. Only these three had no part in the dance. White Bird and Fighting Bear were expressionless, but Bright Feather's face had taken on a sharp, wolfish look, and his eyes were glittering as brightly as those of the dancers. It was as though he had absorbed the frenzied beat of the drums deep within him and was responding in the only way suitable to the dignity of a chief. Looking at him closely, Justin had the feeling that he longed to hurl himself into the dance.

Justin looked away from Bright Feather. Now, reluctantly, he let himself look at Caroline. She sat rigidly upright, her hands on her knees, a figure made out of stone. Only her eyes looked alive, stretched wide and dark and terrified in her colorless face as they followed the frantic motions of the dancers. Seated beside her, Lianne was not looking at the dancers; her eyes were fixed on Buck. As though he was her salvation, Justin thought.

Buck knew that Lianne was looking at him, but the same feeling moved inside him as had moved inside Justin. He could not look at her. Perhaps he would not look at her at all. She represented love and happiness, perhaps children, all the things he would never know now, and the sight of her might prove to be his undoing. His mouth dry, he fixed his stinging eyes on the dancers. A man, suddenly leaping from the circle of dancers, caused him to start.

Justin tensed as the dancers, abruptly ceasing their wild gyrations, drew back to make a clear space for the man. Limbs still twitching, they stood there swaying, their hypnotized eyes fixed upon him.

Not allowing himself to think beyond the moment, Justin studied the man. He was different from the others both in costume and in appearance, and it was obvious from his arrogant bearing that he held a place of some importance in the village community. He was small of stature, almost dwarflike. The upper half of his body, his arms, and his face had been painted in somber colors of dark purple, dark green, and black. A lighter purple circled his eyes and was filled in with a dull yellow. Except for a thick upstanding central crest of hair that extended from his forehead to the nape of his neck, his large round head was completely shaved. The crest of hair was decorated with strings of vividly colored shells. The dangling ends of the strings had been looped back and tied neatly behind his head, presumably so that the shells would not strike his face and impede him. His arms and his upper torso were naked. Below, he wore what appeared to be at first sight a leather skirt, but when he moved, it could be seen that it consisted of four panels that depended from a wide beaded belt. Each panel had been sewn with beads and brightly colored porcupine quills and edged with colored feathers.

The man's circled eyes turned in Justin's direction, lingered there for a moment, and then fixed themselves upon Buck. His lips twitched and then drew back, to reveal sharply filed teeth. But apart from the movement of his eyes and his mouth, he remained motionless. Suddenly he threw back his head; his wide-open eyes seemed to be studying the dark velvet of the star-pricked sky. His face quivered as a series of long, rippling shudders shook his body. Lowering his eyes, he thrust forward his hands, which, previously, he had held clasped behind him. In his left hand he held a rattle, and in his right hand a feather-tipped staff. His face, which had smoothed itself to an empty expression, contorted. Then, with heart-shaking abruptness, he gave a wild shriek. Now, shaking the rattle and twirling the feathered staff, he threw himself into a bewildering series of lightning movements that made up a grotesquely savage dance, chilling in its implications. He gave the impression of having no bones at all in his short body. The dance went on for some time; then, with one last mighty leap, it concluded. Shining with sweat, the dancer threw himself backward and lay sprawled out on the ground, his legs and arms flung wide. Once again, as he looked upward at the sky, the rippling shudders began to shake his body.

Shaken out of his half-trance, Justin was amazed to hear the high-pitched laughter of the women mingling with the deeper tones of the men. The dancer had seemed to him to be a frighteningly sinister figure, but certainly not an object of amusement. He turned bewildered eyes to Buck.

Buck was unsmiling. Like Justin, he found nothing amusing in the grotesque figure. His answer, however, showed that he was well-versed in the ways of the Indian. "They got strange notions, Justin. The job of that painted-up freak is to amuse 'em. He's what you'd call a jester, I reckon. Every tribe's got one of 'em."

A jester? Justin stared at the twitching figure. He looked, he thought, like someone in the throes of a fit. Incredible to think that that man with his macabre painted body, his wild face, his grimaces, and his eerie shrieks was the Indian idea of diversion.

The drums, which had been reduced to a soft, sinister mutter for the final stages of the performance, now exploded into a deafening pitch. The dancers listened with expressionless faces, but it was obvious that the drums carried a message rather than an invitation to the dance, for they made no move to resume. Instead, they retreated farther from the fire, until they had made a large cleared space. What now? Justin wondered, unpleasantly aware of the accelerated beating of his heart.

Again Buck enlightened him. "Our time'll come, Justin," Buck said grimly, "but it ain't yet. Them drums are saying that it's time for the punishment ceremony to begin."

"What happens?"

"This is the time when the Injuns, them that's offended against the laws, are punished. When I was living with the tribe, I saw more'n one of these ceremonies. I can tell you now that you ain't going to be too crazy about what you see." Buck grinned. "Take my word for it."

Justin had never felt less like smiling, but Buck's grin, his deliberately light tone, showed that he was making an effort to keep up his courage, so he curled his lips in automatic response. "You don't tell me!" he answered. "So far, I haven't liked anything I've seen and heard."

Buck nodded. "It ain't no palace of pleasures, I grant you. With a bit of luck, we'll be out of it soon."

"Or dead, Buck."

"Or, as you say, dead. Listen real careful to me, Justin. When you run that goddamned gauntlet, don't run straight. Keep on swerving. That way, it'll make it harder for them to land one on you. You get me?" Buck broke off. "Here comes Fighting Bear," he went on. "Look at his face."

Fighting Bear's expression was more than usually grim as he stopped before them. Folding his hands before him, he said in a tight voice, "Chief Bright Feather wishes you to watch the punishment ceremony."

"Why?" Justin's dark brows rose in faint mockery. "Not that we have much choice, of course."

"No, you do not." The corners of Fighting Bear's mouth twitched with a suggestion of amusement. "The imprisonment and the torture have not robbed you of your boldness, Lawrence." His eyes turned to Buck. "Or you. You are truly men. Had we been of the same blood, I think we would have been friends as well as brothers."

Looking into Fighting Bear's dark eyes, Justin could believe this. The man was the enemy, yet there was something noble about him. He was an Indian, but the cruelty that was so apparent in Bright Feather seemed restrained in him. Strange to experience this liking for him, when soon they would be running the gauntlet, with no expectation of life at the end of it. "I believe that, Fighting Bear," Justin said slowly. "You are of a different stripe from Bright Feather. Yes, it might well have been that we would have been friends."

Fighting Bear's lashes flickered slightly at this reference to Bright Feather, but he answered with his usual gravity, "For those words that confirm my own belief, I thank you, Lawrence. As to why Chief Bright Feather wishes you to observe the ceremony, he believes, should you survive the gauntlet and the test of friendship, that you will spread the word that he is fair and impartial. That you will tell your people that he punishes the Indian offender as severely as he does the white enemy."

A smothered laugh came from Buck. "What!"

Justin was incredulous. "He actually believes that?"

"He does," Fighting Bear answered with unruffled calm. "You see, should you survive, he has given his word that you shall go free."

"And if he honors that word, he will expect his crimes against us to be expunged?"

Fighting Bear's loyalty stirred. "Crimes against you?" he questioned coldly. "You forget that you are the enemy."

"No, Fighting Bear, you are wrong. Buck Carey and I are not your enemies. Do not number us among those white men who have become so."

"I do not know how one may pick out the good seed from the bad, Lawrence. Therefore, until proved otherwise, all white men must be considered our enemies."

"What about the ritual test of friendship?" Buck put in. "Ain't that supposed to tell you what you want to know?"

"Yes, it will tell us, provided you live to take it." Fighting Bear's eyes swept them both. "It is my hope that you will live. But if it is not to be, I bid you farewell. We will not speak together again." Turning away, he returned unhurriedly to his place beside the chief.

"A pity Fighting Bear ain't the chief," Buck said gloomily. "We might have had a chance, then."

"Fighting Bear seems to be the only decent one, Buck."

"No, Justin, you're wrong. Don't you go judging them all by Bright Feather and Little Wolf. Injuns is cruel, but most of 'em are honorable."

"If you say so." Justin's eyes were on Caroline, and his voice was tinged with bitterness.

"I know how you feel," Buck answered quickly, "and I cain't rightly say that I blame you. But if we live, you'll find out that what I say is true."

Justin was about to reply, when his attention was caught by an abrupt movement from Caroline. She had risen to her feet. She hesitated for a moment; then, leaving Lianne still seated, she turned away and walked toward the wigwam she shared with Lianne and three squaws. No one attempted to stop her, and he was relieved to see her go.

"Ceremony's about to start." Buck said.

Justin watched as Bright Feather walked over to the space created by the dancers. Seating himself, he stared straight ahead. He was joined by Fighting Bear, and then, with apparent reluctance, by White Bird. It was obvious that the boy was ill-at-ease, surrounded, as he was, by the malevolent stares of those who still considered him to be a traitor. White Bird seated himself on the chief's left, Fighting Bear on his right. A wave of Bright Feather's hand invited others to join him. Several men came forward and took their places. When a circle had been created, the chief spoke. "Bring forward the first offenders."

A woman stepped forward and entered the circle. She was tall and slender and beautiful, in a feline way. Her long black braids of coarse hair, decorated with copper ornaments, fell to below her waist. Her expression was blank as she went on her knees before Bright Feather. A man followed after her. He went close to the woman and placed his hand lightly on her back.

Bright Feather stared at the woman, and in the silence that had fallen, the woman's quick, shallow breathing could be heard. "Bending Willow," he commenced in a sonorous voice, "you have offended." It was a statement not a question.

"I have offended," Bending Willow answered.

Bright Feather nodded. "You have disgraced the lodge of Stalking Horse, he to whom you were joined by the gods."

"I am guilty."

Bright Feather's eyes grew stern. "You are a wanton. You have given your body to another."

"I am a wanton. I have done this thing of which you speak."

"For this offense, for this insult to Stalking Horse and the injury to his pride, you will be punished."

Bending Willow bowed her head meekly. "I deserve punishment. Your will is mine."

Bright Feather's expression changed. Now his voice became brisk, almost businesslike. "Woman," he commanded, "you will remove the ornaments from your hair."

Bending Willow made no protest. The only trace of emotion was shown in the shaking hands she put to her hair, as one by one she removed the ornaments and placed them at Bright Feather's feet. Her small breasts swung free from their flimsy covering each time she bent.

The woman was guilty, Justin thought. She had admitted it, but this blind obedience to the will of the chief was horrible. He had the feeling that her attitude would have been no different even had she been innocent of the charge. He looked at Buck. "She has no spirit. Why doesn't she protest, try to defend herself?"

"Protest?" Buck answered. "She'd be shocked at the very thought. It's the way of the Injun, Justin."

Bending Willow had removed the last ornament. Now she began unbraiding her hair. She combed it with her fingers and then shook it about her shoulders.

The drums began as Bright Feather turned his eyes to the man who still stood with his hand on the woman's back. "Take her hair," he said in a loud voice.

The words chilled Justin. "Dear Christ!" he said in a stifled voice.

"It ain't what you think," Buck said quickly. "They ain't going to scalp her. And if you're thinking that what you've seen is bad, there's worse to come."

The man to whom Bright Feather had issued the command drew a knife from his belt. Bending over the woman, he began hacking at her hair. It fell about her kneeling figure in thick clumps. Now, for the first time, she showed emotion. The firelight shone on the tears sliding down her cheeks.

His task finished, the man straightened up and replaced the knife in his belt. The woman, after a momentary hesitation, rose to her feet. Standing before the chief, her shorn head lowered, she waited for his next words.

"Your disgrace shall be published, wanton," Bright Feather said, resuming the sonorous voice. "Your hair shall be fastened to a pole just outside our village, so that all who pass will make inquiry. They shall be told of your infamy. Go from me, woman. Get out of my sight. You have disgraced your people and besmirched the honorable name of Stalking Horse."

"I heard, and I obey." Bending Willow turned away. Her cropped head held high, she stepped clear of the circle.

Bright Feather stared at her back with malevolent eyes. "Woman!" he roared. "You will go from my sight on your hands and knees. You will crawl from this village that you have disgraced in the same way. You no longer have the right to walk with pride. I cast you out. Never let me set eyes on you again!"

Justin watched the woman as she dropped obediently to

her hands and knees and began to crawl away. An outcast, poor woman, he thought pityingly. Was there hatred in her heart for Bright Feather, or did she feel that she deserved the harsh sentence? And what of the brave to whom she had given her body? Did he grieve for her, did she grieve for him? Had her infidelity been prompted by lust, or love? He turned his head. "What will happen to her, Buck?" he asked.

Buck sighed. "Eventually she'll die. No other tribe will take her in. No one will feed her. The disgrace alone will kill her. Last case I heard of, the squaw lived only two days. Seems like she just laid herself down and willed herself to die."

Justin found himself unable to speak. The picture Buck had presented horrified him. All of his chivalry, his pity, rose up in protest. A proud people, Buck had said. Too proud to go on living under a cloud of disgrace. That squaw, Bending Willow—she was young and beautiful, she had just begun to live. Would she, too, just lie down and die? he wondered. With hard, bright eyes he continued to watch as the judgment went on. One by one the petty criminals were brought forward to kneel before Bright Feather. One brave, convicted of theft, had his right hand cut off. Another, for the same crime, was struck six times upon the head with a wooden cudgel. The cudgel was wielded with enough force to kill. When the brave finally collapsed, Justin felt a cold wave of horror. Was the brave dead, or merely unconscious? Again he looked at Buck.

"Ain't dead," Buck answered. "They don't strike for the vital spot with a petty thief. Looks bad, I know, but he'll come out of it alive."

"With his wits addled, no doubt?" Justin said in dry sarcasm.

The parade of petty criminals ended. Now it was the turn of those accused of more serious crimes. Gray Wolf, accused of murder, was ordered to lay his head on the flat stone that had been brought into the circle for that purpose. Without hesitation or a single word of protest, he did so. Cudgels again, wielded by three men this time. At a sign from Bright Feather, the men began battering at Gray Wolf's head. They did not cease until the head had been reduced to a bloody pulp that was mixed with the grayish-white matter of brains.

Sickened, Justin watched the men hold up the cudgels as if

for approval of their efforts. Even from here he could see the blood and hair adhering to the wood.

Another brave, who admitted to having raped three women and killed another, was judged and condemned. He too was to be beaten with cudgels until every bone in his body was broken. If, after this, he still lived, he was to be burned to death. Their faces expressionless, the three executioners threw aside the bloodied clubs. Receiving fresh ones, they began to club the brave. For some reason, the victim's facial bones were left intact. Strangely, he was still living when the punishment ceased. He was placed by the fire to await burning. Justin shuddered at his expression of stark agony, and because he still breathed, Justin found that his overwhelming pity was mixed with a strong awe for this tenacity to life. Incredible! After such savage and terrible punishment, the man should surely be dead. Reaction set in as Justin stared at the broken body of the brave. Nausea rolled over him, bringing to every part of his body a cold, clammy sweat. He gritted his teeth, the labored sound of his own breathing loud in his ears.

"Easy, Justin," Buck's soft voice said. "Just keep telling yourself that you cain't do nothing about it, and it'll help you to hang on."

Conquering the desire to vomit, Justin answered him grimly, "I'll hang on, Buck, and to hell with the red bastards." He drew in a deep breath. "But what about that poor devil over there?" he went on unsteadily. "My hope is that he'll die before the next part of the sentence can be carried out." He shuddered. "God almighty, just look at the wreck they've made of him!"

"I'm looking, lad, and I'm with you. He'd be better off dead. One thing, though. You can be thankful that Caroline ain't watching."

"Yes, I can be thankful. She's seen some brutality in her time, we both have. But nothing like this." He paused. "But what about Lianne? She hasn't moved since the trials began."

Buck's eyes went to Lianne. Her hands were resting lightly on her knees; her breathing appeared to be calm, and the eyes with which she viewed the horror before her were unwavering. "I know," Buck answered. "Don't seem right to you, I know. But it don't mean the same to her as to Caroline. She's used to it."

Lianne, the savage, Justin thought. The bloodthirsty little savage. How could a man like Buck possibly love her? Love certainly made for some strange bedfellows.

"Here comes another of 'em." Buck's voice scattered thought.

A tall brave, who answered to the name of Clouded Sky, stepped into the circle of justice. A charge of murder and incest was recited against him. Clouded Sky, answering the charge, lifted his head arrogantly. "It is not true," he said clearly. "Someone has borne false witness. I did not enter the body of my sister. I did not murder her."

Bright Feather's right hand came out, his middle finger pointing stiffly at Clouded Sky. "Let no further lies roll from your forked tongue," he said in a loud voice. "You have ravished the body of your sister, and you have added to your crime by taking her life. I know this to be true."

Clouded Sky's lashes flickered. "Great Chief, I am falsely accused."

"You are guilty!" Bright Feather roared. "Proof has been brought to me."

"What proof?"

"Silence!" Angry blood dyed Bright Feather's face and neck, and his eyes glittered dangerously. "Hear my judgment upon you. Your limbs are to be lopped off. The skin is to be torn slowly from your face, your head, and from what remains of your body. Do you understand the judgment?"

Clouded Sky swayed. "I understand. But again I tell you that I am falsely accused."

Justin was to be spared this particular sight, for at that moment Bright Feather rose to his feet. "The punishment of Clouded Sky will be carried out upon the next rising of the moon," he announced. "Take the prisoner away."

Clouded Sky, the first shock over, seemed to have accepted his fate. His head still held high, he stepped clear of the circle. His eyes turned briefly to Bright Feather; then, shrugging, he went on his way, walking with slow dignity between the two warriors who had been appointed to guard him.

Bright Feather turned his head and looked at the trussed bodies of the white men. "It is time to form the gauntlet." He spoke in a ringing voice. "The white men will run. Only in this way can they prove their courage."

Anger stirred in White Bird. Why did Bright Feather insist

upon this? Surely the white men had proved themselves. But Bright Feather was no longer the friend of his youth. He had become a stranger, a stranger who refused to listen to reason. "I am to run too, great Chief," White Bird said quietly.

Bright Feather's eyes turned to him. Whatever his thoughts, no flicker of expression showed in his face. "I need no reminders, White Bird," he said in a level voice. "What I have said will be. You will run with them."

A bustle of activity began, and Justin, watching, was unpleasantly aware of the increased beating of his heart. What would this night bring? he wondered, his eyes on the man with the broken bones, who was even now being lifted and carried away. He heard the man's groans of agony, and he swallowed against the dryness in his throat.

"Life or death," Buck said, echoing Justin's thoughts. "That's what we've got to look forward to. I wonder which it will be?"

Justin became aware of an overwhelming weariness. "What does it matter, Buck? Either way, we will be free."

"You ain't to talk like that," Buck said sharply. "It sounds to me like you're giving up."

"Perhaps I am."

Buck's amber-brown eyes narrowed. "You cain't give up, Justin, any more than I can. It ain't in you. You think I don't know a fighter when I see one?"

"A fighter?" Justin gave a short laugh. "All the fight's gone out of me."

"No it ain't, and you know it. You'll keep alive, if you can. You'll fight as hard for life as I will. We're sure as hell no good to them gals if we're dead. Think on that."

"You're right," Justin said after a moment. "Goddamnit, Buck, how come you're always right?"

Relieved to see the light of spirit and determination once more present in Justin's expressive dark eyes, Buck grinned at him. "Don't know," he answered.

Justin's lips curled into a responsive smile. "Go to hell," he said lightly.

"Well, now, lad, before this night is over, I just might be doing that little thing."

"And I'll be right behind you," Justin said, laughing.

Bright Feather was angered by their laughter. It was as though they were contemptuous of anything he might do to them. For a moment he was tempted to repudiate his promise to let them go free.

White Bird knew what was passing through Bright Feather's mind. He spoke quickly. "Once I, too, was puzzled by the laughter of these two pale-skins, for it seemed to me to mock at danger. But now I understand. They use their laughter to cover deeper emotions."

"Like fear?" Bright Feather asked.

"Like fear," White Bird agreed.

"It is a strange thing to do, and hard to understand. But then, it is my belief that all pale-skins are mad. There is no dignity in laughter." Allowing his anger to die, Bright Feather lifted his hand in a sign that he was about to speak again. "Hear me, warriors. Should these white men survive the gauntlet, they shall be allowed to go free, and they will take their women with them. I, Bright Feather, have sworn this. Know you all that this promise, made in honor, shall be kept in honor."

Fighting Bear's smile had a faintly cynical twist as he listened. But, surprisingly, he had the impression that Bright Feather spoke in all sincerity.

"Bring forth the white woman," Bright Feather commanded. "She shall stand beside the half-breed. Let their eyes observe the courage of their men, or the lack of it. I have spoken."

"Buck!" Lianne was on her feet. Oblivious of the eyes that watched her, she held out her arms to him. "Run for me, Buck. I love you."

Bright Feather heard the note of hysteria in her voice, and he felt shame for her. "The half-breed woman will be silent!" he said sharply. He turned away from the sight of her ravaged face. "Let all be prepared for the test."

White Bird stood there as if uncertain. Then, without looking at Bright Feather, he limped toward the prisoners.

Fighting Bear followed after him. He had said that he would not speak to the white men again, yet he could not deny his strong compulsion to do so.

"I have returned, my white brothers," Fighting Bear heard the boy say. "I could not come before, for it was not permitted. But I have kept faith with you both. We will live or die together."

Buck stared at the boy. The almost fanatical light in his

eyes made him uneasy. "Listen to me," he said urgently. "There ain't no need for you to take the run."

"I have something to prove." White Bird's head lifted proudly. "And there is one other thing. I do not desert my friends."

"There is still time for you to change your mind, White Bird." Justin did not look at him as he spoke. His eyes were on Caroline, who was now standing beside Lianne. "If Buck and I don't come through this thing, Carrie and Lianne will need you."

Folding his hands together, White Bird looked down at the ground. "No, Lawrence, they will not need me. If you should die, the women are to be given to the warriors. They will not be able to endure such an ordeal, and therefore they will not live long."

"My God!" Justin stared at him in horror. "Is this true, White Bird?"

White Bird saw the agony in both faces, but he could not bring himself to lie. "It is true," he said quietly.

"Therefore, you must live." Fighting Bear spoke for the first time.

"Live?" Justin looked at Fighting Bear with bitter eyes. "You make it sound as though you care."

Fighting Bear shrugged. "Many strange feelings move inside me, and I do not always recognize their meaning. You are white, and I have a great hatred for your race. I cannot deny this. Yet I have found you both to be men of courage, and I admire courage before all else. I think, because of this, that I would like you to live." Without waiting for an answer, he turned on his heel and walked away.

Chapter 25

Justin stumbled through the long lane of white-painted warriors, trying to avoid the clubs that rained blows on his head, body, and limbs, trying to keep his wits about him in order not to be tripped by the cunningly wielded lashing bastinadoes. There was a screaming deep inside his head, the shrill sound all mixed up with the savage throbbing of the drums. It was a woman who screamed. A woman who cried out his name in high-pitched despair.

It was Carrie who cried out to him. Justin almost tripped. Recovering himself quickly, he thought with mounting despair: I must not think about her. I must close my ears to her voice. Above all, I must concentrate on coming out of this alive. There was such an intense, fiery pain in every part of his body. He blinked hard, trying to clear the blood that dripped from the gash on his forehead, blinding him. The slight clearing of his vision enabled him to make out the hunched figure of Buck, who was slightly ahead of him. He was staggering badly; the blood dripping from his lacerated back left a red trail as he went. Behind him, Justin could hear White Bird's distressed breathing. He wanted to turn, to try in some way to aid him, but he dared not. He must concentrate!

A sudden yell of triumph from one of the grotesquely painted warriors caused Justin's heart to thunder in blind panic. He blinked again, and then he saw the cause of the man's excitement. Buck had tripped. With his arms outflung, he was desperately trying to recover his balance. Justin swallowed. His throat felt swollen. He knew it would pain him to bring out sound, but he had to try. He must, in some way, reach Buck, encourage him. He shouted, "Stay on your feet. For Christ's sake, stay on your feet!"

He felt an almost dizzying relief when he saw that Buck

had regained his balance. "Don't worry." His labored reply came faintly to Justin's straining ears. "Look to yourself."

Shuddering, Justin remembered White Bird's solemn warning. "I have seen other white men run the gauntlet," the boy had said. "Since you cannot avoid the blows, you will naturally be in severe pain. Even so, you must be strong. You cannot allow your pain to weaken or distract you. You must not fall, because the warriors will pile on top of you and club you to death. Remember the words I speak now, my brothers. If you reach the end of the line and you are still on your feet, you will be safe. The warriors will respect the fight you have made. They will not touch you."

Justin moaned as a club descended upon his right shoulder, numbing his arm. Must not fall! The words raced through his swimming brain. They were nearly at the end of the line, and the blows had taken on an added viciousness.

"You are nearly there, Lawrence." White Bird's voice, broken and panting, came to Justin's ears.

"See!" a warrior cried. "The Indian brother weakens. He is about to fall!"

A wild yelling that hurt his ears, howls of triumph from the other warriors. Hearing it through his failing senses, Justin felt rage rising hot and strong, giving him a temporary strength. Damn them all to hell! White Bird should not fall, not if he could do anything about it. "White Bird," he gasped. "Grab hold of my belt. Hang on tight."

"No, Lawrence. Save yourself!"

"Do as you're told. Grab hold!" He could say no more; he hadn't the breath. He could hear the stumbling sounds of White Bird's faltering run, his heavy, labored breathing. To help him, he slowed down a little, but he dared not cease running altogether. He must not hesitate more than he already had, or he would be lost. He could only pray that White Bird would heed him. His relief when he felt the clutch at his belt was enormous. His chest heaving, he increased his speed.

Buck cleared the line. Still on his feet, he stood there swaying, watching Justin's labored efforts. Behind him, he could see that White Bird's grip was weakening. The boy was all but unconscious. "Make it, lads!" he prayed aloud. "You must!"

The drummers, seeing that the race was almost run, went

into a frenzy of excitement. Yelling at the tops of their voices, they slapped the palms of their hands hard against the tautly stretched skin of the drums, producing a deafening din.

With the thunder of the drums pounding in his head, his heart feeling as though it was about to burst, Justin came on like an exhausted and overladen mule. Sweat mingled with blood dripped from him, the cords in his throat strained, and his staring eyes seemed about to bolt from his head as he continued to drag his extra burden. He did not hear when the shouting voices changed in tone. Now they yelled to him in encouragement, and cried out his name. He heard nothing but the frantic beating of his heart in his ears, which, mingling with the drums, made a terrifying cacophony of sound. Buck's face suddenly loomed up before him, bruised and bloody, his swollen eyes almost completely closed. It loomed larger, larger than life. Buck! He tried to say the name.

"Justin! Come on, come on!"

Justin heard his name piercing the roar of sound. But why was Buck shouting like that? Couldn't he see that he was trying? Only a few more steps to go, but it seemed like miles. White Bird was a deadweight behind him. Had the boy fallen? Was his body touching the ground? What did it matter, what did anything matter? He must rest!

"Justin, you're beyond the line. You've won!"

That was Caroline's voice, trembling, on the edge of tears. He was beyond the line, she had said. His knees buckled beneath him, and the ground came up to meet him. It must be true, for now her hands were upon him, her tears falling coldly upon his burning face. She was telling him again that he had won. That he had brought White Bird to safety. Now her voice was changing. "Oh, Justin, I love you so much!"

He wanted to tell her that he loved her too, but he was too exhausted, too full of pain to talk. Her face dimmed, and his head fell sideways.

Caroline looked up at Buck. "He's fainted."

Buck nodded. There was a blackness before his own eyes.

"Rest, Buck. Sit down." Lianne's hands pulled at his arm, urging him downward.

Unresisting, he sank down. Justin was safe. White Bird was safe, and Lianne's arms were about him, trying to support him. They had come through the gauntlet. Perhaps they had a chance at a life together? His thoughts became jumbled, and now he was conscious only of the pain grinding into every part of his body. Perhaps he would not survive, after all. His fingers twitched as he made the effort to lift his arms. He wanted to draw her close and hold her tightly, but his arms would not obey his will; his strength was all gone. Tears filled his eyes.

Lianne's arms were holding him. His head was pillowed against her soft breast, and her hand was stroking his hair. He felt a great relief. She held him so tenderly, she understood that a man must sometimes have his moments of weakness, that he could not always be strong. Gratefully he buried his wet face against her and brought out choked words. "So tired, Lianne."

Bright Feather looked down at White Bird. The boy was lying on his back, his wide-open eyes fixed upon him. Bright Feather hesitated; then, surrendering to the urgency in White Bird's eyes, he lifted a hand for silence. All sound ceased as he got down on his knees and bent over the boy. Fighting Bear, looking on, saw the soft look on the chief's face. It seemed to him that Bright Feather had never looked more dignified and noble than at that moment.

Forgetful of the warriors, Bright Feather touched White Bird's damp hair. "You are safe, my brother," he said gently. "Is there something you wish to say to me?"

White Bird's eyes blinked as he struggled to bring out words. "My friends . . ." he managed. "B-badly hurt. You . . . you gave your word."

"I gave my word, and I will keep it. The white men shall be cared for." Abruptly he rose to his feet. "Have you all heard my words?" he asked, looking about him. "The white men will not be harmed. Their wounds will be tended."

For the first time, Fighting Bear smiled with his eyes as well as his lips.

Bright Feather turned and walked away. His mind was preoccupied with the change in Fighting Bear's expression. When he had obeyed the impulse to get down on his knees beside White Bird, he had, in a sense, lowered his dignity. He knew well that a chief does not kneel to a boy, especially one who has been branded a traitor. Fighting Bear always had been his enemy, and he had expected his derision. Instead, he had seen warmth looking from his eyes, approval of his action, something deep in those eyes of his that might be described as liking. Fighting Bear was a strange man, and Bright Feather found his reaction to certain things very puzzling.

Fighting Bear stared after the erect figure of the chief. It is hard for you to change, Bright Feather, he thought. It has always seemed to me that you were born without those qualities that make for a good warrior and chief. Perhaps I was wrong. When you looked at White Bird and placed your hand upon his head, you became a warrior of dignity and compassion. If the coming of White Bird will lead your heart and mind in that direction, then I shall no longer envy you the great position you have achieved, for you will be worthy to become a leader of men. Only prove yourself to me, and you shall have all of my loyalty. I will no longer plan to lead the warriors in revolt against you, for there will be no need.

Bright Feather ordered the white men carried to the healing lodge.

Chapter 26

Justin was smiling as he rode through the blue and gold of the afternoon. Carrie was perched up before him, and behind him he could hear the voices of Buck and Lianne. He reached out a hand to pat the glossy neck of the horse he rode. They were free. The sun was hot on his head; the air he breathed seemed as pure as crystal. He was happy in a way he had never thought to be again. Laughing aloud, he tightened his arm about Caroline's waist and rested his chin on her rumpled blond hair. "Did I remember to tell you I love you, Carrie?"

Caroline's attention was on the black-clad figure on the dispirited-looking horse who was plodding ahead some distance from them. The man on the horse was the only person they had seen on the road since leaving the Indian village. He was apparently without curiosity, or entirely fearless, for not once had he looked back. At Justin's words, Caroline's attention left the lone traveler. Turning her head, she looked at Justin with shining eyes. "You did, but keep on telling me. I will never grow tired of hearing that you love me." The smile left her lips suddenly, and she shivered. "I keep thinking I will wake up and find this is only a dream."

"It's real, Carrie, love. We're on our way home."

"If it hadn't been for White Bird, we would never have . . ."

"Don't think about it, it's over."

"We shall never really be able to forget all we have been through, will we?"

"No, darling, but perhaps we should try."

"I'll try, Justin, I promise." Caroline leaned her head back against his shoulder. "Dear White Bird. He is one I will never forget. I will pray every night for his happiness."

Justin thought back to the White Bird who had entered the

338

healing lodge after their ordeal. It was a very different White
Bird. In the four weeks that had passed since they had run
the gauntlet, he had picked up so amazingly that no would
guess at the ordeal he had undergone. He had, for all his delicacy of constitution, recovered from that grueling race for
life far more rapidly than either Justin or Buck. But it was
not only his regained health that struck one. It was his air of
confidence, the serenity in his eyes that had never been there
before. In this village of enemies, White Bird had evidently
found his place. He looked like a young chief, proud, almost
arrogant of bearing.

Justin smiled. "Why, Carrie," he said tenderly, "that
sounds strange coming from you. You have never been a
praying woman."

"Perhaps I have become one. Truly, Justin, I can't help
thinking that the hand of God was in this."

Her words were lightly said, but there was nonetheless an
undercurrent of seriousness in them. She would never, Justin
knew, become one of those grim-faced, Bible-thumping fe-
males who took their religion so joylessly, but it would seem
that her ordeal had caused her to discover God. He was glad
for Carrie. In all the trials that had beset her, she needed a
faith to cling to. His thoughts went to the parting from White
Bird. Outwardly it had been quite unemotional, but the eyes
do not lie, and there had been sorrow in White Bird's. "I
pray we will meet again, Lawrence," he had murmured, clasping his hand firmly, "but let it not be in war. You and Buck
Carey are my brothers and my friends. It would grieve me
to kill you."

He had meant it too, Justin thought grimly. White Bird
was his friend, but should they ever come face-to-face in
battle, the boy would not hesitate to kill him or Buck. One
who had been declared friend of the Indian should not be
among those pale-skins who battled against them. That was
how White Bird would think, he knew. To him it would be a
betrayal. Had it not been for White Bird, Justin rather
doubted that Bright Feather would have honored his promise
to let them go free. Certainly his expression had been sour
enough when they rode away. It was as Carrie had said—
they owed White Bird a great deal.

"Cain't get enough of this freedom air, can you, Justin?"

The shout came from Buck, who was riding close behind them, with Lianne perched before him. "Ain't it wonderful?"

Justin smiled. "It is, Buck," he called over his shoulder.

Lianne looked at Buck, smiling tenderly. "You have said that you wish to become my husband. Do you still wish for this?"

Buck kissed her serious face. "Sure I wish it. Just got through saying so again a few moments ago. I'm going to put my ring on that little finger of yours and make it all tight and legal." He grinned at her. "You reckon I ought to put a ring through your nose, just so's I can be sure of you?"

Startled, Lianne touched her nose. "Oh, no, that will not be necessary."

"That mean you're going to be a good and faithful wife to me? After a while, when you get tired of me, you ain't going to run off with some brave?"

Lianne looked at him intently. There was laughter in his voice, but his amber-brown eyes were sober. "No, Buck, I will never wish to run from you," she reassured him. "I will love you all my life."

"There's things about me you don't know, darlin'. In some parts of this country I am still a hunted man."

"Are you?" Lianne smiled at him. "One day, when we have much time, you must tell me of everything that has happened in your life."

"It might mean that trouble will come to us someday, sweetheart."

"If trouble comes, Buck, we will face it together," Lianne said firmly.

Lianne's words drifted to Caroline. How Lianne has changed, she thought in amazement. But love was capable of producing miracles, she knew. It had produced one in Justin. Her beloved rogue was now a man of strength and tenderness, and all of his love was given to her. It appeared to have wrought another in Lianne. The little savage had turned into a warm and loving woman. She no longer thought only of herself. It was obvious that Buck was her life, her reason for being.

Justin turned over Buck's words in his mind. "It might mean that trouble will come to us someday," he had said. He was referring, of course, to that long-ago murder of his great-grandfather, Swift River, and to those braves who had grown up with the popular pastime of hunting down Buck Carey, the man who had killed a great chief. Justin frowned thoughtfully. He would be loath to lose Buck, but for his own sake it might be better if he took Lianne and made his home in another part of the country. Someplace where the vengeance of glory-seeking braves could not extend.

Lianne touched Buck's chin with the tip of a finger. "Will you marry me in the church of your white God, Buck?"

Buck's eyes went to the figure plodding ahead of them. "I've got a better idea, darlin'." He gestured. "You know who that man is?"

Lianne shook her head. "How could I know."

"He's a traveling preacher, that's what he is. I know him by them clothes he's wearing."

"You are sure?" Lianne's eyes were shining.

Buck looked into the astonished face Justin had turned to him. "That's right, Justin, he's a traveling preacher. Now's your chance to marry that gal of yours."

"Could it be done, Buck?" Caroline's voice quivered slightly. "Would he marry us?"

"Sure he will," Buck assured her. "His job, ain't it?"

"But could it be that easy?"

Buck grinned at her. "When folks live in the wilds, Caroline, and they got a hankering to get hitched, it had just better be easy."

Caroline's hand touched Justin's, squeezing urgently. "Would you . . . would you marry me, Justin?"

Touched by the look on her face, he pretended to consider. "I just might," he said at last.

"Justin!"

"Idiot child! I'd like to see anybody stop me from marrying you, Carrie, love."

Caroline stared at him for a moment, her smile radiant.

Buck let out a whoop. "Then what are we waiting for? Let's ride."

Later, thinking of that hurried ceremony that had bound them together, Caroline could not help smiling. When they had caught up with the man on the horse, they had found him to be fast asleep. Not even the thunder of hooves had awakened him. No wonder he had not once turned to look their way. Prodded awake by Justin, he had looked at them with dazed eyes. "What?" he had spluttered. "What do you want of me?"

"We want you to marry us," Buck had put in.

"Marry you!" The rotund little man had spoken the words in amazement, as though he had never heard of marriage. "What, here on the road?"

"And why not?" Justin had spoken impatiently. He prodded Caroline with a finger. "Unless, of course," he went on in a laughing voice, "you are suggesting that I bed this woman without benefit of marriage?"

The man had looked horrified. "Certainly not," he snapped.

"Then marry us. You can do it, can't you?"

"I can." Obviously flustered, he cast a sternly reproachful look at Justin and commenced mopping at his forehead with a large and none-too-clean handkerchief. "I would have you know," he announced in a dignified voice, "that I am fully ordained."

"Then that's good, ain't it?" Buck said in a cheerful voice. "It means we'll be tied up nice and tight with no fear of jiggery-pokery."

Giving Buck a look of dislike, the man had thrust the handkerchief into his pocket. After much fumbling, he had drawn out his Bible. "It is dangerous to linger," he muttered. "One never knows. We must hurry." Sliding reluctantly down from his horse, he had bade them do likewise. When they were standing before him, he had cast speculative watery blue eyes in Lianne's direction. "You certain you want to marry this Indian?" he asked Buck. "I'm not sure it's even legal."

Buck's arm went protectively about Lianne, drawing her close to him. "But you're ordained," he said in a dangerous voice. "Ain't that what you just got through telling us? The way I look at it, you can make it legal."

Flinching from the look in Buck's eyes, the man swallowed any further objections he might have made. Confining himself to a look of grim disapproval, he performed the ceremony. The fact that there had been no rings given to bind the marriage had seemed to further upset him. The brief ceremony completed, he had vaulted back on his horse. After ascertaining where they might be found in the future, he told them he would be by that way in about four months' time, when he would expect to collect his fee. "If," he said, picking up the reins and looking furtively about him, "I'm still alive to collect it." His eyes rested on Lianne for a moment. "What with Indians scourging the countryside and killing off God-fearing people, one never knows." Nodding, he had gone on his way with a hurried "May God bless you."

Closing her eyes, Caroline settled back against Justin. They had many miles to go before they reached their destination, but, unlike the preacher, she was not afraid of the journey that lay before them. God had indeed blessed her, for was she not Justin's wife? She had not dreamed she could be this happy. The strong sunlight bathed her in a warm golden glow, and she yawned widely. Even happiness could not hold back the overwhelming desire she had to sleep. The many haunted days and sleepless nights she had spent were catching up with her. Why not let herself sleep? She was in her husband's arms, and they were both safe. When she awoke, his arms would still be about her. Her senses began to haze and drift. She heard Justin's voice saying something, but she was too tired to reply. They had all their life before them. There would be plenty of time for laughter and love and conversation. Her last thought, before her head fell forward in exhausted sleep, was that she would have another child. It would complete her happiness if she could hold Justin's son, or his daughter, in her arms.

When he heard the riders coming, Jim Partridge, from force of habit, had led his horse off the mired narrow track that did duty as a road.

Tom Cross, his companion, had automatically followed him. Standing concealed among the trees, Cross glared at him impatiently. He was an open man himself, and he did not believe in all this skulking and hiding. Partridge was always doing it, so it was evident to him that he must have a great deal to hide.

As he brooded, Cross's iron-gray eyebrows drew together in a frown. His small brown eyes were resentful as he thought of Mr. Markham telling him that he had to team up with Partridge. From the first moment he had glimpsed Partridge's pasty face, his weak blue eyes, and his shock of untidy ginger hair, allied to a meager figure, he had known that he could never like or trust such a man. Mindy, Markham's fat elephant of a cook, had agreed with him about Partridge. Her round prune-black face shining with sweat, she had echoed his thoughts about the man. "Ah purely cain't understand how Master Toby can bring himself to trust that little skunk o' a Partridge. He a bad one, all right. Ah done tol' him more'n once that he ain't welcome in mah kitchen."

With his hands thrust into the deep pockets of the caped greatcoat, which, ignoring the derisive laughter of his friends, he wore in all seasons, considering that it gave him an air, he pondered on Mindy's words. Should he speak to Mr. Markham about Partridge? Thinking of Tobias Markham, with his dark face and his curiously light, almost icy eyes, brought with it a feeling of deflation. No, since he had only suspicions of Partridge's true character to go upon, he couldn't really tell Markham anything. Markham was kind enough, provided you didn't try to go against him, but he was remote, holding his workers at a firm distance, drawing a mental line over which they dared not step. Furthermore, he seemed to trust Partridge. He believed, did Markham, that if anyone could find his runaway white slaves, it would be Partridge.

Cross's lip curled. Didn't Markham ever give up? he wondered. Why was he so fanatical about finding Justin Lawrence and Caroline Fane? There were some folks who insisted that Tobias Markham was in love with the runaway Caroline Fane, but it didn't seem very likely to him. Markham was a cold one. Cold as ice. After all, it had been two years and more since they had run off from the Montrose Plantation. Lawrence had run, so he had heard, after the killing of Moon, the black slave who was his friend. And Eliza, the young white girl that Moon had dared to love. It had been Miss Biddy, Tobias Markham's dead wife, who had been responsible for the two murders. She would have shot Justin Lawrence too, had he not taken the pistol from her. That, at least, was how Cross had been given the story. It had happened before he had come to the Montrose Plantation to work for Tobias Markham. Yes, and now that he came to think of it, there were some rumors floating around about the death of Miss Biddy. Some said that her headlong fall down the stairs was accidental. Others maintained that she had been helped on her way.

Tom Cross shrugged. Murder or accident, it was all one to him. He was paid to work, not to pry into the business of his employer. His mind went back to the two fugitives. Partridge, who had been present at the time, had witnessed the double murder of Moon and Eliza, and he had seen the murderous intent that blazed from Justin Lawrence's dark Indian face when he had closed with the hysterical and drunken Miss Biddy, and he, Partridge, never tired of telling that story. Cross sighed. Partridge had likewise given him the description of Justin Lawrence and Caroline Fane over and over again, until he was fair sick of it. So Lawrence was tall, with black hair and eyes. So he looked rather like an Indian in appearance. So what? Cross knew himself to be a not very observant man, and he really didn't see how he was expected to help Partridge find them. He was tired of the whole affair anyway. He was getting old, and his bones ached from camping out in all weathers. It was true that at first he had had a mild enjoyment in the chase, but that was long gone. All he wanted to do now was to settle down and sleep in a bed at nights. Perhaps he could persuade Markham to provide Partridge with another partner, one who did not mind the rough-and-tumble life entailed in a long search. It would be better still, of course, if Markham decided to give up something that he must surely know by now was a lost cause. The two had vanished as surely as if the earth had opened up and swallowed them. They might even be dead, the victims of a massacre.

An abrupt movement from Partridge drew Cross's impatient attention. "What are we hiding here for, Partridge?" he demanded. "If we're going to hole up for every rider that comes along, we're going to waste a hell of a lot of time, ain't we?" He took a closer look at Partridge. "What's the matter with you? You look like you seen a ghost. This lot coming along are only ordinary riders, ain't they?"

"Ain't nothing ordinary about them riders, Cross," Partridge answered in a stifled voice. "See that big dark fellow riding to the front? That's Justin Lawrence. See the fair woman he's holding? That's Caroline Fane. We got 'em, Cross, we got 'em!" He swallowed. "I knew I'd catch up with 'em sooner or later."

Cross's first flare of sharp excitement had already died. "That's all very well," he said gloomily, "but we got to take 'em, first. He's a big one, that Lawrence. It ain't going to be easy."

"Knows that, don't I?" Partridge glared at him impatiently. "I wish he hadn't got them others with him."

Cross heartily endorsed this. "Who are they?"

"What you asking me for? How the hell should I know? Only thing I can tell you is that the gal looks like a breed."

"That's a big help, ain't it?" Cross said with a fine sarcasm. "Well, you're the expert, Partridge. You mind telling me how we're going to take 'em?"

Casting him a look of cold dislike, Partridge raked his dirty fingernails through the heavy fringe on the sleeve of his buckskin jacket, carefully disentangling the strands. He had never liked teaming up with Cross, and he couldn't understand why Mr. Markham had such trust in the driveling fool. Cross had never pulled his weight—not so far as Partridge was concerned, anyway. He was always going on endlessly about his aches and pains, always mumbling about his age. He was a gray-headed coot, all right, but he wasn't that old. Somewhere in his early forties, he believed. No, Cross didn't fool him for an instant. He just used his age to cover the fact that he was a quitter and a coward. Partridge turned his attention to the other sleeve. After all, no one was forcing Cross to go on with the job. When he first tired of the hunt, he could have pulled out at any time. The truth was, despite his constant whining, he didn't want to miss out on the generous wages Markham paid.

"Perhaps you'd like a brush for your hair, Partridge?" Cross said. "You're so busy with that jacket that you ain't got time to answer my question, I suppose?"

Partridge ignored the sarcasm. "Sure I'll answer you, Cross. We let 'em get by a little way, see. Then we come out of hiding and ride 'em down. Surprise attack. Simple, ain't it?"

Cross's gloom was unabated. "I don't see anything simple about it. What if they shoot at us?"

Partridge clenched his hands in exasperation. "If you'd used your bloody eyes, you'd have seen that they ain't got no weapons."

"Maybe they've got 'em hid. You thought of that?"

Partridge's head, with its untidy thatch of ginger hair, rose arrogantly. "Don't you worry none about me, Cross. I think of everything. It ain't likely they'd have their weapons hid. Too dangerous around these parts. They'd have 'em in plain sight, in the hopes of scaring off an attacker. Another thing, they're just about asleep on them horses. They look plain exhausted to me, which is going to make it a lot easier."

"And after we've rode 'em down?"

Partridge's pale-blue eyes blinked rapidly as he strove to hang on to his temper. "We give 'em a nice kiss all around," he snarled. "What do you think we do? We don't shoot 'em, because Mr. Markham's got his own ideas. He wouldn't thank us none if we was to bring 'em in dead. So we club 'em, see? I'll tackle Lawrence and Fane. You see to the other two."

"All right." Cross spoke sullenly. He didn't appreciate Partridge's constant jibing.

The riders went by. Cross and Partridge mounted. Beneath his legs, Cross could feel the quivering eagerness of his animal to be on its way. He wished he could feel the same. A pity they couldn't shoot at them. It would make the task easier. He leaned forward, peering through the screening leaves. Partridge was right about one thing. All four of them looked to be just about asleep.

Shooting a look at Partridge, Cross drew his club from the saddle pocket. He was somewhat cheered by the weight of it in his hand. He was good with a club; he knew just where to strike. Partridge, to give him his due, was also an expert in the use of the club. A good thing, too. They didn't want murder on their hands. A shiver chased its way down his back as he thought of Markham's reaction, should they bring him the dead bodies of Fane and Lawrence. With a start of unpleasant surprise he suddenly realized that he was afraid of Markham. The man had proved that he could be a good friend, but Cross had the feeling he would make a very bad enemy.

His slight body tensing in the saddle, Partridge gathered the reins into his callused hands. "You about ready?" he said, giving Cross a sour look. Then, by way of encouragement, he added, "We bring in them two, and our troubles are over. You ain't forgot the bonus Markham promised us?"

Cross brightened. Strange, but he had forgotten. Which only went to show that he wasn't money hungry, like Partridge. He nodded almost cheerfully. "Ready when you are."

"Right. If the breed sets up a squalling," Partridge instructed him, "give her a tap on the head. It'll likely be better if I do the same with Fane. Used to be a real wildcat, did that one. Don't suppose she's changed. Come on, let's go!"

His mind wandering in a half-dream, Justin became dimly aware of danger. The thunder of hooves behind him was real! He jerked upright. "Buck!"

"Riders almost on top of us!" Buck's raised voice. "Look out, Justin!"

Justin swung around. He caught a fleeting glimpse of Partridge's well-remembered face, and then he knew. "Montrose riders!" he yelled to Caroline. They were his last words before he descended into blackness.

Jerked from sleep, dazed and bewildered, Caroline saw Justin falling sideways. Screaming wildly, she grabbed for him. She could not hold him! "Justin, Justin!" She scrambled down from the horse. He was dead! she thought, bending over him. Oh, God, he was dead!

Partridge slid down from his horse. Fane was not even aware of him as yet. But with the first shock over, she would be. Lawrence had recognized him, and so, he felt sure, would Fane. And, with that recognition, he'd have trouble aplenty on his hands. He shrugged. There was only one way to deal with trouble, and that was to stop it before it started. Why waste valuable time in subduing her? The sooner they got back to Montrose, the better. On this last thought, his hand lifted and brought the club down on Caroline's head. Stepping back, he stood with his legs apart, looking down at them. He felt a great satisfaction. Lawrence and Fane, the two of them together. After all this time, he had finally completed his mission! Smiling broadly, he turned to Cross.

Cross was on his knees staring at the unconscious stranger. "Buck," he had heard the breed cry out. What was her name? he wondered. Didn't matter much. He was just curious. Probably Floating Lily, or Scarlet Bloom, or one of the other stupid names the Indians delighted in. His eyes turned to look at the girl. She was lying stretched out beside the man, the wind blowing strands of her long black hair across his face. Her face was colorless. A good-looking piece, Cross thought. But what was a dirty breed doing in the company of a white man?

Partridge came nearer. "You ain't killed 'em, have you,

Cross?" he said sharply. "Because if you have, you're on your own. I ain't having nothing to do with murder."

Cross bit back a heated reply. Partridge, that dirty swine! Where did he come off, saying he would have nothing to do with murder? Cross happened to know that he'd killed more than once. Controlling himself, he said calmly, "No, Partridge, I ain't killed 'em. You can believe it or not, but I know what I'm doing." With a stubby finger he indicated Buck. "Got a hard head, he has. I had to give him an extra tap before I could send him to sleep." Rising to his feet, he dusted off the knees of his moleskin breeches. "Well, Partridge, what now?"

Partridge frowned. "Seems like I've got to tell you everything. Ain't you able to think for yourself? Take the rope and tie up your man. Make it good and tight. After you've done that, you can help me with these two."

"What about the breed?" Cross said, giving him a surly look.

"You can leave her untied." Partridge turned away. "We'll be well on our way to Montrose before she comes to and sets him free."

Chapter 27

Tobias Markham avoided looking at the anxiously hovering Mindy. If he gave her an opening, she would interfere, and he had no intention of allowing that. It would be as well if she could sometimes bring herself to remember that she was only a servant.

With an exclamation of pity, Mindy started toward the girl who sat slumped in the big wing chair. Her round black face beneath the starched white headcloth was creased with anxiety, and her fat hands were visibly trembling. "Cain't you let up on some of yore questions, Master Toby? You been at her for three days now, and the pore child is all wore out. Ain't no need for starting in again, is there? Let me take her away and see after her."

Markham's pale eyes lit with a spark of anger. "I have waited a long time for this, Mindy, and you will not interfere."

"Ain't gonna do you no good, Master Toby." Ignoring him, Mindy bent over the girl, her large hoop earrings swinging. "Mindy's here, Caroline, mah honey, so don't you fret." She patted the girl's rigid shoulder soothingly. "Ah ain't gonna let nothing happen to you."

"Mindy!" Markham's voice was sharp.

"Ah means it, Master Toby." Mindy straightened up and looked at him with defiant eyes.

"And I mean this. I will not tolerate your interference. You will go back to your kitchen at once. If I need you, I'll send for you."

Mindy stared at him for a long moment; then her eyes dropped. When he spoke like that, no argument was possible. She loved Tobias Markham. She had loved him for as long as she could remember. She had even murdered for him. But he had changed so much. His mind seemed now to dwell upon violence. Violence, in the shape of her own murderous hands that had thrust Miss Biddy down those stairs to her death, had set him free from his drunken and immoral wife. Now he contemplated another act of violence, believing that eventually it would bring him the love of Caroline Fane. But it wouldn't. Only hatred and bitterness could result from such a deed. Mindy shivered. If only she had the courage to tell him that she had overheard him talking to Partridge. "I want Lawrence dead," he had said. "There are many dangers on the plantation, and it might be that he will meet with a serious accident." The burst of mirthless laughter that came after these words had chilled her. "Should he meet with an accident," he had gone on, "it would be pleasing to me. There would even be an extra bonus to be picked up."

"Mindy!"

Mindy started out of her thoughts. "Yes, Master Toby?"

Markham's pale eyes narrowed. Why did she look at him like that? For an uneasy moment he had the thought that she knew everything that passed through his mind. His plans for Lawrence. His plan to marry Caroline. But, no, he told himself, she might guess his intentions toward Caroline, but she could not know about Lawrence. Even if she did, it did not matter too much. She was a murderess. She had killed his wife. It was true that she had done it out of her love for him, but it was still murder. For such an act he could have had her flogged to death. But he had been grateful to her, and he had stayed his hand. She was always interfering. Much more of it, and he would see that her crime became a matter of public knowledge. Or, perhaps, if he merely threatened her with exposure, it would prove sufficient to quell her. He had found that one could not live beneath the shadow of murder and remain the same. His dreams were still haunted by the memory of Biddy lying naked at the foot of the stairs, her head twisted at a grotesque angle. He had hated Biddy, insane drunkard that she had been. He had wanted her out of his life. He had brooded on her to the point where he had believed he was going insane. And, yes, he could not deny it, there had been those times when he had planned murder in his mind. But he knew now that he would never have lifted a hand against her.

The rustling of Mindy's black gown startled him out of his thoughts. Her soft, dark eyes had widened, and they were fixed on his face. She looked frightened. He felt cold suddenly. Mindy, his childhood playmate ... For a moment he felt a piercing regret for the vanishing of that love and trust that had always been between them. To cover his sudden surge of emotion, he cleared his throat and spoke to her harshly. "I was under the impression that I told you to go, Mindy. Why are you still standing here?"

Mindy's glance slid away. "Ah'm sorry, Master Toby. Ah'm going now."

With a last look at Caroline Fane, Mindy turned about and went over to the door. There was a shivering inside her. There was nothing in the strange, pale eyes of the man she had once adored. His love for the slave wench seemed to have turned his brain. For a long time now, the expression in his eyes had been cold, almost merciless. It was as though a stranger looked from them. He had become a man she did not know, did not want to know. As she fumbled blindly at the doorknob, she felt the onset of her old superstitious fear. It was the atmosphere in this house that had changed them all. This Montrose, with its air of brooding evil, this terrible place of death and destruction, misery and despair. Miss Biddy lived on within these walls. She could feel her hovering, malignant presence. Turning the knob, Mindy opened the door. She hesitated a moment longer, her trembling hands smoothing her starched white apron; then, blinded by tears, her head hanging, she went out into the hall and closed the door softly behind her.

Markham stared at the girl in the chair. She sat there like one frozen. She seemed emptied of emotion, drained of life. He frowned. He had never really understood the strong emotions Caroline Fane aroused in him, and so, for lack of a better word, he had called it love. But was it love or only desire? Even now, seeing her seated there before him, he could not be sure. But either way, he would have her, he determined. He did not want her as his mistress, but as his wife, so it might well be love he felt for her. He thought of the long days and nights when she had been gone, the weeks, the months. He had not been able to put her out of his mind. The thought of her had colored his every action, every word he had spoken.

Markham moved nearer to the chair. She was thinner than he remembered her. There were deep hollows beneath her cheekbones, and her face was drained of color. She looked up at that moment, and he saw that he had been mistaken in believing her to be drained of life. The wide brown eyes, her chief beauty, were full of hatred and defiance.

"Caroline." He reached out his hand to take hers, but she drew it back sharply. "There is no need to look at me like that," he went on with an unconscious note of pleading in his deep voice. "You are quite safe. You must know that I will not punish you. When have I ever treated you as a slave?"

A faint scornful amusement touched her mouth. "This is the third day you have brought me to this room, Mr. Markham. I have answered all your questions, I believe. As for the rest, you merely repeat yourself. I tell you again that I want no favors from you."

Insolence! Markham's hands clenched in a spasm of anger. "How dare you speak to me like that! I could have you flogged."

"As you had Justin flogged? Oh, yes, I know about it. You had him flogged, and afterward you ordered that he be chained."

"He is a slave. My property. He ran away. Do you think I would allow him to go unpunished?"

"Then why not punish me?" she flared. "I too am a runaway slave, Mr. Markham. Have you forgotten that?"

"No, I have not forgotten. Are you so anxious to be punished, then?"

Caroline sat up straighter in the chair. "Yes, yes!" She spat the words at him. "Anything to get away from you!"

His swarthy face darkened. "You know that I have no wish to punish you, Caroline."

"What you do to one, you must do to the other." She hesitated. "Where is Justin? What have you done to him?"

Markham's mouth hardened. "He is in the slave jail, naturally. He mends fast, for already he is recovering from the flogging."

"And when he recovers fully, you will punish him again, I suppose?"

He was blind to the fear in her eyes; he heard only the sneer in her voice. His control left him. "Yes," he shouted. "I will punish him again and again until I break him. Either that, or I will have him put to death!"

He heard the choked sound she made. His anger lifted, enabling him to see the terror in her eyes, the blind, groping movements of her hands. So he had managed to touch her at last.

Rage exploded inside him. That look on her face! Did she, then, love Lawrence so very much? He wanted to strike her! He lifted his hand and then let it drop back heavily. Mastering his anger, he answered her in a calm, cold voice. "I would be within my rights. You know the laws governing master and slave."

"Yes, I know the laws." With a quick movement she came to her feet and stretched out her hands in pleading. "You would not kill him? Say that you would not!"

"I might. It depends upon you."

"On me?" A faint note of eagerness crept into her voice. "What is it you want of me, Mr. Markham? I will do anything!"

Markham did not answer her. He walked past her and sat down in the chair she had vacated. As she turned about to face him, he studied her closely. In her overwhelming terror for Lawrence, she looked almost demented, he thought. Her face was pinched and white, and her big brown eyes were burning with terror. Her blond hair was untidy, spilling down in a bright stream to touch the shoulders of her white buckskin tunic. He felt a spurt of irritation. Why did she continue to wear that squaw garment? He had offered her Biddy's gowns. He had told her that she could alter them to fit her. She had refused. When he had asked her why she insisted upon wearing the Indian tunic, since it must surely have many bad memories for her, she had said to him, "Because it is mine, Mr. Markham. It is the only thing I own now."

The only thing? he thought, his fingers massaging his aching forehead. And he had wanted to give her everything!

"Mr. Markham." Her eyes were upon him, urgent, compelling, fiercely willing him to answer.

He looked away. She must wait for her answer until he had had time to think. He shouldn't have spoken at all. It was not the right time. He tried to concentrate, but he found that only one thing emerged clearly. He had changed since Biddy's death; he was harder, less inclined to mercy where his slaves were concerned, but for all that, he was not really a vicious man, and he did not want Lawrence's death. No matter what he had told Partridge, he did not. There had been too many deaths already. Biddy, Selina, Moon, poor pathetic little Eliza. No, all he wanted was to remove Lawrence from Caroline's life once and for all. If this could be accomplished without his death, so much the better. An idea occurred to him. He could cancel Lawrence's papers of bondage. He could send him away. Should he speak now, or would it be wiser to wait? He had meant, of course, to give her time to settle down. He had planned to drop the idea into her mind little by little. He hesitated, but found the temptation too great. Now was as good a time as any. "You say you will do anything to save Lawrence, Caroline—did you mean it?" He found himself startled by the hoarse note in his voice. It sounded like somebody else speaking through his mouth.

The way she looked at him reminded him of a small, wary animal who scented danger. Uncertainly she moved a step nearer. "Y-yes, anything."

He smiled at her. "You can marry me, Caroline."

For a moment she just stared at him, her face registering blank amazement. Then her eyes came alive with an expression he could not define. He had expected a passionate protest from her, and instinctively he had braced himself to receive it. Instead, all she said was, "And how will my marrying you help Justin?"

Lawrence again! First and foremost, always him. Would she ever stop loving him? The man's face rose up before him. The stormy, dark eyes in the handsome, swarthy face, the thickly curling black hair, the tall, lithe figure. Yes, Lawrence would no doubt be a figure of romance in the eyes of most women. But he himself could give Caroline so much more. With Lawrence her life would be chancy at best. His mouth tightened as he thought of Lawrence's words when he had ordered the flogging. "You want Carrie, Mr. Markham, I have always known that. But she will never belong to you. Even if you kill me, she never will!"

Markham's fingers began to massage his forehead again. But she would belong to him, she would! He would see to it.

"Mr. Markham, I asked you how it would help Justin?"

"Caroline, listen to me. If you marry me, I will cancel his papers of bondage. He will be a free man. He will be able to go where he pleases, without constantly having to look over his shoulder."

"Without me?"

"Without you. I thought I had made that quite clear."

Caroline nodded. "You did indeed, Mr. Markham. Very clear. I just wanted to be sure that I understood you."

So calm, he thought, so collected. For a moment, as he watched her walk over to the couch and sit down, some of the tension lifted and he even experienced a mild touch of amusement. Whatever he had expected her reaction to be, it was certainly not this. He spoke to her lightly, allowing his amusement to show. "What, Caroline, no melodramatics?"

She had been looking down at her hands. At his words, she raised her eyes and looked at him closely. "You want melodramatics, Mr. Markham? Tell me, is it melodramatic enough for you if I tell you that I would rather die than marry you?"

She had made him angry again. Why did she insist upon doing that? He said sharply, "It will not be you who will die, my dear Caroline."

Her hands clenched tightly on her lap. "Why do you wish to marry me, Mr. Markham? I have been accused of murder, as you know. The murder of my husband, Thomas Fane."

The word brought back images of Biddy lying at the foot of the stairs, Mindy, her black face shining with sweat, saying, "Ah did it for you, Master Toby! Ah wants you to be free, to be happy!" Oh, God! He shuddered. Would he ever be free of memory? "You were innocent of that charge, Caroline," he said thickly. "You told me so."

"And you believed me?"

Some of the burden lifted, and with the easing there came a desire to laugh. He understood that she was trying to put fresh doubt into his mind. "Yes, Caroline, I believe you to be innocent. Whatever else you might have been, you are no murderess. Put your mind at ease, my dear. I will not be afraid to lie beside you at night."

"No?" Rising, she walked over to the window and stood there stiffly, staring outside. "But you should be afraid, Mr. Markham. You really should be."

"Threats, Caroline?" He got up and joined her at the window. "What are you trying to tell me?" he said, placing his hand upon her shoulder. "That you will murder me if you can?"

Leaving his question unanswered, she shrugged herself free of his hand. "If I refuse to marry you, what will happen to Justin?"

"You know what will happen."

"You will kill him, you mean?"

He nodded. "I will have him killed."

Caroline turned about to face him. He winced before the expression in her eyes. "I could still refuse," she said in a colorless voice, "so how would killing him help?"

"Let us say that his death will compensate for your loss."

"What has happened to you, Mr. Markham?" she said in a bewildered voice. "What has caused this change in you? You used to be a kind and generous man. I don't know you any longer."

Murder happened, he wanted to shout at her. A scream in the night, a body bumping down the stairs. "For once, Caroline," he answered her without a trace of his inner emotion, "I am determined to get something for myself. You can marry me or not, just as you please, but I will not change my mind about Lawrence."

Her eyes searched his face. "I believe you."

"Then you will marry me?"

Her mind darted here and there, seeking a way out. What could she do? She dared not tell him that she was already married to Justin. Were she to do that, she had the feeling that he would order his death immediately. Still playing for time, she stammered, "J-Justin will never believe that I prefer m-marriage with you to a life with him."

His face was expressionless. He would not allow her to know how much her words had hurt him. "It matters little what he believes. You need not even see him, you know. Once I have your promise, I will present Lawrence with the canceled papers of bondage. Call it a wedding present to you."

She was trembling so violently that he feared she would fall. He put out a hand to steady her, but she jerked away. Losing her head, she screamed words at him. "You fool! Don't you know that Justin will kill you?"

"You hope he will, I know." A smile curled his lips. "But I can take care of myself. As a slaveowner, I have had enough practice. I agree that Lawrence is a violent man, but he is also an intelligent one. He would know what his end would be if he laid hands upon the master of Montrose."

"He wouldn't care. Don't you understand that?"

"He would care. If it came to a question of his own life, you would find that he would care very much."

"No! You don't know him."

He laughed outright. "My dear, it is only in storybooks that the hero dies for love. I fear you invest Lawrence with too much nobility." He waited for her to speak. When she said nothing, he went on, "Well, are you going to marry me?"

Her mind was in a fever. She could no longer doubt that he meant what he said. She must lie to him for now. She must pretend to agree. Perhaps, later, she would be able to think of a way out. "Yes," she said in a dull voice. "If marrying you is the only way to save Justin's life, then I say yes."

Markham stared at her. Now that he had won, he felt curiously hollow inside, mean, vindictive, and he had never had cause to feel that way before. Even now, it was not too late to draw back. Perhaps he could tell her that he had not meant it. That whether or not she chose to marry him, Lawrence would be perfectly safe. He opened his mouth to speak, hesitated, and the impulse was lost. Deliberately he closed his mind against reason. He wanted her, he always had, and he would have her. There must be something in his life to make up for the years of unhappiness.

"Why do you want me, Mr. Markham?" Her voice was rising again. "Why do you want to marry someone who hates you? Someone who is in love with another man, who will always be in love with him?"

"Lower your voice!" he said sharply. "I can hear you perfectly well, so there is no need to scream at me."

"Miss Biddy used to scream like that, didn't she, Master Toby?" a voice said from the doorway. "You remember how Miss Biddy was always screaming?"

Markham swung around to face Mindy. Now it was he who trembled. Biddy—her insane screaming that had gone on day and night, that terrible sound! He moistened his dry lips. "What are you doing here?" he said harshly. "I didn't send for you."

"Ah knows that, Master Toby. But when ah hears Caroline screaming like she done, ah figure that she's had enough. So ah come to take her away."

Markham took a quick step forward. He wanted to strike that beaming black face. It was something in the smile, the quality of it, that stopped him. It was not really a smile, it was more like a fixed grimace. Looking into her eyes, he wanted to cry for her, for himself. She suffered, poor Mindy, even as he did. Biddy was still here. She would never let them rest! He put his hand to his throbbing head. "Yes, Mindy," he said in a dull voice. "Take Caroline away. Look after her." He tried to muster a smile. "She has promised to marry me, you know."

Mindy's shoulders sagged. In that moment she looked defeated, older than her years. Even the rich black of her complexion was tinged with gray. "Yes, Master Toby," she answered him. "Ah've known what was in your mind from the first day she come back. It ain't right what you a-doing to her and her man. You knows it ain't."

"Be quiet!"

"Ah be quiet if that what you a-wanting, but that don't make it right. There been enough lives ruined in this house." Without looking at Caroline, she held out her hand to her. "You come along with me, mah pretty. Ol' Mindy'll take real good care o' you."

Caroline's eyes softened. Dear Mindy! Like a child, she ran to her and placed her hand in the fat black one. "Mindy, I—"

Mindy's fingers curled warmly and comfortingly about Caroline's hand, but her eyes were still on Markham. "Don't say nothing yet," she bade her. "Now ain't the time, child." She turned her eyes from Markham and led Caroline from the room.

Chapter 28

The mattress beneath her felt hard and lumpy. It had no comfort to offer her aching, twitching body. The aching, though it affected her body, was not really a physical thing, it was the result of an overburdened conscience that would not let her rest. The twitching, she surmised, was caused by frayed nerves. Nevertheless, it frightened her to have her body shake and jerk like someone in the throes of a fit.

Sighing, Mindy heaved herself over onto her back. She fixed her burning eyes on the black square of the window. She hadn't slept a full night through since the death of Miss Biddy. She kept on remembering herself as a young girl, lying in Master Toby's arms. For a little while he had loved her. Later, when he had turned from her, putting the barrier of color between them, she had humbly accepted, and she had gone on loving him. She loved him still. All she had ever wanted was for him to be happy. That was why she had pushed Miss Biddy to her death.

Mindy's lips quivered. It hadn't made him happy. Hers was the guilt, and yet he seemed to have assumed part of her burden. Perhaps because he had wished so often that Miss Biddy would die, her murder had become like a canker eating into his soul, turning him old overnight, warping him, until he became someone she scarcely knew.

Mindy put a hand to her mouth. Tonight, with the memory of Caroline Fane's white face and desperate eyes to give her courage, she had gone to Tobias Markham's room, hoping to reason with him. For more than an hour she had rehearsed the things she was going to say to him. "You cain't force love," she would tell him. "Just 'cause you got a paper that says you own them white folks, it don't mean you can start in tearing their lives apart. They ain't dogs or mules, they is breathing, loving people. You ain't got no right to do 'em as you're doing. Don't matter how much you love that Caroline chil' or how much you do for her, she ain't gonna forget about Lawrence. How you gonna be happy, with her hating and resenting you and all the time pining for her man? Ah tell you, Master Toby, it cain't be done."

His room had been empty, and so she had never uttered the carefully planned words. She went to the one other place where he was almost certain to be. She found him lying full-length in the narrow strip of field just beyond the house. It was a favorite place of his. In Miss Biddy's time, when the woman had been reasonably sober, he would sometimes sit with her in the small field enjoying the cool of the evening.

Her approach had been so soft that he did not know she was there until she sat down beside him. She put her hand on his shoulder. "It's Mindy, Master Toby."

At her touch, he had started violently. "Go away," he said in a muffled voice. "I must be alone for a while."

Braving his anger, she had not moved, nor had she removed her hand. "It seem like you never want Mindy near you these days." She stroked his ruffled hair gently. "Mindy is the only one who is really loving you, Master Toby. Ain't you knowing that yet? Ah would give up mah life for you if ah thought it would help you and make you happy again. Only it ain't no use, is it? There ain't nothing in this world that's gonna make you happy."

It might have been that her words had touched a vital spot of agony, for suddenly he was clinging to her. "Mindy! Mindy!"

She felt his tears cold against her neck, and she held him gently, wanting to help him but not knowing how. It was partly his heavy drinking, she knew, that had caused the outburst, and partly his guilt about Miss Biddy that would not let him rest. How many times she had said to him: "Planning murder in your mind don't kill, Master Toby. Ah done it. Ah pushed her down them stairs. So why you got to go on feeling so badly? Ain't as if you loved her. Ah could understand if you had." But no matter what she said, she could not seem to reach him.

"Mindy, help me!"

"Ah ain't knowing how, Master Toby," she had answered him. "But why you wanting to add to that load you're toting?

You'll be feeling a lot better if you let Caroline go, if you let them both go. Ain't they got a right to their happiness?"

She had felt him stiffen against her. "No! You don't understand, Mindy. I need her."

"What you a-needing is a wench to love you, and that ain't Caroline. You gonna find plenty of gals just hankering to be Mrs. Tobias Markham."

He was silent for so long that she began to wonder if he had fallen asleep. When he finally did speak, his words stabbed at her heart. "I wish I were dead, Mindy. I'm so tired. So unhappy!"

Her arms tightened about him. "You ain't to say that. You hush up!"

"Scolding again, Mindy." He had tried to laugh, a difficult, painful sound that made her shiver with pity for him. "You know, I wish I had the courage to take my own life."

"You're pitying yourself, Master Toby, that's what. Ah ain't caring if you punish me for saying it, 'cause it's the truth."

He had not been angry. "Perhaps you're right, Mindy. But I think it's a little more than that. I feel as if life is running away from me, leaving me in a limbo. Can you understand that?"

Her fear for him came out in the form of anger. "No!" She almost shouted the word at him. "You knows that ah ain't understanding that kind of talk."

"I'm sorry, Mindy." He had smiled at her and touched her face with his hand. Then, raising himself, he had kissed her. He had taken her body many times, but for the first time in all those long and aching years since he had taken Miss Biddy as his wife, he had joined his lips to hers. "Dear Mindy. Dear, loving, faithful Mindy! I think that you are the only one I have ever truly loved."

For a moment she had not been able to answer him; then she had said in a voice husky with pleading, "Will you come to me tonight, Master Toby?"

"Yes, Mindy, I'll come."

She did not doubt that he would come to her eventually, but it would not be for some hours. She knew his habits now, those habits that had been formed since the death of Miss Biddy. At this very moment, she knew, he was sitting in his study drinking and brooding. Mindy closed her eyes tightly.

He did love her. It might be only in a certain way, but he did love her! She hugged the happiness of his words to her, reliving them, cherishing them. And then, ugly and startling interruption, those other words he had spoken sounded in her head again. "I wish I were dead!" Oh, the memory of his face when he had said it!

"Jesus God," Mindy began, her words echoing in the silence, "take away mah master's unhappiness. It ain't his fault. You know ah done killed Miss Biddy. Ain't minding if you punish me, Lord, 'cause ah deserves it, but I'd be 'bliged to you if you'd show ol' Mindy a way to help Master Toby."

She lay there for a long time, her eyes closed, her hands clasped together. Gradually the agonized lines in her face smoothed themselves out. She had received an answer. She knew what she had to do. All her life she had done what was best for her Master Toby, and she would do her best for him now.

She got out of bed. The floor felt cold beneath her feet, and she shivered slightly. She stood there for a moment, wishing that her head would stop aching. It had been aching for days now, and the constant pain was making her short-tempered and irritable. She picked up the old worn-out coat lying across the foot of the bed and thrust her arms into the sleeves. She used the coat as a robe, and though it was tight on her bulky figure and she could not button it, she refused to discard it. She clung to the garment because it had once belonged to Tobias Markham. She gave a sudden soft chuckle. Here she was whining about the pain in her head, when it really didn't matter anymore. They were all going to be happy again, so why waste precious time in thinking about her throbbing head?

Crossing over to the door, she opened it and peered outside. The corridor, lit by flickering candles, was deserted, the doors lining its length tightly closed. Walking along the corridor on her way to Tobias Markham's room, Mindy was smiling, because once again she could hear his words sounding in her head: "I think that you are the only one I have ever truly loved."

Mindy paused before Markham's door, letting herself remember the sweet pressure of his lips on hers. She did not tap on the panel; she knew there was no need. Opening the

door, she went into the room. The round of keys hung on a
nail over the bed. She took them down and thrust them in the
pocket of the coat. Even if, for some reason, Tobias Markham should come into his bedchamber, he would not notice
the keys were gone. As was usual with him these days, he
would be too befuddled by drink.

Mindy stepped back into the corridor and closed the door
behind her. Retracing her steps, she felt no guilt. She was doing this for Master Toby. She walked the length of the corridor, turned to the left, and mounted the steep flight of stairs
that led to Caroline Fane's room.

Caroline lay on her back, a shaft of moonlight across her
face. Bending over her, Mindy placed a gentle hand across
her mouth.

Instantly Caroline's eyes opened, looking up wide and
startled at the dark shape above her.

"It's all right, chil'," Mindy whispered, removing her hand.
"Don't be afraid. It's only Mindy."

"Mindy, what are you doing here? Is something wrong?"
Her eyes dilated. "Justin! Is it about Justin?"

"In a way. But no need for you to be frightened. Ain't
nothing wrong with him, far's ah know."

"I don't understand."

"You don't have to. You just do like ah say. You're going
away from Montrose tonight, you and your man. Get yourself dressed. Hurry!"

"But—"

"Ain't you wanting to get away from Montrose?"

"Oh, yes, Mindy, but—"

Gripping her by the arm, Mindy pulled her from the bed.
"No time for talking. Ah explains later."

Caroline nodded. Without another word she scrambled into
her clothes. Going out of the door, she asked only one question. "Why are you doing this?" she whispered.

Mindy paused at the head of the stairs. "Ain't doing it for
you, but for him, Master Toby."

Down the stairs, picking their way carefully. The occasional creak of their descent sounded as loud as a pistol shot
in Caroline's ears. Across the hall to the big door. The door
made a groaning sound as it opened. Caroline moistened her
dry lips. Tobias Markham was in his study. She had seen the
light beneath his door as they tiptoed past. What if he should

come out and find them? She was so afraid that she hardly noticed when Mindy closed the door and urged her forward. The night air felt cool against her flushed face, and some of her panic lifted. Even so, she was in such a fever to get away from the house that she missed the first step.

Mindy caught her arm, preventing her from falling headlong. "What's the matter with you, gal?" Mindy whispered fiercely. "Get ahold of yourself, 'less you a-wanting to wake ever'body up."

"I'm sorry." They were some distance from the house before Caroline spoke again. "What if Mr. Markham should find out that you helped us, Mindy?"

"He ain't gonna find out."

"Mindy, you can't be sure of that."

"Yes, ah can. Ah knows what ah'm doing."

Seated on the wide wooden bench that did duty as a bed, Justin stared down unseeingly at the stone floor. His eyes felt heavy, but, obstinately, he refused to let them close. The wounds of the flogging were all but healed, but his body was still tender, and he had no wish to lie down on the hard wooden bench. Besides, how could anybody be expected to sleep in this stifling atmosphere? It was heavy and foul with the mingled odors of the previous occupants. The only air came from a slitlike window set high in the wall, and it did little to disperse the smells.

He got up and began to pace restlessly. At least he could move about freely tonight, which was something to be thankful for. But why had Markham sent Partridge to remove the fetters? What was supposed to happen now?

He returned slowly to the bench and sat down. As always, his mind went immediately to Caroline. His only comfort was the knowledge that she had not been punished. Markham had told him so, and he had no reason to disbelieve him. Not, at least, in that one thing. Full circle, he thought bitterly. They had gone full circle, and now they were back where they had started, with no prospects of escape this time. He had never been a particularly superstitious man, but he could almost believe he had been born under an evil star, and even worse, Caroline perforce was touched with his ill luck. But Markham couldn't keep him in this cell forever. Once he was out, his mind would begin to function again.

When Partridge had entered the cell to remove the fetters, he had asked him, "What happened to my friend and the girl who was with him?"

"Don't know." Partridge had seemed nervous. His pale-blue eyes blinking rapidly, he had backed to the door. "I left 'em lying, that's all I can tell you."

"Then they could be dead?"

With the door opened and himself poised for flight, Partridge obviously felt safe, for his familiar cockiness of manner returned. "Who knows? Could be dead. Cross is right handy with a club." He went out quickly. The key grated as he locked the door.

Yes, Buck could be dead. Lianne, too. Justin buried his face in his hands. He seemed to bring bad luck to all. Paul, his brother, had died because of him. Carrie had suffered, was still suffering, and now Buck and Lianne had been added to the list.

He was jerked out of his black thoughts by the sound of the key turning in the lock. He rose from the bench as the door swung open. "Mindy! Carrie!" He stared at them in blank astonishment. "What are you doing here?"

"Justin!" Caroline ran to him and flung herself into his arms.

He held her fiercely close, but he did not take his eyes from Mindy's face. "What is happening?" he said quietly. "Does Markham know that you have come here?"

Mindy shook her head. "He'll know soon enough. Don't just stand there cuddling that gal. You got to get out of here. Now, you remember what ah tell you, Master Justin. You got to go by way of the lower pasture. Ain't no guards that way. You'll see two horses in the field. You take 'em. They ain't been branded yet, so nobody can holler 'horse thief'."

Justin released Caroline. "You'll have to come with us, Mindy. Carrie and I can ride double."

Mindy shook her head. "Cain't," she said simply. "Cain't never leave him. Master Toby is mah life."

"And what you are doing might well *mean* your life. Come with us, Mindy."

"No. Ain't leaving. Master Toby won't do nothing to me, so don't you be fretting 'bout that. Ah've always known how to handle him." Mindy took a step nearer to him. "And you ain't to be fretting and studying on them slave papers Master

Toby's got on you. Ah'm gonna tear 'em up when ah gets back to the house. Ah knows where he keeps 'em."

"Mindy, you can't! Don't you understand that what you are doing is sheer insanity? Markham could not only take out fresh papers, but he could also have you flogged to death."

"Could, but he won't."

"Why won't he?"

Mindy looked away. "Just won't, that's all."

"I don't like leaving you behind. For the last time, I ask you, beg you, to come with us."

"And for the last time, ah tell you ah ain't leaving." Mindy's head rose proudly. "Master Toby won't be taking out fresh papers, and he ain't about to have me flogged. Loves me, he does. He done tole me so. Oh, it ain't in the way you love Caroline, but it's still love."

"I'm sure of that, Mindy." Something had been niggling at the back of Justin's mind, and now he brought the thought out. "How did you get in here without being stopped? Where are the guards?"

Mindy smiled. "Them guards are where they always are when the master ain't looking. They're in one of the huts playing cards." She cast a look behind her. "Could come out at any time, though. You get along, now."

"Mindy!"

"Don't say no more. Ah've given you mah answer."

"Thank you, Mindy." Justin took her briefly in his arms.

Caroline kissed her cheek. "God bless you, Mindy."

Her eyes glistening with tears, Mindy stood aside to let them pass. "Go quickly," she bade them. "And be careful."

Mindy closed and locked the door. She stood there for a few moments longer. When she could no longer see their shadowy forms, she turned and made her way back to the house.

It was nine o'clock in the morning when Prudence, the kitchen girl, worried by the absence of the cook from her domain, made her way to Mindy's bedroom.

Outside the door, Prudence hesitated. Mindy was always very kind, but just lately she had been irritable, snapping at her for the least little thing. She hoped Mindy would not blame her too much for disturbing her. Making up her mind, Prudence tapped on the door. Receiving no answer, she tapped again. When there was still no answer, she opened the door and entered the room. "Mindy." She stopped short, her mouth dropping open. Mindy lay in the bed, her eyes closed, one arm holding Tobias Markham close.

Prudence swallowed. Her eyes round and startled in her black face, she approached the bed hesitantly. "Mindy." She put her hand on the woman's shoulder. "Wake up, Mindy."

Mindy did not wake up. Leaning closer, Prudence saw that she wasn't breathing. Terrified, she put out a shrinking hand and touched Tobias Markham's face. His flesh was as cold as death!

Prudence sprang away from the bed. Screaming, she bolted from the room. "They's dead! Master Toby and Mindy, they's both dead!"

Some half-hour later, Benjamin, the chief houseman, entered the bedchamber. He stared at the two dead faces for a long moment. Then, turning away, he picked up the jug from the table beside the bed. He swirled the remaining contents, his thick lower lip jutting thoughtfully as he saw the sediment at the bottom.

Replacing the jug, Benjamin turned and looked at the servants crowding the doorway. "It look to me like Mindy put one of her special powders in that jug," he announced. "She was always saying 'bout how unhappy Master Toby was, so ah reckon she decided to die and take him with her."

Prudence burst into noisy sobs. "What we do, Benjamin, what we do?"

"Well, for one thing you can stop that bawling, gal," Benjamin said sternly. "Ain't seemly to be taking on like that in the master's presence."

"But he dead!"

"Don't make no difference." With slow, majestic steps, he went toward the doorway. Awed by his calm demeanor and his air of authority, the servants drew back to let him pass.

Chapter 29

Buck's keen eyes spotted the two riders from a long way off. For a moment he could not believe what he was seeing. He had been watching the roads and scouring the countryside hoping for just this moment. Laughing, exuberant, he flung his dusty hat in the air. Catching it again, he jammed it back on his head. "It's them," he shouted to Lianne. "It's Justin and Caroline. I knowed that sooner or later, if they could, they'd be making this way."

Lianne came running, her black hair flying. "Where, Buck, where?"

"There." Buck pointed down the hill. "See 'em?"

Her hand shading her eyes, Lianne looked in the direction he was pointing. "I see two riders." Her hand dropped. "But it could be anyone."

Buck grinned at her. "Only, it ain't just anyone, it's them. I seen the sun shining on Caroline's hair."

"I wonder how they managed to get away from those men?"

"Don't know, but I aim to find out." Buck looked lovingly at Lianne. Catching her in his arms, he kissed her soundly. "Mount up, Mrs. Carey," he said, releasing her. "Let's go meet 'em."

Lianne frowned. "Now that they are free, they will be expecting to go back to the settlement. How can we tell them that the place is in ruins and that my people have massacred all the settlers?"

Buck sobered. "We'll just tell 'em, that's all. Ain't no other way around it. Anyway, we've got to get on back to the settlement and start burying them people, so they'll be seeing it for themselves."

Lianne shuddered. "Buck, must we go back? I do not like to look upon dead people."

"Nor do I, honey. It's got to be done, and that's all there is to it." He touched her cheek gently. "I thought you were over that spirit nonsense."

"I am," Lianne defended herself quickly. "But sometimes I cannot help being afraid."

"I ain't gonna let any harm come to you, ever." Buck kissed her again. "You believe that, don't you, darlin'?"

"I will always be safe with you." She smiled at him. "I know this to be true."

Releasing her, Buck mounted his horse. Holding out his hand, he pulled her up before him. "Let's go meet 'em."

Justin looked up sharply. "Rider coming down the hill," he exclaimed.

Caroline's hands gripped the reins tightly. "A ... a Montrose rider?"

"Not coming from that direction, no." His eyes narrowing, he leaned forward in his saddle as the rider drew nearer. "Carrie!" His smile flashed. "Carrie, it's Buck, and that's Lianne in front of him. Listen to him yelling. He'll bring out every Indian for miles around."

With his arm about Caroline's shuddering shoulders, Justin stared with bleak eyes at the still faintly smoking ruins of the settlement. People were lying everywhere, and they were all dead. Even the children had not been spared. His eyes fell on a blond woman. Frances Hunter, her name had been. She was lying on her back, her face twisted into an expression of horror, her sightless eyes staring upward. An arrow protruded from her breast, and another from her neck.

Buck stooped and picked up a child's toy. He held the little wooden horse between both hands. "Them Injuns ain't spared a one, the bastards!" Blindly he handed the little horse to Caroline. "Justin, you notice something different about this massacre?"

Justin shook his head. "No, Buck," he said hoarsely, "this is the first massacre I've seen."

"I was forgetting. Wish I could say it's the last you'll see, but cain't."

"What's different about this one?"

"The Injuns left 'em their hair. They usually scalp 'em."

Justin's eyes met his. "White Bird?"

"Could be. Likely they let him have his way on this raid. Won't last, though. Next time they come down on a settlement, they'll take hair."

Justin's face tightened. "Let's bury them, Buck."

It was late before they finished putting the last pitiful body into the earth. Buck had hacked out some crude crosses, and he had placed one at the head of every grave.

Caroline touched Justin's bowed shoulders with a loving hand. "Come away now, darling. We did all that we could for them. It's over."

Buck turned to look at her. "Ain't over, Caroline. The fight for this land is just beginning. I aim to be a part of it."

"And I," Justin said. He lifted Caroline onto her horse. Mounting himself, he looked at Buck and Lianne. "Shall we go?"

Buck nodded. "We're ready."

Keeping close together, they rode away, heading into the path of the sunset. They did not look back.

About the Author

Constance Gluyas was born in London, where she served in the Women's Royal Air Force during World War II. She started her writing career in 1972 and since then has had published several novels of historical fiction including SAVAGE EDEN, available in Signet. She presently lives in California, where she is at work on her new novel.

CONSTANCE GLUYAS

A BREATHTAKING SAGA OF TEMPESTUOUS LOVE AND RAGING PASSION THAT SWEEPS ACROSS TWO CONTINENTS

This is how the wildly passionate love story of beautiful Caroline Fane and the daring, flamboyant Justin Lawrence began. This is where the inner fires of burning desire united two lovers in a breathlessly romantic alliance of never to be forgotten love and tenderness. . . .

(#J7681—$1.95)

by the author of

Rogue's Mistress

More Big Bestsellers from SIGNET

☐ **THE KILLING GIFT by Bari Wood.** (#J7350—$1.95)

☐ **LOVER: CONFESSIONS OF A ONE NIGHT STAND by Lawrence Edwards.** (#J7392—$1.95)

☐ **WHITE FIRES BURNING by Catherine Dillon.** (#E7351—$1.75)

☐ **CONSTANTINE CAY by Catherine Dillon.** (#W6892—$1.50)

☐ **THE SECRET LIST OF HEINRICH ROEHM by Michael Barak.** (#E7352—$1.75)

☐ **FOREVER AMBER by Kathleen Winsor.** (#J7360—$1.95)

☐ **SMOULDERING FIRES by Anya Seton.** (#J7276—$1.95)

☐ **HARVEST OF DESIRE by Rochelle Larkin.** (#J7277—$1.95)

☐ **THE PERSIAN PRICE by Evelyn Anthony.** (#J7254—$1.95)

☐ **EARTHSOUND by Arthur Herzog.** (#E7255—$1.75)

☐ **THE DEVIL'S OWN by Christopher Nicole.** (#J7256—$1.95)

☐ **THE GREEK TREASURE by Irving Stone.** (#E7211—$2.25)

☐ **THE GATES OF HELL by Harrison Salisbury.** (#E7213—$2.25)

☐ **TERMS OF ENDEARMENT by Larry McMurtry.** (#J7173—$1.95)

Other SIGNET Bestsellers You'll Enjoy Reading

NAL/ABRAMS' BOOKS
ON ART, CRAFTS AND SPORTS
*in beautiful large format, special
concise editions—lavishly illustrated
with many full-color plates.*

THE NEW AMERICAN LIBRARY, INC.,
P.O. Box 999, Bergenfield, New Jersey 07621

Please send me the ABRAMS BOOKS I have checked above. I am enclosing
$_____(check or money order—no currency or C.O.D.'s). Please
include the list price plus 50¢ a copy to cover handling and mailing costs.
(Prices and numbers are subject to change without notice.)

Name_____

Address_____

City_____State_____Zip Code_____
Allow at least 4 weeks for delivery